GW00669843

NOCTURNE

By the same author

UNDERGROUND

NOCTURNE

Mark Chadbourn

DAMAGED COPY

GOLLANCZ HORROR

GOLLANCZ HORROR

First published in Great Britain 1994
in hardback and paperback
by Victor Gollancz
A Division of the Cassell group
Villiers House, 41/47 Strand, London WC2N 5JE

© Mark Chadbourn 1994

All rights reserved. No part of this publication
may be reproduced or transmitted in any form or
by any means, electronic or mechanical
including photocopying, recording or any
information storage or retrieval system, without
prior permission in writing from the publishers.

The right of Mark Chadbourn to be identified as
author of this work has been asserted by him in
accordance with the Copyright, Designs
and Patents Act, 1988.

A catalogue record for this book is
available from the British Library.

ISBN 0 575 05791 2 (hb)
ISBN 0 575 05793 9 (pb)

Typeset by CentraCet Limited, Cambridge
Printed and bound in Great Britain
by Cox and Wyman Ltd, Reading

*This book is sold subject to the condition that it shall not,
by way of trade or otherwise, be lent, resold, hired out, or
otherwise circulated without the publisher's prior consent
in any form of binding other than that in which it is
published and without a similar condition including this
condition being imposed on the subsequent purchaser.*

For June Mavis Chadbourn
(1933–1992)

Acknowledgement:
For Elizabeth, who always gave the best
advice, and who was there in the
Crescent City when it happened.

*Of course, everybody in the city of New
Orleans was always organization-minded,
which I guess the world knows. And a dead
man always belonged to several organizations,
such as clubs, and, well, say secret orders, and
so forth and so on. And every time one died,
why, nine out of ten, there was always a big
band turn out when the day he was supposed
to be buried – never buried in the night,
always in the day . . .*

*'Rejoice at the death and cry at the birth' . . .
New Orleans sticks close to the Scripture.*

Ferdinand Lamott *Jelly Roll* Morton
to the US Library of Congress, 1938

PART 1

Eyesight to the Blind

*Behold, I shew you a mystery; we shall
not all sleep, but we shall all be
changed.*

I Corinthians (15:51)

Chapter 1

BANG, BANG. BANG, BANG. The sound, like hammers.
BANG, BANG. BANG, BANG.

Rising through the fog like a swimmer striking out from the depths, he left the grim, grey world behind him and focused on the light. His passage from somewhere-that-wasn't to somewhere-that-was came with a slow awakening, a laborious throwing-off of chains that wanted to hold him back and keep him in the safety of oblivion. At first there was the noise, constant, rhythmic, leading him up out of the darkness with an insistent, unnerving tug.

Bang, bang. Bang, bang.

For a moment he had difficulty distinguishing if it was a memory, a fading echo from the twilight world, or if he was actually hearing it, and in that moment it suddenly seemed frighteningly important that he knew. But as the other sensations surged around him the anxiety faded and was replaced by an awareness of a bright new world. There was light, a stroboscopic flashing through his eyelids, light, dark, light, dark. A metallic, sticky taste encircled his sluggish tongue. The smell of oil, heat and dust cocooned him. His fingertips slid over smooth wood, cracked upholstery, warm from the sun.

He opened his eyes.

The pieces of the picture fell into place slowly, drifting through a mind cobwebbed by too long without conscious thought. The flashing was sunlight through the window opposite him, interrupted at regular intervals by something outside the vehicle in which he was travelling.

Blank acceptance gave way to growing shock. On a gut level he knew it wasn't right; the strangeness of the sensations jarred and he looked around quickly, groping dully for memories that would not come. He appeared to be in a trolleycar or tram, gently rocking through a strange landscape. The images were commonplace, but his mind rejected them.

You are not seeing this, it told him. *You are not here. It is a dream.*

He blinked once, twice, swallowed, closed his eyes and listened to the electric hum.

Bang, bang. The wheels rattled along the rails. Bang, bang.

When he finally dared to open his eyes once again, the conductress, a black woman in a smart grey uniform, was looking at him quizzically. He looked at her, right through her, and then out of the window as his whole world skewed.

In the distance skyscrapers gleamed against a powder-blue sky, soaring towers of glass, metal and concrete. Closer to him was a carpet of smaller buildings, their jumbled roofs and towers and the odd mix of architecture suggesting great age. Two worlds side by side, old and new. It wasn't London. It didn't even look like England.

With the mounting panic, fear and disorientation came over him in a second. His thoughts collapsed like a house of cards as he desperately shuffled through the pack for something which would tell him exactly what he was seeing. The last image he could recall clearly was a cold, grey day in South London, standing on a wet pavement waiting for a bus.

This wasn't London.

'What's the matter, honey?' The conductress' voice was heavy with the accent of the southern United States.

Her voice re-triggered the panic and he suddenly wanted to leap from the trolleycar and run until he could find a dark place to hide. His fingers gripped the arms of his seat, anchoring him to reality, and then he concentrated so hard his head ached. He could remember his name: David Easter; his age: twenty-seven; and every detail of his life until a few weeks ago. Then there was nothing. No, that wasn't quite true. There were flashes of remembrance, like the starbursts behind eyelids just before sleep came, but little to link then and now. An ocean of foggy greyness lay in between and he could pluck nothing from it.

'Where am I?' It sounded a pathetic question in the still air of the trolleycar.

The conductress looked around the empty carriage, eyes wide with theatrical amazement, but her broad smile was kind with no

12

hint of mockery. 'You're in The Big Easy, honey. The city of your dreams.'

He stared at her blankly.

'You Brits!' She laughed. 'You like your jokes! The Big Easy. That's what we call New Orleans 'cause life here *is* easy.'

'New Orleans?' David repeated her words as if they were a foreign language, feeling like a cartoon character who had just had a safe dropped on his head. He laughed. No, he didn't believe it. It was a joke. Someone was setting him up.

'You really don't know? Where you going, Mister Englishman?' A note of concern was suddenly evident in her voice as she watched David's face.

He shook his head slowly. 'I . . .' Dazed, he shrugged in reply.

'You going to Bourbon Street? To see the sights? I guess you're dressed for somewhere classy. That's a nice suit.'

David glanced down. He was wearing his best suit, almost a grand's worth of fine cloth, specially tailored to his specifications; long in the sleeve, baggy in the crotch, pleats and cuffs. Dressed to kill. His jazz suit, the one he wore for his *special* nights out at Ronnie Scott's or the Jazz Attic. 'My wedding and funeral suit.'

'You come to me first before you go gettin' married.' She chuckled deeply.

He felt comforted by her friendliness; it was something to hang on to while the world fell away.

'You won't have any trouble findin' a place to stay,' she continued. 'Mardi Gras's come and gone. The hotels are empty now, and a good sight cheaper. If you came a couple of weeks ago you wouldn't got no room for love nor money. You tourin' around?'

He nodded noncommittally.

'You don't look too sure!'

'I'm touring. Seeing the sights.' In his daze, his thoughts drifted briefly back to London. 'I've always wanted to come to New Orleans,' he added truthfully.

You can't be in New Orleans, his mind told him.

Her eyes narrowed. 'It seems to me you got a problem, honey. You were in a dream when you got on here. Girl trouble, maybe? Men always say that's the only kind of trouble, but they don't

13

know anythin'. Well, you came to the right city. The Big Easy is a good place to forget.'

'I want to remember.' David looked down. His small, beat-up suitcase was there, clutched protectively between his heels. He didn't recall packing it. Logically, it was still tucked under his bed, gathering dust. Nausea twitched in his stomach.

'You can remember here too! Just take life easy, let it all wash over you. This is a city for lovers and dreamers. You one of those, honey?'

A twinge. 'Isn't everyone?'

'Not many, believe me.' She smiled and looked out of the window, riding with the jerks and bumps like a sailor long at sea. 'But when I meet someone that is, that lights up my day.'

David could control the panic no longer. It was making him feel ill, like the disorientation that came with drinking six pints on an empty stomach.

I've got to get out of here, he thought anxiously. *I'm going mad.*

Calliope music, jaunty and uplifting, blared out nearby, followed swiftly by the blast of a steam whistle. David strained his neck to look behind him and saw for the first time that the trolleycar ran along the bank of a wide, grey river.

Not the Thames. Too wide, too slow.

He glanced back at the conductress who had the benignly baffled expression of an adult watching children at play. *New Orleans?* That would make it the Mississippi.

He shook his head. No, no, he was starting to fall for it, the big practical joke that someone was playing on him. Any minute now Jeremy Beadle would leap out and whip off his false beard. 'Surprise! We drugged you and transported you overnight to New Orleans!'

Sure . . .

A steamboat, as white and proud as a wedding cake, bobbed gently against its moorings on the slow, grey waters. The name 'Natchez' was emblazoned on its side. Tourists crowded on the deck, grinning and waving.

'My stop,' he said. There was a note of hysteria in his voice. The effort of creating a façade of normalcy was eating away at him inside. 'Thanks for the ride.'

'My pleasure, honey. You enjoy yourself, be good and come and see Monica soon, y'hear.' She winked as he passed. Before the trolleycar moved on, he could hear her humming deeply and melodically to the empty seats.

The waterfront was hot and David had to shield his eyes from the glare off the white concrete. Warm, florid air blew in from the river, smelling of mud and rotting leaves. The languorous drift of the water was soothing, but despite the tranquil setting, the panic was still there, ready to sweep up and overwhelm him if he allowed it.

What had happened to him?

Up it came like a geyser, the boiling soup of his emotions. And then he was running, across the tracks, down a ramp, towards the city, desperate to expose the lie, the big lie that was driving him to the brink of insanity.

People stopped and stared at him as he passed, some stepping back from the wide-eyed and frightened runner like he was a rabid dog. His arms flailing, he careered directionlessly into the heart of the city where everything only added to the madness of his situation. The shops and restaurants were not English. A sign in one window said PO-BOY $2. Another advertised POPCORN 50 CENTS. The clothes and fashions were not those of the West End. Even the haircuts, the faces themselves, screamed at him that he was far, far from home.

Crowds swarmed around, hampering his headlong dash and he careened off people like a pinball, barked obscenities dogging his heels. And still he kept running as if to stop would force him to admit where he was: that he had been transported thousands of miles without knowing it, that his memory had been scoured, that his mind was collapsing.

The streets around him were small, the buildings crowding in close. The very air reeked of age, the odour of accumulated years piled up high, grumpy and unmoving. Drifting through it were other scents, the fragrance of flowers and of lush vegetation carried on the breeze from somewhere beyond the city, the spicy aromas of cooking food.

A man jumped into the gutter to avoid him, preferring the

danger of metal in motion to the human projectile. David rounded a corner and was confronted with another street which offered no escape other than that of the bars which were everywhere, their interiors dark and inviting, promising seclusion and forgetfulness. Still David ran. His feet ached, his throat burned. The world of technology and real things where people did not suddenly wake up in another country was represented by the skyscrapers in the distance. He headed towards them.

A few yards later a hand snaked around his upper arm and yanked him suddenly to a halt, whipping him around so that his neck cracked and his knee joints flared. He was face to face with a short man with bulging eyes and breath that reeked of beer and cigars.

'You're gonna get hurt,' the man said.

'What are you talking about?'

'They're all around. Can't you see them?' The man's eyes darted about, pupils reduced, whites showing. David could see madness there. 'I saw you,' he continued. 'You know. I can tell . . . you know . . .'

David wrenched his arm free and sprinted back into the flow of people, but the man's words stayed with him and as he ran a creeping paranoia closed around him. He could feel the prickle of eyes upon his back.

People were watching him. Glancing around, he saw them every now and then. Faces loomed out of the crowd, out of doorways, or dark alleys, pale faces with glassy eyes. And they were all watching him. Why? Why were they staring . . . ?

The fear made David crash into a wall and he stayed there, hugging the brickwork for dear life. An over-sized car glided by, its suspension low to the road, as gleaming and efficient as the day it had rolled from the production line in Detroit.

He could doubt it no longer. He was in America.

The knowledge replaced his wildfire panic with a Mogadon acceptance. When he left the security of the wall his legs felt leaden and he found himself trudging like a wino back into the crowds.

His memories of London were so close, of the people, the streets, the pubs, friends, work. That was all he knew. And yet

16

here he was, in New Orleans, as if a magic carpet had whisked his sleeping form away . . .

He paused outside a shop stuffed with antiques, tables and chairs, boxes, candlesticks, ornaments, anything which could be classified as *old*. In the window hung an ornate mirror, framing his pale face. He stared at it, examining it closely, noting the dark rings under his eyes, the hollow cheeks. He looked terrible. Running his fingers through his lank hair, he felt the last vestiges of grease applied several days ago. Things must have been bad if he had not paid any attention to his appearance. He always ensured he was looking good. What had happened to him?

Think about it, he told himself. Get it straight in your head.

My name is David Easter. I live alone in Brixton, in a one-bedroom flat at the top of a decaying mansion that should have been condemned years ago. I work in a record shop. I hate my job because it's dull and boring and because there's no way out of it. I hate losers and people who say 'This is all there is.' I like Indian food, Guinness and dressing well. I like jazz. I love jazz. It's the only thing in a grey, dreary world worth living for. I don't see my family and I have only one friend, Willie Hobbes; but he's a very good friend, the best, and we're partners in crime in the search for fun and freedom. I feel . . . what? Lost. Lonely. Sad. Angry. Bewildered. I can remember all that. Why can't I remember how or why I travelled three thousand miles? I've never been out of Britain before.

Until now. So what *has* happened to me!

David hammered the wall next to the shop window, but the pain did little to ease his torment. The worst thing was his eyes. They didn't even look like any eyes he remembered. They were staring and haunted, as if they had looked on monstrous, terrifying things.

Perhaps they had. How was he to know? And why New Orleans? Why not Amsterdam or Paris or Cairo? Was it something to do with his love of jazz? His longtime dream of visiting the mecca of his music? The ghost in the mirror stared back at him, giving nothing away.

He turned slowly now and looked around. Four kids tap danced in the gutter. There was music in the air and a sense of abandon,

17

of horizons enlarging. New Orleans! It was at once disturbing and exciting. He stepped out into the flow of people and allowed himself to be carried along.

It was some time later when he found himself sitting on a bench in a large square, unaware of the time that had passed. For what could have been hours he had been wandering dreamily through an alien world, watching the Martian faces with fascination. This city was vibrant and alive, with music billowing out from every bar and crackling with the energy of *les bon temps roulent*. The character of New Orleans was writ large in every face and building. And he was in the French Quarter, the old part of the city, home to the Mardi Gras, the music and the pleasures of the flesh. Admitting it to himself left his stomach churning.

In the centre of the square, a gaudily dressed man with a wide-brimmed felt hat opened a case and took out a gleaming saxophone. And then as the sun blazed down he began to play a bright, simple tune, swaying from side to side with his eyes closed.

David gently massaged his temples in the hope that it would relieve the pressure in his head. The situation had to be examined logically. He remembered Brixton, his flat, his job at the record store. Christmas had been a laugh – too many drinks in Covent Garden. New Year, yes, that was there too. Willie, good old Willie, had thrown the party of the year. And then . . .

His head hurt. What had happened then? He checked the date on his watch. March. Nearly two months missing. Two months and three thousand miles. Anxiously, he checked through the possibilities. An injury of some kind, a blow to the head that had damaged his memory? Maybe he had been mugged. Tenderly he felt his scalp. There was no bruising or soreness. A breakdown of some kind? He could not think of anything which could have pushed him that far.

Why he was in New Orleans wasn't the only question. There was also the niggling subject of *how* he'd got there. Short of robbing a bank he would never have had the funds to fly from London to Louisiana. Any spare cash he had was spent on clothes, music or beer.

And even more worrying: what was he going to do now?

He stood up and wandered a few feet in one direction, turned around and walked back and then headed in another direction, afraid of making the wrong choice.

David's thoughts were disturbed by a gangling man who hyperactively bounced up to him on the balls of his feet with all the grace and restrained power of a basketball player. Expensive Raybans shielded his eyes, but he was grinning broadly, his teeth pearly white against the blackness of his skin.

'Hey, man,' he shouted. 'I can tell you all about your shoes.' He clutched a small plastic bag close to him.

David ignored him. He wanted time to think, time to find an anchor. The hustler, however, had no intention of leaving him alone. He danced from foot to foot in front of him, tapping with his toes and heels, a street-level Fred Astaire.

'Your shoes, man. I can tell you exactly where you bought them. Which state, which city, which street, which shop.'

'Don't bother,' David snapped.

'I'm an expert. I know everything there is to know about shoes.'

David was shaking, actually trembling with the strain, and he felt his knees would buckle. 'Go take your foot fetish to someone else. I . . .' The words stumbled and died on his lips.

'You need a rest, man. This sun is too damn hot. Just sit back while I shine your shoes. We'll talk, sort out your problems. Problems – they're my bag.'

The hustler refused to move. David had no drive to argue and like a man too long without food, he allowed himself to be led back to the bench where he flopped down and covered his eyes with his hands. 'OK, OK. Jesus. What's your pitch?'

Through his fingers David saw the man's grin grow wider. 'Let me clean your shoes, man. Two bucks, that's all. Best shoeshine you'll ever have.'

David shook his head. 'Look . . . I haven't got any money. I—' Subconsciously, he slipped his hand into his pocket and felt the crinkle of notes. Separating one from the roll, he eased it out. A crisp, new dollar bill.

Where had he got a roll of US currency?

'If you can find another one of those, we've got a deal!'

Wearily, David agreed. Why argue? Nothing made sense any more. He should just go with the flow, pretend he was in Alice's Wonderland where even the bizarre seemed normal. He looked down at his shoes. The shoeshine man was right to pick on him. They were thick with the dust and scuff marks of travelling and his feet felt sweaty and exhausted within them.

Out of his plastic bag, the shoeshine man plucked a handbrush and a grey, stained rag which he flourished and snapped in the air. 'Nice shoes, man,' he said, brushing vigorously. 'Expensive. Good leather, tops and soles. I can see you're a man who likes quality and knows how to dress sharp. You're English, right? And these are the shoes of an English gentleman. You got them in London, right? Definitely London. Quality shoes, man, only from London.'

'Close. Edinburgh.'

'That's what I said, man. Edinboro. Is that your home town?'

'No,' David replied distractedly. 'I'm from London.'

'You here on holiday?'

'Maybe.' His gaze drifted around the square before settling on an incongruous building at one end, a cathedral. 'I can't remember.'

The shoeshine man stopped his frantic buffing motion and peered at David through his sunglasses. 'You can't remember? What's wrong?'

David's words floated out, almost to himself. 'It's like . . . someone's taken a scalpel and cut out part of my memory. This is New Orleans! I can't think of any reason why I should be in New Orleans, but here I am. I haven't been out of London for two years. I can barely afford the bus fare into the West End. I must be going mad!'

'Hey, slow down!' The shoeshiner seemed excited at the prospect of a good story. 'You've got, like, no memory and all that shit?'

'I came round on the trolleycar. It was like waking up from a deep sleep. There are bits and pieces from the last few weeks in my head, but that's all. Christ, I can't even remember landing at the airport. Maybe I hijacked a plane. Maybe I went mad because my job is so boring and life is so fucking dreary. I could have robbed a bank, fled the country and come to New Orleans to live out my days in the sun.'

'If that's right, the price of this shoeshine just went up.'

There was someone watching them.

Near the cathedral, with the sun behind him, a man stood motionless, his head turned in their direction. At another time David would have ignored him, but he felt something, an icy tingling that left him uncomfortable. Paranoia, he thought. But the sensation continued, like a subsonic buzz.

He's just a tourist, David thought.

He still went cold. Squinting into the sunlight, he plucked out details from the dark shape. The man was tall and his skin was black although it had a strange sheen to it in the bright sun. His hair was pomaded back in a hopelessly outdated style, glinting in the rays. Unusually, in the warmth, he wore a heavy, dark suit, stylishly cut, and a white shirt. Not a limb moved.

'You know that guy over there?' David asked the man at his feet.

The shoeshiner glanced around him. 'No one who knows me's gonna come down here, man. Just get tourists down here. In the day . . .'

David looked for the watcher again, but a crowd milling towards the riverside blocked his view. When they had passed by, the place where he had seen the tall man was empty.

'Whatever's happened, man, there are plenty of worse places you could be.' The shoeshine man continued the conversation, unaware that David's attention had wandered. 'What about your name? You must remember that?'

'Easter. David Easter. I know my home address, my post code, all the basics. It's just details. There's something . . . I don't know . . . something important I should be remembering. Christ, why am I telling this to a total stranger!' The panic continued to rise and fall within him, the swell of a mighty ocean, just one step away from a tidal flood.

"Cause I'm a good listener. Sounds to me like you went and got yourself mugged. Happened to my cousin Jake. Coupla guys jumped him, beat him round the head with a tyre iron and took his wallet. Ten lousy bucks, that's all he had. Ten bucks, man.

Shit, can't get many shoeshines with that. My brother found him three days later, sleeping on a park bench. Jake didn't know him from Adam. Didn't even recognize his wife.' He paused, slapping a shoe with a range of different strokes. 'So, where are you staying?'

'I don't know.'

'You checked your pockets? Might be something in there. A clue or some shit like that.'

This was so obvious that David was surprised and embarrassed that he hadn't thought of it before. In his left pocket was his passport and a thick book of American Express traveller's cheques; he glanced at them without letting the shoeshiner see them. Behind them was a travel agent's card wallet. An itinerary was stapled inside.

'The Sonesta Hotel,' he read out loud.

'Sonesta? Good hotel, man. Classy. It's down on Bourbon. Maybe you did rob that bank.' He looked at David over the top of his sunglasses. 'Hey, if you're looking for a guide around town, I'm your man. I know all the jumpin' joints. Best clubs, best bars. You wanna hear good music, I know where. You want some blow, I can find it. An' if you want a good woman, I can get that too. Bebop, blow and babes. Shit, man, I can even take you to all the tourist spots. Don't go with any of those guys on Jackson Square. They'll rip you off. I'm your man. Word.' He finished his spiel with a final flourish of his rag.

'Thanks, I'll bear that in mind.'

'You can find me anywhere between here an' the river workin' my patch any day, man. The name's Moose.' He held out his hand.

David looked at it, and then shook it. Having done so, he immediately delved in his other jacket pocket. His fingers moved over the familiar shape of his wallet and settled on a piece of card, one corner crinkled and bent. Gently, he pulled it out. It was a photo, recently taken, but obviously well travelled, its edges a spiderweb of creases. A hot flush swept over him; he wanted to laugh and cry at the same time.

The picture that had triggered this explosion of feeling showed him sitting on the couch in his flat, his face bright, his arm around a woman. For some reason David could not bring himself to look at her face. Anxiously, he pushed the photo back into his pocket.

'Something interesting, man?' Moose asked.

'Maybe.' David bottled his emotions back up tightly. His throat burned. 'Thanks for the shoeshine. I like to look my best.'

'You're lookin' sharp, man.'

David handed over two dollars and added another one as a tip. Moose tucked them immediately into a moneybelt. 'Don't forget, man.' He slapped David's shoulder. 'I'll be down here working my patch. Just ask for Moose.'

The sun was hot on his neck as David crossed the square and headed towards a café. He had to control himself, had to be logical. If his memory was going to return, it would do so in its own time. Meanwhile, he knew his primary concern was to find a bed, a roof and some food. And that meant finding the Sonesta Hotel.

He took a detour to a tourist booth and bought a guide to the city. Looking out across Jackson Square to the French Quarter, he had a brief feeling of vitality and excitement despite his predicament. The magic of the city was as evident to him as if every building had been lit by neon. New Orleans, the city of jazz! One of his fantasy destinations whenever he'd thought about escaping from London.

Nearby a horn player stood on the kerb, wringing out subtle emotions and brilliant colours from his instrument. Passers-by rewarded him by tossing coins and notes into a shoebox at his feet, small payment for bringing a brief glimmer into their lives. Occasionally he paused to wipe a sheen of sweat from his brow and exchange jokes with the children who ran up to stare at him.

David walked into the Café du Monde, finding it both bustling and laid-back at the same time, and took a table close to the pavement where he could hear the street music easily. He ordered a *café au lait* and some hot, square doughnuts dusted with mounds of castor sugar which the waitress called 'beignets', parted with a dollar sixty, and watched the crowds pass by on the sidewalk: the tourists, the locals, the hustlers, the musicians, black, white, fat, thin, young, old – the insistent, jumping beat of the city.

It was a moment of peace and relaxation briefly replacing the panic – until he remembered an attractive, smiling woman on a crumpled photograph.

Even in the comfort of his room in the Sonesta Hotel, easily found on Bourbon Street, he could not bring himself to look at the photo straightaway. He felt he needed time to prepare himself. It was a key to the door which would open the labyrinth of his hidden memory and it frightened him. He knew that once he unlocked that door something unwanted would eventually crawl out of the dark. He didn't know what it was, but he knew it was in there. Waiting.

Hanging his jacket carefully on the back of a chair, he turned to the suitcase he'd found on the bed. The contents were a revelation; he could not remember packing. At first there were only the essentials: a few changes of underwear and socks, toiletries, a pair of 501s, a couple of t-shirts. But as he got further and further down the case, a feeling of disquiet crept up on him.

Gingerly he half moved a t-shirt. Nothing seemed out of the ordinary, but alarm bells were ringing in his head. His memory might be locked away, but it was still speaking to him in abstract terms. And it was telling him that something in the case was bad. He was shaking once more.

Christ, what a state I'm in, David thought. Nervously, he turned away, switched on the TV and turned the sound low, letting it drone in the background in the hope that the noise would calm him. Leaning against a chair, he eyed the suitcase cautiously as if it might leap from the bed and bite him.

Come on! he told himself. *It's only a suitcase, for God's sake.*

At first he thought his subconscious was finally about to speak to him, but the feeling receded and he knew the only way to find out what was frightening him would be to look and see. He stepped forward, stared at the t-shirt for a second while his stomach did a flip, and then he plucked it away.

At the bottom of his case was an old, white shirt, no longer white. It was splattered with dark stains across the front, huge,

24

encrusted spatters which gave the appearance of army camouflage.

Blood.

His own? But he had no cuts on his body. Feeling sick to the pit of his stomach, he flipped the case shut so he did not have to touch the shirt. He locked it with trembling fingers.

Sitting on the edge of the bed with his head in his hands, strange images came alive in his mind, but when he focused on them, they disappeared, teasingly insubstantial. All part of his disorientation. Something had dragged him a world away, some powerful force, but he had no idea what it could be. He could not face it either.

He slumped back on to the bed and stared at the ceiling, waiting for it to crash in upon him. Then he closed his eyes and tried to wish all his questions away.

Later, he went for a drink in the bar to calm his frayed nerves. The Sonesta was a quiet, refined oasis amid the seedy glamour of Bourbon Street with its strip joints and bars and 24-hour party people. The foyer was marble, the furniture expensive and understated. David felt like an impostor. He had never stayed anywhere as classy before, where the bellhops still called him 'sir', but the room was reserved in his own name.

In a quiet corner, he drank a cold beer and steeled himself. Then he withdrew the photo from his pocket once more, but this time he forced himself to examine the woman's face.

She looked familiar, although he could not recall her name. Tantalizingly it hovered on the edge of his memory. What did emerge surprised him with its intensity. Sweeping emotions, sudden and destabilizing, a yearning to have her there next to him so he could touch her skin, stroke it, feel its warmth and silky texture. In the photo she was smiling, but only slightly, enigmatically even. One corner of her mouth twitched up, hinting at secret knowledge, hidden depths. Her eyes glittered darkly and seductively. Black hair in a stylish bob gleamed richly.

They had been close, hadn't they, some time during those lost weeks? And, more than that, she had stolen his heart.

In a sudden flash of remembrance, he knew she had been forced to leave him. And he *knew*, although he did not know how, that she had come to New Orleans. The details of their relationship were still hidden, but the emotions he felt for her returned to swamp him. He would have followed her to the ends of the earth – and in a way he guessed he had. She had been the one thing in his life that he treasured and for some reason she had left it.

A nameless woman, his life, his love. Where was she now?

Chapter 2

'There's nothing physically wrong with you, as far as I can see.'

The doctor switched off his pencil flashlight and stopped peering into David's left ear. 'No bumps or scars or obvious signs of any injury. I can X-ray your head if you like, but I don't think we'll find anything. You say you've not been experiencing constant headaches . . .' He shrugged. 'From the symptoms I don't think it's anything serious.'

'So what is it? Are you telling me it's psychological?'

'Could be.' The doctor returned to his leather swivel-chair and looked at David across his desk. He had a deep brown tan and blue eyes like an ageing West Coast surfer. The hotel had found him and arranged a quick appointment after David had woken in a panic and realized there were still no signs of his memory returning. Once over the initial shock, he had envisaged a whole host of hideous causes and a medical examination seemed the only way to put his mind at rest.

'Have you heard of the term "fugue"?' the doctor asked.

'It's a musical expression, isn't it?'

He nodded. 'But it's also used in psychology. Fugue is a condition where someone loses their identity and wanders away from the home environment. It's not as rare as you might think.'

'But I haven't lost my identity. I know who I am. And I came here looking for my girlfriend.'

The doctor held his hands in the air. 'I'm not saying I have all the answers. I deal with the body, not the mind. You would need to see a specialist to take it further.'

David considered this and asked the big question. 'If that *is* the problem . . . what caused it?'

'A trauma of some kind, I would guess – emotional or physical. The mind can cope with sudden shock by shutting down many functions to repair itself and to prevent the stress of further attacks.

27

It might be something as simple as you being unable to cope when your girl said she didn't want to see you again.'

'She wouldn't have said that.' David surprised himself with the vehemence of his denial.

'How do you know that? You told me you could barely remember anything about the woman. I sense in your response a certain amount of self-denial. Perhaps you should consider that area.'

'I know I love her.' He surprised himself again when the words came out.

'How?'

'I . . . just feel it. It's so strong, it's the only thing I *can* feel and it seems like it's getting stronger. I can't recall any facts or images . . . anything about her. But I do keep getting waves of abstract impressions, emotions, that sort of thing. I don't know . . . it's so difficult to put into words.'

'That's understandable. Your mind doesn't want to be acting in this way so it's sending out signals to let you know things are OK really.'

'Will my memory come back?'

'It will, but don't ask me when. It could be tomorrow. It could be twenty years from now. You might find it returning in piecemeal fashion, a little here, a little there, over a period. Then again, if you found the right trigger it could all come back at once.'

'If I found *her* . . . ?'

'That would probably do it.'

Find the woman. In his mind the words were burning, six foot high, kerosene-doused and roaring.

David checked his watch. Noon. New Orleans was six hours behind London so Willie would be home from work, jazz blaring loudly from his hi-fi, a can of cold Kronenbourg safely warming in his hand.

The dull grey patch in his mind, what he had come to call the Fog Zone, had not shifted, but Willie would know what had happened. He knew everything David did. They had been friends since school, teaming up in the playground – the gawky kid with the dour expression and bad attitude, and the bespectacled kid with the smart mouth and the fading Scottish accent. David had got them out of the fights that Willie's mouth had got them into. They had studied for exams together and dropped out together, much to their parents' irritation and despair. And as their disillusion with London life grew, it was Willie who had introduced David to jazz. The music had saved him. It had brought colour into grey days and nights, and it had introduced him to stylish clothes instead of drab fashions, as well as passion and excitement. It had given his existence meaning at a time when he was in danger of immersing himself in drugs or drink to cloud his mind. And then, five years ago, they had vowed to escape to New Orleans. To live out their days in a haze of cool beats and hot tunes, honkers, screamers, beboppers, wild women, Wild Turkey and Dixie. Sure. Willie would know what had happened. He knew everything.

When was the last time he had seen him?

There was something there, in the centre of the Fog Zone, like a drowning man waving frantically. David concentrated, focusing tightly on it, but it was just out of reach and all his effort would not bring it closer. The man drowned.

In his room he dialled Willie's number; it was the only phone number he had in his head but he knew it was Willie's. There was silence as the signal leapt the transatlantic gulf. Through the window he could see a blue sky unmarked by clouds. In Brixton it would be twilight, chilly, probably raining.

The ringing began. He would pick up soon. It was unlikely he would be out. Willie was a creature of habit: in from work at the same time, eating his meal on his lap in front of the TV regular as clockwork. David let it ring for a full five minutes before hanging up.

For some strange reason, he felt irritated when he thought of London. He had always hoped to leave the capital, but that still didn't explain the strange desire never to go back there which had come over him as he'd hung on the phone. At least while some mysterious force was paying for his stay in New Orleans, he *didn't* have to think about England. There were other ways of tracing his missing love without spending hours waiting for Willie to come back from having a good time.

Later, as he stood out on the sidewalk in Bourbon Street smelling the mixed aromas on the warm breeze, a strange thought flashed into his head.

This is the beginning. Who knows where it will end?

It was not his thought, he was sure of that. It was a cliché from a thousand romance novels. But there it was. He walked out into Bourbon Street. It was not the way he would have chosen to find himself in the city of his dreams, but that wouldn't stop him doing his damnedest to enjoy it.

The street life and the sights were mesmerizing, but David's thoughts kept rolling back to a female face. Every now and then he would stop his random tramping and pull out the photo, staring intently as if those features would suddenly unlock his memory. She was the key.

As he passed a newspaper dispenser, he automatically dug out a few coins and pulled a copy of the *Times-Picayune* from the machine. 'Now in its 157th year', it said proudly beneath the masthead. He riffled through the pages of the New Orleans rag, and as he did so an idea began to come to him.

He returned to his hotel room and dialled the paper, asking to be put through to the newsroom. Establishment figures always made him faintly uneasy, but he was prepared to suffer if it brought him closer to his goal. The suffering wasn't too great; everyone exuded Southern charm. He hung on for the City Desk secretary, the Features Department secretary and then the assistant features editor while they tried to decide what to do with him. Eventually he found himself talking to a feature writer who went by the name of Lynsey Kane.

'What can I do for you?' she asked politely. Her voice was like honey.

'I'm looking for someone,' David replied, working himself up for his spiel. 'My name's David Easter. I'm from England . . . London. I'm trying to find a woman from New Orleans whom I met back home.'

'Have you thought about taking out a small ad?' The reporter's voice had developed a slight iciness. David could tell she was thinking, *Don't waste my time.* He had to get to the point.

'I have, but this would make a good story for you. I was in an accident. Hit and run. I lost my memory.' He paused and then added hastily, 'I didn't have any identification with me, see? I ended up in hospital for a while and everyone who knew me thought I was dead. Or something.' He was sweating. He never felt convincing lying. 'To cut a long story short, the woman I was in love with was so heartbroken she left England and came back to her family home here before I could let her know I was still alive.' He paused and waited for a response.

'Go on.' His heart skipped. She sounded interested now.

'Part of my memory returned – you know, my name, personal details – but I still can't remember *her* name. I've spent everything I could earn to come here and look for her. All I've got is a photo. I thought maybe you could publish it, tell my story and that she'd read it and get in touch with me.'

Before he had barely finished speaking, the reporter said, 'Come into the office. We'll talk about it. I can't promise anything. I need to interview you fully before I can make a decision, but if your story holds up, well . . . we'll see.'

David scribbled down the directions to the office and then hung up. The success of his scam had given him an adrenaline buzz. It could work, as long as *she* read the paper. He smiled to himself.

Then he had a more ominous thought which leapt into his mind without warning: as long as she was still alive.

Sunlight shimmered on the waters of the Mississippi as it rolled towards the sea. David stood by the railings for almost fifteen minutes, transfixed by the eddies, the soft, sleepy lapping against the dockside, and the impenetrable grey-green colour that hinted at dark and secret depths. He felt at peace looking out across the expanse of water to the far bank, the warm wind gently raising the hairs on the nape of his neck. For one moment, all that mattered was the slow, steady passage of time marked by the river's flow.

He had slept deeply and long, free of dreams, well-refreshed and ready to establish a base in the city. If the worst came to the worst and his mystery woman was not located easily, he knew he might have to stay in New Orleans for days, even weeks. That would cost money, and it would not be too long before the traveller's cheques ran out. The hotel had been pre-paid for two weeks so at least he didn't have to look for another place to stay immediately. Of course he could return to London at any time – the airline ticket was in his travel agent's wallet – but that wasn't a real option. With each hour that passed it seemed increasingly important that he find the woman in the photo, even if it meant leaving his own life on hold.

Moose was easily located, on his turf, hassling the tourists for dollars. David could hear his endless patter long before he saw him, a hip-hop beat of words bouncing out of a human sound-system. When he saw David approaching he nodded to him discreetly and finished shining the shoes of an elderly man in a brown, ill-fitting suit.

'Hey, man, how ya doin'?' He tucked a five-dollar bill into the belt wallet under his shirt.

'Fine. I decided to take you up on your offer.'

'That's what I'm here for, man. I'm a regular public service.'

'I need a job.'

'But you ain't got no green card, so we gotta be careful, right?' Moose grinned. 'Sure, no problem. I know just the place. Man owes me a few favours.'

'I'll see you right.'

'Twenty-five bucks a week out of your wage packet.'

'Twenty-five dollars? Indefinitely? I'm not a charity, Moose.'

'This is business, man. I gotta make a living. Got a lot of mouths to feed.'

'OK, OK. Twenty-five bucks.' A blast of the steam-boat *Natchez*'s whistle punctuated his reply.

Moose snapped his fingers loudly and laughed. 'You made the right choice, man. Stay here for a while. Take it easy, find out what the city's really like. You don't need all that tourist shit.'

'All I need is to find my friend.'

'You'll find her at Charlie's Place, man. That's where I'm

takin' you. Everybody goes to Charlie's Place – an' if they don't then you bet your life someone who does will know them.'

'Charlie's Place?'

'That's your new place of work, man. Your new employment centre.'

Charlie's Place was in one of the French Quarter's quieter streets. From the outside it resembled an abandoned store, ignored by shoppers who had moved on to more fashionable establishments. The door was ratchety and looked as if a single push would burst it from its hinges. Above it a large fan turned slowly, a dying rattle of age behind a wire grille. On either side two large windows of grey, dusty glass had been boarded up from the inside. It was a quiet place, a secret place; there was no sign outside.

David felt a tingle of excitement at the prospect of entering an historic New Orleans jazz club. During his years of dreaming on damp Brixton nights, the American city's clubs had attained a mythic quality; he did not care if the reality dovetailed from that; the fantasy was enough to fire his dreams. The rundown appearance of Charlie's Place did not destroy the magic. Even on the doorstep he could smell the atmosphere of bebop, the breeding ground for the Jazz Age.

Moose pushed open the door and led him into the dark confines. A rickety table had been set up just inside for the ticket seller and further on David could just discern the dull gleam of the rows of bottles behind the bar. The club itself was cramped. Fire regulations ensured most French Quarter venues were on the ground floor and Charlie's Place was no exception.

At a table in front of the bar, a buffalo-like man in his late fifties was writing in a large ledger, his sausage-like fingers awkwardly clutching a delicate fountain pen. Pneumatic muscles bulged out from beneath his shirtsleeves, but beer and junk food had turned his belly to rolls of shirt-stretching fat. His skin was so ebony it was almost lost in the surrounding gloom. Only the tight grey curls of his hair provided any outline. The red glow of a well-chewed cigar signified slight head movements.

'Charlie?' Moose said with uncommon politeness. 'I've got just the guy you're looking for.'

A disinterested grunt drifted towards them.

'Don't be like that, Charlie. This is the word.'

He tugged David's sleeve until he was standing before the club owner. Charlie looked up, his slow, white eyes showing no emotion above the rippling of his jowls. Gradually he stopped writing in the ledger like a clockwork toy winding down, and with a smack of his lips he deposited his cigar in the ashtray.

'What have we got here?' He drew the words out lazily and David could not tell if they were laced with contempt or humour.

'This is the man, Charlie. He needs a job. He's from England. London Town. Be good for business, Charlie. Folk love the way they speak.'

Charlie's stare was unwavering. Eventually he said, 'Say somethin', boy.'

'Mary had a little lamb.' David looked the nightclub owner directly in the eye. 'Its fleece was white as snow.'

Charlie flipped his lizard eyes on to Moose. 'The kid's got an attitude.'

Moose clapped his arm around David's shoulders in an overt display of camaraderie. 'Spirit, Charlie. The kid's got spirit.'

'You call it spirit. I call it an attitude.' He turned his attention back to David. 'So whaddaya want a job here for anyhow, kid? I'll tell you now, I don't want any dopeheads or pushers. No pimps, no dips and no petty thieves. You hear what I'm sayin'?'

'I hear.'

'You ever smile, boy? With a face like that you'll be scarin' off the payin' custom. That's one goddamn surly attitude.' Charlie snarled angrily, hawked and spat a wad of phlegm on the wooden floor.

'Aw, he don't mean nothin', Charlie. He's just messin'.' Moose moved sinuously around the table, his feet just a step away from a dance. 'He's got skills. Back in London he was the best barman in town. Folk used to come from all over England for his highballs. Ain't that right, Mis-ter Easter?'

David nodded. Charlie was unmoved. He replaced his stogey in his mouth and returned to work on the ledger. Moose danced a few more steps to the other side of the table. 'An' he's a hard worker, Charlie. Whee-ew, all that energy! Floors'll get swept faster than a hurricane. That's right, hurricane speed from Hurricane Easter!'

'You're startin' to piss me off, Moose.'

'Aw, give him a chance, Charlie. Have I ever sent you anybody who ain't the best?'

If Charlie agreed he didn't show any sign of it. 'You know what this club is, boy? It's a jazz club with a bit of ragtime an' a touch of bebop thrown in for good measure. I expect all my employees to have a good groundin' in the music. What can a li'l ol' white boy from London Town know about the jazz?'

'Everything,' David replied. *Arrogant jerk*, he thought. 'I know everything about jazz.'

Charlie laughed a deep, mocking chuckle. He turned to a new page in the ledger.

'Ask me.'

The nightclub owner looked up in surprise, his expression slowly changing to narrow-eyed curiosity. 'You what, boy?'

'Ask me a question. Anything about jazz. Anything you want. If I can't answer it, I leave. If I do answer it, you give me a job.'

This time Charlie's laughter was clean and hearty. 'You hear that, Moose! Let's make a deal! Haw, haw, haw, snk, snk.' He sucked on the cigar and obscured his head in a thick cloud of smoke. 'OK, boy, I'll make it an easy one 'cause I like you.' His eyes narrowed slyly. 'Lemme see now. Yeah, right.' The concentration on his face reflected the effort of dragging the question from the depths of his memory. 'Which old jazzman used to play of a night at Lulu White's bordello up in Storyville?' He laughed. 'Take your time, boy.'

'I don't need to. Jelly Roll Morton. He used to earn more than a whole band for his solo piano work.'

'Whee-oo.' Charlie was quietly impressed, but he buried it quickly. 'Best of three then, boy, as we agreed.' Charlie waited for David to argue before continuing. 'What . . . no, who . . .' Charlie paused and thought deeply. 'Right. Who released Blue Blues and Arkansas Blues on the ol' Brunswick label?'

'The Mound City Blue Blowers,' David replied sharply. 'Red McKenzie, Jack Bland and Dick Sleven.'

'I stand amazed.' Charlie and Moose both laughed raucously,

doubling up at the waist and hooting with obvious surprise. 'You won it fair an' square, boy,' Charlie admitted. 'You know your music. I'll give you your job, but don't you forget I'm doin' you a big favour. It ain't gonna be legal 'cause I'm damn sure you ain't got no green card an' if the immigration comes snoopin' round then I wash my hands of you, you hear me?' David agreed. 'I 'spect Moose here wants his reg'lar deal so I'll pay him straight from your wage packet. Save you havin' to worry about it.'

Moose gave David the thumbs up from behind Charlie's back. 'What's the wage?'

'Don't you worry about that, boy. I won't cheat you. My word is my bond.'

The door swung open with a crash. A tall blonde made an entrance like a forties movie star and marched up to the bar. She was wearing high-tops, tight black ski pants and a silk shirt knotted at the waist. Her hair was pinned up on top of her head and tumbled down loosely like a mushroom cloud. 'Yo, Charlie.' Her face had the hardness of a downhome Veronica Lake.

'How you doin', Arlene?' Charlie turned back to David and whispered, 'An' I don't want you slippin' it to the waitresses neither.'

'I'm clean living, Charlie.'

'You make sure you stay that way.' His attention was already wavering. He picked up his fountain pen to return to the accounting and added, almost as an afterthought, 'You start at nine tomorrow night. Don't be late. You get your money at the end of the week.'

'Say, Charlie,' Arlene yelled over from the bar. 'You hear about the stiff?'

'What stiff?'

'They fished him out of the river this morning. Said it looked like a truck had run over his head.'

'Probably drunk as a skunk with his head on the tracks listenin' for the streetcar comin'.'

Arlene lit a cigarette, screwing up her eyes as the smoke drifted across her face. 'No, it's got to be the Mob, Charlie. They destroy the features so the victim can't be traced.' Her throaty laugh transmuted into a cough. 'I read that in the *Enquirer*. And if he was hit by a streetcar, how come he ended up in the river?'

'Chickens do it all the time, man.' Moose snapped his fingers and put his arm around David's shoulders. 'Hey, Arlene. You got some new competition for gratuities.'

'Hello, Arlene.'

She flashed David a smile. He estimated she was in her mid-thirties, but she had that lived-in look that came from drugs, drink or too much work for too little pay. There were dark smudges under her eyes.

'You better show this snot-nosed punk the ropes, Arlene,' Charlie growled. 'Wouldn't want him to screw up on his first night. What *is* your name, kid?'

'David Easter.'

'Well, don't fuck up, boy, or you'll be crucified. Haw, haw, hyuck, hyuck, huck.'

As David walked over to Arlene, Moose whispered in his ear, 'I'll be in touch, man. See how you're gettin' on. Might be able to do more business, right?' Then he was loping across the room with giant strides towards the door, the anticipation of another deal already lighting in his mind.

Arlene stubbed out her cigarette as David approached. She reached out and shook his hand with a tough, street grip. 'Pleased to meet you, David. You're a Brit, right?'

He nodded. 'From London.'

'God, London. I'd love to visit London! I dream about it all the time – Carnaby Street, London Bridge, Buckingham Palace. Better than this goddamn dump,' she added in a conspiratorial whisper. 'So what's he got you doing?'

David shrugged. 'Who knows? He only hired me for the novelty value. But my shoulders are broad. I can live with it.'

'That probably means you'll be doing everything.'

'The jobs no one else wants?'

'Right. And there are plenty of those. Charlie's Place is real popular. Every night is like Christmas at Macy's, and everyone gets drunk by ten. But Charlie's fair, y'know. He doesn't rip us off. So why are you hanging out here? This isn't the kind of joint I'd expect a nice guy like you to work in.'

'Appearances are deceptive. And I need the money. I'm planning to stay in town for a while. I'm trying to look up an old friend.'

'So, where's home?'

'The Sonesta.'

'Yeah? And you're working here?'

'I've got to find somewhere else to stay soon – *and* I've got to find the money to pay for it.' The prospect was daunting. He was starting to enjoy the comfort of the Sonesta.

'I might be able to help you.' Arlene rifled through her purse. 'I've got a friend who's got a room free. The guy who was sharing with her walked out in the middle of the night. He stuck her with all the bills. If I can find her a new roomie before she advertises, I'll be her friend for life. Maybe she'll lay off asking for that loan back.' She scribbled down a number on the torn-off top of her cigarette packet. 'Her name's Beth. She's cute, but she'll give you a hard time.'

'I hope I pass the inspection.'

She rested her elbow on the bar and her head on her hand, letting her gaze wander across his face. 'I'll tell her you get my seal of approval.'

'I'm honoured.'

She smiled. 'Listen, I've got to talk to Charlie. I need an advance and I just bet he won't give it to me.' She took her lipstick and a small mirror out of her purse. 'But if I smile sweetly . . . I'll see you tomorrow night.'

'This snot-nosed punk has to learn the ropes off someone.'

'I'm glad you've got a sense of humour,' she added. 'You're going to need it working here.'

David left Charlie's Place with a palpable sense of relief. It was as if he had replaced some of the life that had disappeared. London did not seem such a loss, nor did his job at the record shop; he had lost interest in both of them anyway. Now he had an island of security at the centre of the typhoon. But despite all that, he couldn't shake the feeling that hidden in his memory was a terrible secret.

Something dark and filled with blood.

And something that might just save his life.

Chapter 3

The bloody shirt in his suitcase haunted David's waking hours. Several times he moved the case from under the bed to the wardrobe and back again in a futile search for a hiding place where it could be forgotten. His only escape from his thoughts was in the ruler-straight streets and twisting, hidden alleys of the French Quarter, exploring them obsessively as he waited for the interview at the *Times-Picayune* which he hoped would lead him to the woman in his photo. Occasionally he would entertain a vision of just bumping into her on the street, browsing in one of the cluttered bookshops or staring into the windows of the art galleries on Royal Street. Sometimes he even thought he caught a glimpse of her at the end of a dark alley or walking on to an ornate balcony, tending the verdant hanging baskets and floral displays. It was never her.

Breathing behind the brick of those timeless streets was every fantasy he'd ever nurtured during all those days when he lay in his London apartment listening to the rain on the window. This was the magic of the Quarter. The locals called it the Vyoo Carray, a perversion of its French name, Vieux Carre, but to David it was simply a wonderland – untouched by developers or the harsh realities of the modern world. It was alive; he could hear the walls breathe, softly, in-out, in-out, like sandpaper whispers on the edge of his perception. The past was living. The present did not exist. The air did not smell of chemicals and fumes; it smelled of must, seeping out through the pores of the huddled old buildings. It smelled of age.

David broke his meandering tour when his stomach told him, pausing at a dark bar on Chartres Street. Its walls were yellowing and cracked and a wooden sign bearing the name The Napoleon House creaked over the door. He ordered a Dixie beer and, from the menu, a heavy Italian sandwich called a muffuletta.

'This is an historical place.' The dry, rustling voice disrupted his concentration. On the next table an old woman was leaning in his direction, her face brown and shrewish, her hair a mass of grey wire pulled back and tied with a bow. Half-lens glasses gave her the appearance of a cultured academic. 'It dates back to the seventeen hundreds. Did you know they hatched a plot here to rescue Napoleon from St Helena? The French émigrés wanted to bring him triumphantly to freedom in New Orleans. They even prepared a room upstairs for the little emperor. They filled it with the finest furniture, paintings and drapes to befit his status. He never came.'

'Those dictators – they're so unreliable. Too busy invading other countries or rotting in prison to remember their friends.' After the intensity of his solitary brooding, he was happy to talk to another person. 'I like the atmosphere,' he added. 'You need history when all you see each day are burger bars and parking lots.'

She lifted a wooden cane and tapped it on the edge of his table. 'If you like history, young man, you have come to the right place. The past lives on in New Orleans. Nothing ever really dies here.' She whispered behind her hand, 'There's magic in this city. I myself am nearly two hundred years old.'

David smiled politely at her eccentricity.

'Life is full of strange, inexplicable things,' she continued. 'We must celebrate them. That is why we have Mardi Gras here – to celebrate the strange. In my purse . . .' – she tapped an aged black leather bag – '. . . I have artefacts of great power. There are things in here which would make your hair curl. I have a stone statuette of a Native American god who tells me great secrets. I have a talisman once owned by the Comte de St Germain.' She paused, waiting for the wonder to dawn on his face. When it didn't she added, 'Oh, my dear, another unbeliever. There are so many people who can't see the wondrous things around them. Well, I must be away now. The spirits are calling.'

She downed her Bloody Mary, bid David goodbye and tottered slowly out of the bar. Several customers nodded at her as she passed. A harmless eccentric, David told himself, but her words had nevertheless disturbed him.

As the lunchtime crowd increased, he retreated into himself.

His gaze wandered aimlessly around the room, eventually falling upon a grey, ageing photograph, framed and displayed with others at the end of the bar. He couldn't distinguish it clearly, the way the sun fell on it through the open shutters, the drinkers occasionally obscuring his vision, but it seemed to him that it featured a woman holding something. And she was surrounded by strange shapes, an eagle, an angel. The more David focused, the less he could see. He squinted, feeling things shift in his own mind. It reminded him of something – something hidden in the Fog Zone. It reminded him . . .

And then he had it, realization coming like a slap to the face.

A Tarot card.

He pulled the photo quickly from his pocket and, sure enough, there on the table in the foreground was a pack of Tarot cards. She had been obsessed by them, hadn't she? He remembered now. It was one of the first things she had told him at the start of their relationship. Gradually a scene crystallized from his memory: his room, late one evening, alcohol, music, low lights, the woman slowly shuffling a deck she had pulled from her travelling bag.

'This is my card,' she had said.

It was there, floating in front of him. Card number five, *Travel*, the French translation – *Voyage* – written above it.

Her words had perfect clarity, as if she had only whispered them in his ear a moment ago. 'This card is called The Gospel – it's very important. You know why? Because it's the emblem of success in love as well as career. It's got its sights set on heaven.' Her laughter had seemed strange, almost bitter. 'It's also the card of travellers. You turn this card over and you know that your journey will prove beneficial. It means other things too – reconciliation . . .' But now the words trailed back into the Fog.

As David drained the last of his Dixie, he marvelled at how the subconscious mind worked, throwing up its own hints and pointers while the conscious mind was wandering round in circles. If she was obsessed with the Tarot perhaps she had visited one of the readers in the city? And if he took the photo around, someone might recognize her, remember a name, an address. It was a long shot, but it was worth pursuing while waiting to see if the newspaper would play.

On the way out of The Napoleon House, he inspected the picture that had inspired him. There were no eagles or angels. It was simply a portrait of a young man in a black suit standing in a doorway.

On Bourbon Street, not far from the hotel entrance, was Marie Laveau's Voodoo Shop. It already had a special fascination for him. He had passed it several times and on each occasion he was amazed that it actually existed, there, in the centre of the tourist zone. It seemed that even the dark religion of Africa and the Caribbean was a tourist attraction these days. It sold charms, spells, mojos and gris-gris to housewives from Poughkeepsie and scholars from Birmingham, anyone who wanted to win a distant heart or deflect the evil eye. At the centre of the window was the biggest charm of all, an American Express sign.

The shop was dark, but the woman behind the counter was bright and good-natured. She gave David a list of names and numbers of Tarot readers in the city and advised him which ones to try first. The most important, she said, was a woman called Dauphine.

David tried three readers on his way to Dauphine, but without any luck. They all promised a great deal, that they could eventually lead him to his lost love, but it was obvious there was little substance to their guarded offerings. He had already decided on a different approach when he arrived at Dauphine's place on Barracks Street on the east side of the French Quarter.

She had the prettiest house on the street. The filigreed balcony was festooned with flowers, large, colourful blooms, overflowing hanging baskets dripping with water. There were tiny coloured pennants along the guttering and in the centre of the balcony was a wind chime which tinkled melodically with each breeze along the quiet street. A lone wooden chair was positioned for a view of the sunset.

A stately black woman answered the door. David was immediately struck by her eyes which seemed to pierce to the heart of him. She rarely blinked and when she did her lids moved up and

42

down like a lizard in the sun. There was an air of lazy summer days about her and it was not just the way she moved her hips slowly from side-to-side as she walked, tugging at the material of the red-gold-and-green wraparound dress.

She led him through to a cool, dark study at the rear of the house. It smelled of rose blossom. Bric-à-brac and ornaments filled every available space, a cornucopia of tiny interests, of statuettes and pictures and ornate jewellery, candlesticks, plants and urns. Dauphine sat in one of the antique Regency chairs which stood on either side of the dark, mahogany desk.

'Please.' She motioned to the other chair. 'Sit.' The atmosphere made David feel uneasy and a little apprehensive.

As he sat down he was aware of her studying his face intently. Something about her gaze made his flesh creep, an impression that she was burrowing through his skin, his bone, into the depths of his brain. He stared back at her, offence as defence, while his fingers twined nervously in his lap.

'What can I do for you?' Her voice was like oil, but everything else about her put David on edge. He felt she already knew why he was there, what he wanted, all his innermost private thoughts.

'A reading. I want to know about my future.'

She shook her head.

'What? You're not going to do it?'

'That's not what you want to know. People who come here, they want to know somethin' specific. Are they gonna get rich? Are they gonna fall in love? Some even wanna know when they're gonna die. No one says, "Tell me about my future."'

Her gaze had turned cold, laying his deception bare. David felt chastened, but before she could terminate the audience, he said hastily, 'OK, I'll be more specific. I want to know if I'm going to get back together with the girl I love.'

Dauphine nodded thoughtfully, weighing his words. Then she picked the pack of Tarot cards from the centre of the desk and held them out to him on the palm of her hand. 'Cut the cards.'

As he took them, he felt something squirm in his mind. A memory. The woman, his love. It burst forth, white hot from the Fog Zone and then receded just as quickly, leaving behind a hollow feeling at the pit of his stomach. Although he had come to expect any memory of her to be joyful, this one wasn't; there was a darkness behind it, a nagging doubt that he was unable to identify.

If only he could remember.

Dauphine took the cards and dealt them out on the desk in a pattern which she called The Crucible. As each lushly illustrated card was turned up on the dark wood, David felt himself pulled in a little more by the images, dragged down into a gothic world of skulls and demons and hanging men.

Finally she said, 'There we have it.'

'Is it good or is it bad?' David didn't really care about the answer. He just wanted to get to a point in the conversation where he could ask about the woman in his photo.

Dauphine didn't reply. Her face remained still and calm, but just for a second he saw something shift in her eyes that made him cold. Suddenly the ritual did mean something to him. There was a voice in his head telling him it was important. To listen, to listen carefully. For several minutes she stared at the cards as David's apprehension grew, and when she did finally speak her words were measured as if all emotion had been wrung out of them to protect him. 'You got . . . troubles. No doubt about it.'

'You can say that again.'

'This card . . .' – she pointed to one featuring a knight on a horse – '. . . is what we call the signifier. It speaks about the here and now. It represents change, separation, risky journeys. It tells me someone has left you an' now you're suffering.'

David had never really believed in the power of the Tarot, or astrology or skrying, or any one of those mystical things, but there, in Dauphine's dark parlour, that world suddenly seemed the most reasonable of all.

'Go on,' he said hesitantly. Once again she stared at him, and this time he had the unnerving feeling someone was standing just behind his shoulder. He resisted the urge to turn around.

'There's a hurricane out there shakin' everythin' up, and great sadness. And more.' A shadow passed across her face. 'Much more.' She turned over another card, tapping it with a long, painted fingernail. 'This card is The Sky. It represents secrets and what secrets hide, the truth. Of all the cards, this here is the most mysterious. There's mystery surroundin' you, a mystery at your heart. You're headin' for a surprise meetin' and a sudden discovery.'

A surprise meeting! A sudden discovery! David felt a swell in his heart.

'The girl. We . . . we were separated. By accident.'

'Now we get to the heart of it.'

'Will I find her?'

She searched the cards once more. 'It's not easy to see. This one . . .' She touched a card with a number four in the corner and the word 'Revelation' above the illustration. '. . . means you're going to lose something, but it shows you've got what it takes to face up to it. A secret, a bitter secret, is goin' to be revealed. It's goin' to upset you, I won't hide that from you. Maybe even do you some harm.'

She *was* hiding something from him. David could see it. Blunting the blow of her words. The chill within him grew colder as he chewed over what she'd said, sifting the hints of failure and despair. He needed to find the woman who loved him, of that he was certain. He could not afford to fail.

Subconsciously, he reached out to touch Dauphine's hand in appeal, but she withdrew it quickly, allowing him only a fleeting contact. He had the sensation of brushing a peach stuffed with ice.

She pointed to another card. The word 'Violence' was at the top. The chill within David turned to a faint nausea. 'This is the worst card here for you. It signifies Evil Force.'

A memory . . . almost . . . almost, blood . . . noise. The room whirled around him, and he clutched on to the edge of the desk until his fingertips hurt. The memory fell back once more, leaving a disturbing psychic aftertaste.

'Whenever I see this, I feel my bones go cold.' Dauphine's voice seemed far away, droning. David fought to centre himself. 'It's a card that is harmful. It speaks to me of violence and hard effort with nothin' to show for it. It speaks of people who can't control themselves . . .' Her voice trailed off as if she'd been about to say more, but had caught herself at the last moment.

David shook his head a little too much. 'No,' he said with a hard, defensive smile. He paused, thought a moment, and then said again with more stress, 'No.'

Violence, she had said.

His head was hurting, pounding at the temples. Bang, bang. Bang, bang. Something was creeping forward from the Fog Zone, snarling in the swirling mists, building up speed, ready to rend and tear, to force its way out into the light. He rubbed his forehead, still shaking his head.

No. He *didn't* want it to get out. He *didn't* want to remember.

The deft touch of Dauphine's hand on his was like an electric shock, snapping him away from the dark thoughts. David looked the Tarot reader in the face and said, 'I'm afraid.' He didn't know why or of what, but he could taste the metallic edge of fear in his mouth.

'You poor boy.' For the first time there was emotion there, but it was pity. 'The cards are just a guide. A warnin', if you will. These things aren't writ in stone.'

'I can't remember.' It was all he could think to say. Dauphine and the cards had stirred things within him, but rather than the warm flush of happy memories, something bitter and twisted had surfaced. He couldn't give it form yet, but he could sense it. And he knew, whatever it was, that it was something best forgotten.

As if to confirm his thoughts, Dauphine waved her hands over the cards and said, 'You better listen to me now, though. There're some real strange forces around you. Everythin' I see here tells me danger. What you gettin' yourself into?'

'Nothing. I just want to find my girlfriend.'

Dauphine's expression lightened a little. 'They call this the city of love. If you were meant to find your sweetheart here, the spirits will bring you together.'

'I have a photograph.' He handed the snap over to her. 'She's into the Tarot. You might have given her a reading.'

Dauphine's hand paused as she reached out for the picture when he laid it on the table. It was almost imperceptible, but David noticed. 'Do you know her?' She took the photo without replying and stared at it for a long minute. Finally David asked again. 'Do you know her?'

'I know her.' Her voice was steady, impassive. David felt a tingle of excitement.

'Where can I find her?'

'I don't know. It's been months since she was here. Every few weeks she'd come to see me to have her cards read. She never told me where she lived.'

'Months?'

Dauphine nodded.

'But I met her in London.'

'She's a N'Orleans girl, no doubt about it.'

That answered one question: *why New Orleans?* He had met her in London and she had returned home. And for some reason he had followed her.

'Do you know anyone who knows her? Anyone at all?' David could feel the desperation adding a jarring note of tension to his questions.

Dauphine shook her head. 'She was a quiet one. She never spoke much about herself. She just listened to what the cards had to say.'

David watched her carefully. Her eyes held his stare and for a while he almost believed her. Then there was a flicker, the merest loss of concentration, and he knew she was lying. She could see from his face that he had penetrated her façade.

Why was she lying? What was there to hide?

'I need to find her, Dauphine. I don't know anything about her because of my memory loss, but I've got this feeling that we were meant to be together. It's stronger than anything I've ever felt in my life.' That was the bizarre truth.

'I just tol' you,' she stressed. Her voice was like piano wire.

'Tell me everything. I need to know.' He watched her face darken. 'Tell me.' And then, suddenly, a question from nowhere, one which seemed to have no root in logic. 'Is she alive? Or is she dead?'

'Worse than dead.' Her voice crackled angrily, releasing the tension.

'What are you trying to say? What are you keeping from me?'

'Hush!' She paused, reining in her emotions. 'You don't know

47

anything. You don't *want* to know. She's dead to you. Leave it at that. Forget her.'

David snapped at the absurdity of this, 'Forget her! How can I forget her when I can't remember her? You've got to help me!'

'I don't know where she is. And that's the truth.'

'But you know something about her!'

She shook her head with a note of finality. 'You better be careful what you're messin' with, boy. You're way out of your depth.'

These ominous words made David pause, and in the lull his anger subsided and was replaced by the fear he had felt before, only this time it was stronger. 'What are you talking about? I'm only looking for a girl.'

Dauphine shook her head.

'What more is there?' Now he was almost pleading, yet somewhere deep inside him he realized he *knew*. There was a churning and roiling in the Fog Zone like two wild dogs fighting. His heart started to pound. He had to get out, away from cold stares and secrets, into the sun. He stood up, almost knocking his chair over in his haste.

He was surprised when Dauphine leaned over and held his hand again, this time tightly, with sympathy. 'Don't you forget what the cards said. This is an old town an' it's different from any other you'll be in. It doesn't forget its past as easy as other places. Sometimes it remembers the past as easy as if it was today.'

David withdrew his hand sharply, the panic within him growing. And he let Dauphine lead him to the door with a speed that was in contrast to her earlier languor, as if she could no longer bear to have him on her premises. She closed the door firmly, but David knew he would be back at some point, to prise her secrets from her.

He turned into the empty street. The distant cry of the *Natchez* steam ship echoed mournfully across the rooftops, but in his head David could still hear another sound. A banging. A harsh, angry banging.

'This whole deal sounds like some cheap romantic novel.'

Lynsey Kane eyed David suspiciously. She was just how he'd

imagined her from her voice: hair dyed an auburn gold, green eyes that reminded him of a cat, soft tan, and a smart, well-cut business suit just to let everyone know that, however she looked, she was no bimbo. Her crisp manner had David squirming.

'I know what it sounds like. Would I make up something like that?'

'I don't know.' She looked him in the face, eyes half-closed, and thought for a second. 'Unless you've got some perverse desire to get your face in the paper.'

'Not me. I'm the shy, retiring type. I wouldn't be here if it wasn't absolutely necessary.'

'Tell me again why it's necessary.'

'Because I love her.' He laid the picture on the desk between them and stared at the woman captured by the camera, her smile, her eyes. There was a shimmer in his memory and for a second he thought her name was going to leap to his lips. It fell back, as so many other memories had done, but he knew then it would only be a matter of time before he recalled who she was.

Evidently the sincerity in his voice was enough to convince Lynsey Kane. She switched on the mini tape recorder and put it in front of him. 'Tell me what you remember,' she said with irony obvious only to David.

The interview lasted only twenty minutes, but that was all the time it took David to spin his yarn about the love that spanned continents, with enough romance and drama to give it the colour that would ensure the paper printed it, and enough truth to achieve what David wanted. If Margaret Mitchell had been writing in the 1990s it would have done her justice, he was sure of it.

When Lynsey switched off the tape there was silence in the interview room apart from the murmur of computer keyboards from the newsroom without. Eventually she said, 'You must love her a great deal.'

'I do.'

She nodded, obviously moved by the sentiment, before returning to her businesslike approach. 'We should have it in the paper pretty soon. It's a slow news period . . . no disrespect to you, of course. I'll get our picture desk to arrange a snap of you and to copy your photo. We'll run the two side by side.'

'Do you think it will work?'

She shrugged. 'You won't have a better opportunity. If she doesn't read it, somebody who knows her will. Just one word of warning.'

'What's that?'

'There are a lot of nuts in N'Orleans. And they're worse than the ones in LA or New York, believe me. They've been out in the sun longer. They could come calling . . .'

'I can look after myself.'

'Don't underestimate the people of this city just because it looks pretty. There's a lot of violence out there. A lot of brutality.'

Something shifted suddenly in the Fog Zone, responding to her words. There was a rushing in his ears like the sound of a jet taking off. He could almost remember. It was so close.

'. . . find her, let me know,' Lynsey was saying. 'I'll write a follow-up.'

'I will,' David lied. He stood up and shook her hand, but all he could think about was the word that had triggered the explosion in his memory. For the second time that day.

Violence.

By 11 p.m. Charlie's Place was a bubbling pot of passion and energy, customers shoulder to shoulder, wall to wall, calling for beer and bourbon in raucous voices above the vibrant music of the house band, The Dedication All-Star Ensemble. Half of the club nearest to the stage was reserved for drinkers at tables only, but Charlie had sidestepped his own rules by packing in at least ten people to each table. David had not stopped moving for two hours. His shoulder ached from holding a drinks tray above the bobbing heads and his feet were sore from tramping back and forth. When he wasn't walking he was swabbing up a never-diminishing pool of spilt beer and water behind the bar.

But the music kept him going. The crash of the drums, the anguished blare of the sax, the guitarist, inventive and wild, his face contorted in concentration. Sometimes David would stop whatever he was doing and watch until the calls for service grew too loud to ignore.

His first night would have been much more difficult without Arlene to help him. She had eased him into the job gently, with tips, directions and secret knowledge, whispering advice when she could see him about to make a mistake. David liked her; because what you saw was what you got; because she was a decent human being; but basically because she made him feel a part of life again. She had an undeniable charisma that charmed the customers and soothed the violent and the drunk. They loved her. She was getting five times as many tips as he was.

The barman, Dean Pozner, was a different matter. He had taken an instant dislike to David and made no attempt to hide it. His nose visibly wrinkled when Charlie introduced them, a cartoon awareness of a bad smell which changed rapidly into a sneer. David didn't care much for him either. Dean had the bearing of a school athlete who knew he was the best, complete with the swagger and the arrogance. He had cultivated an All-American image, clean cut, smart, dull haircut, but there was an impression of nastiness behind the front.

'Oh, he's OK,' Arlene had said. 'He just doesn't like strangers.'

'Strangers don't like him either,' David had replied.

Charlie had been visible irregularly throughout the evening, but he mainly kept himself to himself in his tiny, smoke-choked office behind the stage. Arlene said he entertained himself with a bottle of Jack Daniels and the latest copy of *Hustler*.

By 3 a.m. the club began to thin out a little as the clientele moved on, to their beds, to parties or to the secret drinking clubs tucked away in hidden basements around the Vieux Carre. The All-Stars, sweaty and exhausted, shifted their equipment from the stage and lumped it into the back of a garishly spray-painted van outside, their upbeat rhythms replaced by the drone of a TV set.

Soon only the hard core remained, secluded, glassy eyed, in the shadows, or slumped in their seats next to beer-pooled tables.

'This is where it gets fun,' Arlene whispered in David's ear. He could smell the spices of her perfume, heated by her high body temperature. 'When there's no music to distract them, they get fresh, violent or sick.'

'I don't think many will get fresh with me.' David leaned against the wall, enjoying a brief respite from work. He had located a safe spot around the corner from the bar, away from Dean's watchful eyes.

'Don't count on it, sweetie. I've already seen a couple of them eyeing your butt.'

'You flatter me.'

Arlene checked no one was about to order and then lit a cigarette. 'So, enjoy your first night?'

'Enjoy isn't quite the right word. It was an experience.'

'Yeah, well, that's what life's all about, right? I just switch my mind off when I get in here. Pretend I'm Robby the Goddamn Robot. *Herez your beer, zir.* It'd drive me nuts otherwise. Don't suppose you'll be sticking around long, huh?'

'Just till I find my friend.'

She smiled tightly. 'Got to be a woman, right?'

He nodded.

'Want to tell me about it?'

'One day. When it's quieter.'

'Hey, maybe we could do lunch. Just like they do in LA.'

'Sure. I'd like that.'

'It's a deal.' She crushed her cigarette underfoot and waved to a fat, bearded man in a stetson who was gesticulating wildly. 'All right, you fat shit, I'm not on wheels,' she said without once loosening her glossily false smile. 'Got to keep the customers happy. Even if they are geeks and losers.' She added, almost as an afterthought as she walked away, 'I won't forget that lunch date.'

David watched her manipulate the Cowboy like a teacher with a small child. A few jokes, a brief flirt and he was eating out of the palm of her hand. As he watched her admiringly, Dean's head appeared around the corner of the bar.

'Any danger of you doing any work tonight, Easter?'

'About as much danger as of you having an intelligent thought, pondlife,' David said under his breath. He picked up a tray and began to fill it with glasses and bottles.

There was a dreamy quality about the club by that time of night. The air was thick with tobacco smoke, filtering the few lights into an otherworldly ambience of shadows and half-seen faces. Drinkers moved in slow motion to the toilet or the bar, concentrating on limb coordination, their eyes inward looking. Slurred voices twisted words into unintelligible shapes.

David moved quickly among the tables, plucking off dirty glasses and taking the occasional order. Beer had mostly gone out of fashion and the requests were usually for the hard stuff.

He turned from a table towards the bar and suddenly stopped in his tracks. Something was not quite right. He looked around him, his skin prickling. Everything seemed to be normal, or as normal as it got in Charlie's Place. Yet some kind of sixth sense, some preternatural device, was still tightening his stomach in protest.

He dismissed it and moved on. That business with Dauphine had got to him. He had had the creeps all day. There were strange resonances going on within the Fog Zone. The cards and his memories were calling to each other.

There it was again.

This time his sixth sense had given him a shock that had made him physically shiver. A wave of paranoia came over him. Someone was *watching* him. Slowly he turned through 180 degrees, scanning the shadowy reaches of the club, his ears ringing, muscles taut. Then he saw him.

Sitting alone in a distant, gloomy corner, far from the stage, was the man he had seen in the square just after his arrival. Unlike before, and despite the darkness, David could make out his features. He in turn was watching David as he moved about the room, his large white eyes unblinking like a bird's beneath his shining, pomaded hair. He seemed to be in his late twenties although it was difficult to tell at that distance. For a second their eyes locked and David felt a coldness rush into him. It seemed like he had stepped into another world with the rest of the club as hazy as if a fog had closed in on it. All he could focus on were those unblinking eyes.

Two things happened. The man's mouth, framed by heavy, hollow cheeks, began to grow wider and wider, turning from a slight smirk to a dark grin that revealed all of his white teeth. At the same time David felt a movement on the tray he was holding.

He looked down. An empty glass was vibrating, almost imperceptibly at first, but then faster. As it did so it began to move, slowly and jerkily towards the edge as if it was being dragged by invisible hands. David was transfixed. Gradually it reached the side of the tray before plunging off to shatter on the floor.

The man was still grinning, wide, like a tiger. He raised a hand slowly and beckoned.

He wants me, David thought, but it was a notion that seemed to come from without him. He began to take a step forward.

A loud crash near the stage jolted him back to reality. The Cowboy had flung his bear-like arms around Arlene and had wrestled her on to his lap where she was struggling like a wildcat. He was braying with laughter, his one free hand attempting to grope her while at the same time trying to plant his blubbery mouth on her lips. The table had upended, showering beer and broken glass across the floor.

The other drinkers looked on, amused; it was just another part of the floorshow. At the bar, Dean put down his cloth and watched nervously. His eyes kept darting towards the closed door of Charlie's office. There was an annexe off that room where Charlie's two minders went to relax. They had retired when the crowd had started to thin out.

'Get off me, you creep,' Arlene yelled, her voice lost in the noise from the TV. She somehow managed to wrestle her arm free and in a flash raked her nails across the Cowboy's cheek.

He howled like an injured dog and dumped her on the wooden floor where she landed awkwardly. His cry of pain turned to a snarl of anger when he heard the other drinkers laughing at him.

The Cowboy pulled back one booted foot and swung it at Arlene, catching her on the elbow. She gave a piercing cry and curled up into a ball, clutching her arm to her chest. David could tell the Cowboy was not about to stop. His face held an expression of sadistic glee as he raised his boot again.

David moved quickly. He covered the distance between them in four strides and barged the Cowboy solidly on the shoulder. The collision jarred every bone in David's body, but it was enough to send the Cowboy flying backwards across an empty table. He rolled over it and hit the floor like a sack of coal.

David dropped to Arlene's side and began to help her to her feet. There were tears of pain in her eyes, but she was grinning. 'He's going to have a hell of a headache tomorrow,' she said.

'He probably doesn't feel pain.'

The Cowboy's boot caught David squarely on the side of his head. For a second he could see nothing but random flashes of purple and gold. His hearing had virtually disappeared – sounds were muffled and distant. He could feel, though. Fire rushed through the nerve endings in his cheek and jaw, and there were barbs of pain where slivers of glass bit into his hand.

When his vision cleared, he saw Charlie's security team bearing down on the Cowboy. They were like a force of nature; nothing could stop their progress. Two concrete punches dropped the Cowboy before a threat could leave his lips and then he was dragged, unconscious, to the door.

A hand grabbed David by his collar and pulled him roughly to his feet where he swayed like a drunken sailor. 'Never,' Dean said an inch away from his face. 'Never get involved yourself. Fetch Mac and Pete. That's your lesson for the night.'

Arlene pushed the barman out of the way with unconcealed annoyance. 'Are you OK? That creep's feet were made of iron.' Her fingers felt ice-cold on his blazing cheek.

'Nothing major surgery won't cure. How are you?'

'I won't be carrying much with this arm for a few days.' She touched her elbow and winced.

'You better get it seen to. It might be broken.'

'It was very sweet of you to help me,' she said softly. 'I'm not used to knights in shining armour.'

'If I was wearing my armour, my jaw wouldn't be swelling up to the size of a basketball.' David touched it tenderly. 'I need a drink.'

The bourbon numbed his mouth, but he knew he would be paying a price for his heroism the next day. As he massaged his cheek with his tongue, his mind suddenly snapped back to the man with the slicked-back hair at the back of the club.

His table and chair were empty. David glanced around, but he couldn't see him anywhere. The paranoia he had felt had not gone. David remembered the man's chilling stare. And the way the glass had seemed to move of its own accord.

Who was he? What did he want with David? For some reason, David dreaded the answers. His life was getting too off-kilter. After the years of boredom and repetition, he was not ready for it.

That night he even saw those staring eyes in his sleep. They haunted him, burrowing into his mind, into the Fog Zone. There was a movement, a shaft of light, and then he realized, in that lucid way that some dreams possess, that the woman's face was there.

Even in his sleep he could feel his excitement. He was remembering. It was coming back to him.

He was in a club in London and it was the night they met . . .

Chapter 4

Her eyes were green. Powerful, swirling, fascinating.

The first glimpse of her in the mirror behind the bar, beneath the tequila and whisky bottles and the rows of gleaming glasses, was enough to intrigue him, but he had to look into the depths of those eyes to be really hooked. David always thought you could read the mind of a person that way. Cut through the fluff and the guff and the presented faces to get to the heart of the matter. Most people he met in his day-to-day life had flat, cold eyes like nailheads, emotionally dead.

Fermay Grey's eyes were alive, but they gave nothing away.

It was a quiet night in the club. A few of the regulars hovered near the back of the long, low room, hanging out, as he was, to check out the obscure New Jazz quintet from North London. They'd had a couple of reviews in the specialist press, enough to pique his interest, but evidently not enough to pull the crowds.

The air was filled with the Jazz Attic's familiar aroma of must, stale beer and smoke. It was gloomy, as always, and there were corners where the few discreet lights never penetrated. David positioned himself against a pillar and watched the roadies going through their motions. A touch to the drums here, the moving of a guitar there, the flicking of switches, on-off, on-off. It seemed to be a tedious job, night after night the same, but if one of them had asked David to join their closed society, he would have gone instantly. Brixton would become just another gig, to be left far behind when the next one beckoned.

He had tried to explain his feelings to Mick Gittings in the shop as they unpacked the latest arrival of records and loaded them into the racks.

'There's too much reality in the city, Mick,' he had said as he scanned the jazz selection. 'It closes in around you. Mundane things become really important because that's all you see. You start to think that that's all there is. There's no time for wonder. Or mystery. Or magic.'

Gittings had stopped midway through sliding a Morrissey album into the 'M' section. He looked at David and narrowed his eyes. 'Are you on drugs?'

Are you on drugs?

That summed it up, didn't it? In Gittings' view, in everybody's view, you had to be off your face to want something more than the bleakness of days behind the counter and nights in front of the TV, counting the pennies until there was enough for an evening out.

And then there was Michelle. Or Maureen, or whatever her name was. A lousy one-night stand, reeling drunkenly out of the pub and back to her squat for a few minutes of unpleasant grunting and groaning. He only did it because she pressed him and he thought it might brighten up an otherwise dull evening. And now she was pregnant, or she thought she was. She didn't even know if she wanted it. But she did know she wanted to move in with him, whatever his name was.

Brixton. Fun City. In London's swinging capital.

Now, as he waited for the band to come on, the DJ played the maudlin, late-night sound of Mood Indigo. It was a strange selection, the swell of damp emotion dispelled any faint spark of excitement or tension.

David noticed her as the familiar melody tugged at his feelings. In the sparsely populated club with its audience of restrained aficionados, she stood out like Gianni Versace at C&A. From a distance he watched, at first surreptitiously from the corner of his eye, and then openly when he realized she could not see him.

Her clothes were stylish and smart, expensive, though not in a vulgar way. Her fingers were long and slim, musician's fingers perhaps, or maybe an artist's, and their delicateness mirrored the deft poise of her cheekbones. She was attractive, although no more or less than many other women he saw around town, but for some reason his gaze was magnetically tugged back to her.

There was sex, definitely. Unbeckoned, his thoughts raced electrically in that direction. He imagined them in bed, running through his portfolio of favourite positions, her legs wrapped tightly around him. Fingers teasing the back of his neck, running down his spine. He was shocked by the intensity of the image.

There was something else, too. She had an aura that made her stand out in the crowd. There was a sense of mystery and secrecy.

She turned towards him and smiled. For a moment he thought she had read the carnal images in his mind. It took him by surprise and brought a brief flush of embarrassment. He shivered, almost from excitement.

Through the speakers, Eddie Jefferson picked up the beat. 'Show a little mercy, Think what it would do to my poor heart,' he pleaded.

'Can you hear the emotion in that voice?' The faint scent of her perfume had alerted him to her presence even before she spoke. When he turned she was close at his side, looking deep into his eyes.

'Are you a fan of Eddie Jefferson?'

'I love all music that's got soul.' *Good looks and good taste*, David thought. *A dangerous combination.* She sipped her drink. There was something almost predatory in the way she was looking at him. 'You don't mind me coming over to talk to you, do you?'

She was American. David recognized the accent of the southern states. 'No, I don't mind.'

'I know it's forward, but I liked the look of you.' David blushed and she laughed, putting her hand to her mouth. 'You've got an artist's soul. I saw that right away. Also, a very nice suit.' Her fingers touched his lapel, feeling the texture of the cloth, hypnotizing him. White, slim fingers. He imagined them shaping clay on a wheel, smudging thick paint on a canvas. Massaging his back.

'It's my wedding and funeral suit.'

'Oh? And which one is this?' He watched her lips move, a teasing smile just a hint away.

'The band will probably think it's a funeral when they come on.' He took a swig of Michelob from the bottle. 'I just meant that I wear it for special occasions.'

'So what's the special occasion?'

'I try to make every night out special.'

She turned down her flirtatiousness and looked at the stage. 'I don't mean to be pushy. You looked like an interesting guy and I wanted someone to talk to. I've been on my own all day. It drives you nuts, y'know. Not being able to speak. Any longer and I'd just explode.' She smiled. 'I like to chat.'

David shrugged and took another swig. He was not used to being picked up; he found it a disorientating experience. 'Feel free.'

'So . . . What's your name and what do you do and where do you live and blah-blah-blah?'

He thought about lying. The bald facts of his life seemed too uninteresting and he wanted to impress her, but whenever he tried to fabricate he always ended up embarrassing himself by getting the detail wrong. 'David Michael Easter. I work in a record shop. I live just down the road in a damp flat which may lack salubriousness, but which has a modest rent.' There it was, the sum total of his existence in three grey sentences. He wouldn't have been surprised if she'd walked off there and then.

The band came on to a smattering of polite applause. 'So what about yourself?'

'Too boring for words,' she replied.

'Compared to my adventure-packed resumé, you mean? At least tell me your name.'

She considered his request briefly and then replied, 'Fermay Grey.'

'That's unusual.'

'It is.' There was an impenetrable wall around her. David tried vainly to read something in her face, but her smile was

60

her disguise. She swayed her head in time to the music. 'They're quite good, aren't they?'

'Not bad. Technically they're not up to scratch, but at least they're not bound by tradition. I like to see people doing something fresh. You like jazz?'

'It's part of my heritage. Back home it's difficult not to like jazz.'

'Where's back home?'

'The Crescent City. New Orleans, Louisiana.' She pronounced it N'Awlins. 'Have you been there?'

'No, but I'd like to.' He laughed. 'That's an understatement. It's the city of my dreams.'

She didn't seem wholly to agree with his sentiment. 'You should go,' she said with some understatement. 'For the music. For the food. For the people.'

'Tell me about it. I'm planning ahead. I've already got the checklist in my head. I want to visit the Jazz Museum and Preservation Hall and get drunk on Bourbon Street. You know, all the tourist things.'

'Don't worry, the locals do it too.'

When she relaxed, there was a freshness and honest joy about her that was appealing. Her smile came easily, but she seemed guarded about her life. David, acutely aware of time ticking away, decided to be blunt in his questioning. In two hours the club would shut and then he would have lost his chance.

'Are you over here on holiday?'

'Vacation, yeah.'

'Alone?'

'Alone.'

'You're not the easiest person in the world to get to know.'

'I'm sorry.' She bit her lip nervously. 'It's just that I'm a very private person. It takes a while for me to, you know, open up.'

'I can appreciate that. You talk to some of the people here and you'll get their life story, the intimate details of their sex life and their childhood traumas before the second drink. I'm not prying. I'm just curious about people.' He paused, and then decided to chance it at the risk of sounding corny. 'I'm curious about you.'

For a moment he caught a flash of something in her eyes that unnerved him. 'Don't worry,' she said, aware that her comment wasn't as inviting as he would have liked. 'I don't want to be left alone.'

He drank beer, she tequila, and by the end of the evening they were both swathed in the soft, warm haze of inebriation. With each glass downed she became more tactile, accidentally stroking the back of his hand, touching her lips against his earlobe when she whispered to him, brushing her breasts against his arm, yet he found out nothing else about her. His questions were deflected, politely but definitely, and if he did press the point she would yawn theatrically until he turned the conversation to something more superficial.

For his part, David was hooked. He wanted her more than anyone he had met in months, perhaps even years. She was amusing, exciting, intelligent, sexual, all of those and more. One night would not be enough, he knew that before the band had played their final encore and the DJ had switched to his 'Talkin' Loud' albums.

Naturally she consented to go back to his place. No, that was wrong. She had not consented; she had *asked* him.

They hurried along the chill streets, laughing at stupid jokes and ridiculous observations like teenagers on their first big night out. By the time they reached his attic flat, he had her shirt half off and was kissing her so hard he saw stars. Finding the condom was amusing, penetrating her was ecstatic. Their orgasms were never quite simultaneous.

And if he had dreams, he could not remember them. He awoke to the sound of faint singing from the next room, soft, mournful. He did not recognize the tune, but it plucked at his thoughts in that demimonde between dreaming and wakefulness; he almost caught himself humming it. The clock radio's lurid digital display showed that it was 3.45 a.m. and the warmth on Fermay's side of the bed had already faded. As he pulled himself to a sitting position, he was dimly aware of scratches across his back, sore and throbbing against the cold wood of the headboard, but his thoughts were soon drawn back to the reedy voice that drifted languidly from the lounge.

The song. What was the song? He had never heard it before yet it seemed as if he had known it all his life.

Rising, he walked slowly to the door, aware of his nakedness in the cold dampness of the room. Fermay was sitting on the floor in the centre of the lounge, illuminated by a single shaft of moonlight like the sole performer on a stage. She hugged her knees to her, her skin milky white, and though her eyes were open, David had the impression that she was still asleep. He dropped down next to her and put his arm around her shoulders. She was icy cold.

'Fermay?' he whispered into her ear.

She seemed gradually to become aware of him, her eyelids flickering, her stare becoming less distant. Eventually she said, 'I'm so lonely.'

David kissed her gently on the top of her head. 'Come back to bed. It's warmer under the sheets. You'll freeze to death out here.'

'There are ghosts all around,' she continued, a note of anxiety underlying her dreamy tone. 'I can't get away from them, wherever I go. I don't want to be on my own. I just want peace.'

David helped her to her feet and let her lean on him as he guided her back into the bedroom, wrapped warmly together.

Her troubled tone faded. 'David, let me stay with you,' she asked, drifting gently back to sleep.

'Do you miss him?' Fermay twined her fingers around David's in the depths of his overcoat pocket and gave them a comforting squeeze.

'All the time. There isn't a day goes by when I don't think about him in some way or other. I remember him when I was a kid, when we used to do things together. Just silly father and son things, football on the lawn, building model aeroplanes, you know. Or I think about him when I was older and he'd gone into himself for one reason or another and we weren't that close. I wish I'd spoken to him more.'

The path wound its way through the centre of the graveyard, mottled with sodden, brown leaves and broken at irregular intervals by large puddles which they had to step over gingerly. Behind the wind which gave life to the spindly, black bodies of the trees along the far wall was the steady thrum of the dual carriageway. His father's grave was in the furthest corner from the church.

'How did he die?'

That was the wrong question. The one he couldn't consider. He remembered the blood too clearly. The slumped body. It had haunted him for so long, in sleep and in his waking hours, the memory of what had happened, the guilt at what he had done. 'Not now. Another time.'

'Hey, I'm sorry. Tell me if I'm prying. I just wanted to know the details so I could help you. I want to give you support, David.'

She had already, more than she knew. Every time he had been to the graveside, he had felt so weak he never knew if he would make the last few steps. This time he felt stronger. She made him stronger.

She had insisted on coming. She said she couldn't let him go alone. For the first time, he actually felt someone cared about him, enough to help him through the bad times.

'Thanks for coming,' he said suddenly.

She squeezed his hand again. 'It's you and me against the world, kid.'

The grave never changed in winter. There were often fresh flowers in summer when his mother made the effort, but in the cold, dark months David guessed he was the only visitor. He looked at the black marble cross that always reminded him of plastic and the simple gold letters: MICHAEL PORTLAND EASTER, RIP, SADLY MISSED BY A LOVING WIFE AND SON. How much hypocrisy could be wrapped up in just a few words.

Fermay stood at his side and put both arms around him tightly. Her warmth was comforting in the cold wind. 'I've never been here with anyone else,' he said. 'It's too near to me, too raw. But I'm glad you're here.'

'We're both similar people, Davey, you and me. We lock the real us away so it can't get hurt. But we can show each other.'

'Are we going to make it work?'

'Of course we are.' She pulled his head next to hers and put a hand on his cheek. 'Nothing's going to hurt you . . . either of us . . . ever again.'

David wondered if his father was watching, if he forgave him.

'You can cry if you want,' she said.

Back in the city he felt the excited relief of a schoolboy who had escaped the dentist's chair without a filling. After the oppressive emotions of the morning, he felt they needed some light relief, so he took her to a little café in Great Compton Street where they could talk and make fun of the Soho bohemians. They were still feeling their way with each other, learning responses, delving into likes and dislikes, but even then it seemed like they would fit together like a peg in a hole.

The café was dark with plenty of nooks and alcoves where visitors could hide away. In the early sixties it had been the haunt of rock and roll groups building the foundations of the new music. David and Fermay sat on a bench seat near the window and drank cappuccino. Outside they could see a grinning tramp holding out a dirty hand for any spare change from the tourists.

'I wonder what he's so happy about.' Fermay leaned across the table and smudged the frothy moustache from David's top lip with her thumb.

'You've got to laugh, haven't you. At the absurdity of it all. All the money around this city and that poor bastard can't get enough for a bottle of cheap wine.'

'It's sad.' She watched the tramp with concern for a moment. 'Life's so bad for him, yet he's grinning.' She looked back at David with serious eyes. 'Are you lonely?'

'Lonely? No, not really. Willie's always around to kick me if I start moping. He's my best friend. My only friend, really. We've got the same interests – jazz, drink, having fun. I could never be lonely with Willie around.' It sounded like a lie even as the words left his lips.

'No other friends?'

'I never needed anybody else. People are so untrustworthy, dull, miserable, pick an adjective. I know what I get with Willie. It's always been just the two of us.'

'Well now it's the three of us.'

'How about you? Lots of friends back home?'

'No. I had a very sheltered life. I didn't go out much as a kid so I never really got a chance to mix with other children my age. I had a personal tutor who taught me at home so I didn't have to go to school. Consequently,' she held her hands in the air, 'I never met anyone.'

'That's tragic.'

'Not really. Because I never had companionship, I never really missed it. Oh, sometimes I got a bit blue, but, you know, I wasn't *yearning* for a little friend of my own.'

'So you mixed with adults all the time? What about fun and games?'

'Yeah, I guess it made me kind of serious. I used to play on my own a lot. When you live like that it really helps you to develop your own imagination. I created my own little world, my fantasy world. Hey, Lewis Carroll had nothing on me! I was the princess locked up in the big, old, creepy castle. I had all my little magical friends to help me stay one step ahead of the wicked old grown-ups.'

'Did they have names?'

'Sure they did, but you don't think I'm going to tell you, do you!' She cuffed him lightly across the forehead and laughed.

'Ah, g'wan.'

She ignored his mocking. 'I suppose I did grow up before my time. Too serious, too thoughtful. That's why I go crazy so often now I'm out in the big world.'

'I haven't seen you go crazy.'

'You've only known me two days. Just wait! Ever since I

got out of that house and on the road I've been acting like I'm in the biggest playground of all. I want to experience everything. Have fun! Get drunk! Dance on tables!'

There was a look of wonder and enchantment on her face that was almost childlike. David's heart went out to her in an instant. 'But what happens when you go back?'

She leaned close to him conspiratorially. 'Honey, I ain't never goin' back!'

When she looked into his eyes like that he felt his logic and his sense of cool turn belly up. He wanted to pick her up and swing her round the room. 'We get on pretty well, don't we? I know it's only been two days, but . . .'

'Well, you know what they say.'

'What's that?'

'There's only one soul-mate for you anywhere in the world. Ninety-nine per cent of people never find theirs, poor suckers. But when you do, you know straightaway.'

'Like a punch in the face.'

'Like an Acme safe on Wile E. Coyote's head.' They laughed together, but Fermay's eyes remained serious. 'Don't go walking out on me now, boy. I've found a new drug, and I'd just die without it.' She seemed to be joking, but there was an obvious undertone of truth.

'No way,' he said sincerely. 'It's you and me now.' The atmosphere suddenly seemed too heavy, filled with the weight of the future. He changed the subject quickly. 'OK. It's time we found out some more about each other. Ready for twenty questions? First subject: favourite movies.'

She thought for a moment. 'Old ones. Black and white. Romance. Music. Fred Astaire and Ginger Rogers. *Top Hat. Flying Down To Rio*. Busby Berkeley. You?'

'Big productions, eh? I'd never have guessed. Old and new for me. *The Maltese Falcon, Fistful of Dollars, Blade Runner* . . .'

'Tough guys with a gun facing the world to save a broad. Yeah, I *would* have guessed! How about music?'

'You know the answer to that. Any kind of jazz, some soul and blues. Sinatra. What do you listen to?'

Her face darkened briefly, inexplicably, but her smile returned before he could question it. She was about to answer when her attention was suddenly caught by the tramp outside. An expensive-suited City-type had almost pushed the old man into the gutter in his eagerness to avoid giving him any money. 'Excuse me a minute, hon.' She stood up and squeezed past David to get into the aisle.

A second later, David saw her on the street, dodging among the cars to the other side of the road where the tramp stood. They huddled in conversation for a moment and then she turned and flashed David a grin. A second later the tramp started to sing. It was some old Irish melody, thundered out with a drink-cracked voice and theatrical flourish, one arm extended in mock passion. At the same time, Fermay started to dance; seductively, humorously, idiotically. Anything that would catch the attention of the passers-by. She was completely unselfconscious, like a little girl playing, but she knew what she was doing. A cheeky grin, a flirtatious wink, a pleasant smile, and soon the coins were dropping at their feet. One man, lost in thought, walked past without contributing. Fermay ran down the street, grabbed him by his sleeve and dragged him back, cajoling him until he handed over his loose change.

As David watched her perform, he was entranced. He had no idea what was happening to him. Of all the women he had dated in his life, he had never felt so strongly so quickly. And, he couldn't quite put his finger on what had hooked him. Maybe it was like she said – they were soul-mates.

After ten exhaustive minutes the tramp had amassed more money than he had probably taken in a week of begging. He stooped to pick up his earnings and then turned to Fermay and kissed her on the hand. She did a dainty curtsey, waved to a couple of applauding tourists, and then headed back.

There was another smattering of applause in the café when she returned to her seat. She was flushed and out of breath, but she seemed pleased with her achievement.

'I didn't know you were such an entertainer.' David went

to order another cappuccino, but there was already a complimentary one on its way.

'Oh, I have many secret resources. You should see what I can do with Shakespeare.'

They laughed, then kissed. At that moment, the world seemed perfect.

The memory was receding. Even in his sleep David could feel the Fog Zone closing him off, and he fought it, trying to grab hold of that instant of happiness, of Fermay's face, of her kiss. But eventually it slipped away. All that was left was blackness, woven through by the bleak sounds of haunting music, and then a thunderous noise like the crash of an enormous drum, pounding on monotonously until he thought his head was going to explode.

Bang, bang.

Bang.

Bang.

Chapter 5

MURDER VICTIM – GANGLAND LINK?

The headline leapt out from the front page of the *Times-Picayune* over a brief report detailing the developments, or lack of them, in the investigation into the body fished from the river two days earlier. As Arlene had so graphically described, its head had been virtually crushed to paste. The story carried details of the postmortem and a comment from the police chief that the cause of death was 'numerous blows with a blunt instrument'. The corpse had not yet been identified. The paper expounded the theory that it was a gangland killing, but the brutality of it had surprised even the New Orleans PD, no strangers to brutality.

'Welcome to Fun City.'

He looked up from the paper to see Arlene standing on the other side of his table in the hotel restaurant.

'Mind if I sit down? Don't worry, I've already eaten breakfast. I'll just have a coffee.' She called the waitress over and ordered a decaf.

'This is a surprise.'

'I wanted to thank my shining knight again – and to see if he needed his jaw wiring up.'

David tried to appear blasé, but it was too painful. His jaw was the size and tenderness of an overripe melon, a cacophony of pain ringing around his ear to remind him constantly of the Cowboy's boot. 'What can I say? It hurts like hell, but I don't think it's broken.'

'You were very brave. No one else would have tried it. They're all too scared of someone pulling a knife or a gun.'

'Maybe I'm stupid. I didn't think of that.' He hadn't, and the thought made his stomach dip. 'I just acted on impulse.'

'Hey, don't worry, women like that in a man.' She pulled out a compact and checked her make-up, smudging her finger with precision along the edge of her lip. 'So, your reward for bravery above and beyond the call of duty is, you get me as guide for the day. Great prize, huh? Better than a purple heart any day.' David began to protest, but she hushed him. 'I insist. If you've got anything else to do, do it later. You've got to relax, give your jaw a chance to heal. I thought we could go down to the Jazz Museum – I know how much you like the music. We can mingle with the tourists and you can tell me all about yourself. Then I'll take you for lunch to a little place I know. This afternoon you can choose.' She paused and frowned. 'Stop me if I'm being too bossy, right? My boyfriend always says I try to run his life. He should be so lucky. If I was in control he might be something better than a worthless bum.'

'No, that's fine. You lead, I follow.' Despite the pain, he was in a good mood, a truly good mood, for the first time since he had arrived in the city. He knew her name.

Fermay Grey.

He rolled it around in his mind, savouring each syllable, relishing its lyrical quality. How could he ever have forgotten it? Their first meeting was crystal clear in his mind, reinforcing his belief that they had been very much in love. It gave him hope that the rest of his memory would surface in quick succession, making him whole once more.

The previous night's lucid dreaming session had also left him with another, more disturbing impression – of a haunting tune which set his pulse racing whenever he attempted to recall it. It was the tune Fermay had been humming, insistent yet plaintive, but his attempts to reproduce it with a whistle failed miserably. It was as evasive as mist, but it wouldn't go away.

'Hey! This is you!' Arlene had picked up the paper and had been absently flicking through the pages.

Eagerly he took it from her and saw his dark features staring from the centre of a page near the back. Fermay's face was there too, slightly fogged by the grainy image blown up from the snapshot he kept in his pocket.

Arlene snatched the paper back with a giggle. 'My workmate is famous. Boy, aren't I the lucky girl,' she said in mock wonder. She glanced over Lynsey Kane's short article and then added, 'So this is what she looks like. She's pretty. You go well together.'

71

'We do. Or we did do.' David could barely contain his excitement. He was convinced the article was the key which would lead him back to Fermay and unlock his memory. She was so close he could almost smell her perfume.

Arlene's face grew serious as she read the piece. 'Is this story true? It's, like, so romantic.' David thought she was going to cry.

'Bits of it are true. Some of it's made up because I wanted to make sure the paper would publish it. The truth? I have lost part of my memory and somehow I became separated from Fermay. That's the woman, Fermay Grey. I remembered her name last night.'

'Jesus, David. This is so bizarre. You reckon she's here in New Orleans?'

'It's hard to explain, Arlene . . . It's all buried in my subconscious. I feel she's here and I'm sure that's why I'm here too. This is her hometown. I don't remember getting to the city. My memory is really badly screwed up. But, no, I don't know for certain that Fermay is here.'

'So you could just be fooling yourself.' She bit her lip. 'That sounds awful . . .'

'No, you're right. I *could* be fooling myself, but I daren't think about that. I've just got to trust in my instincts.'

'Wow. It's the screwiest thing I ever heard. And the sweetest.' She looked at him in a different light as she handed the paper over. 'I wish someone cared about me that much.'

David folded the paper so the article was at the front and he could see Fermay's face at a glance. 'I just can't shake the feeling that there's something else important I should be remembering. Every time I see her face it gets me like someone twisted a knife in my guts.' He looked up at Arlene and smiled dismissively. 'Oh well. I'll find out soon enough.'

It was a lazy spring day, sunny and warm but with a fresh breeze blowing from the river which stirred the unique, ancient odours of the French Quarter. Arlene was bright and inquisitive, firing questions breathlessly. David felt slow-witted in comparison.

Under a covered piazza in the French Market, a lone pianist teased a ragtime tune from battered ivories. His lips curled back from his teeth in ecstasy, his head rocking backwards, his eyes screwed tight, playing to an audience of ghosts. Pools of water lay around his feet where the café owners had hosed yesterday's dust into the gutter. The notes drifted out mournfully across the empty square.

The Jazz Museum occupied a few rooms in the old US Mint which took up the whole 400 block of Esplanade Avenue. It was a solid brick slab, a fort that kept the world out and culture in, hunkering into view as they walked along Decatur Street on to Barracks Street, its regimented windows glinting in the morning light.

'What's that?' David pointed to an old russet-coloured trolleycar parked in the courtyard next to the building. It looked out of place, marooned.

'That's the Streetcar Named Desire. You know, the one Tennessee Williams wrote about? They saved it from the wrecker's yard. Sorta turned it into a monument. Cute, ain't it?'

'Nothing ever really dies here, does it? It's all recycled for posterity.' David thought for one moment that there was someone sitting in the trolleycar, near the back. He half glimpsed a figure hunched over the seat, looking out, but when he squinted to bring it into closer detail, the carriage appeared empty. A trick of the light.

Inside the building it was quiet, almost reverential. A sign pointed to the Mardi Gras Museum which was just across the hallway, but David was only interested in the jazz rooms.

'Have you always been a jazz buff?' Arlene asked.

'Pretty much. It started as a statement. When all the other kids at school were into pop or rock, I wanted something which would make me stand out in the crowd. They used to think I was mad when I raved about Cannonball Adderley while they were drooling over Genesis or some other dross. Funny thing was, the more I played the music, the more it took me over. It reflected everything I believed in my life, even as a kid. A total disregard for authority, creativity, wild leaps of imagination.'

'Pardon me. I thought it was just music.' Her laughter deflated all the gravitas in his statement. He looked at her, offended at first, and then laughed along with her.

'You should lighten up. You're too serious.'

'I've always been serious. Life makes you like that. It's not exactly a bundle of laughs, is it?'

'I thought I was a downer. What's so bad about your life?'

Dark thoughts flashed through his mind, unbidden. He visibly flinched. 'Things.' He forced the thoughts back. 'Come on. I've waited years to see this.'

There were only three people in the museum so early on a Sunday, a husband and wife and their child. The wife looked bored, snapping gum loudly and obsessively hitching up her leather skirt. Her husband had a thunderous face beneath the kind of flat cap that was fashionable for a month or two in the seventies. He was loudly proclaiming that the exhibits did not meet his extremely high standards. 'We came all the way from Missoula for this? This is crap.' Adding for emphasis, 'It's worse than crap.' Their child ran wildly among the display cases making aeroplane noises.

'It's amazing what you see when you haven't got a gun,' David said.

Arlene laughed. 'You crack me up, Davey.'

Another memory: Fermay used to call him Davey when she was playfully patronizing him.

David's attention was soon swallowed up by the exhibits. The museum traced the history of jazz from its origins among the African and Caribbean slaves to the present day. There were aged musical instruments, cracked fiddles, battered trumpets, laid out like religious artefacts which, to many people, they were. They had been touched by gods. There were black and white photos, speaking of fun and music and booze and lights, shouting down the years. There were maps and words, scrawled letters, signatures of icons. There was a note from a ten-year-old Harry Connick Jr, explaining how the jazz legends of New Orleans had shaped his life. There were bizarre nicknames like Leadbelly, Jellyroll, Satchmo. The gods of music.

David was entranced. He wandered through the rooms slowly, transfixed by every display, drinking in each word, until Arlene, New Orleans, even Fermay were forgotten.

The Family From Hell were arguing loudly on the other side

74

of the room. 'This is a *family* holiday and you are *not* going to hit the bars on Bourbon Street,' the wife snapped, hands on hips, face dark with fury. The husband murmured something inaudible. 'No, not even for a *little* while.' He blushed and sheepishly looked away. In the meantime, their brat had careered into a display cabinet and was building up to show off the full power of his lungs.

The distraction disappeared into the background the moment David saw the photograph. Time stopped, leaving him standing in a silent vacuum; all he could see was the picture swamping his entire vision. It was in the centre of a glass showcase, the black and white image fading on once-creamy paper now turned brown. At first David could not tell what it was that had fired the nerves along his spine, but his gaze was fastened on to the photo like a hook in a marlin.

As his vision swept back and forth along a row of heads, he saw it. A face, eyes staring, mouth grinning.

The face of a dead man.

The photograph showed six men, all bursting with the fullness of youth, proud, arrogant even, with the world lying before them and their imposing musical prowess. Their hair was slicked back. Their suits were smart and stylish, shiny black contrasted by crisp white shirts. Beneath the picture, in blocked brown letters, it said: *The Hot Jazz Ensemble, Lola Harmon's, 1910,* followed by a list of names.

The face was there, second from the right, handsome, confident. It was the man he had seen at the back of the club on the previous night. The man who had watched him in Jackson Square on the day of his arrival.

A dead man.

The inscription said his name was Carlton 'Buffalo' Marsayle. He had not aged one year. No lines had crawled around the eyes, no silver had wisped its way into his hair. It was a face frozen in time.

David felt besieged. Was it not enough to have lost part of his memory? Did he now have to see hallucinations of dead people? He clung on to the showcase until his knuckles grew white.

Arlene was at his elbow, her soothing fingers on the back of his hand. 'What's wrong?'

He pointed at the photograph. 'I've seen that man.'

'Where?' She asked the question as if she meant to say 'So what?'

'When I first arrived here. Then in the club last night.'

Bending forward, she read the inscription. '1910? You can't have. He'd be dead by now.'

'I know.' His mouth was dry.

Arlene caught at his arm. 'Hey c'mon. I'm not used to people telling me they've seen a ghost.'

'I'm *not* saying that I saw a ghost,' David said with irritation born of embarrassment and fear. 'I'm saying . . .'

Arlene gave him a hug. 'If you said you saw him, then you did see him. Y'know, I've read a lot about these experiences. What star sign are you?'

'Aquarius. What has that got to do with anything?'

'There you are then! They're the sensitive ones. Maybe you picked up on this Marsayle guy's vibrations. He might be trying to tell you something.'

'You sound like some Californian New Ager who's O.D.'d on mineral water and vegetables. Ghosts don't exist.'

It was Arlene's turn to be offended. 'I was only trying to help.'

They agreed to let the subject rest for a while and spent another half hour in the Jazz Museum, but David's initial enthusiasm had long since withered away. He glanced at the displays half-heartedly, twitchy, the slightest sound making him start. Eventually he took Arlene's arm and led her into the corridor outside the room.

'OK, Davey,' she said. 'Let's get some lunch.'

Then the world slipped away from him for the second time that morning. He had glanced, not even aware that he was doing it, into the Mardi Gras Museum on the other side of the corridor. He had little interest in the annual *Fat Tuesday* celebrations and had no wish to view the exhibits. But there, standing half obscured behind a life-size storeroom dummy dressed in a colourful Mardi Gras costume, was Buffalo Marsayle.

His eyes were locked firmly on David's.

In one instant, the real world did a flip. Marsayle was summoning him, although no words passed between them. David could feel the pull, the words COME TO ME blazed in his mind, but he was terribly afraid that if he went he would never return.

The figure moved further back into the museum.

David followed. His first tentative step became a quick pace and then a run, his legs not energized by conscious thought. Then he was sprinting through the Mardi Gras Museum towards the rapidly disappearing form.

Around him, he was aware of the history of the Mardi Gras celebrations passing him by. Huge figures loomed like mythological gods. Costumes of bygone eras, blinding with blues and golds, feathers and velvet. A thing with a giant, misshapen papier mâché head hovered threateningly near his elbow. There was the heavy aroma of cloth and paint and history.

And death. He could sense it as he ran.

When they suddenly reached the final room of the museum, Marsayle was motionless near one wall. David watched his hand raise slowly to a picture on the wall. Then the jazzman snapped his fingers.

The sound was like the boom of a jet. In one second, the feel of a warm, modern museum returned.

David was left rooted to the spot, staring at the place where Marsayle had stood. He felt stunned.

Arlene's hands were on him, comforting him. 'David, are you all right?' Her voice expressed more than concern.

'Did you see it?' he croaked.

'Did I see what?'

'Him. Buffalo Marsayle.'

There was a long pause that said more than words. Then, 'I didn't see anything, David.'

He pulled himself away from her and walked slowly forward to where Marsayle had been. There was a faint coldness in the air, a memory. And the picture on the wall.

It was a watercolour of a man in long flowing robes, his head shaped like a bird's. The beak was long and wickedly curled, the eyes beady and black. The inscription said, *Costume of the Krewe of Aidoneus, King of Carnival, 1939.*

Next to the picture was a large frame which merely contained a small piece of white card. On it was printed, 'Carnival, from the Latin *Carnisvale* meaning *Farewell to the Flesh*.'

Chapter 6

By the time twilight had fallen on the city, the fear had finally left him, but it had been some task to drive it from his system. He had looked into the eyes of a dead man and they had looked back, telling him of nightmares and horrors he had never dreamed existed.

All afternoon David had sat with Arlene in the quiet of his room, worrying he was going insane. Arlene had calmed him eventually, stroking the nape of his neck and holding his clammy hand until he had slowly emerged from his troubled state. David guessed she thought he was cracking up. What did it all mean? he'd asked her. A dead jazzman? That picture? The Krewe of Aidoneus?

'Who knows what it means, David?' Arlene had said. 'The krewes are the secret societies who arrange the Mardi Gras. I've heard mention of Aidoneus, but that's all. Maybe it was trying to tell you something.'

Pat O'Brien's bar on St Peter Street was the perfect diversion. There was a shamrock on the logo and an atmosphere that would have made Dublin proud. As early as 7.30 p.m. a swell of bodies moved through its maze of rooms. In the bar at the front, a statuesque woman brassily sang old standards to a choppy but virtuoso piano accompaniment. Bodies filled the doorway, clapping and calling out for old favourites. The warmth of humanity was reassuring.

The courtyard at the back was quieter, but the waiter could only find one empty table, within the splash zone of the central fountain. David felt comforted by the balmy evening and the hiss of hot gas which powered the flaming torches. They added a discreet, flickering light to the court's corners. All he wanted to do was drown the vision of Marsayle's face in alcohol until he could lose himself in the exhausting bustle of Charlie's Place again.

David demanded the most alcoholic drink on the menu and the waiter brought him a Hurricane cocktail, a mixture of rum and exotic fruits with enough alcoholic power to tranquillize a rhinoceros on the hoof. Arlene had a mint julep in a long glass.

'Hey, look.' She sipped it with exaggerated haughtiness. 'Now I'm a real Southern Belle.'

David smiled. 'You're not from here?'

'No way. I was born and raised in Crystal City, Texas. I'm a proud daughter of the Lone Star state.'

'So what brought you to New Orleans?'

'A bus.' She laughed at the flimsiness of her own joke. 'And the hope of earning a decent wage and finding the man of my dreams.'

'Was it worthwhile?'

Her eyes dropped. 'Sure,' she said dismissively. 'Well . . . you know how much Charlie pays. I mean, it's not going to buy me a limo and diamonds, but, y'know, it's a living.'

'What about the man of your dreams?' David watched the flames from the torch make playful shadows across her face. The movement of light and shade wiped the dark tiredness from around her eyes and gave her something of the bloom she must have had in her teens.

'Scuba. He's OK.'

'Scuba?'

She blushed. 'It's some stupid jock name. The meatheads he used to hang around with in high school gave it to him because he was . . .' – a sneer came quickly to her lips – '. . . a champion muff diver. Cute, huh?'

'I'm sure he's very nice.' It was a noncommittal answer, but it seemed to be what Arlene wanted to hear. She returned to her julep without comment. There was something about her that made David feel secure and at that moment he needed that feeling badly. 'If this thing with the newspaper doesn't work,' he told her, 'I don't know what I'll do.'

'Have you tried the phone book?'

'There's about a million Greys. I checked before breakfast. But if I have to I'll phone every one of them.'

Arlene leaned across the table and held his hand. 'I'm always

80

here, Davey. If you need me.' She paused, suddenly embarrassed, and withdrew from the honesty of the contact. 'Don't worry so much. If you think you saw Marsayle, then you did. Don't question it. It's not as crazy as you think, y'know. This is New Orleans.' She laughed. 'A ghost on every corner, just like hot-dog stands.'

He smiled weakly in reply.

'Think of the folks back in England. They'll keep your feet on the ground whenever you start having black thoughts.'

'Sure.' The lack of enthusiasm in his voice was unmistakeable.

'What's wrong? No one back home? No friends?'

He shrugged. 'I tried to call a good friend a couple of times, but there's been no reply.'

'Maybe he's gone away for a few days.'

'Maybe.'

'You don't like talking about yourself, do you?'

'No.'

'Why not? You can trust me. I'm a simple kid. I won't play mind games with you.'

'I believe you.'

'Then . . . ?' She waited for a reply and when she didn't get one she let out a frustrated sigh. 'You are sooo annoying.'

'Arlene, you wouldn't love me if I wasn't enigmatic.'

'Don't you believe it,' she said sulkily, but her eyes sparkled.

Charlie greeted them with a grunt when they walked through the door of the club, a smouldering cigar shoved in one side of his mouth. His piggy eyes flickered from David to Arlene and back.

'I hope you ain't disturbin' my workers, kid,' he said as he passed.

'I wouldn't dream of it, Charlie,' David said after him.

'That's Mr Charlie to you, boy,' his voice floated back throatily.

The night's work was hard, although not as eventful as David's first. The crowd was smaller, par for the course for a Sunday he guessed, and there were no undercurrents of violence. David had half expected the Cowboy to be back, looking for revenge, but there was no sign of him.

At closing time, there was a sudden shout. 'Hey, Arlene!' The voice boomed across the empty bar, drowning out the sound of wooden chairs clumsily being thrown on to tabletops.

Arlene's face fell. She quickly covered up with a weak smile. 'Hi, honey,' she said.

A tall, broad-shouldered man with shoulder-length curly black hair strode towards the bar. His leather biker's jacket pulled uncomfortably across his biceps and chest like a second skin. Two days' stubble darkened his jaw, bringing out the whiteness of a broad grin that exuded confidence. He thrust an arm around Arlene's shoulders and pulled her to him, planting a big kiss on her lips.

Arlene wriggled free, her cheeks flushed. She touched her hair and flashed an embarrassed glance at David.

'How ya doin', baby? Glad to see the old Scooby-Doo?' He continued to massage her shoulder with a giant hand.

'David, this is Scuba, my . . .' Arlene began to say 'boyfriend', but then thought better of it. 'Scuba, David's visiting from England. Charlie gave him a job here.'

'Hey, a limey!' Scuba crushed David's hand in a wringing sportsman's shake. 'How are you doing, old chap?' His attempt at an English accent had obviously been learned from Dick Van Dyke's cod-Cockney chimney sweep in *Mary Poppins*.

'Fine,' David replied, singularly unimpressed.

'Is my old lady here lookin' after you?' He pulled his property close to him with another flex of his muscles. Arlene grimaced. 'She's a real catch, ain't she?' He winked at David. 'Hey baby, any chance of a beer?'

'No, there is no chance of a beer.' Charlie's voice boomed over David's shoulder. 'How many times do I have to tell you? No drinks after time.'

'Come on, Charlie. Just one Dixie. No one'll know,' Scuba whined. There was something about the way he pawed Arlene that set David's teeth on edge.

'Shouldn't you be out stealing hubcaps, boy? Goddamn juvenile delinquent. Get outta here.' Charlie walked back to his office, looking as if he had swallowed vinegar.

'Fuckin' nigger,' Scuba said under his breath. His eyes grew murderous before that simple childlike expression returned to his face. 'Come on, baby, let's go. I've got some beers back home. Let's party.' He grabbed her wrist and started to drag her towards the door.

'Scuba,' Arlene protested. 'I'm still working. I've got to clean up here.'

'It's OK, Arlene,' David said. 'I'll finish off for you.'

'Hey, kid! Limeys are OK, y'hear. Come on, Arlene.' Scuba flashed a cheesey, vacant grin before tugging at her arm once more.

Arlene looked at David pleadingly and then she relented, allowing herself to be pulled in Scuba's wake.

David started work early the next day to help Dean store the weekly delivery of booze. As usual, the barman treated David with open contempt, avoiding eye contact and going about his business in sullen silence. David made no attempt to communicate with him; if Dean wanted to be unpleasant that was his choice. David had other things on his mind.

As they transported crates of Dixie from the storeroom to the bar before the club opened, David lost himself in the monotony of the work, daydreaming about Fermay. He was disappointed that he had not received a call in response to the newspaper article. He kept telling himself it was only one day and not everybody read their paper from cover to cover immediately, but he couldn't stop his spirits falling.

On his fifth trip to the bar, he suddenly stumbled over something in his path. Pain exploded in his shin and he went sprawling to the floor as if he had been poleaxed. His crate of Dixie sailed through the air (he remembered it later in slow motion like some Looney Tunes cartoon), finally bursting open with an explosion of glass when it crashed against the boards further along the corridor. He heard Dean's mocking laughter before he saw the empty beer crate strategically placed near the doorway to the storeroom.

'What are you doing, lame-o?' Dean's amusement turned to a sneer. 'You're just a first-rate fuck-up.'

David snapped, the stress of the previous days finally getting to him. He launched himself at Dean with a rugby tackle, catching the barman in the stomach with his head. The two of them rolled out into the bar like some Wild West brawlers, and if Charlie had not chosen that moment to emerge from his office it would have deteriorated into a full-scale fight. David was almost disappointed. He wanted to lash out, to punch and kick until all the pent-up frustration had been drained from his system.

Charlie bawled them both out and then Dean snidely pointed out that David had broken an expensive crate of beer with his 'lame-o clumsiness'. Charlie gave David another dressing down which he took with his anger burning inside him. He knew there was no point arguing with Charlie when he was riled. Dean watched from the other side of the bar with a sly grin on his face. Afterwards he came over to rub salt in the wound.

'Stay away from me, Dean.' David could barely restrain himself. 'I'll fucking kill you! I swear I will.'

'Big talk, faggot. You're living on borrowed time. You have been ever since you walked into this joint. I'm sick of foreigners coming in here and getting all the best treatment.'

'What's the matter? Can't take the competition?'

'Fuck you. And stay away from Arlene.'

David's laugh brought colour to Dean's cheeks. 'That's the real reason for all this, isn't it? You've got the hots for Arlene and you're afraid she's going to fall for someone with more style, wit and charisma than you. You must have a very depressing life worrying about all those candidates.'

Dean drew his fists up spontaneously, but David wasn't about to get into a fight with Charlie already in a foul mood. He smiled mockingly, both of them knowing he had won.

As he walked away, he could feel Dean's eyes on his back until he had crossed the floor and entered the lavatory. The room was spartan with plaster-cracked walls and dripping taps. There were no windows, and the single bulb which hung on a frayed cord had been malfunctioning for more than a day; Charlie had still not got around to calling in an electrician. A loose wire or a short circuit caused the bulb to flicker on and off constantly, throwing the room from darkness to light and back again, an irritating effect that distorted the senses. David shivered in the chill, dank air.

He filled one of the basins with cold water and began to douse his face until his anger slowly dissipated. He hated to lose his temper and he wasn't going to let Dean have that power over him. Gradually, he realized he felt calmer.

With that thought, there was a sudden sensation of falling that was horrifyingly familiar. He fought back, but reality was tumbling away from him.

He brought his head up sharply from the basin and looked into the mirror in front of him.

Buffalo Marsayle was there.

David let out a brief cry of shock and whirled around to find that Marsayle was standing in the corner near the cubicles. The air around him almost seemed to crackle with tension. In his black suit and white shirt he looked like a churchgoer in his Sunday best. David could see the sharpness of the creases, the shine of the buttons. It looked too real.

The lightbulb continued to flash, on-off, on-off, one moment illuminating the pallid face, the next plunging the room back into darkness.

David could almost have coped with it. Almost, if not for the eyes. Their stare was so wide, so powerful, and in it he saw madness and pain.

'What do you want?' David croaked. There was no reply.

Then, during a moment of darkness, he heard Marsayle move towards him. Just a couple of paces, but it was enough.

It's coming for me, he thought.

With his own feet scrambling for traction on the lino, David suddenly jerked into life, heaving himself towards the door. He had a sudden vision of Marsayle moving quickly, laying a heavy, cold hand on his shoulder and dragging him back, icy fingers closing around his throat. Then, unbelievably, he had the door open and he was out.

It slammed behind him with enough force to shake the wall. David kept going until he was out on the sidewalk in the warm air. The sun was huge and red, disappearing behind the silhouette of the skyline. He looked up at it and prayed for the morning to come quickly. He could no longer face the night.

Fat droplets of rain were marbling the sidewalk and bursting noisily against windowpanes when David finally slipped out of the club at the end of his shift. There was the smell of hot dogs and popcorn in the air, triggering memories of funfairs in England. But the alleys that led off the main streets were as black as pitch and when the wind channelled through them, it howled in a mournful, despairing voice. In the distance the sound of an occasional car echoed through the city's business district, but there, on the Eastern edge of the French Quarter, it was deserted.

David pulled up the collar of his jacket and walked into the wind, thinking about Fermay, about Arlene. He had buried the terror of his latest confrontation with Marsayle beneath the reality of serving beer and swabbing floors until his shirt was damp with sweat. Some thoughts could only be confronted in the warmth of the day.

He followed an erratic route towards the Sonesta, avoiding the main thoroughfares where the drunks would be picking themselves up and preparing to move on. The grid system made it easy to understand the layout of the Vieux Carre but even so he felt he had a natural feel for the place, a memory, perhaps, from another life.

He aimed to head along Ursulines Street and then cut through to Bourbon, but at the junction of the two roads he halted suddenly. Slowly, he turned in a full circle. He was alone and nothing moved, but an image of Buffalo Marsayle's grinning face flashed in his mind and he shivered. The darkness around him seemed like a giant cloud of evil that was slowly spreading across the city.

There was something out there. He could no longer stand his ground. Whatever it was, it was getting closer and it was speaking to him on a level beneath the senses. He started to walk, slowly at first, but then faster, moving to the centre of the road away from the shadows that clustered on the sidewalk.

He walked quicker, almost jogging. He could sense evil, that was the best way he could describe it. An overwhelming presence moving in on all sides like a fog.

Overhead he could hear the screech of a bird, only it wasn't like any bird he had heard before. It rose and fell, rose and fell, like the hunting cry of a raptor, filled with menace and an almost human loathing.

Something was searching for food.

David looked up, past the sodium streetlight glare and the rooftops, scanning the sky for whatever it was. It sounded enormous. At any minute he expected to hear the thunderous beat of powerful wings, but there was nothing apart from that chilling cry. Even so, the evil, whatever it was, was almost breathing down his neck. And as he looked behind him, the streetlights seemed to dim.

The last few days had whittled down his rational mind. A primal fear overcame him as he gave in to the pervasive atmosphere, and then he was running, like a child in the dark of the night, not knowing what he was fleeing or why. Only when he reached the comforting lights of the hotel did he feel safe from whatever was out there, loose in the city.

From his window, the skyline looked bright and modern above the archaic rooftops of the French Quarter. He tried to tell himself that this was the atomic age, that he was a superstitious fool, but every time he closed his eyes Marsayle was looking back at him. And then he knew that anything was possible.

Anything at all.

Chapter 7

The ring of the phone jarred David out of a troubled sleep. It was 8 a.m. precisely. At first he thought he was in London with Fermay lying warm beside him, but when he contentedly stretched out a hand he found only a cold, empty space.

He fumbled for the phone, still heavy with exhaustion. It had been only four hours since he had climbed into bed, tired from the gruelling work at the club.

'It's reception, Mr Easter. There are two gentlemen here to see you.'

'Who are they?' His head was too fuzzy to comprehend who could be calling on him.

The receptionist held the receiver to one side as she quizzed the visitors. 'They say they're here about a newspaper article, Mr Easter,' she said shortly.

An electric burst of excitement cleared the woolliness from his mind in an instant. 'Tell them I'll be down in about ten minutes.'

David showered and shaved with nervous haste, dressed in his best suit, freshly cleaned and pressed by the hotel service, and then ran to the lift. When he stepped out of it, reception was empty apart from two men who had their backs to him. They looked like Mafioso, a pastiche of New York Wise Guys with expensive Italian suits, broad shoulders and slicked-back hair. Their bodies were stiffly erect, the kind of stance that came from too much packed muscle, and one of them wore aviator sunglasses despite the delicate light. They didn't look like anyone Fermay would know.

David slowed his step as he approached, but they turned before he was within ten paces of them. The one with the sunglasses spoke first, his voice confident and powerful. 'Mr Easter. I recognize you from your photograph.'

'You're one up on me.' David shook his hand.

'I'm Mr Lynch. This is my colleague Mr Frantz.' Smiles came

quickly to their faces, but the signals they were sending out were not friendly. David found it difficult to read them; they seemed like robots, efficient and emotionless. 'We represent Mr Eugene Broussard. You may have heard of him. No? He's a very important gentleman in this town. He read the article about you in the *Times* and he'd like to meet you.'

'Can he help me?'

Lynch gave a lizard smile. 'Mr Broussard would be quite happy to talk to you at length. We have a car waiting outside. If you'd like to accompany us . . . ?'

There was something about the duo which made David instantly suspicious – they were too slick, too friendly, too groomed – but his eagerness to find Fermay overcame any doubts. Walking a few paces behind them, he found himself at the back of the hotel where a long black limousine was waiting. The chauffeur, who was dressed in a full uniform complete with peaked cap, started the engine when he saw them.

'Your boss obviously likes to travel in style,' David said.

Lynch merely smiled in reply, holding open the rear door so David could slide along the leather seat. Frantz climbed in next to him and Lynch sat in front next to the driver. The car moved off so smoothly David could barely tell they were in motion, turning out into the French Quarter's streets which were almost empty of tourists at that time of day.

'So, who is your Mr Broussard?' David addressed his question to Frantz, but the answer floated back from Lynch who spoke without turning round.

'Mr Broussard is a businessman, but he is particularly respected in the city for his many charitable works.' Implicit in Lynch's comment was a demand for instant respect for his superior.

'I'm lucky he's got time to see me.'

Lynch ignored any sarcasm in the comment and added, 'That's right. Mr Broussard rarely sees anyone outside his immediate circle.'

The car glided quickly out of the Vieux Carre across Canal Street, heading west. Neither Lynch nor Frantz spoke unless David asked them a direct question. He sensed almost contempt beneath their superficial politeness. They passed through the edge of the business district and a run-down area of town before turning into the broad, leafy thoroughfare of St Charles which led into the Garden District. The opulent mansions, once the home of plantation owners and Southern Belles, were surrounded by acres of lush, green lawns – calm, relaxing space in a city where that commodity was at a premium, and a world away from the cramped, jumbled confines of the French Quarter. There was an air of casual wealth and genteel attitudes.

'Does Mr Broussard live around here?' Lynch nodded. 'Nice area if you can afford it.'

Lynch swivelled in his seat until David could see his own reflection in the aviator sunglasses. He exuded the faint aroma of sandalwood. 'Mr Broussard feels comfortable here. He's worked hard. He likes to enjoy the things he's earned.'

The St Charles streetcar rumbled down the centre of the avenue, reminding David of his arrival in New Orleans. It seemed like transport for the poor so they would not set foot in the land of the rich. He was concentrating on the natural beauty of a black girl seated at the rear of the trolley when the car swung across the road and into a driveway. Frantz was out and had opened David's door before the limo had come to a halt. It reminded David of films showing secret servicemen in the President's entourage.

'If you follow me, Mr Easter, I'll take you directly to Mr Broussard.' Lynch marched ahead without waiting for an answer.

The house was enormous, gleaming white in the sun. Huge windows added to the impression of size, and colonnades stood on either side of the door like some Greek temple. Above David's head, filigreed balconies overlooked the gardens and street. After the icy air-conditioning of the car, the morning heat pressed down heavily and he was pleased to enter the refreshing coolness inside the mansion. It was just as impressive within. The reception area had an Italian marble floor which created echoes like the inside of a cathedral, while ahead of him was a magnificent staircase with a mahogany banister. He could see a dazzling crystal chandelier in a room to his left where oil paintings hung in heavy golden frames.

Lynch led him into a darker room to his right, a study lined with books and filled with antique furniture and ornaments. Heavy velvet drapes hung each side of a floor-to-ceiling window looking out over the lawns.

There was a man sitting in a high-backed leather chair next to an empty, stone fireplace. A large, leather-bound volume was open on his lap. He closed it noisily.

Eugene Broussard was a bizarre figure and in other circumstances David might have been forced to stifle a laugh. He was around sixty with tanned skin that had turned leathery, it clung tight to his skull like horsehide and David was reminded of Californian geriatrics who felt they could hold on to their youth through bronzing. It was his hair that was the most striking. It had been permed tightly and dyed blond, a pastiche of some twenty-year-old surfer from the seventies and it was so incongruous that it glared like a beacon. But whatever his immediate reaction told him, David soon realized this was not a comical figure. Broussard's eyes crackled with cold fire beneath his glowering brow, and though he was smiling it was the smile of a cobra. He seemed too big for his age; an amalgamation of bone and muscle, radiating power that could crack out at any time. His suit was expensive Italian cloth, his tie fine silk. There was a single diamond on his tie-pin. A cigarette was clenched between two fingers, held flamboyantly high.

'Mr Easter,' he said with a trace of sibilance. 'Do come in. Please take a seat. Coffee?'

David stepped forward. 'Yes, please.'

Broussard nodded to one of his men at the door. 'Why, your photograph didn't do you justice,' he continued. 'You're quite a handsome devil, aren't you. And what a nice suit. Where is it from, if you don't mind me asking?'

'London.' David felt relieved. You could trust a man who recognized good clothes.

'Clothes make the man, they say.'

'You have a very nice place here.'

'Ah,' Broussard said with a dismissive wave of his hand. 'I like to be comfortable. I work hard and it is very nice to have some luxuries around for those odd moments of relaxation. I'm sorry

. . . would you like a cigarette?' He took a compact wooden case from his pocket. 'No? It's one of my few vices.'

The coffee arrived and Broussard poured David a cup from a silver pot. The flunkie stepped back silently to the doorway.

'Tell me, Mr Easter. How do you like our city?'

'I love it. The people, the music, the culture . . . it has everything I ever dreamed of.'

Broussard nodded, his smile so tight it resembled a fixture on a mask. 'Many tourists come here. People from all over the world. They are attracted by the very things you mention. In a way, N'Orleans is a very European city. The Spanish and French influences are obvious, but there are other more subtle things . . . an air of sophistication and, as you say, culture. But many people leave without seeing the true side of N'Orleans, Mr Easter. The city is like a woman, if you can forgive me for being so clichéd. It presents one face of glamour, but many others are hidden beneath and not all of them are so pretty.'

David nodded politely. All he wanted to talk about was Fermay. He was so eager to be led to her, he could barely restrain himself, but he didn't want to risk offending Broussard. He could bide his time. She was so close he could almost smell her perfume.

Broussard rose gracefully, surprising David anew with his hulking presence. With a serpentine sway of his hips, he glided over to one of the bookcases; his fingers, as he ran them along the rows, were thin and long, almost unnaturally so, and they didn't seem to fit the rest of his body. An array of rings that on anybody else would have seemed unaccountably vulgar gleamed in the sunlight. Gold and silver, moonstones, opals, and diamonds, ornately designed and plain. Eventually those delicate fingers came to rest on one particular volume which he plucked eagerly from the shelf. He found the page he was looking for instantly.

'Do you like books, Mr Easter?'

'I prefer music. Jazz.'

Broussard smiled while he read. 'Ah. The Devil's music. Lucifer has all the best songs. I am not an educated man myself, but I strive to better myself. Books are one tool I use. I read voraciously.' He gave David a brief supercilious glance. 'You should read more, Mr Easter. It's good for the soul. It drives the beast out of us.' Returning to the book, he traced a line with his finger and said without looking up, 'This is particularly interesting. It is a history of N'Orleans and it is quite remarkable because it highlights some of the more unsavoury elements of our rich past.' He looked David up and down and moistened his lips. 'The unsavoury is always quite exciting, don't you think? Do you mind if I read you one of the tales?'

'Sure. Why not.' David was baffled by the man's eccentricity, and felt wrong-footed.

'You see, I believe it illustrates the point I was just making, about the true face lying behind the glamour.' He moistened his lips once more and began to read. '"There is a house at 1140 Royal which was always one of the most opulent in the French Quarter, but like many images of finery and sophistication it had a darker face beneath. During the early nineteenth century it was renowned for the magnificent parties thrown by its owner, Delphine LaLaurie, attracting the *crème de la crème* of New Orleans high society. Delphine herself was a woman of great standing, signifying all that was right and proper in culture, genteel attitudes, sophistication. She was a Southern beauty who attracted the attention of men from all over the city. Her bearing marked her as a woman who set herself apart from the common herd.

'"One night in 1834 a fire ripped through the house. The neighbours, terrified for the great woman, broke down the locked doors and searched the elegant mansion. Locked within one of the rooms, in darkness and filth, were seven slaves. They were all starving, their rib cages protruding through their skin. All of them had been chained to the wall in positions guaranteed to cause the most excruciating pain. The neighbours were horrified, even in those times when many people considered slaves to be no more than animals. One of the rescuers summed up the feelings of society when he told the local newspaper, *I wouldn't even treat a dog like that. No sir, not even the lowest beast.*

'"Madame LaLaurie might have been forgiven her cruelty, and her society friends might have escaped looking into a dark mirror, if the newspaper had not suggested that she might have lit the fire herself, happy to see the wretches die in blazing agony.

93

'"One night a crowd gathered outside the LaLaurie home. They wanted her punished for her transgressions against humanity, and if the law wasn't about to dole out retribution, by God, they were. Tempers flared, the mob surged forward, hammering on the doors and windows.

'"Suddenly an enclosed carriage burst out of the driveway, the driver thrashing the horses to force a path through the crowd. Madame LaLaurie escaped justice by fleeing to Europe where she stayed until she died. Her last wishes were to be buried back in New Orleans, with which her family reluctantly complied. But the hatred generated by the most heartless daughter of a proud city meant that even then, several years later, she could only be interred in utmost secrecy. Many said that if her burial had been general knowledge, within twenty-four hours her corpse would have been dug up and dragged through the streets."'

Broussard shut the book and held it to his chest, closing his eyes and raising his head in pleasure. 'Ah, Madame LaLaurie,' he whispered. 'Such sophistication, but so dangerous. People misjudged her because of the way she looked, Mr Easter. It was a foolish thing to do.'

Broussard returned to his seat with a broad smile on his face. David was growing impatient. 'That was very interesting, Mr Broussard, but I don't see what it has to do with why you brought me here.'

'No,' Broussard said, still smiling. 'Fine, then. To business.' He paused. 'I don't like it, Mr Easter. At all.'

'You don't like what?' David tried to read Broussard's face without any luck.

'This . . .' Broussard held up the paper containing the article and then tossed it dismissively on to the coffee table. 'Please don't hound my ward, Mr Easter.'

'Your—'

'Leave her alone.' His voice was quiet, but the words contained the power of a threat. He ended the sentence with another smile which somehow made it even worse.

'I don't understand.' David searched Broussard's face. His pretence of familiarity had fallen away as if a cold wind had swept it from the room. Now his eyes glittered like ice and David realized Broussard had all along been quietly mocking him, playing with him.

Broussard drew on his cigarette, his stare clinical. 'I simply cannot allow any person off the street to see my ward. Do you understand me now, Mr Easter?'

'I didn't know Fermay was your ward, Mr Broussard.' David felt an edge rise in his voice, but he didn't try to disguise it. 'I met her . . . in London. We became very close. I had an accident . . .' He shrugged, '. . . whatever . . . I lost some of my memory. Somehow Fermay and I were separated. I'm not sure what happened but I ended up here, in New Orleans, and I presume in some subconscious way that I was following Fermay. I have no evidence that she is here, but I can *feel* it. If I was just "any person" I would not have gone to such lengths.'

'How romantic. Well, I'm sorry to disappoint you, you having come so far and all.'

'You don't have to take my word for it,' David snapped. 'Just ask Fermay. She'll tell you how much we mean to each other.'

Instead of becoming annoyed at David's outburst, Broussard seemed to become more interested. 'Why, Mr Easter, you are the passionate one. The simple answer is that I do not consider you worthy of my ward's attentions.'

'You don't know anything about me!'

'I have learned from the good book, Mr Easter. "For the Lord seeth not as man seeth: for man looketh on the outward appearance, but the Lord looketh on the heart." And in your heart I see an immature boy, low-born, lacking mettle. Besides, the woman has more important things to do than waste time seeing—' he paused as if searching for the right description and then said simply '—people like yourself.'

David didn't like the way he said *the woman*. It was bleached of emotion like he was talking about one of his flunkies. 'Don't you think Fermay should make that decision?'

'No, I do not. My ward does what I say, as she always has. She is dutiful, more so than I could have expected in any child of my own.'

'Is she well?'

Broussard remained mute; his smile teased David with a score of possible answers.

'Is she here?'

'That is no concern of yours.'

David could feel his temper rising in the presence of Broussard's unyielding condescension. His almost theatrical bearing only enhanced his confidence and calmness. There was a flicker around his mouth, a dart of sadism at his probing of David's soft, fleshy parts, triumph, glee. But then something else happened, fleetingly; David almost missed it. Was that weakness? Worry? A flash and it was gone, but to David it was a flaw in the magnificent façade.

'Tell me, Mr Easter,' Broussard began cautiously, 'while you were with my ward in England, did she say anything . . . about her life here? About me, perhaps?'

'Not that I can remember. As I said, my memory isn't what it should be. Should she have?'

Broussard dismissed David's question with a twitch. 'But your memory could return at any time?'

'So the doctor said.'

Broussard nodded thoughtfully. He stood once more and swayed across the room with his hands behind his back, pausing at one of the tall windows to look over the green serenity of the garden. It seemed for a moment that he had forgotten David was there. When he did finally speak his voice was steady and quiet.

'You have arrived here at a very inopportune time, Mr Easter. I am a businessman and my current plans are complex. They will require my utmost attention and concentration over the coming weeks. I really cannot afford to be diverted.'

'I'm not going to cause you trouble. All I want is to see Fermay.'

Broussard turned and walked slowly towards David. With the hazy light behind him, his unyielding skin made him seem like a shop dummy. 'Of course you will cause me no trouble, Mr Easter.' The stresses in Broussard's voice made David turn cold.

'I can wait to see Fermay until you have more time. If you can give me some indication of whether she's here . . .' He almost said *whether she's alive*. 'For my peace of mind. Whatever you might think, I do care about her.'

Broussard carried on walking until he was standing behind David. The sound of his breathing had increased and there was a faint rasp when he drew air in. David did not turn round, although he could sense Broussard moving into his area of personal space. When he stopped, he was so close David could feel the heat from his body. The scent of his aftershave was a little too spicy and occasionally David thought he could smell a tinge of sweat beneath it.

Broussard stood there for a moment in complete silence. David felt unnerved and he couldn't decide whether he should turn around or keep looking ahead. Then Broussard rested his hands on David's shoulders. David's breath caught in his throat. He wanted to shake Broussard off, but he was rooted to his seat by the audacity of the man. Broussard moved those slim fingers slightly until the tip of one on each hand touched David's neck above the collar. They were as cold as ice and David jumped as if a cattle prod had been jabbed against him. Broussard pulled his hands away instantly and stepped back a pace before walking round to face David once more.

'Really, Mr Easter, this is getting so suburban. I have no doubt that you care about her. But you have to understand that that is of no interest to me. Do you know what I see when I look at you, Mr Easter? I see small-town ideas and small-town ambitions. I see weakness. I see failure. I really cannot afford to spend too long with someone like that. The taint might be catching.'

David bristled, but he controlled himself. He didn't want to give Broussard the advantage of seeing him lose his temper.

'I concern myself with things so far beyond you I might as well be your god, Mr Easter. My ambitions are epic. And I don't like weakness.'

David sized Broussard up. Behind the mincing exterior he could see another man: a brute, bullying, arrogant. In his eyes there was animal cunning, a hint of sadism. The odour of menace lay behind his expensive aftershave.

'I don't understand your attitude, Mr Broussard. If you don't like me, I would have thought you would have done something

97

for Fermay's sake. But it seems to me, looking at you, that you're afraid of me in some way. I don't know why. But I can see it as plain as the nose on your face. You're afraid that if I got together with Fermay it would disrupt your life.' Broussard gave no sign that David's words had any effect on him. 'You may be a big man around here, Mr Broussard, but you have no power over me. If you won't take me to Fermay I'll get to her some other way.'

Broussard sighed and stood up once more. 'You really are an irritant, Mr Easter. There are so many other things you could be doing with your life. Having fun, dancing, drinking. Instead you're sailing into dark, uncharted waters.' He wandered past the bookshelves until he found the one he was looking for, and pulled out a large book bound in milky leather. There was a gold cross on the front. The leather was badly stained. He opened the Bible and returned to his seat. 'I love reading the Good Book. So many homilies, so many lessons for the blind lumbering herd. All the rules for a good life are here. Why, sometimes I even consider them myself. Do you read the Bible, Mr Easter?'

'I don't want to play any more of your games, Mr Broussard. I'm trying to stay polite, but it's not easy. I'm interested in one thing – meeting your ward. And I can't see for the life of me why you can't allow us to get together. You've not given me any good reason.'

'I am a sophisticated man, Mr Easter. A cultured man. But please do not take me at face value. Do not believe that because I like fine things and fine people that I do not have a solid vein of steel at the core of my soul. Do you recall the story of Madame LaLaurie? Never judge a book by its cover, Mr Easter.'

'I didn't think a man of your bearing would stoop to threats, Mr Broussard.'

He laughed. 'Needs must when the devil drives. I won't threaten you, Mr Easter. Nor will I warn you again. You must take the consequences of your actions on your very broad and handsome shoulders. I should point out that when it comes to discipline, I'm with the Good Book. And when it comes to repelling someone who has damaged me in any way, well . . .' He flicked through the pages and found the verse he wanted. '"Life for life, Eye for eye, tooth for tooth, hand for hand, foot

for foot, Burning for burning, wound for wound, stripe for stripe."
That covers just about every eventuality, does it not?' He closed
the Bible and stroked the leather as if it was velvet. 'A lovely
volume, is it not? Perfectly bound. Flawless leather. It's a shame
about the stains. Do you see them, Mr Easter?' Broussard traced
the dark streaks with a well-manicured finger. 'It's blood. The
blood of the previous owner. Such a terrible thing. This Bible is
the only reminder I have of him. The poor, poor man.'

As David looked at the stains he felt a pounding in his head. A
sudden flash of a white shirt, splattered darkly.

'"As for man, his days are as grass: as a flower of the field, so
he flourisheth." I know my scripture, Mr Easter. It has a poetry
to it, does it not? "The Lord gave, and the Lord hath taken away;
blessed be the name of the Lord." Such a gentle way of looking
at death. How far removed from reality it is.' He leaned forward
until David could smell his breath, an unpleasant tint of over-
cooked meat. 'Go back to your little home in England, Mr
Easter. Forget about my ward. And if you remember anything
she said to you during your brief time together, forget that too.
Your life will be so much better.'

David felt a deep chill at the very heart of him. Broussard's
eyes were heavy-lidded above his smile. Their stare made David
feel dirty.

'I can see a hardness in your eyes, Mr Easter. Or shall I call
you David, now that we're better acquainted. Now that we have
an *understanding*. You're thinking about opposing me. You're
thinking "What right has he to tell me what to do?" Well, think
on that very carefully, David. This could be a pivotal moment in
your life. You could return home to your mundane life and
things would run along much as before and sometimes you would
sit and think of this moment and say to yourself, with some relief,
"Yes, I made the right decision." Or you could persist in your
half-baked, idealistic plans . . .'

Broussard nodded in the direction of the door and within a
second David felt a presence at his back. 'Is that it? The audience
is over?' David felt scared, out of his depth, but his pride would
not let him whimper off into the shadows. 'This isn't just
about me wanting to see Fermay. If it was, you wouldn't have

99

overreacted like this. You're a businessman. You're used to weighing up situations and giving the right response. It's something more. Whatever it is, Mr Broussard, I don't care. I'm not going to rock the boat. I only want one thing – Fermay. And I'm not leaving town until I get her.'

Broussard nodded. 'You've made your position very clear, David.'

Broussard smiled and returned to the pages of the Bible as if his visitor had already left the room. David waited for a moment to see if there would be any goodbyes, but when it was obvious the pleasantries had been dispensed with long ago, he stood up. Frantz was so close to his elbow as he walked out of the room, he expected to be grabbed by the arm at any moment.

In the hall, a sudden giddy feeling came over him as some of the tension escaped. He breathed deeply for the first time in a quarter of an hour, but he would not be happy until he was out of the house, on his way back to his room. His dreams of a quick reunion broken, his exasperating search would have to continue, both of those things and more were still wrapped up inside him. He would think of them later. When he felt safe. When he had escaped.

Frantz moved ahead of him to open the door outside, and as he passed by, David felt a sudden constriction across his chest. There was a bloom of heat across his back and neck, and the certain knowledge that someone was watching him. He thought it was Broussard who had emerged to see him off the premises, but when he turned round there was no one else in the hall.

Frantz reached the door, his fingers on the handle. The sensation grew stronger, almost too much to bear.

Stop looking at me! he wanted to shout.

David looked round again, his stomach churning. Along the hall to the rooms at the back. Nothing. Up the glorious staircase to the first floor. Nothing. And then he saw it. An enormous gilt-framed mirror filled a huge portion of the wall near the foot of the stairs. David glanced unconsciously at his reflection and felt his blood run cold.

There were other faces in the mirror, scores of them. Men,

women, children, young and old, all of them haunted, filled with horror and hate. All of them looking at *him*.

David stopped mid-step, his breath freezing in his lungs. Their gaze was so cold, so intense. In the glass, they seemed to fill the hall behind him, packed tightly, a multitude with wild hair, and slack, gaping mouths. Yet when he looked over his shoulder there was no one there.

And when he looked back, the mirror was empty.

Back at the hotel he dialled Willie Hobbes in London. He had decided it would be the last time he would try. He had had enough of being reminded of his old life, of the grey, mundane existence which Broussard had so easily identified. He wanted to go forward into a bright new future. Again there was no reply. And although he wanted to tell Willie so many things about New Orleans, he was almost relieved. For some reason he had almost not wanted Willie to answer.

Lying on his bed, he wondered what could he do now to locate Fermay? He had banked so much on the newspaper article coming up trumps that he had no alternative plan. Broussard certainly knew where she was, but David wasn't going to get any help there; and if he didn't move quickly, Broussard might even become a major obstacle.

He felt an overwhelming sense of love for Fermay. He almost couldn't believe that he felt so strongly. The emotions were like a powerful wave, but there were no memories to back them up. It was all locked within the Fog Zone.

Chapter 8

'This is the beginning. Who knows where it will end?'

Fermay rolled the words out in a theatrically portentous voice. 'One of us has to say that.' She laughed mischievously and at that moment appeared to David ten years younger than the woman he had met in the Jazz Attic. 'It's written. When you're embarking on a passionate love affair you have to say *This is the beginning. Who knows where it will end?* or you get thrown out of the Romantics Union.'

'I think I'd rather be a blackleg.'

'Don't be so pompous.' She cuffed him gently on the side of his head.

David restrained his smile. The rules of the game insisted on deadpan expressions. Horseplay between lovers always made him feel faintly nauseous, but there he was, doing it himself with all the underlying coyness and cosiness that he despised. Somehow with Fermay it didn't matter. It wasn't coy, it was romantic. It wasn't cosy, it was dangerously passionate.

She had been with him a week, her thin suitcase tucked under the bed, her small selection of clothes packing one end of his wardrobe. He had expected a degree of annoyance when the feeling of enclosure crept up on him, but so far it had not materialized. He guessed, though he dared not recognize the thought, that it never would.

David surreptitiously watched her reflection in the mirror on the pub wall opposite as she sipped from her pint of Guinness. Those eyes still fascinated. In fact the fascination had doubled because they had yet to give up their secrets.

There had been no repetition of the first night's sleepwalking. He was pleased. It had frightened him. There had been something about the accompanying glazed stare that had warned of deep, dangerous currents in Fermay's psyche. Her failure to recall ever having left the bed when he broached the subject the next morning did little to assuage his worries.

'You're not thinking about your father, are you?' She gave his hand a concerned squeeze.

'No. Not this time.'

'Good, because you dwell on it too much. You've been on your own too long worrying about these kind of things. You need somebody to look after you.' Her hand felt warm and comforting on his. 'You know, David, you can talk to me about it any time. It must have been a terrible thing to go through. I just want you to know that I'm here for you.'

'Thanks, Fermay.' He meant it sincerely.

'And I want you to know that I'm having a great time here.' Her eyes sparkled. 'There are so many places to see. Kensington Park was wonderful.'

'It was wet and bleak.'

'No,' she corrected him with mock sternness. 'It was wonderful. I could almost imagine Peter Pan stealing the children there.' She downed some of her Guinness. 'So, this friend of yours . . .'

'Willie.'

'Willie. What's he like?'

'I told you. He's a good bloke. He likes music, a good drink, a laugh . . . what more do you want?'

Fermay appeared on edge. She searched the shapes in the Guinness head for augurs. She had asked him about Willie four or five times since he had arranged the meeting in the Prince of Wales, adding that she was always nervous of meeting new people. David was keen that his best friend should get on with her, but Fermay seemed quite happy to cut themselves off from the rest of the world.

'Don't worry.' He gave her thigh a secret squeeze under the table. 'You'll get on like a house on fire.'

'I guess I'm a little shy.' She smiled nervously.

'You were good enough when you came over to talk to me.'

'That was different. I had a good incentive then. Believe me, I wouldn't have done that for anyone.'

'You'll like him, Fermay,' David said calmly. 'Trust me.'

She dropped her chin on her chest, hiding her face with her hair. 'I'm not used to trusting people.'

'Did I lie to you when I said Guinness was a great drink? No. Did I lie to you when I said I was the world's most knowledgeable jazz freak? No, I did not. Did I lie to you when I said . . .'

'David, shut the hell up!' She butted her head gently against his.

'What I am trying to say is that I am eminently trustworthy.'

'Well, that's reassuring to know.' She looked at him in such a way that he knew her statement was not ironic.

At that moment, Willie surged through the door, a whirlwind in black, trailing water behind him. The rain and wind gusted in until he slammed the door forcefully. His dark hair was wet, but not yet plastered to his head which always annoyed him because it revealed his receding hairline. His horn-rimmed glasses were streaked with water. His long coat billowed out in batwings behind him as he strode forward, nodding to the landlord. He wore his leather biker's jacket zipped tightly beneath it.

'What a night!' He swung his coat off, spraying water across the table. 'And you won't believe what I saw.'

Fermay watched his face intently.

'Willie, this is Fermay.'

Willie shook his coat and threw it over a stool. 'Pleased to meet you. David hasn't stopped talking about you. The only thing that's managed to wind him up as much as you, is music.'

'Come on, Willie. You know that's not true. I can't stand her.'

'OK, now we've got the pleasantries out of the way, let me tell you what I saw.' Willie took off his glasses and cleaned them on his sweater. He looked strange without them, like a rodent, his saturnine features appearing stretched, misshapen. David could see why he chose the large spectacles with their unmistakable intellectual appeal.

'Go on then. I suppose there'll be no rest until you get it out of your system.'

'It was . . . like . . .' He was fumbling with his words in his excitement. 'A bird-man. Or a man-bird.'

'What are you talking about?' David mocked.

'No, no, listen. I turned off the High Street and took a short cut through the back streets to get here. I thought all those high warehouses would keep some of the rain off. The gusts were sweeping in between the buildings like Hurricane Hilda had arrived.' He turned to Fermay. 'Winter is not the time to be in Britain.'

'Autumn, spring and summer aren't much better,' David added.

'I digress. I was coming around the back of the market when I saw him. He was standing just inside an alley that runs down the side of one of the warehouses. I suppose he thought he wouldn't be seen in the shadows, but the street-lamp caught his head and shoulders. Now get this, he was dressed like a bird! I mean this guy had a fuckin' bird's head on or something. Long beak, feathers, the works. Can you believe it? Maybe he was going to a fancy-dress party or something – I don't know. But it's not the kind of thing you expect to see on a rainy night in Brixton. I tell you, it scared the living daylights out of me. A fuckin' big bird. I thought I'd wandered on to Sesame Street.'

'Have you been on the mushrooms again?'

'I swear to God, David, that's what I saw.'

They looked at each other incredulously and then burst out laughing in unison at the ridiculous image. It took a few seconds before David realized Fermay was not laughing with them. He glanced at her and saw an unmistakably nervous expression on her face.

'What's the matter?' David asked.

She ignored him and looked directly at Willie. 'Are you sure?' Her breathing had suddenly become shallow.

'I saw it with my own eyes, Fermay. Some dickhead wearing a bird mask. People and their private lunacy never fail to amaze me.'

105

'Fermay?' David touched her forearm reassuringly. She recoiled as if she had been burned.

'So soon,' she said in a tiny voice. 'So soon.'

Willie was staring at her in incomprehension. 'It was only a man in a bird mask, Fermay. It's not a relative of yours, is it?'

'Fermay?' David continued undeterred.

Her eyes suddenly focused on his face. 'I'm sorry,' she said. 'It's reminded me of something . . . a bad experience. Excuse me.' She stood up quickly, banging clumsily into the table, and hurried to the toilet.

'What's wrong with her? Did the stork molest her on the way to the family nest. Or get this, maybe she's got a mortal dread of being brought before the Beak.' Willie snorted at his own joke.

'Ah, give it a rest. You sound like Paul Daniels. She's not normally like this. She's just a little highly strung.'

'Highly strung? She's hanging off the Telecom Tower. What is it with her?'

David raised his hands in the air. 'Don't ask me – I'm just dating her.'

'Dating? That's an interesting euphemism that I haven't heard for a while. Well, I'm sure you know what you're doing.' He paused before adding, 'but that has never stopped me offering a word of advice. After all, I am your best friend and that's what best friends are for – to offer advice which might be a little . . . unpalatable . . .'

'What are you going to say? That I'm making a fool of myself by falling for someone so quickly?'

'You said it, David. You *have* only known her a week. At this stage you're normally trying to think of ways to break off the relationship, not asking them to move in with you.'

'What do you know? The last time you had a deep emotional experience you had to pay for it.'

'Don't have a go at me.' Willie made a stay-back gesture with his hands. 'I just want to help. If you don't want to hear my advice, you don't have to listen. I mean, she does seem a

106

little flakey. She might be one of those neurotic types who—'

'Just wait until you know her a little better, OK? You're always jumping to conclusions.'

'Until *I* know her better? Anyone would think you'd been seeing her for a year, not seven bleedin' days. You're talking about her like you're ready to get engaged. What is it with you? What the hell's come over you so suddenly?'

'Just let it drop, Willie.' David was angry at Willie's response and frustrated that his introduction to Fermay hadn't gone better. 'I like her, that's all that matters.'

'OK, OK, no problem.'

The strained atmosphere had disappeared before Fermay returned, but her appearance would have dispelled it anyway. She had changed. There was a grin on her face and confidence in her movement. 'Can I get anyone a drink?' she asked brightly.

'I thought you'd never ask,' Willie replied. 'Sol, and don't forget the lime.'

'Sol, it is. And another beer for you, Mr Easter. I want to get you drunk tonight.' She turned back to Willie. 'He's at his best when he's drunk. He drops all his inhibitions.' She succeeded in making David blush. 'Jesus, he even allows some affection through.'

Her fingers stroked the back of David's neck, cool and strong.

By 11 p.m. and after several drinks, Willie and Fermay had found some common ground and were chatting sociably, although there wasn't the obvious bonding for which David had hoped. The subject of New Orleans found them in fine voice, a place which Willie dreamed about as much as David, and he quizzed Fermay intensively about the city.

Jazz was the other thing which they all loved. When he was on the subject, Willie couldn't stop himself ranting about his private obsession, his collection of hard-to-find recordings, and then he fired questions at Fermay about the location of any record shops in New Orleans where he could pick up rare discs.

'Does anyone there know anything about The Lost Record?' he asked excitedly.

'The Lost Record?'

'Yeah, you must have heard of it. The rarest jazz record there is with only one copy in existence.' David had listened to Willie rave about it on numerous occasions until he had learned to switch off when the subject was broached. 'It was recorded by Hound-Dog Johnson. I would love to own that record.'

'I think it's a myth,' Fermay said smiling.

'I'm not so sure. You always hear someone talking about it at record fairs or markets, normally some spotty little trainspotter in an anorak, but everyone believes it existed at some time. Nobody knows where it is now.'

'Maybe you'll find it when you visit New Orleans.'

'And then I won't be able to afford it,' he replied resignedly. 'Isn't that the story of my life.'

On the walk home, David asked Fermay what she thought of his friend, but she wouldn't reply. Her mind was elsewhere; she appeared distracted, jumpy. When they arrived back at the flat, she locked the door as soon as it had closed.

That night, after their usual, passionate bout of love-making, she rested her head on his shoulder and said, 'I feel like you're the only person I can trust, David.' Her voice sounded small and frightened; a little girl.

He hugged her silently. Emotions were a hidden land to him and the words to describe them did not come easily. It was not as if he was embarrassed by them, just that he felt numb. It was a cold, dead feeling that had been with him for almost as long as he could remember.

'It's been so long since there was someone I could turn to,' Fermay continued. 'It's hard when you've only got yourself to rely on.'

'Don't you have any family?' He instantly regretted touching on the taboo subject of her past, but the question had slipped out before he'd thought about it.

For once she didn't mind. 'Both my parents are dead.'

He had a sudden image of his own father and mother and drove it from his mind. 'What about friends?'

'No real friends. Just people who look after me.'

'What does that mean?'

'They care for me for their own reasons.' Her body stiffened as she became aware that she was revealing too much.

David did not ask any more. He could feel the barriers crumbling, slowly but surely, and that gave him more joy than he had felt in a long time.

Fermay woke him at 3.10 a.m. She was naked on a chair in the corner of the bedroom, her body snow-white in the half light, and she was humming a familiar tune. There was a quality to the rising and falling of the music, like the breathing of a giant beast, that both excited and disturbed him. Her eyes were wide open, but she appeared to be asleep.

David clambered out of bed, shivering in the cold, and put his arms around her as he had done a week previously. 'Come back to bed, you're dreaming,' he whispered.

She looked at him with sudden lucidity. 'They're coming.'

'Who are coming?'

Her eyes glazed over once more and an answer never came. David had been aware since their first meeting that she was troubled, but now he wondered how deeply her problems lay.

With an effort he pulled her to her feet and she allowed herself to be led back to the bed. Her eyes closed as soon as her head touched the pillow and her sleep was instantly peaceful. But for that one moment when she had looked at him, David had thought she looked scared.

More than that. She looked terrified.

Chapter 9

New Orleans basked in the balm of a midsummer evening all day
long. The streets never became oppressively hot, but nor did it
rain. The mood in the streets was of laziness and reflection, but
David could not find peace anywhere within him. Broussard's
subdued threats hammered away at the back of his head. And the
terrifying world ushered in by Buffalo Marsayle always seemed
ready to crowd in around him.

David lounged in one of the seats overlooking the cathedral
and closed his eyes. Fermay's face hovered in the darkness,
teasing him, igniting a yearning deep within him. It was that
which drove him on, his passionate determination was stronger
than any fear.

David was convinced Fermay had returned to her guardian and
was staying at Broussard's mansion in the Garden District. His
only hope was to watch the house and wait. Sooner or later she
would come out, to walk in the sun, to head into town, and then
he would seize his opportunity.

He was pulled from his thoughts by activity in one corner of
the square. A musician was playing an accordion accompanied
by a marionette attached to the instrument by strings, jigging
madly to the shanty. Closing his eyes, David drifted with the
music. He felt exhausted. Jackson Square had become something
of a refuge for him during his stay. It reminded him of Covent
Garden with its street performers and artists plying a trade that
stretched back hundreds of years. A gang of punk rockers with
leather jackets and torn t-shirts placed the scene firmly in the
twentieth century, but even they harked back to the bands of
vagabonds that begged for change in public places two centuries
earlier.

He opened his eyes when the music stopped. The vista had
changed. New performers had appeared on the scene, different
tourists passed before him. One character caught his eye, a

110

juggler who performed on the cathedral steps. He was dressed all in white with black pom-poms down the front and he was sporting garish white face-paint with heavy, black make-up around the eyes. It gave him a nightmarish appearance. His skill was undoubted; balls and then skittles whirled through the air in a dazzling display of dexterity. David was fascinated by the way the objects magically seemed to find their way back into the juggler's hands.

His attention wandered from the juggler to the stooped old buildings that lounged around Jackson Square, and then beyond, across the cracked, creaking rooftops of the French Quarter to the steel and concrete city that enclosed it. He suddenly became aware that something was happening across the breadth of New Orleans. It felt like it was changing. He could smell something foul in the wind, like the stink of a dead cat hidden in a roadside ditch in high summer.

It had started two days earlier, when he was heading home from Charlie's Place and he had experienced the bizarre sensation of a black tide begin to move across the city. The next morning it seemed to have gone, but it had only been lying dormant, waiting to consolidate its grip. He had never considered himself particularly sensitive, but he could feel a charge in the air like the blanketing hum of power before a big storm.

Looking around, he could see other people felt it too. Many were blithely unaware, happy, untroubled, as they always had been. But in the faces of some was etched a mute, uncomprehending fear. Even in the glare of the sun, their eyes flickered nervously towards the shadows. Occasionally they would glance behind them as if they were afraid they were being followed. Tension. Fear. The inexplicable knowledge that *something* was moving closer.

David felt hot and sticky and a little sick. He had never believed in the supernatural before, but now he could not ignore it. When he had woken on the streetcar, he had stepped into another world. Or perhaps he had always been there, but had never recognized it before? Had the events which led to his memory loss suddenly opened his eyes?

As he rose to head back to the hotel and lock himself away in his room, he noticed that the juggler in costume had stopped performing and was now watching him. The crowd had dispersed and he stood in front of the cathedral, a skittle in each hand, staring at David with those black-rimmed eyes in a white face.

David shivered and hurried away.

Moose was harder to locate that morning. David had scoured Jackson Square and the waterfront, but the fixer was nowhere to be seen. He finally found him overseeing an open-air card game at the back of the French Market, taking cash from passers-by with a joke and a flourish of his own peculiar energy. David sat on a wall and waited for the game to finish before calling Moose over to ask for his help.

Marsayle had been preying on David's mind constantly and ever since the manifestation in the Mardi Gras Museum, he had come to see himself as the victim of a haunting. There was one thing in particular which nagged him. The picture. *The Costume of the Krewe of Aidoneus*. Marsayle had pointed to it as if it bore some significance. Everyone David had spoken to since had said the krewes were harmless, groups of society people or business-men who gave up their time to ensure the Mardi Gras ran smoothly. They might keep their identities secret, but they did nothing more threatening than decorate their own floats for the parade and raise money for charity. Few had heard of Aidoneus – it was not one of the most prominent krewes – but David was determined to discover more. Marsayle had shown the picture to him for a reason.

Moose came over when he had fleeced just enough money from the tourists so that they left the game in irritation but not realizing they had been conned.

'So what can I do for you, man?' he said breezily. 'You don't want your shoes shined, right?'

'I'm looking for some information, Moose. A history lesson.'

'History I can do. To tell you the truth, man, shining shoes is the least of my many skills. History is right up there with blendin' the honies.'

'I want to find out about a Mardi Gras krewe called Aidoneus.'

Moose's brow furrowed slightly, but just enough for David to realize he had heard of them. 'Don't know nothin' about them, man. Now I can tell you about Comus . . .'

'No, it's got to be Aidoneus.'

'Comus are good. Or Rex.'

'Aidoneus.'

Moose laughed. 'Looks like I'm losin' ground here. Why don't you go to the library, man? Plenty of books there about the Mardi Gras.'

'Because I want to find out things that library books would never tell me. Like . . .' David paused. What could he say? *Like why dead people are interested in them.* He let the sentence hang in the air.

Moose held up his hands in resignation. 'OK, man, but you're playing with fire.'

'What do you mean?'

'Aidoneus are bad news. I don't know much, but I know *that*. Krewes are respectable, any Joe Public will tell you that. Street guys know different about this gang. Aidoneus use all that charity shit as a front. They got a nasty streak running right through them and that's the word.'

'Nasty in what way?'

'Nasty in every way, man. Drugs, prostitution, and . . . Let's just say they're not nice people, man. Nobody crosses them. Even the slimiest, double-dealing hustler on Bourbon knows that. People get hurt.'

'Who's behind it all?'

'Don't know, man. Don't *want* to know. They like their secrets to stay secret. Anybody gets too close they fall into the river or get hit by a truck, you know what I mean? They're powerful people, believe me.'

'I need to know more.' The familiar cold nugget at the bottom of David's stomach told him he was on the right track.

Moose shrugged. 'It's your funeral, man. I know folk who know everythin'. Where Ronnie Reagan got his hair dyed. Who wrote Ollie North's speeches. Why Mickey Mouse sounds like a girl. You make it worth my while, man, an' I'll find some sucker to give you the lowdown on Aidoneus.'

David slid a few notes into Moose's hand. It was all his spare cash and he watched reluctantly as it disappeared into Moose's moneybelt.

'That'll do as a down payment, man.'

They shook hands and Moose disappeared into the crowd like a ghost. David was sure Moose would come up with the goods, yet he felt apprehensive at what he would find. What connection was there between a long-dead musician and a group of modern gangsters?

And what did it have to do with himself?

He had barely gone two blocks when he realized he was being followed. As he turned a corner, he glanced back down the street towards Jackson Square and saw Broussard's men heading towards him. They were trying to appear nonchalant, but the stiffness in their bodies left David in no doubt of their attentions. He looked ahead of him and thought about losing himself in the crowd, but he knew it would be futile. They would only wait for him at the hotel. Apprehensively, he turned back to face them.

'Mr Easter.' Lynch greeted him with a tight, false smile. 'We didn't think you'd still be around.' He laid a heavy hand on David's shoulder with a grip just tight enough to be threatening.

David chose his words carefully. Before the menacing mass of Lynch and Frantz, he started to regret that he had not taken Broussard's warnings seriously. 'I've still got a few things to sort out.'

'Mr Broussard asked us to reiterate his statement yesterday that there is really nothing for you here in New Orleans.'

'You're telling me to get out of town? That's a little melodramatic, isn't it?' He fought to control his temper. *Don't mess with these people*, he told himself. *You'll regret it*.

Lynch's smile slipped a little. His grip on David's shoulder grew tighter. 'You should listen to what I'm saying. I'm trying to be nice . . .'

'If he gave me Fermay, I'd be out of here on the next plane. With her by my side.'

'That isn't possible, Mr Easter.' They moved in closer and David found himself backing up against a wall. 'This is a difficult time for Mr Broussard. He doesn't want you around town complicating matters. I suggest you cut short your visit *immedi-*

ately. I wouldn't want to run through this again with you. Do you understand?'

All pretence of amicable advice disappeared with the last three words. Lynch spat them out like bullets as his fingers dug deeply into David's shoulder. His grip was like a steel clamp. David looked from one to the other, but he was not about to argue. They faced him for a second or two longer, letting their threats hang in the air, before turning silently like robots to walk briskly back in the direction of Jackson Square.

David breathed deeply and rubbed his shoulder. How far would they go? he wondered. A beating? More than likely. He had to get out of the hotel as soon as possible, go somewhere where they couldn't find him. He remembered Arlene mentioning a friend with a spare room. She had even scribbled down a number, but for the life of him he couldn't remember where he had put it. He would have to ask Arlene again that night and then hope that he could stay out of Broussard's way until he was reunited with Fermay.

As it was, Arlene came over to him during a lull, worried by his nervous appearance. 'Hey, are you OK?' She held his upper arm and looked into his face with concerned eyes. 'You look terrible. Do you want to talk about it?'

He shook his head. 'What is there to say? Strange things are happening – situation normal in the Easter household.'

'Wow, David, I've never seen you like this. Is it that . . .' She paused, struggling for words that would not make his problems sound too incredible. '. . . y'know, what you saw? The guy? The dead guy? Because, y'know, if I can help . . .'

He smiled. 'Thanks, Arlene. Yeah, you can help me by giving me the number of that friend of yours who has a room to rent. I lost the piece of paper you wrote it on.'

'Beth? Sure, the room's still free.' She wrote the number on a bar receipt, and added the address.

'I've got to get out of the hotel. You know that bigshot businessman I saw? Fermay's keeper? You may find this hard to believe, but he's taken an instant dislike to me. In fact, he dislikes me so much he's prepared to have his monkeys take me out and teach me a lesson.' He looked at the number and tucked the paper into his pocket. 'I'll call Beth first thing.'

'You'd better leave it till the afternoon. She's out at work till three. She's a teacher. Is that too late for you? 'Cause if there are any problems you can always crash at my . . . our . . . place.'

'Thanks again, Arlene. I should be OK till three.' David noticed a worried look on her face when she spoke of her home. 'So how are things with you?'

She moved further behind a post where they could not be seen and opened a soda bottle she had secreted in her pocket. 'Oh, you know . . . life goes on.' David was suddenly aware how tired she appeared. She looked away, and when she looked back her eyes were wet.

'What is it, Arlene?' It was David's turn to give her arm a comforting squeeze.

Arlene brushed away a tear as if it was a sign of weakness which could not be tolerated. 'Oh, David . . .' She stopped herself and then looked at him seriously. 'Can I trust you, David?'

'Of course you can.'

'I mean, real discreet, like? I've got to talk to someone about it. It's driving me nuts. It's about Scuba.'

'Oh, him.'

'Yeah, I know he's a jerk. You don't have to say anything. God knows why I stay with him – I must be a real sucker. David, he's tied up in some dirty business. I'm worried, y'know, I'm worried he's going to get himself killed.'

'What is it?'

'Drugs. He's bringing it into town for some local gang. All I know is there's some lab out in the swamps where they mass produce crank and cut the pure coke that's smuggled into the port from the south. Scuba's always had this thing about getting rich easy. I keep telling him you gotta work for the things that matter in life, but not Scuba. He's too goddamn lazy. See, he's not a bad guy, David. He just wants it all without getting off his butt and growing up. He's got this beat-up van from when he was in a rock band. Some guys came up to him one day and asked him if he'd run errands for them, if you know what I mean. At first it was just small stuff, a few ounces here, a few there. I guess they were just testing him. I told him he was crazy getting involved with that shit anyway, y'know. I mean, I've seen what it does to people. You gotta be responsible. He told me to mind my own business.' She touched her jaw subconsciously. 'Then it got worse and worse. He was bringing in kilos, packing the van to the roof. It was like he thought he could never be caught, like he was indestructible or something.' She took another swig of soda to lubricate her dry throat.

'You said you were worried he might get killed. If the cops catch him he won't die. He won't see much daylight, but he won't be dead.'

'It's worse than that, David. Today he was threatening to hold off a shipment, park up his van with a full load in a warehouse until he got more money. He thinks he can blackmail them into making him rich.'

'What is he – nuts?'

Arlene shook her head, the tears threatening to pour forth. 'I'm sick with worry, David. What am I going to do? I don't want anything to happen to him, but he won't listen to me.'

David put an arm around her shoulders and she slipped in close to him, her head gently nodding against his. What should he say? That Scuba was a small-time crook and a big-time loser and she'd be better off without him? He couldn't hurt her feelings in that way. 'You've got to use some psychology on him, Arlene. Appeal to his ego. Tell him only punks and leg-men do the kind of dirty work he's doing. Tell him he's losing your respect. Withdraw his bedtime rations. There are plenty of tricks you can use.' He couldn't resist adding, 'You're smarter than he is.'

She leaned closer and whispered in his ear, 'You say the sweetest things. I'm not too sure how Scuba will go for any of that, but I'll give it a shot. Uh-oh, here comes trouble.'

Arlene pulled away and quickly pretended she was wiping her tray clean as Charlie lumbered across the room. 'Hey, you two,' he bellowed. 'Get to work. What am I payin' you for?'

'Thanks, David. You're one of the good guys,' Arlene whispered before hastily moving back out into the crowd.

*

117

David's nerves were still fraying when his shift ended. There was a sense that something was *wrong*, a gut feeling like the one soldiers spoke about before combat, the one that told them which way the battle was going.

Out on the street, the night was warm. Clouds had banked up low over the city, obscuring the moon and stars. There was going to be a storm, he thought. The air still crackled with electric tension. He regretted that Charlie's Place was so far from the main tourist area.

The first thing he noticed was the streetlights waxing and waning and then winking into the background until they became little brighter than candles.

He stopped and stared. The air seemed foggy, although the night had been clear. Details were blurred.

No, he thought with sudden realization.

A band of pressure tightened across his chest and before he could do anything, the shadows rushed out of the side alleys to swarm around him. He wanted to run, but it was too late. His blood vessels were filled with lead – it took all his energy to make just one step. All he could do was stand there.

The silence was oppressive as if it, too, was nervously waiting. The blood fizzed loudly through David's head and he caught his breath, and then came the sound of madness.

This time it was not Marsayle and it was not silent. He heard its high-pitched screeching laugh long before he saw it shamble out of an alley, '*Eee, eee, eee.*'

It lurched out of the shadows into the golden pool of a streetlight like a drunk, its mottled, dirt-flecked suit hanging so loosely from its frame it was like a ship's sail fluttering in the breeze. Its black skin had turned almost white in whatever afterlife it existed, flapping in ribbons on the lower left side of its face so the yellowing bone of its jaw and teeth were exposed to the night.

Slowly it advanced. One step, two steps, relentless, moving towards him, fingers opening and snapping shut again and again.

David had to face it in the loneliness of the night.

'What do you want?' he said hoarsely. How many times would he have to repeat the question before he got an answer. 'What are you going to do to me?'

The advance continued until David thought his heart would burst. His tongue had swollen and seemed to fill his whole mouth.

The spirit stopped when it was ten paces away from him, its laughter trailing away in a dying cry. With its head rocking from side to side like some hideous mockery of a jazz musician keeping time, it let its slack jaws fall apart and it said, 'Your daddy . . .' There was a pause as if it had trouble forming the words.

'Your daddy says hello.'

David dropped to his knees. 'No, Dad,' he whispered. 'I'm sorry. I didn't mean to do it.'

When he looked up, the spirit was gone. There was only a faint smell of earth in the air. For a moment he stared at the cold space and then he clambered to his feet, and ran, directionlessly, crazily, through the city streets as the tears ran down his cheeks.

His father . . . !

Only in the quiet of his hotel room did he finally rest and there he cried for a full hour for the soul of his father, feeling the memories he had been seeking come back in force however much he now tried to bury them.

Chapter 10

'He's out there, David. You better watch out.'

Arlene manoeuvred him until he had a clear sight through the crowd. The Cowboy sat on the far side of the club, his stetson pushed back on his head at a couldn't-care-less angle. He was laughing heartily so that his jowls rippled beneath his bushy beard.

'Why did Charlie's boys let him in?'

'Charlie has this policy which says no one can be blamed for getting drunk. "It's a fact of life, Arlene. Men gotta get drunk." That's what he always says. Everyone gets a second chance, even the guy who threw up outside his office.'

'And that includes a fat bully who tried to beat up two of his employees?'

'Everyone.'

After the madness of the last few days, David was almost happy to see the Cowboy's corpulent, grinning face across the room. It was reality, hard, tough and dirty, pulling him back from terrifying thoughts about his encounter in the street and the nightmares he had had about his father's suffering.

'He's probably not here to cause any trouble. He looks like he's just enjoying himself.' Even as he said it, David didn't quite believe it.

'Yeah, right, like he doesn't carry a grudge for being made to look a jerk in front of the whole bar. Get real, David. He's out for trouble. There's a whole bunch of his meathead friends there and they're knocking down beer like it's going out of style. I'm going to warn Charlie about it. If Mac and Pete keep an eye on things they can move in before it starts to turn nasty.'

'While you're at it, why don't you tell Dean they're giving big tips on that table? He might want to swap places with you for the night.'

'You're evil, David,' Arlene said, laughing.

As the night progressed, both David and Arlene steered clear of the Cowboy's table. Charlie agreed that another waitress should serve it – Millie was in her late thirties with a no-nonsense manner and years of experience of dealing with drunks. Charlie was convinced that not even the most argumentative punter would get on her bad side.

David kept his eye on the Cowboy and his cronies as he went about his business. There were five of them in all, each one of them an odd mix of beer belly and muscle. They were rednecks drunk in the worst possible way, with humour decreasing and aggressiveness increasing in direct relation to the amount of alcohol consumed. Despite that, there was little sign of them doing anything worse than loudly abusing the band. They didn't even acknowledge David and Arlene's presence in the room. By 1 a.m. the tension had dissipated enough for David to relax.

'One of us overreacted and it wasn't me,' he said as playfully as he could manage when he and Arlene took their nightly break in their usual hiding spot.

'So I'm cautious. So sue me.' She lit a cigarette and inhaled deeply. 'Shit. I've got through ten of these in the last hour. My throat feels like I've swallowed a razor blade. Hey, did you call Beth?'

'She had her machine on all day. I left a couple of messages, but she never got back to me.'

'Yeah, that's Beth.'

He had a sudden bout of anxiety that time was running away from him. How much longer would Broussard give him before he started flexing his muscles? 'I'll call round tomorrow afternoon,' he said. Ideally he could stay out of the hotel all day and move straight into Beth's before work. 'Hey, how's Scuba?'

She dropped her head and looked at the floor. 'He's OK.' Then she added, 'I don't want to talk about him. Say, are you doing anything for lunch tomorrow? There's this great place not far from here – best gumbo and crayfish étouffée in N'Orleans. We could go round to Beth's after that.'

David was warmed by her enthusiasm. 'OK. It's a date.'

Surprisingly, she blushed. 'Great. I'll meet you outside here. 1 p.m. Don't be late.'

David could feel Arlene watching him, smiling, as he weaved through the drinkers to the toilet. Her loneliness was obvious, to him at least, and he could see the burden it placed upon her. Scuba couldn't help her – he was one of the causes – and there was no one else, apart from himself. Arlene had gone out of her way to help him, and now he would do anything he could for her in return.

At the toilet entrance he paused hesitantly. Whenever he swung open the door he wondered if he would see Buffalo Marsayle within, waiting with grasping hands. As always he waited until someone walked in before him. He would follow, do whatever he had to do quickly, and be out, ignoring the thin film of sweat coating his back. At least Charlie had finally got around to fixing the flashing light.

When he turned around from the urinal a couple of minutes later, the room was suddenly crowded.

'How you doin', boy?'

The Cowboy and his four friends had slipped in quietly and were standing in a line next to the cubicles. The man David had followed left quickly, his hands still dripping from the wash basin. A tall, pony-tailed bruiser with tattoos up and down the length of his arms took up position next to the door to deter anyone else from entering.

David's throat tightened, but he kept a cool head. As if they weren't there, he stood in front of the mirror, took out his comb, and began to flick back his greased hair.

'You fuckin' faggot,' the Cowboy sneered. David ignored him. 'Hey! Anyone in there? I'm talkin' to you, boy.'

David knew his only hope was to stall for time until the failure of people to get into the lavatory alerted Mac or Pete. In the mirror he could see their brutal, unintelligent faces distorted by hate. He finished combing his hair and turned around.

'What do you want?'

The one with the ponytail guffawed. 'It speaks! The faggot speaks!'

The Cowboy could see no humour in the situation. His face was darkened by hurt pride, his eyes glowering. 'We'll do this nice and quick, boy. You've gotta learn your lesson, not to fuck with your betters. You hear what I'm sayin', boy? Nobody fucks with me.'

'Get him, Kenny,' another of them said. He pulled out a switchblade. The click of it opening sounded like a gunshot to David's hyper-alert senses. 'Get him good.'

The Cowboy took off his leather belt and wrapped it tightly around his fist. His muscles flexed in a macho show of strength. He looked directly into David's eyes.

'What's it like to be the only man alive who speaks fluent Cromagnon?' David said.

The Cowboy's eyes flickered with bovine stupidity until he decided it was an insult. Then he lunged forward, roaring like a beast. David noticed the scars on his cheek where Arlene's nails had raked him, still raw and painful. The Cowboy's blow was filled with power, but it was the punch of a drunk man and telegraphed from the second he pulled back his fist. David dodged it easily. The Cowboy grunted, narrowly preventing his hand smashing on to the wash basin.

His friends realized it was not going to be the one-sided fight they had expected. They moved in as one, grasping for David's arms and legs. He punched and kicked out, backing into the corner.

This is it, he thought. *I'm a dead man*.

The door burst open a second later. Mac and Pete roared in, fists flailing like comic-strip characters. Behind them David caught a glimpse of Arlene's frightened face. She had raised the alarm just in time.

The other four turned to confront the club's bouncers while the Cowboy continued his attack on David, determined to get his vengeance. His fist crashed into a shoulder, sending a momentary explosion of pain up David's neck. He had suffered worse and he responded quickly. His first blow slammed into the Cowboy's face, mashing his lips into his teeth. The second powered into his cheekbone just below his eye. The Cowboy spun sideways and fell to the floor, dazed.

As David nursed his aching fist, the one with the switchblade realized the odds were diminishing quickly. With a guttural snarl, he aimlessly lashed out with the knife. There was a sickening tearing noise. A stifled cry. And then blood spurted across the room in a bright red arc, splashing across the front of David's apron, staining it like camouflage. Mac dropped to his knees, his eyes wide with shock. There was a sudden frantic scuffling as the four thugs realized what they had done and fought with each other and Pete to get out of the cramped toilet. They stampeded across the club like wild men, lashing out at anyone who got in their way.

Mac was thrashing around the floor like an epileptic in a growing pool of blood. David moved quickly. He ripped off his apron and fell to the bouncer's side. 'Mac!' he yelled. 'Stop moving! You're making it worse!'

Pete joined him, grabbing Mac's arms while David tried to staunch the spurting blood. It was a futile task. The thug's random attack had severed Mac's jugular.

Arlene was there at his side, tears of shock streaming down her face. 'It's gonna be OK, Mac,' she said. 'There's an ambulance on the way.' He didn't seem to hear her. His wild eyes were focusing on another world.

Arlene was half right: an ambulance crew were on the scene within minutes, taking over with machine-like efficiency.

David grabbed Arlene's arm and led her out into the club. 'Come on,' he said. 'There's nothing we can do here.' She burst into tears, resting her sobbing head on his shoulder.

They watched silently as the medics rushed Mac out on a stretcher to the waiting ambulance. David couldn't read their blank faces, but he could see from the stillness of the body that Mac had gone.

'Why did it happen?' Arlene asked as she dabbed at her eyes. 'I mean, Mac didn't have anything to do with this. The Cowboy was after you or me. Mac didn't deserve to get it.' She was trembling from the shock.

David couldn't answer her question. He thought of the way violence had exploded out of nothing with random brutality and he found parallels with his own life. He recalled his father once again. His face, drained of blood, was in his thoughts with increasing regularity.

The Cowboy, at least, had not escaped. A group of drinkers

from the bar had leapt on him as he ran out of the toilet, and pinned him down until the police arrived. He was led out of the club cuffed and still dazed.

Only later, as things gradually returned to normal, did David notice the blood stains on his clothes. They were splattered there just like the stains on his shirt. For a second he almost remembered something else at the core of the Fog Zone, something vital, but then it slipped out of his grasp.

The Presbytere on Chartres overlooking Jackson Square was another of the New Orleans buildings dedicated to the worship of time. It was originally intended to be a home for the cathedral priests until the Louisiana State Museum bought it for the new church of the living past. Artefacts were stored there in reverential silence allowing the casual browser to phase into a long-gone world.

David wandered through the maze of rooms, aware that he had taken to grinding his back teeth. Stress. Life in the city was getting to him.

The atmosphere in the Presbytere helped to calm him briefly, its exhibitions of painting and pottery and antique pianos allowing him to forget the violence, the hauntings and intrigue that had come to form his daily diet. It was a place where a footfall could be heard two rooms away. Dust motes were suspended in the sunbeams which broke through tall windows. In the reception hall, an attendant waited quietly for the next visitor, a ticket at the ready.

He thought of Mac and felt sad, even though he didn't really know him. There had been so much blood. It had taken an hour to swab it off the floor. The mops and paper towels had merely transferred it from one place to another until the whole floor was stained red.

Arlene had been difficult to console, partly because she liked Mac, but mainly, as she told him later, 'because it could have been you lying there in that pool of blood, David.' He had felt flattered by her concern and he told her so. It seemed to cheer her a little.

He checked his watch. Only half an hour until he met her for lunch. He had left the hotel early in case Lynch and Frantz arrived to 'escort' him to the airport, and the Presbytere had seemed as good a refuge as any. He didn't want to be late for Arlene so he returned to the reception hall, pausing briefly by an intriguing, intricately designed tapestry which detailed life in New Orleans. It was based around a series of maxims and proverbs, each one illustrated with a small, delicately stitched picture.

One of them caught his eye. Next to it was the legend, *The Devil is a Gentleman*.

A security guard near the door coughed, disturbing the warm, sleepy peace of the room. Nearby someone was whistling.

The Devil is a Gentleman. Honied words. Warm handshakes. The Prince of Lies. For some reason, David thought of Broussard.

Perhaps he should have had two minds about stepping into the Presbytere, given that it was a centre dedicated to keeping the dead alive. What more pale, restless spirits might emerge from the museum's nooks and crannies to torment him? What better place to find them than in a building packed with their possessions? But the closest he had come to seeing one was the juggler with the death's-head face who performed on the cathedral steps next door.

Outside, looking across Jackson Square, he was forced to shield his eyes against the brightness of the sun. He looked around for the juggler but he was no longer entertaining the crowds. Their eyes had met briefly as David entered the Presbytere and it had felt like an unwanted introduction.

Down the steps and into the mass of tourists, David felt suddenly alive once more. Dodging the gawpers and performers, he set off towards Charlie's Place where Arlene would be waiting for him. For one brief moment there was a clear view ahead of him through the milling tourists and suddenly his stomach clenched. At the end of the corridor of bodies he could see them waiting. Frantz and Lynch stood in the shadows under one of the covered walkways at the side of the square. They were trying to look inconspicuous, but their Mafioso appearance stood out like a four-alarm fire among all the t-shirts and denim.

David pushed his way into the crowd, his heart pounding faster, but Frantz and Lynch saw him and moved forward quickly, their jaws set, their eyes hidden behind sunglasses. To his left he saw Broussard's black limo, parked illegally on Chartres with clear contempt for the law. The windows were too dark to tell if there was anyone inside.

He pushed against the crowd furiously. Someone swore at him. Another jostled him back. As he started to wriggle his way through in the direction of the waterfront, he felt a hand grab his collar roughly. Lynch hissed in his ear, 'Get in the car. Now. Or you'll be sorry.'

David was not about to wait for the threat to be put into effect. He yanked his jacket free and marched quickly away without looking back, leaving Lynch cursing under his breath. If they wanted him, they would have to catch him and he had given enough muggers, pushers and police the slip in Brixton to know they would have a run for their money. Anyway, how much could they do in a busy, daytime street?

He ducked suddenly into St Anne Street and began to walk as quickly as he could towards lakeside. After a couple of blocks he stopped and looked behind him. Frantz and Lynch had moved out from their cover and were striding up the street in pursuit. When they saw David staring at them they stopped in their tracks, evaluating the situation, before continuing at an even quicker rate. David moved off at a breathless pace, quickly breaking into a jog.

His suit was not the ideal outfit for running through the hot streets, but at least Frantz and Lynch were equally constrained. He turned along Bourbon Street towards downtown, away from the crowds.

The sound of Frantz and Lynch's running feet echoed behind him as they stepped up the pursuit. The further he got from the tourist area, the more sparsely populated were the streets. He had gambled on a few stragglers wandering off the beaten track in search of hidden sites, but at times he and his two pursuers were the only people in view.

With the sweat soaking through his shirt, he took a sudden detour lakeside, then uptown and then back towards riverside so he had gone in a full circle. Frantz and Lynch were managing to keep up with him and even seemed to be drawing closer. As he rounded the last corner he dodged quickly into an alleyway he had seen earlier. It wouldn't take long before they realized where he had gone, but the brief respite was all he needed to shake them.

The dark alleyway led into a small paved courtyard, through a wrought-iron gate which hung open. It was quiet, peaceful and cool and for a second David thought about hiding there until he heard Frantz and Lynch run past the entrance to the alley and then come to a halting stop when they failed to see David ahead of them.

Instead, without waiting for them to turn back, David moved quickly across the courtyard and into another alley on the opposite side. The tension left a lump in his throat the size of a melon, but he was almost laughing with the vibrancy of it all, the excitement of the chase and the thrill of being ahead. He felt like one of his childhood heroes from the old movies he used to watch with his father on sunny Saturday mornings – *The Thief of Baghdad* or *Robin Hood* or *Jack The Giant Killer*, always out-manoeuvring the villains.

The sunlight blinded him when he emerged from the alley and it took him a second to get his bearings. During the hours spent alone in his hotel room, he had virtually memorized the tourist guide he had picked up on his first day; all the streets in the Vieux Carre *and* all the sights. He looked up and down the street. He was on Royal.

And then he noticed it, just across the road. 1140 Royal. The old LaLaurie home with the dark past which Broussard had described so graphically. David felt his flesh creep without any particular reason. His eyes scanned the dark, lonely windows, searching for a mark of its past. The building was now luxury apartments, eagerly sought after by New Orleans' wealthy, but although he could see nothing extraordinary about the place he could feel a strange, dark attraction. Like lines of force trembling just beneath his feet, threatening and warning but at the same time pulling him in magnetically.

He could hear the force field whispering to him, its voice growing louder the longer he waited there, telling of sorrow and pity, hatred and suffering. It said Madame LaLaurie still walked through the house, her immortal soul enduring the punishment she escaped during life.

David never heard the car draw up behind him. The house had him in its spell. A blow hit him squarely at the base of the skull like a jackhammer, a thousand fiery stars exploding before his eyes. When he opened them again he was face down on the sidewalk, the concrete cold against his burning head, a ringing in his ears like a hundred solstice bells.

Rough hands grabbed him and flipped him belly up. He was looking at himself. The image receded as Lynch's head came into view, David's face framed in each of the lenses of his aviator sunglasses.

'Mr Easter. You made me break into a sweat. I don't like doing that.'

'Fuck off,' David mumbled through cotton wool.

'Those are the magic words.'

Frantz and Lynch pulled him to his feet and dragged him towards the car. The window slid down with a hum.

'I don't normally accompany my boys on such mundane tasks, Mr Easter,' Broussard said with a thin smile. 'But I wanted to ensure you had a good old N'Orleans send-off.'

'I'm not going anywhere,' David replied defiantly.

Broussard laughed patronizingly. 'You are indeed going somewhere, Mr Easter, and you will be going there in style. It would have been fitting to have involved you in my business, but the time is not ripe. As it is, we have a suitable replacement.'

'What are you talking about, Broussard?'

'What I am talking about, my young sir – and I will ignore your lack of respect at this juncture – is that your normal life is over. You are at a moment of change, of transmutation, from base metal into gold. Say farewell to the mundane and greet the glorious. You are about to journey to another place. And I think, in fact I am sure, that it will look very much like hell.'

On cue, Frantz levelled another blow at David, this time catching him on his ear which flared with pain. David fell to the ground once more, aware that the street was empty. Lynch powered his foot into David's ribs and then into his stomach. David gagged and rolled into a protective ball.

Thoughts stumbled through his head. *Get up! Run! Fight back!* but the blows were coming in too quickly.

Then, in one moment, the pain disappeared into the background until it became the sound of a lone drummer heard from behind an oaken door. All his thoughts were focused on what he saw above him as he sprawled on the pavement. Frantz and Lynch's grinning faces occasionally popped into his field of vision, but David was staring past them, up the wall of the house to a first-storey window.

A woman was looking down at him. Her face was contorted with such malevolent glee that her natural beauty had been destroyed. Her eyes bugged out wide in white porcelain skin and her mouth formed a giant 'O' which was either a silent scream of pleasure or an ear-splitting shriek of horrific joy. Even from that angle David could see the hatred in her face. She wanted him to die, painfully. She wanted to see him ripped limb from limb. Briefly her mouth slipped into a little knowing smile. She was aware that he could see her.

Chains of the heaviest metal hung like magnificent jewellery from her dress of silk and taffeta. One slim, aristocratic hand was raised to the glass.

Suddenly his view was obscured by the sole of a leather boot smashing into his face. The last image he carried into unconsciousness was of Madame LaLaurie laughing maliciously at his suffering.

Into the darkness he went, like a swimmer striking out for a distant shore. Faces passed him by in the inky sea, but as always there was one that stood out like a beacon. Fermay. Deep in the heart of the Fog Zone she stirred, calling to him . . .

PART 2

The Lonesome Road

*Faith is the substance of things hoped
for, the evidence of things not seen.*

Hebrews (11.1)

Chapter 11

'David, it's your responsibility.'

The girl had eyes of steel and a voice of flint, but he did not flinch as she harangued him on the Brixton street corner in the pouring rain. The water trickled down his back, gluing his t-shirt to his body. Overhead, the clouds were an impenetrable mass of grey that blanketed the dead streets. There was an insipid sense of hopelessness and futility about it. All he wanted to do was to get away.

'David, are you listening to me?' She must have done some detective work to establish his identity; the last time they had parted she seemed to be under the assumption he was called Darren. Or Donald. Or something. She had only actually called him by name a couple of times.

'I'm listening, Shelagh.' It wasn't Michelle or Maureen after all. Now wasn't life full of surprises. He knew she was called Shelagh because she had made a point of introducing herself when they met. Shelagh. With a gee aitch. She knew he wouldn't have remembered either.

'Well? What have you got to say then? I'm pregnant. Definitely pregnant. The doctor says so.'

She was lying, of course. The basic stupidity of the lie made him dislike her even more. Admittedly, he had been drunk during their seedy, loveless encounter, but not so drunk that he hadn't used contraception. Shelagh, however, *had* been too drunk to realize. He hadn't even wanted to sleep with her in the first place, but she had badgered and cajoled him all evening at the club and then followed him home and threatened to make a disturbance on the doorstep unless he let her stay the night. She had made out she was joking, but David had had his doubts. He knew it was a weak thing to do, but as he told himself the next day: what else was there? He had truly believed at the time that that was as good as it got. How could he have been so stupid?

'So, Shelagh, would you like to get married?' he said in a voice that captured the weariness he felt. He wanted to get this whole scene over as quickly as possible and return to Fermay.

It had all been planned from the moment she had laid eyes on him, he could see that now. He discovered the reason only two days ago when he heard she had been given notice to leave her squat, but he could have guessed it from her face, from the slyness which she struggled to hide but which managed to claw its way back to the surface every few minutes. He realized her ploy had been borne of desperation – it was tough being homeless. But he hated being lied to. He loathed being manipulated by someone who simply *didn't care*.

'Don't be fucking stupid,' she snapped. 'Marriage is just a male ploy to keep women in chains.'

Her hair was in dreadlocks which had probably been knitted together months before. Dirty and greasy, they clung to her skin in the rain like dead rats' tails. The clothes she kept hidden beneath the fourth-hand army parka were shapeless and drab, a camouflage of grey and green for the dole queue. Even her skin was drab; pebble dashed on her chin with scarlet zits, it had the chalky sheen of a speed freak. And everything on the surface matched what lay within.

How did he ever become stimulated enough to take her to bed? That's the demon drink for you, he thought philosophically, cheap currency in the loveless relationships of Brixton's sub-culture.

'So what *do* you want?' he asked calmly.

'You've got to take me in. It's your responsibility. You've got to look after me until . . . until I've made up my mind if I'm going to have it or not.'

'Or until you decide to tell me the "doctor" was mistaken, you mean.'

Shelagh's face erupted in sobs and she kicked him sharply

on the shin. Then she spun on her heels and marched away in the direction of the high street.

He was not a bad person, David kept telling himself, but within his mind wriggled a doubt that his treatment of Shelagh had been sadistic, punishing her for all the wrongs or imagined wrongs that he felt had been dealt him. He could have let her down a little more gently, couldn't he?

Fermay would be laughing if she could hear the arguments in his head, he thought wryly. It was so typical. Even when he was convinced he had acted reasonably, he felt guilty about it.

He met Fermay at The Monument in the City. It was just one more port of call on her whistle-stop tour of the capital's sights. She was hungry for all the tourist attractions, with the enthusiasm of a schoolgirl on her first day in the capital.

'I want to see it all, David,' she had said underneath the space-exploration exhibit in the Science Museum, gripping his arm with wide-eyed optimism. 'Every last bit of it. It's all so exciting! There's so much history, so much culture.' She had kissed him on the cheek and then had leaned forward and whispered in his ear conspiratorially, 'And I want to find out everything about it because it's *your* town.'

When he emerged from the tube station, he was surprised to see the rain had stopped and the clouds had been swept away by the chill winter wind. The crowds heading out of the City offices for lunch were thick, but he had no trouble spotting Fermay. She was wearing a short black skirt and a baggy claret blouse that she had picked up in a store in Covent Garden. Over it she wore a thick charcoal coat, almost to her ankles, as protection against the January cold. David was still surprised at how little clothing she had brought with her, only a few necessary items stuffed into a suitcase that had seen better days. She claimed she had only intended to stay in Britain for a few days, but something in her voice had given him the impression that it was not the whole truth.

'How're you doing?' she said, greeting him with a kiss and

135

a hug. Her arm instantly snaked into the crook of his. 'Thank God you're here. All these people were starting to drive me nuts. They were crowding around me.'

'Fermay, this is England's biggest city. There are supposed to be crowds.'

'I know, but I don't have to like them. I just want to be on my own.'

'Thanks a lot.'

'On my own with you, honey,' she cooed mockingly.

In the face of Fermay's whirlwind, his thoughts about Shelagh had been swept away. 'Couldn't keep away from the shops, huh?'

She was laden with two carrier bags and a long cardboard tube gripped tightly between her left arm and her rib cage. 'I thought I'd spend all my savings at once so you'd be forced to find me a job.'

A *frisson* of excitement crackled up his spine. If she was thinking about a job, she was thinking about staying around a while. He had delayed asking her when she was returning home, not wishing to consider it himself. In fact, he had decided that when she announced her intention to leave he would ask to go with her. There was nothing in London to keep him. This job idea was better than he could have believed. He quickly moved on to another subject, afraid that if he laid her statement open to inspection, it would prove to be a joke and his hopes would be dashed.

'Who leads the way?' He motioned to the entrance to The Monument. Over his head, the stone tower commemorating the start of the Fire of London soared up higher than the surrounding buildings.

'You do, because you're the hulking he-man around here. I'm just a lickle girl. And I want to watch your butt going up those stairs.'

'Sexist bastard.' He stepped through the doorway and began the climb.

At the top Fermay leant on the guard rail and looked out into the hazy distance. She breathed in deeply, filling her lungs, and then she sighed. 'Isn't it wonderful,' she said. All

David could think about was the thick London pollution she had inhaled. A breath of wind licked at her hair, pulling a strand across her face. She ignored it, her concentration focused on the scenery as she scanned from the City across the East End and the river rolling thick and grey beneath them. David reached out and tucked the strand behind her ear.

'I love this city so much.' Wonderment coloured her face. 'There's a magic here, David. In the buildings, in the people. Can't you just feel it? I could spend the rest of my life here, just walking around, looking and talking, so much to see and do. Don't you feel that anything can happen here?' She looked back at him, her eyes sparkling, and his stomach flipped.

'Sure,' he said drily. 'The lame will walk and the blind will see.'

'You're a dirty cynic, David Easter.' Her gaze drifted out over the rooftops once again. Then she said, 'I've brought you a present.'

'Why?' he said in surprise, and then realized it sounded a little ungrateful. 'It's not my birthday.'

'Because I love you.' His muscles clenched; it was the first time she had said those words to him. He felt a surge of rapture, confident for the first time that Fermay's feelings were as deep as his own. Perhaps it was true love, like the romantics always said. It had happened so quickly. Suddenly he couldn't imagine life without her. 'Haven't other people bought you presents just because they love you?' she continued.

'No,' he replied truthfully.

'Then enjoy the experience.' She handed him the cardboard tube which had been tucked under her arm.

He took it gratefully, uncorking the plastic top with cold fingers and removing the rolled poster within, careful not to crease it in a sudden gust of wind. Turning away from the guard rail, he pulled it out to its full width. Five repeated images of a woman were stretched out, duplicated in Warholesque style. Each image had been altered wildly with different crazy designs and bright, exciting colours. Beneath the women were the words *Queens of Carnival – New Orleans*.

'It's great.' The design fascinated him.

'I thought you should have a piece of New Orleans to accompany your other piece of New Orleans.'

'A most excellent idea. Really, it'll look striking on the wall of the flat.'

'Good, but you can't have it yet. I'm going to get it framed for you. It has to be presented properly and it has to be protected.' She reclaimed it and returned it to its tube.

Far below them a taxi honked angrily at another car. People hurried along the streets to London Bridge, but The Monument was theirs alone. Fermay leaned back against the guard rail and smiled enigmatically. 'Glad you like the present, Davey, because now it's payback time.'

'What do you mean?'

She puckered her lips. 'Kiss me, you fool. Then take me home to bed.'

'Kissing? Here? It's a public place,' he joked.

'Can you think of anywhere better, with a wonderful view like this?' She turned around and rested her elbows on the rail, wiggling her rear at him seductively. 'Come and get it while it's hot.'

David stepped forward and gripped her hips. 'Now *this* is a wonderful view.'

Overhead the gulls swooped and soared in a chill sky, warmed by a golden sun haze. She turned and put her arms around his neck. 'Nothing's ever going to hurt you,' she whispered in his ear. 'I'm going to protect you.'

He thought it was a strange thing to say, but before he could reply he was lost in the warm depth of her kiss.

David gripped the wheel and concentrated on the speeding vehicles around him. The noise was deafening and exhilarating, the clangs, the hooters, the electric hum of motors, the constant bass thud of the music thundering through distorting speakers. He had lost sight of Fermay, but he knew she was hunting him down.

It had been her idea to come to the funfair on Clapham Common. 'I've never been to one before,' she had pleaded.

'Never been to a funfair? Which planet are you from?' he had replied.

She had looked hurt at his comment and mumbled, 'I've had a sheltered life.'

How could he have resisted her when that innocent joy turned to childlike disappointment? She had seemed like a child as long as he had known her, demanding to experience everything and anything with the hunger of a youngster let out of the house for the first time. David found it difficult to reconcile that side of her with the Fermay he had first seen at the Jazz Attic, the knowing, seductive woman, worldly-wise and cynical. There seemed to be two different people fighting constantly for supremacy in one body.

David hated funfairs; he disliked anywhere where having fun was a prerequisite for attending. 'Nobody really has fun at a funfair,' he had protested. 'They just pretend that they do.'

'That's just you,' Fermay had retorted. 'You don't have fun anywhere.'

Her comment had stung him. Was he really so dour? And so he had accompanied her, determined not to enjoy himself in case she thought he was making an effort for her.

His dodgem car whirred around the rink, avoiding the leaden vehicles controlled by dads and sons and young lovers. The dodgems was the only funfair ride he did enjoy; it allowed him to cause mayhem without punishment. There was a vicarious thrill in releasing all the pent-up aggression which had fermented during the long, uneventful days in the record shop. He had few other opportunities to uncork the bottle.

He suddenly spied Fermay in her car on the other side of the rink. She was smiling mysteriously and pretending she hadn't seen him. Then, as he coasted around after her, she turned her wheel sharply and ploughed straight across the centre of the crowded floor.

There were shrieks and laughter as cars careered out of her way. She was determined not to deviate from her path. David could only watch in surprise as she hurtled towards him like a torpedo toward a drifting ship. Her dodgem struck his car square on with a bone-jarring impact, lifting it off the floor. When Fermay finally came to a halt, David's car was at an angle, one side resting halfway up the front of her vehicle.

There was laughter and hoots from the crowds around the edge of the rink and David felt the heat of embarrassment rise up from his neck to his cheeks. He folded his arms and looked at her. 'Thanks a bunch.'

'That'll teach you to be such a tightass.'

One of the operators ran over and unhooked David's car with a grunt. 'She got you fair and square there, mate,' he laughed. 'I've never seen this happen before.'

'She's a test driver for JCB,' David replied.

'Isn't he a misery goat!' Fermay said to the operator. 'He just won't loosen up.' A thought seemed to come into her head and in one movement she stepped out of her car and pushed David back across his seat. Before he could speak she had planted her lips on his and was kissing him passionately, her tongue teasingly flicking into his mouth. A cheer rose from the audience they had attracted, quickly drowned out by catcalls and whistles.

Then she pulled away and smiled. 'Time to stand up and meet your audience, Davey.'

After he managed to escape into the crowd without too much embarrassment, he pursued Fermay across the funfair until she collapsed on the wet grass, giggling uncontrollably. They rolled around mock-wrestling like two children until they finally came to a halt with Fermay on top.

'You really got one over on me there,' David said. 'My trousers were so tight I was thinking about paying for another ride until everything subsided.'

'You were lucky I didn't unbutton your fly. I'm sure all the young girls watching would have liked to have glimpsed your gear lever.'

David laughed. 'Five days I've known you and I still haven't the faintest idea who you are. The moment I think I've got you sussed you do something that throws me completely.'

'You wouldn't want me to be predictable, would you? Anyway, I feel the same about you. The difference is, I know everything that's inside me, and I don't think you've got the slightest idea what's lurking inside you.' She tapped him on the breastbone. 'There's another you all chained up inside and I want to free him.'

'What are you talking about? Another me?'

'I can feel him. It's the real you. Everyone has one big secret and that's yours, but it's a secret even to you.'

'You're nuts.'

Fermay smiled knowingly.

'You're saying I don't know myself? That's very insulting.' She raised one eyebrow.

'You're nuts.'

'You've tied up the real you because you're afraid to let him out into the world. That's very sad, Davey. You're stifling yourself through fear. Of what, I don't know.'

'What makes you so perceptive?'

'I've always been very good at looking into people's souls. Why don't you tell me about it? Then we can work to free you together. I'd like to be the one who makes you whole.'

'Tell you what, I'll talk about me if you tell me about you.' Fermay's face clouded over, her eyes darting away nervously. 'Everyone has secrets, right? Well you seem to have more than your fair share,' David continued. She sat upright, her clothes stained from the wet grass. 'What's the matter? It's suddenly different when we're talking about you, isn't it? What makes you so special?' David felt the warm flush of irritation. Why did he care that she wouldn't talk about her past? He had never bothered before when any woman had insisted on maintaining her secrets, usually in an obvious

141

attempt to conjure some kind of mystique that would keep him hooked.

'Come on,' she said dismissively. 'I want to go on the big wheel.'

'No. I want to talk. I want to know why you change the subject whenever I ask you anything about the here and now.'

'Don't do this to me, Davey. Don't push me.'

'You want to help me. Well, I want to help you, but I can't do it while you keep so many secrets from me.'

'No.' That was all she said. Her eyes were wet. She stared into David's face for a moment, shaking her head slowly from side-to-side, before turning on her heel and marching off into the crowd.

David felt suddenly churlish and bullying. Of course she had a right to her privacy. Why did he try to force it? 'Fermay!' he yelled. 'Don't walk off like that.'

But it was too late. She was gone.

David found her an hour later. It was surprising how someone could lose themselves so effectively in somewhere as compact as a funfair. He had scoured every ride, circling the site at least ten times until he saw her leaning against a tree in the shadows, watching him intently as she wrestled with whatever was going on inside her head.

'You can't keep running away, you know.' He stood in front of her, forcing her to meet his gaze. 'I shouldn't have pushed it. I'm sorry. But if you disagree with what I'm saying or doing, we should discuss it. It doesn't help if you run off and lose yourself. The problem will still be there when you get back.'

There was a faint quiver around her mouth. Then she said, 'It's a luxury to be able to run away.'

'I won't ask you about your past again. Tell me in your own time.'

She gave no indication when that would be. Her arms slid around his neck easily and she nuzzled up to his throat. 'Let's not argue again, David.'

'Everybody argues some time.'

'Not us. I don't want us to argue. This is special and I'm not going to let anything ruin it. I've never . . .' She paused, choosing her words carefully. 'I've never had anyone who's cared for me before. And I've never cared for anyone. My world didn't allow much opportunity for that.'

'It's funny how we've got on so well, so quickly. I mean, five days! It's pretty intense.'

'Well,' she said, smiling, 'maybe it was meant to be.'

'Yeah, maybe we were meant to save each other from fates worse than death – dull, normal lives with no excitement.'

'A normal life would be nice.'

'That gives me a frightening image of ending up like my parents.' His voice carried the humour, but the prospect did scare him. 'I have enough trouble coping with the idea of spending the rest of my life with one person.'

'Oh? Imagine spending the rest of your life not with one person.' Her smile was pale and her eyes sad. She gave him a look which suggested her quiet disappointment at his comment and his stomach knotted. Her words wriggled into his mind, firing a chain of thoughts that made him realize she was right. It suddenly became a blinding revelation, a vision of emptiness, of unconnectedness stretching on to the end of his life.

He put his arm around her and squeezed her shoulders. 'You're very perceptive Ms Grey. I think you might just open my eyes.'

'If I can save just one person then my job has been done,' she said ironically. 'Come on, I still want to see the view from the top of the big wheel.'

'Seven weeks W. F.' That stood for With Fermay, David told her as he handed over the present between the grand stone columns of Covent Garden. It was an LP featuring the track 'Watermelon Man' by Mongo Santamaria, one of her favourite songs, as she had told him on several occasions. She was overjoyed at the gift, and surprisingly a little tearful. No one ever bought her presents, she said.

It was a bitingly cold day with a hint of snow in the air. Winter had returned to the land in force two days before, covering the north country with a dense blanket of white but leaving London relatively untouched. David and Fermay had been tempted out that Saturday morning by the brightness of the sun which belied the iciness of the cutting winds. Fermay had laughed at the two florid circles that had appeared on David's cheeks and the way his nose had turned almost scarlet so that he looked like a Disney cartoon, but she held his hand in the warm depths of her pocket and squeezed it every now and then as they walked.

David had bought her the record in a spontaneous rush of affection as she browsed in one of the area's numerous clothes shops. It was the only way he could show how he felt about her. Later they had a cappuccino at the Central Café and tried to wring some of the cold from their hands.

'In some ways London is really like New Orleans,' Fermay mused, holding her cup between both palms. 'New Orleans has a European feel about it. In other ways it's really different.'

'Are you homesick?' Her eyes snapped back to his face as if they were steel-sprung.

'No,' she said adamantly with an undercurrent of annoyance at what she considered a stupid question. 'I have no desire to go back there at all.'

'Not even a little one?' he teased.

'No, not even the slightest, tiniest, weeniest twinge. There's an atmosphere there at the moment.'

'What kind of atmosphere?'

She shook her head and David wondered if this was another subject which fell in the barren land of conversational no-nos. 'There's, like, a black cloud over the city. It's just hanging there, getting bigger and bigger . . .'

'What is this? The weather report?'

For once she didn't laugh at his feeble joke. Her face was graven, like she had learned of a death in the family.

'OK, I won't play the fool,' he said. 'Tell me what you mean.'

144

She shook her head once more, this time wearily. 'I can't explain it David. Except . . . there's something bad going to happen there. Soon, I think. Maybe very soon.'

'Bad in what way? Crime? Riots? Pollution?'

'No, nothing like that. Or maybe everything like that.'

'This is all very confusing. Why don't you just come out and say what you mean?'

'Oh, it's just me, David,' she said with a laugh, suddenly brightening. It didn't fool him. 'I got gloomy there for a minute. New Orleans used to be so bright and happy, a year-round Mardi Gras, but then it started to change. There was a feeling of . . . wrong things happening.' Another nervous laugh. 'I don't know how to explain it.'

'Is that why you left?'

She paused. 'Yes. Yes, it is.'

'So you weren't on holiday? You were getting out of New Orleans for good?'

'Yes. I didn't mean to lie to you, but I didn't want to answer questions about why I was leaving.'

'You've still not explained it very well.'

'No.' Another pause. 'Let's just say it was the right time to leave home. I intended to travel around, spend a few weeks here, then move on. Paris, maybe. Barcelona. Milan. But now . . . now I'm going to stay here. With you.' She leaned across the table and gripped his hand tightly. David felt something more than affection there, as if to her he was an anchor preventing her from spinning off into space.

'All this talk of black clouds has made me very chilly,' David said. 'Come on. Let's go for a walk.'

He led her out into the large, open piazza, milling with shoppers and tourists despite the razor wind. There was suddenly an air of foreboding about her. But a crowd had gathered in one corner of the piazza and David could hear laughter and cheers. Fermay had heard it too and she was soon pushing through to see what was at the centre, happy with eagerness, once more the little girl. The darkness had slipped from her shoulders in an instant.

When David finally reached her she was in the front row,

145

watching one of the street performers go through his routine for the tourists. Fermay's face was like white stone, her body strangely cold to his touch. The mime artist mirrored her; white face with coal-black eyes, devoid of all emotion, as he came up against a ghost wall and juggled ghost balls.

'I don't like this, David,' Fermay said without looking in his direction. Her gaze was a lance of fire between her and the mime artist and she would not, or could not, break it.

When her whole body shivered, more from the repressed emotion than the cold, David grabbed her and led her back through the laughing crowd. She was walking in mud until he got her out into the open spaces of the piazza.

'What was wrong back there?'

She looked dazed. 'He reminded me of someone.'

'Of course he reminded you of someone! All these mime artists look the bloody same! It might have been Marcel Marceau for all I know.'

'David,' she said anxiously. 'Thanks for the record.'

'You already thanked me for it.'

'I want you to know how much it means to me. It's the sweetest thing I've ever been given.'

'Your upbringing must have been particularly poverty-stricken.'

She took his hand and led him, as he had led her, away from the piazza to the quieter side streets, eventually pausing in the doorway of the Africa Centre. A muscular man in a red-gold-and-green t-shirt pushed past them carrying a huge amp. The aroma of spicey food drifted out from the restaurant.

Her expression was serious, like a preacher. 'David,' she began, 'I want you to know that if I ever have to leave . . .'

'Leave?' Her words were a jolt of electricity. 'You never said anything about leaving.'

'I'm not planning to, David. Please just hear me out.'

He consented, feeling his heart thump madly.

'I want you to know that if I ever have to leave, for whatever reasons, that I love you.'

He wanted to believe it more than anything else in the

world. At the same time he could not escape the tolling-bell sound of those words: *leave you*. There was something ominous about them, whatever Fermay said, a suggestion of probability rather than possibility, and he was struck by a deep fear that his loneliness and insularity would return.

It was an effort to harden himself to his thoughts, but he managed to smile and say, 'I love you too.' The words sounded strange coming from his lips.

Fermay rested her head on his shoulder and gripped him tightly until he thought she would never let go.

'What could possibly make you leave?' he asked trying to sound casual.

Her reply sounded distant. 'There's always something in the background waiting to ruin happiness.'

'That's a very morbid thought.'

'I can't help it. Life makes you think things like that. The way I see it, the natural order is designed to make pain and suffering come out on top and if you want to get any joy for yourself you've got to fight tooth and nail for it.'

'I thought when you mentioned leaving, you were thinking you might have to go home. To New Orleans.'

'I'd never go there of my own volition. Never. Whenever I think about it, all I can remember is unhappiness and ... that's why I never talk about it.'

'Fermay,' he said softly, 'one day you're going to have to tell me what happened to you there. If you've suffered, I want to know. I want to try to help you forget it. I don't want to see you bottling it all up inside. It's going to tear you apart.'

'Tear me apart,' she repeated, punctuating it with a humourless laugh. 'Before I came to London I never thought there were things like happiness and love and tenderness and any of those qualities that make life worth living. I thought they were just fantasies that you told children, that you pretended, like Santa Claus and the Easter Bunny. They certainly weren't part of my life.' She turned her head so she could look into his face. 'Now that I've found they do exist I don't want to let go. I'm like a Born-Again who's suddenly discovered God exists, and I'm desperately afraid that someone will take it all away from me. One day I will tell you about me, David, but I'm frightened of saying something that might drive you away. That's why I always play dumb when you question me. There's nothing nice I can tell you and if I can't tell you anything nice I don't want to say anything at all.'

'I don't care for you just because of the *nice* things, Fermay. People are made up of good and bad, light and dark. I'll never really know you until you tell me those things you're hiding. I'll always feel there's something missing, like a lost memory.'

The man who had been carrying the amp pushed by them again, looking sheepish for interrupting their intense conversation. When he had gone, Fermay said, 'Everything is great right now. Perfect, for the first time in my life, and to even think about the past would cast a shadow.'

'I can understand that. But you will tell me about it one day?'

'Sure.'

'Promise?'

The answer was obviously prised out with the greatest reluctance. 'Promise.'

'No more talk of leaving?'

'None. I'm just a natural worrier. Everything's going to be fine.' She added, 'I was afraid you were going to run away when I said I loved you.'

'A few weeks ago, with somebody other than yourself, I would have done, but I've been thinking about what you said . . . about not spending your life with one person. It made me realize what a jerk I've been. The thought that the future would be just like the past, without ever getting close to anyone, always being alone, for ever . . . it's too frightening. I've been looking at my feelings more honestly since then. So . . . I'm glad you said you loved me. Because I love you and if it wasn't reciprocated I'd go mad. Like you said, once you've found something good you don't want to lose it.' He laughed nervously. 'Listen to me. I sound like someone out of fucking *Brief Encounter*!'

'That's a relief,' Fermay said. 'I thought I'd never get through your thick skin. Now there's just one more thing to do.'

'What's that?'

'Seal it with a kiss. You and me against the world, kid!'

'You and me against the world.'

The biting wind swept across the piazza towards them, trailing snowflakes in its wake. The sun had disappeared behind grey, wintry clouds, and the world was growing dark. Fermay and David's kiss lasted for a lifetime, in a strange doorway in a cold place, as they held on to each other for dear life.

Chapter 12

Darkness.

'Where'mI?'

All encompassing, impenetrable. Like looking into the abyss. Awake? Or asleep? Dreaming? Fermay wasn't there any more. No one was there. Just him. In the dark.

'What'mIdoin'?'

His body was pain. He could no longer break it down into its component parts; the individual instruments seemed lost in the symphony that played his nerves at maximum decibel level. His body had gone deaf. He wouldn't even attempt to move. Perhaps he couldn't. Perhaps his spine had been shattered, trapping his mind in a shell that no longer responded to the electrical impulses from his brain, useless machinery with the computer program still running. Perhaps it was worse.

Perhaps he was dead.

How long had passed since his last thought? A second, a minute, an hour, a day, a week? Longer? Consciousness was ebbing and flowing as he was carried along in a turgid river of black. There were things he had to do, places he had to be, but it was easier just to lie back and float.

The voice had been talking to him for a long time. Or perhaps it had only just started. If he concentrated he could make out words as they nibbled at the edge of his mind, some burrowing in deep, others buzzing away unheeded.

'. . . and life's sweet. Smellin' the jasmine. Drinkin' lemonade on a summer evenin'. A woman to hold. Life's sweet.'

'What about life?' His voice materialized somewhere outside of him.

There was silence for a moment as if he had frightened the

speaker away. Then the voice spoke once more. 'Life is what you do while you're queuing up to die.'

'That's morbid.'

'Morbid. But true. Don't mean you can't enjoy it though. Like I said, smell the flowers an' kiss the women.'

'I had a woman once . . .'

'Well excuse me if I interrupt you there, boy, but what's so unusual about that? We all had women.'

'She was . . . she is . . . special.'

'They're all special, in their own way. Women are a different breed to men. They live with secrets for so long, they're always afraid to tell you the truth.'

David thought about that for a moment and decided it was true.

But still the darkness came and went, a giant ocean stretching out all around him, its swell buoying him up, sweeping him down, so that he was like a cork, directionless, uncontrolled. Occasionally, when the movement slowed, he realized the voice was still talking and he was replying. The conversation came and went like the crackling of a badly tuned radio. Its subjects were concepts which he did not want to consider but which he could not avoid – life, death, what lay between and what lay without. David tried to fight it for a time, but he soon found it easier to go with the flow.

'. . . The Lord would probably say – an' I'm not tryin' to put words in His mouth here – that He's already laid down the plan an' man in his ignorance has decided to ignore it.'

'These things always come down to free will and choices,' David replied. 'The more intelligent and knowledgeable people become, the more likely they are to disbelieve and disobey.'

'Now, is that your definition of intelligent? Doesn't sound too intelligent to me. Why risk your soul just because one afternoon you were layin' in the sun an' decided there isn't a Lord?'

'This whole soul-punishment-reward thing is a completely lame concept. It doesn't hold up to close inspection. You do good, you go to heaven. You do bad, you go to hell. What about the people who do OK? What about the people who do bad for a

151

good cause? The soldier who shoots a commandant to save the lives of people in a concentration camp? That soldier has sinned by killing, but he ultimately did good by relieving suffering. As a system, it just breaks down when you look at it closely.'

'If there isn't a Lord, what's the point in the soldier fightin' anyway? Why doesn't he just take his gun, hold up a few liquor stores, kill a few people he don't like, rape a few women and . . .'

'You can't use human motivations as an argument for the existence of God.'

'Why not?'

'. . . worst moment in my life. You know how some things lodge in your mind so that they're always there, floating to the surface whenever you relax? This was one of those. I know I'll never be able to get away from it. There's this thing I do whenever I feel the images coming to the forefront – I start naming all the records in my collection one after the other until the memories go away. Sometimes it works, sometimes it doesn't.

'It was just after 11 p.m. It was a warm summer night and I was heading home from the pub. I was buzzing because I'd been celebrating something or other – I don't know, just being alive. I was still living with my parents then. I remember walking back and looking at the stars and thinking how great everything was. Now I can see it as the last day of my childhood, but back then I thought I'd grown up a long time before.

'The pub was a good two miles from home, but because it was such a nice night I'd decided to take a few short cuts and walk home. I had real difficulty getting over the fence into the playing fields – too many pints of Guinness. If I'd been any less pissed I'd have thought to walk a hundred yards up the road and use the gate. I landed in a heap on the other side, thought I'd broken my neck at first. It's true what they say: you're indestructible when you're drunk. As I lay there I noticed a car parked under the trees on the other side of the football pitch. It caught my eye because it was so unusual. They would have to have driven over the whole length of the playing field to get there. Anybody who had gone to that amount of trouble to park out of the way must have been up to something . . . and I knew what. I keep blaming it all on the alcohol, but it's true. If I'd have been sober I never would have gone for a look. I crept . . . staggered more likely . . . across the pitch, keeping as low to the ground as I could. They were certainly having a lot of fun. The car was bouncing up and down on its suspension like it was fitted with a trampoline. I'd never had any desire to be a peeping tom before, but right then I was so thrilled I could barely control myself.

'I could see movement behind the glass so I sneaked up and pressed my face against the window. The couple were middle-aged. The man was balding with a roll of flab around his midriff. He was pounding away at the woman like it was a marathon, grunting and sweating with the strain. She had her legs up around his neck, stilettos scraping the roof. She was wearing stockings, but not much else. I thought how saggy her breasts looked.

'Then the man came. He raised his head and chest in triumph. I thought what an old dickhead he looked. At that age I couldn't imagine older folk having sex. As he moved, I saw the woman's face for the first time. It was . . . it was . . .'

'Yeah? Who was it?'

'It was my mother. The man wasn't my father. I ran from there, and then . . .'

'An' then?'

David remembered and then forgot. There was a sudden sweeping feeling of claustrophobia, of being pulled beneath the waves of the black sea. Why did he think about his mother? At least he had stopped the memory before the worst thing.

Yes, the worst thing of all.

'Aidoneus?'

'You stay clear of Aidoneus!'

'Why?'

'You know what Aidoneus means, boy?'

'No.'

'Aidoneus is the Devil.'

'. . . y father. Oh God, I don't want to think about that.'

'What happened?'

'No.'

'Tell me what happened?'

'. . . knew all along my mother was having an affair. The only way he could cope with it was by pretending everything was normal. Oh God, oh God, why did I do it? He just buried it all inside him, like if he didn't talk about it, it wasn't real. But it must have been eating away at him like cancer, destroying everything he held dear. As long as I didn't know about it, he could just about fool himself. I was the only thing holding his pride . . . his self-respect . . . together. That pure love a son has for his father, that view every kid has that his father is a hero . . . as long as he had that, he could keep going. But I wrecked it. Like the fucking selfish, thoughtless little bastard that I am, I smashed that illusion down.

'And then I killed him.'

There was a surge and a dip. The swell of the sea subsided and he was being carried forward, heading confidently in one direction. Ahead of him shapes loomed out of the darkness, rocks, outcroppings. *I'm getting out of here*, he thought, without wondering where he was. Or where he was going.

'Do you believe in ghosts?' David winced as he spoke as if someone had attached an electrode to his forehead. This was the area that he didn't want to visit. Bordering on the Fog Zone, it was the place where he stored all the twisted, unpleasant things that had happened to him. This was where his mother and father lived. And right now it was more crowded than it had ever been in his life. Buffalo Marsayle was there, white eyes staring out of a pale, dead face. And that other thing, that shrieking, half-decomposed thing that had confronted him in the street. Madame LaLaurie laughing malevolently, her long aristocratic fingers grasping for his throat. This was the place he wanted to avoid at all costs, but the irony was that he had to pass through it to get to where he wanted to be.

'Heh, heh.' The voice chuckled in the darkness. 'I believe in a lot of things . . .'

'Don't start that again. Why can't I ever get a straight answer?'

154

David swallowed and continued. 'I believe in them. I've seen them. I always thought they existed. As a kid I used to scare myself thinking about them. But as I grew older I decided they were really just echoes of past life, recordings playing over and over again without any conscious thought of their own. Now I've seen them I know they do think, that they've got some kind of . . . life. They can see me and I can see they want me. Why? Why can only I see them?' A note of hysteria entered his voice.

'Maybe,' the voice replied thoughtfully, 'you're closer to them than other folk.'

'What do you mean?'

'Maybe you took a step into their world at some time and now you can't get out again. Maybe they won't let you get out.'

No, he didn't believe that. When could it have happened?

'Maybe they want you to do something for them.'

'But they all seem different. There's no consistency to their actions.'

'Well, maybe they're just like real, livin' folk. Different personalities, different outlooks. Some are mean as hell an' some are regular guys, some want to talk your head off an' some just sit an' stare, some are jokers an' some are serious as a church minister.'

'They scare me.'

'Maybe you should be scared, boy. Maybe you should be very scared. After all, you don't know what they want. You better hope they haven't got it in for you. Heh, heh, heh. Ain't nothin' worse than a restless spirit with a big hate for one of the livin'.'

'Maybe I'm just going mad.'

'That's the easy answer, boy. You keep tellin' yourself that. Heh, heh, heh.'

Marsayle's face was there in his mind's eye. He couldn't tell if it was accusing or benign, but he knew it wanted something from him and he was afraid it was something he couldn't give.

Suddenly he was receding from the voice as if he was being propelled down a wind tunnel and for the first time there was a sense of reality and of something outside him. He could feel his body, wracked with pain in every limb, and he was aware of himself within his body. It was like he had been in a dream and had suddenly awoken. For the first time he wondered where he was. Before it had not seemed to matter. It was dark.

He opened his eyes.

It was still dark, an impenetrable darkness, like space. The air was dry and musty. He was lying on his back and the surface beneath him was hard and stoney, but it was smooth and obviously man-made.

He stretched out his hand and felt a pile of dry wood next to him. He stretched out the other and felt a cold stone wall. Stone hung above him too, a mere foot above his head.

He was enclosed.

Broussard, Frantz and Lynch suddenly came to mind. The chase. The LaLaurie house. The beating. With a flash of insight he realized they had imprisoned him somewhere, in a cellar, or a coal hole, probably under Broussard's mansion. The realization was followed instantly by a panic attack, tightening across his chest and throat in flaming bands. 'No!' he yelled, scrambling madly along on his back until the soles of his feet rested against another wall. He slammed them against it wildly. The hollow sound told him it was probably the door through which his unconscious body had been shoved.

How much air did he have? Did they intend to kill him by interning him and leaving him to die of slow suffocation? It seemed a frighteningly real prospect.

The fear spurred him into action and he began to kick out at what he guessed was the door panel, hammering his feet against it, this time in powerful, rhythmic blows until his soles felt battered and painful through his shoes. He was starting to hyperventilate at the terror of being trapped, but he concentrated on the beat of the kicks, the pounding of a funeral drum, to drive it from his mind.

He wasn't getting anywhere. For all he knew, the walls might be two-foot thick. He stopped for a moment and rested in the claustrophobic darkness. He imagined himself hundreds of feet underground, enclosed by rock, the weight of it pressing down until he felt like his chest would be crushed.

Was the air growing thin? He couldn't tell. The pressure on

his chest increased. With renewed vigour, he started to kick out at the wall once more.

Perhaps if he yelled, someone would come to his aid. At that point he would even have been happy to see Broussard and his men. He screamed until his throat was raw and his breath came in huge, juddering gasps, but there was no response from the other side of the wall.

There was a wetness in his shoes which he knew was blood. He couldn't carry on much longer. A few more kicks, maybe only five, was all he could muster. After that . . .

One kick. Nothing.

Two.

Three. The pain. He could no longer feel any difference between his feet and the beaten meat of his soles.

Four.

David had almost convinced himself that he was going to die when the fifth kick brought a loud crack which echoed through the dark. He stopped for a moment and rested, praying that it was the door beginning to give. When he tried once more, it was unmistakeable. The crack sounded like a gunshot.

Fired by newfound hope, David somehow redoubled his efforts. One blow, two blows, three blows. Now he could feel the headway he was making. Four blows, five blows. There was another crack and a piece of the door shot out. Sunlight streamed in, forcing him to cover his eyes at first. Four more blows smashed away the remainder of the stone door and he was able to wriggle out of the confined space on his back.

The full sunlight blazed like a nuclear explosion. He screwed his eyes shut and propelled himself forward.

The moment his feet touched the ground he fell to his knees in pain. He could barely walk. His entire body felt like it had been through a mangle and his eyes were blurred and puffed from the blows laid upon them by Frantz and Lynch. Slowly his vision cleared and he was able to look around for the first time.

He was in a cemetery.

The mausoleums stretched out ahead of him in rows for as far as he could see, neatly tended white houses in a suburbia for the dead. *The bastards!* They really had tried to kill him.

He lay sprawled against his own personal house, coming to terms with the shock of his close call. Above him he could see the gaping black hole where he had kicked out the door where the bodies were inserted. He was thankful that in New Orleans they buried their dead above the ground because of the high water table. If Broussard had had him interred six feet under he would never have seen daylight again.

He inched his way up the side of the mausoleum, wincing at every sudden movement, until he could look into the burial hole. Gradually his eyes adjusted to the dark within.

There was one moment of creeping awareness and then horror, rising like a black well bubbling to the surface. The dry sticks he had felt next to him as he lay in the tomb were not wood. They were bones. A rib cage shattered and browned with age. But hadn't he seen something else when the light suddenly streamed in? Something hulking near the far wall, glimpsed out of the corner of his eye? Hadn't he seen the briefest illumination of white bone and of grey skin?

Then he remembered the conversation as he'd hovered in and out of consciousness. He'd thought it was a dream.

But it wasn't.

It took David almost two hours to get back to the Sonesta. The journey out of the cemetery alone accounted for more than half that time, as he inched his way painfully through the maze of mausoleums, resting on them for support whenever he thought he would collapse. His watch told him a day had gone by since the attack by Broussard's men. He had lain with the remains for almost twenty-four hours.

At one point near the cemetery's perimeter he had startled a woman standing in front of an ancient tomb. It was covered with crosses and writing scratched into the ancient stone. The woman looked like a crow, all bone and black clothes, one hand resting on the marks as she mumbled with her eyes closed. When David passed she whirled suddenly, her eyes wide with shock. With a shriek she had begun to spit at him and make signs to ward off the evil eye.

His pain enclosed him like a blanket. The white stone tombs

158

formed their own white landscape detaching him from reality. Occasionally he half glimpsed fleeting shadows on the edge of his vision and he wondered, obliquely, if they were the tombs' residents slowly coming into focus as they moved into his world, or he into theirs. Through it all, his mind kept centering on the conversation that had taken place in the dark of the mausoleum, snatches returning like overheard gossip. It seemed to him that with each encounter with the dead, his own life was fading, becoming less real, less vital. He'd begun to accept what was happening to him in the same way that someone accepted news of a terminal illness; with initial shock and horror and then placid resignation.

As he lurched out of Lafayette No 1 Cemetery into the street, he realized passers-by were shying away from him like he was the walking dead. His clothes were a mess, stained with blood and tomb dirt, and his face was swollen and battered. At least Broussard's boys had not touched the cash in his pockets, but it took him a long time to flag down a cab that was prepared to stop for such a disturbing sight.

As the taxi wended its way back to the Sonesta, David realized the cemetery was in the Garden District, only a short distance from Broussard's mansion. He wondered how many more of the man's enemies lay rotting in the graves of others, never found again. For once his luck had held out. If the tomb's door had not been aged and structurally weak it would have been his resting place for ever.

When he'd started on his search for Fermay he had never guessed it would take him so close to death. Now the stakes had been raised and he knew if he crossed Broussard and his men again he would not be so lucky. It would have been easy to pack his bags and catch the next flight to London, but David knew he could never do that; he couldn't leave without Fermay. There was a bond between them that transcended love. His world only had meaning when he was with her and for that reason alone he could not give up.

Even if his life depended on it.

Chapter 13

'Oh my God, David! What happened?'

Arlene stood in the doorway of David's hotel room, a look of horror on her face.

'It's my new look. It'll be all the rage in the summer.'

She followed him back to the bed, noticing his surreptitious glance at his face in the mirror: two black eyes, a split and swollen lip, puffed cheeks, abrasions, scratches and bruises – a hideous Bosch parody of his real face.

'David, how can you joke about it? You look like Frankenstein!'

'Frankenstein's Monster, actually, but I get your point. I found out The Big Easy isn't as easy as everyone says. In fact, it's pretty hard.'

'Who did this to you?' David thought he could see tears in her eyes. 'The Cowboy?'

He shook his head. 'A couple of Neanderthals called Frantz and Lynch. They took exception to my stunning good looks, my staggering intellect and my stylish fashion sense.' The bed gave him some relief, seeping into the dull ache that was his body.

Arlene perched on the edge next to him and gently brushed the hair from his forehead. Her concerned expression was quickly hidden by a happy-go-lucky smile. 'What are you getting yourself into?' she asked softly.

'I'm so close to finding Fermay, Arlene. I've found her guardian. I've found where she lived and could be living now. If I could just make contact with her . . . But this jerk who claims to have raised her won't let me anywhere near her. He felt so strongly about it, he had this done to me. I'm not that bad a catch, am I?'

'No. Not that bad.'

'There's something happening here that I don't understand. I thought it would just be a simple matter: find Fermay, get back together, get my memory back, return to London. But the deeper

I get in, the stranger it seems. Maybe she was running away from it all. She turned up in London with hardly any clothes – that suggests she left in a hurry. If these thugs are prepared to go to this extent,' he pointed to his face, 'Christ! They even tried to kill me – then I'm starting to wonder exactly what she was caught up in.'

'Maybe it's time to let it drop, David. What's going to happen next? Are we going to find you floating in the river?'

David dismissed this with a shake of his head. 'I'm not giving up on Fermay. I'll just have to be more careful from now on . . . now that I know what I'm up against.'

Arlene bit her lip. 'I was so worried when you didn't turn up for lunch. We all were . . . when you didn't make work.'

David couldn't imagine Charlie or Dean being too worried. 'Have I still got a job?'

'Charlie likes you. He thinks you bring some class to his dump. If you tell him what happened, he'll be OK.'

'I'll tell him tonight.'

'You can't go in like this!'

'I need the money. If he doesn't want the Elephant Man waiting tables, I'll work in the storeroom.'

'You're the stubbornest person I know.' She lit a cigarette and took a seat next to the window where she kept a careful watch on him. 'So what are you going to do now?'

'First thing is to get out of here. Broussard . . . Fermay's guardian . . . he knows I've got a room here. He thinks I'm worm food at the moment and I don't want to dispel that notion. If he does find I'm still around I don't want him sending the Monkey Brothers to pull me out of bed in the middle of the night. I've got to move to your friend's place.'

'Don't worry, I'll sort it out for you.'

'OK. After that . . . I don't know. Do you think I'm crazy?'

'Crazy for this girl.'

'No, I mean in the head.'

'Eccentric, maybe, but no more than anyone else in this nutty city. Why?'

He shook his head. 'I can't work out what's happening to me. Back in England the most unusual thing I had to cope with was winning on the slot machine down at my local. Now I feel like someone's ripped up the script of my life and written me another one that doesn't make any sense at all.'

'Losing your memory is bound to be a shock.'

'It's more than that.' If he could admit it to himself he would have said that Fermay was the catalyst. All the inexplicable things that he was experiencing had begun after he'd met her. 'I feel like I'm in a haunted house movie, only it isn't a house that's haunted, it's a whole city. There's a ghost on every corner. There's some freakish thing that should have been long dead shuffling out of the shadows every time I turn around. If I wasn't crazy before, a few more weeks here would soon have me ready for the rubber room.'

There was a despairing note in his voice that made Arlene wince. 'If you can see these things, David, you should take it as a gift,' she said reassuringly.

'A *gift*? To have every day turned into a nightmare?'

'It's happening for a reason.'

'That's what I'm worried about.' His head swam, forcing him to close his eyes.

Arlene stubbed out her cigarette and stood up, cutting short his morbid brooding. 'You better get some rest, David. You want to look your best for Charlie, right?' She laughed and then suddenly bent forward and kissed him on an unbruised part of his cheek. 'You take care of yourself and don't worry, I'll sort it all out with Beth. We'll have you moved in before work.'

'Thanks, Arlene. I really appreciate everything you're doing for me.'

'Hey, don't mention it. I'll be the first one to remind you about it when I need some help.'

When she was gone he felt lonelier than he had done in a long time, and also more afraid. Being on his own frightened him. He was afraid to look in the mirror and see something looking back that was not his face. He was afraid to pick up the phone in case he heard a strange, dead voice on the other end. He was afraid to step into the bathroom only to hear the door lock behind him.

He tried to rest, but sleep would not come.

*

Beth was the kind of woman who fell in love quickly then fell apart when the affair ended. Attractive with brown, lustrous hair and full lips, she was a twitchy mass of neuroses, never relaxing, skinny as a bird, with a permanently smouldering cigarette pinned between two fingers. Her gaze skittered over David's features and then hid in a neutral corner of the room as her words tumbled out at a breathless pace. She was a teacher. David wondered what her pupils made of her.

'So, like, I've seen more attractive guys.'

'I don't always look like this. I'm a regular Adonis when I'm not going ten rounds with Mike Tyson.' David tried to smile pleasantly, but his aching face pulled it into something close to a grimace.

'Yeah, well, it's not your looks I'm interested in. I just want a guy who pays the rent on time and who isn't a nut.'

'He isn't a nut, Beth,' Arlene interjected. She flashed a 'keep your mouth shut' look at David.

'Yeah? What kind of average guy gets beat up like that?'

'An unlucky one,' David replied. 'This won't happen again, I guarantee it. I've learned my lesson. No more street-fighting.'

Beth shrugged and pecked at her cigarette. 'S'OK. I can have you out on the street as quickly as you came in. Since Arlene's given you the vote of approval, I suppose I can take a chance. That's your room over there. It's cramped, there's damp on the ceiling and you can smell the gumbo from the restaurant two doors down when the window's open, but you already knew this wasn't the Hyatt. You get your own key, but if you wake me when you come in late I'll have your ass.'

'Fine. You won't even know I'm here.' The room was big enough for its single bed, a chest of drawers and little else. One small window looked out over the neat picturesque streets on the eastern edge of the French Quarter; it was quieter there, away from the tourist trap of Bourbon Street, and Charlie's Place was only a short walk away. Broussard would have difficulty finding him.

'The rent's thirty bucks a week,' Beth said, leaning against the door jamb, her cigarette hanging from the corner of her mouth.

David tossed his suitcase on the bed and peeled off a few notes from the rapidly decreasing wad in his wallet.

'Another good thing about this place is that I'm only a few blocks away,' Arlene said hopefully.

'That doesn't mean you've got an excuse to drop in with Scuba,' Beth said sharply. 'You know you're always welcome here, but I still won't have that thing you call a boyfriend messing up my place.'

Arlene looked downcast. 'Sure, Beth, I know that. Scuba's *persona non grata* in my place too.'

'Is he in trouble again?'

'When's he ever out of it?'

'Do you want to talk about it?'

'No.' She smiled at David. 'I've already bent someone's ear about Scuba. I'll let it slide for a while. Pretend he doesn't exist. Maybe he'll just fade away like a bad dream.'

'I don't know why you don't just dump him.' Irritation crossed Beth's face.

'Me neither.' Whenever she spoke about Scuba, Arlene's face took on a beaten look as if she had resigned herself to his presence like a monkey on her back. 'David's got his own relationship problems.'

'All relationships are problems,' Beth said bitterly. 'What's yours?'

'Girlfriend missing, presumed alive, somewhere in New Orleans.'

'Did she walk out on you?'

'We were separated by accident and now I'm trying to track her down. Only her guardian can't stand the sight of me and he'll do anything to make sure I don't get in touch with her – including having me beaten up and dumped in a cemetery.'

'Wow!' Beth looked impressed. 'Romeo and Juliet.'

'From hell,' David added sourly.

Charlie looked at David with abject disbelief, shaking his head from side to side so slowly that he appeared to be moving at half speed. 'You got to be jokin', boy.' Each word was chewed over and rolled out for maximum effect. 'Whatchoo think my customers are goin' to say when they see you comin' up to the table? Shit! You'll give folk a heart attack. You're a mess, boy, a goddamn mess. How'd you get into this state anyhow?'

'Two thugs jumped me, beat me up, left me for dead. Nothing I could do, Charlie. I didn't ask for this.'

'Let me give you a word of advice, boy. You see trouble, you run the other way. I heard how you jumped in when Arlene was gettin' mauled by that dick in a cowboy hat. That kinda stuff's all right in the movies, but you don't do it in real life, y'hear me? Folk don't bounce like rubber. They get hurt. They get turned into hamburger like you. Guys out there got guns 'n' knives 'n' blackjacks 'n' shit. Now whatchoo gonna do if someone pulls a gun on you?'

David nodded, trying to appear repentant. 'It won't happen again, Charlie.'

'You're damn right it won't! I can't use someone who's always gettin' beat up until they're too ugly to be let out.'

'Give me a second chance, Charlie. I know I missed a night, but it won't happen again, really.'

'This ain't no charity, boy.' He sucked on his cigar and cursed when he realized it had gone out. 'All right, all right, this time I'm a sucker. You can work in the stockroom till you look like a human being again. But not tonight. You go home – get some rest. Maybe it'll make you think twice about bein' a hero if you lose a night's pay.'

Outside the office in the bar, Dean appeared from nowhere and grabbed David by the arm. 'Looks like somebody got to you before I could, Easter.'

'Give it a rest, Dean. I haven't got time to practise my one-syllable words.'

'Always the smart guy, Easter. How do you think Arlene feels when she looks at you now? Are you worried about giving her nightmares? That's what you get for pushing your nose in where it's not wanted.'

David shrugged off Dean's hold on his arm and walked away without rising to the bait. *Let him gloat*, he thought. It wasn't important. In the light of everything else that was happening it wasn't important at all.

He turned to go to the toilet and then stopped suddenly, his hand hovering in mid air. It was early. The club wasn't open yet and there would be no one inside. Marsayle's face reflected in the mirror returned to him with a jolt and he almost turned away. Yet he hesitated, heeding a desire to sweep aside the feeling of being a victim with an act of bravado.

He went inside.

It was uncommonly clean after the swabbing given to it in the aftermath of Mac's stabbing. More importantly, there was no sign of anything out of the ordinary, no odd atmosphere, no hairs prickling on the back of his neck.

Standing at the urinal, his thoughts switched uncomfortably between Fermay and the apparitions that were haunting him until he could no longer concentrate.

He took a step back and felt something sticky beneath his foot. He was standing in a pool of viscous liquid, a growing pool. It seeped along slowly, surrounding his feet, red-black. He knew what it was.

Blood.

Hesitantly he turned around, his heart hammering in his chest. The room was no longer pristine, the white tiles polished. There was blood splattered up the walls like a shotgun blast. It dripped from the ceiling where it had also splashed. Drip-drip-drip. Into the pool on the floor which stretched out to one of the cubicles.

Don't look! his mind screamed.

Lowering himself to his haunches, he peered under the door. Two polished black shoes were at the centre of the red stream, the blood running over them to continue the flow.

Don't look!

An aching curiosity battled with the natural fear within him, and won. He moved forward, no longer operating consciously.

He paused at the door, hearing his breath rasp in the stillness of the room. There was no sound. He couldn't even hear any movement outside in the bar. The door was not locked. He touched it with his fingertips and it swung backwards and forwards slightly.

Don't look! Don't look!

Tentatively he pushed again, harder this time, and the door

swung open a few inches until it came up against whoever was within. David pushed harder and the obstruction moved, increasing the blood flow. There was now enough space to look inside. Through the gap he could already see a black jacket sleeve and a white cuff poking from beneath it. The hand at the end of it was originally black, but now a bloodless grey.

There was still time to leave, David told himself. He could walk out and head to the bar for a stiff drink, driving what he had seen to the back of his mind. Leave it for someone else. But the blood held him, chained him to the spot. He pushed the door again and looked.

Mac sat on the toilet, wearing the same bouncer's uniform he'd had on when he was attacked. His face was as grey as his hand and David could see where the knife had severed his jugular. The blood still pumped out in slow, rhythmic gouts, a weak spurt after the initial geyser David had seen during the fight. He felt as if the last two days had not happened, as if it were only minutes since the Cowboy's attack.

Then Mac opened his eyes.

David started, then froze, transfixed by the cold, dead stare. Before he could step back, Mac's hand shot out and gripped his wrist so tightly David's fingers began to go numb. The skin on that grey hand had the texture of dead fish, but the power within it was incredible.

David was hypnotized. All he could do was stare deeply into Mac's unblinking eyes as the dead man dragged him into the cubicle. He could not move. Out of the corner of his eye, he saw Mac's other arm begin to shift slowly, rising towards his throat. The movement was enough to break the spell and suddenly he was wrenching at his wrist, kicking and yanking until he ripped it free from the iron grasp. He fell backwards, away from the cubicle, and winded himself as he hit the floor.

The cubicle door slammed shut with a bang, but from within a sonorous voice like slabs of stone rose up.

'*Get out of here! Back to England! If you don't you'll die!*'

There was a sudden wild thrashing and howling as if the apparition was spinning madly from wall to wall, trying to break out. David did not wait to see what happened. He dragged himself from the floor and ran out of the door into the club.

Leaning against a pillar he slowly regained his composure. It had touched him! He rubbed his wrist where the circulation was slowly seeping back. Now the apparitions were no longer like mist, insubstantial things that flickered across his vision like ghost images on a TV set until they faded away. With growing unease, he wondered if they gained more substance the more he progressed into their world. Now they could hurt him.

They could kill him.

The next few nights passed without incident. David was strung out and tense after his experience, and unlike earlier occasions he was finding it difficult to recover. Each manifestation was a stone placed upon his shoulders and the last confrontation was the one that had driven him to his knees.

Arlene had said to him one night, 'What's wrong David? You don't laugh any more.' So he had bought a tape of his favourite jazz tunes and he played it over and over on Beth's tape deck while she was out at work. It was a futile attempt to give him a view out of the pit into which he felt he was being driven. At the same time, he stared at the photo of Fermay, hoping it would spark some buried memories that would help him escape to the life he once knew.

Broussard was his only link to Fermay. David had taken it upon himself to keep watch on the mansion several times a day, checking the comings and goings for any sign of her. So far he had had no luck, not even the briefest glimpse from his discreet vantage point far up the street.

David had decided not to talk to Arlene again about the haunted visions that had plagued him; he was sure she would think he was going mad. They had made him afraid. Afraid to look anyone in the face for fear he would discover they were dead. Afraid of being alone.

She had done everything in her power to rekindle his love for life. She had taken him out for lunch, accompanied him on numerous sightseeing trips, trawled the record shops with him, even sat with him during his long hours of surveillance of

Broussard's mansion. At first he had feared bumping into Lynch or Frantz again, but as time passed those worries waned. It was a big city, and as far as they were concerned he was rotting away in somebody else's grave.

Dean had moved on from being a minor irritant and had now taken it upon himself to persecute David every moment they were together. His glee at the beating David had taken was unrestrained, prompting him to stoop to new depths of mockery and abuse. David found it increasingly difficult to summon up one-liners or acid comments in response. Dean had always been an easy target, but even that was getting beyond him.

As for Arlene, she had her own problems with Scuba which did not seem to be lessening. David provided her with a sounding board to air her grievances and worries and on most occasions that seemed to be enough to keep her in high spirits. He found her easy-going and warm, with a loyalty that cheered him, but her charms were all on the surface with none of the deep, dark pools that had attracted him to Fermay.

Their relationship reached an uncomfortable turning point on a warm, muggy night five days after David's confrontation in the club's toilets. Arlene returned to Beth's apartment with him in the early hours after finishing work. She wanted to kill an hour, knowing that by that time Scuba would be asleep and she would not have to talk to him. David had offered her a cup of coffee and a chance to chat and unwind which she had accepted with relief and surprising gratitude.

Beth had long gone to bed when they arrived so they tiptoed through the lounge, giggling like schoolchildren, and settled in David's tiny room with a cheap portable radio turned on low to some all-night station. There was no room for a chair in the bedroom so they both lounged on the single bed, comfortable in their proximity, but careful not to touch. A warm breeze blew in through the open window, carrying the verdant scent of a New Orleans night.

'Do you feel safe here?' Arlene asked him. Her voice was husky after the chatter of the club. The remnants of her perfume still clung to her hair.

David looked around the box-sized room. 'Safer than anywhere else in this city.' There were no mirrors for uncommon reflections, no dark corners for unwelcome guests. 'As long as Broussard never guesses I'm alive. That's the main thing.'

'David, what are you going to do about Fermay?' The question came out of the blue. 'Ever since you got here you've been saying how much you want to see her, but . . . y'know, I don't want you to take this the wrong way . . . it's like you're not exactly breaking a sweat to find where she is. It's like you don't really want to find her at all, you're just fooling yourself that you do.'

'*Of course* I want to find her,' he stressed, almost as if he was convincing himself. But wasn't there a little truth in what she said? Something in the depths of the Fog Zone seemed to be restraining his efforts, clouding his mind whenever he tried to think of new ways to search for her. He kept telling himself it was the by-product of his lost memory, but he had his doubts. It was like his subconscious knew something that was influencing his waking mind. 'At the moment I'm doing all I can do,' he continued. 'I don't know what else there is.'

'Yeah, maybe . . .' She didn't sound impressed. 'I just want you to know that if you are, y'know, losing interest in her then . . . y'know, I'm here for you.'

'I know you are, Arlene.'

'No, David,' she stressed. 'I mean I'm here for *you*.' She surprised him by leaning forward and kissing him. His hand automatically went to her hair as her mouth became softer, her kiss more passionate. There was a gentle romance to the act, but also something more, a hint of desperation that added a *frisson* of dark sexuality which made his belly tingle. He almost allowed his hand to drop to her breast, but then, very reluctantly, he caught himself and pulled away.

'What's the matter?' Her voice sounded hurt.

'I can't do this, Arlene.'

'Oh shit,' she said. 'I've done it again.' There were tears in her eyes and she began to roll her legs off the bed and sit upright, frustrated and angry at herself.

David grabbed her arm and pulled her back down next to him. 'Don't get the wrong idea. This isn't any reflection on you. It's me. I find you attractive, Arlene. I find you very attractive and I

170

like you probably more than I will admit to myself. If things were different, there wouldn't be a problem.'

'What is it then?'

'What it is, is Fermay. I can't put it into words what she means to me, Arlene. Without her I'd . . . I don't know . . . I'd just run down slowly and die. If someone had told me six months ago that I would say that about anyone I would have laughed in their face. But you don't realize what capacity you have for change until you've experienced something . . . perfect. Don't get me wrong, Fermay isn't perfect as a person, but she was perfect for me. Finding her was like a junkie who'd been withdrawing for days suddenly stumbling across the ultimate drug. Once you've tasted that high, nothing else can satisfy your need.'

'She's only a woman, David,' Arlene said in a small voice.

'To understand what she means to me, you have to understand me. Before Fermay I'd never met a single woman I could love. I didn't even believe in love. I was frozen, dead, with all my feelings trapped inside me where even I didn't know they existed. I'd never experienced love with my family. My mother and father tolerated each other at best. They rarely had time for me. I ended up burying my feelings and when I grew up, that's where they stayed.

'Somehow Fermay freed them. I don't know how – it wasn't an obvious thing – but I'll be eternally grateful to her for saving me from a world where nothing had any meaning. That's why I need to find her. That's why she's the *only* thing that's important to me. Because without her I have to go back to that meaningless world where relationships are just sex that slowly gets worse and worse until you want a new warm body to perk up your excitement.

'I've given everything to Fermay, Arlene, and I've burnt all my bridges. I *can't* go back to what I was before. And to be true to her and everything that I believe in, I can't go with you, not even for a night. You wouldn't want that, would you?'

She said no, but David felt she meant yes. Her eyes were still wet, but there was no more self-anger. 'If anybody else had said that, David, it would have been bullshit just to get out of being with someone who doesn't turn them on. But, hey, I know I turn men on!' She laughed wanly, before adding, 'I just need to hear you say it, David. Do you like me?'

'I like you a lot.' He kissed her. 'You're my best friend in my new life, Arlene.'

'And maybe if you and Fermay don't get back together . . . ?'

'Maybe. Who knows?'

'It's just that I get lonely sometimes.'

He pulled her close to him so that their bodies fit snugly together and then he held her, stroking the hairs on the back of her neck. 'You know you can stay here if you want to, Arlene. We can stay like this. You don't have to go back to Scuba if you don't want.'

'I'd like that, David. It's nice to feel that somebody cares.'

They soon fell asleep, with the radio still droning in the background, Sinatra and sixties love songs floating in and out of their dreams. And though it was Arlene he held, and Arlene's hair he smelt, and Arlene's body that aroused him, it was Fermay who controlled David's dreams.

Chapter 14

'Close your eyes.' Fermay's smile was bright and mysterious.

'What are you going to do to me?'

'Close your eyes!'

Reluctantly David acceded. It gave him a giddy feeling like he was standing on the parapet of a bridge. He hated putting himself in someone else's hands, even Fermay's.

He could hear rustling. 'If you so much as half open one eye, your testicles are toast.'

'Another fine product of Lady Jane's Swiss Finishing School, etiquette and delicate language a speciality.'

'OK, now you can look.' Fermay was holding a large, flat present wrapped in colourful paper. David knew what it was before he took it and felt the hardness of glass beneath.

'My poster!'

'I told you I'd get it framed for you. It's a gift for life so it has to be durable.'

His fingers ripped the wrapping paper in two swipes and then he was holding it up proudly near the lamplight, slowly twisting and turning it to get the best perspective. 'Non-reflective glass, too. You went to town.'

'Only the best for you, sweetheart.'

Queens of Carnival – New Orleans leapt out at him from beneath the image. 'Thanks. It means a lot to me.' He could look at it for hours.

'That's good. It's our bond then. The link between me and you.' Her voice had grown soft and serious.

'Like a ring?'

'Sure.' She paused. 'Like a ring.'

They stared at each other for a while, afraid to speak. Eventually David looked around his dingy flat and asked, 'Where shall we put it?' The cramped bedroom with its damp walls was not an option. That left the small lounge which

173

was stuffed with ragged, dying furniture, rescued from the junk heap or thrift shops.

Fermay rested an erect index finger on her chin and knitted her brow. She looked like a cartoon from *The Beano*. 'Over there? No, that wall's too cramped. You don't want it too close to the window. There! That's fine.' She pointed to a space on the wall. It was above the sofa which was threadbare and reaching the end of its days. 'It'll stop people looking at that thing.'

David held the picture against the wall for effect and from his cramped perspective agreed that it looked right. Better than that. Perfect! His flat had been transformed.

'OK. Now what do I hang it with?'

'A picture hook is the normal requirement, but failing that I guess a simple nail will do.'

David rifled the kitchen drawers and then searched the flat from top to bottom, but he couldn't find a nail or a tack and he knew he didn't have a hammer.

'Downstairs will have one,' he said hopefully. 'They've got everything. The old man's a DIY freak. His living room looks like Texas Homestores.'

'No, it's an omen,' Fermay said. 'It shows that we shouldn't hang it without a proper ceremony – especially as it's going to be so important to both of us. We've got to prepare for it. Have a party! We could do it on Saturday. Yeah, that's right! We could invite your creepy friend Willie, get some wine in and make it a special occasion. What do you say?'

'Fermay, you turn everything into a special occasion.'

'You've got to enjoy your life, haven't you. Saturday it is, then. That'll give you plenty of time to get your hammer and nails from Mr Fixit downstairs.'

David carefully placed the picture behind the sofa where it wouldn't get damaged and then he said, 'Why did you call Willie creepy?'

'Because he is.'

'In what way? Why don't you like him?'

Fermay sighed. 'I don't like people who aren't what they seem. Willie's nice as pie to your face, but there's always a

174

hidden agenda with him. He doesn't really care about anyone but himself and what he wants. Everything is just a sham.'

'That's not true. I've known him nearly all my life. We're the best of friends. We never had any problems until you came along.'

'That's because until now you've both wanted the same things. You've been two little kids in a very big playground, all fun and games and laughter. Well now, David, you're growing up and your friend Willie doesn't like it.'

Was it true? He shook his head. 'No . . .'

'Tell me, David, is Willie gay?'

'Hang on a minute.' David was shaking his head furiously. 'You're only doing this to mess up my friendship with him.'

She smiled. 'Surely you wouldn't think any worse of him if he was.'

'No, of course not. It wouldn't matter at all. But if he had kept something like that from me, after all these years, I'd have to re-evaluate how deep our friendship was. You know that!'

'Yeah, I know!' Fermay giggled like a teenager. 'Maybe I'm just being mischievous. It's just that sometimes he seems so jealous of you and me. Jealous in a lover sense.'

'I've never been aware of it,' David said dismissively. 'So stop trying to cause trouble. I don't have to choose between you and Willie, you know. We can all carry on together.'

'Maybe you should ask him that.'

'Stop it.'

But he couldn't prevent himself thinking about what she had said and briefly he disliked her for it.

On Saturday morning Fermay and David went shopping in the West End and then to the Barbican to see an exhibition of photos by Annie Leibowitz. They arrived just before lunch and missed the crowds which pleased Fermay immensely, and then they lingered before their favourite pictures without worrying about being jostled or overheard. Afterwards they bought coffee and sat out on the piazza, commenting on what a hideous, soulless monstrosity the Barbican was. The

175

sky was a dull, featureless grey streaked with white. Everything seemed bleached of colour, like the photographs they had just viewed.

David bought a danish, gnawed at it half-heartedly and then began to flick chunks towards a lone pigeon that was pecking rhythmically at unseen granules. It stopped mid-peck and cast a greedy eye at the tidbit before darting forward hungrily.

'Don't do that, David,' Fermay said with slight irritation.

'What?' he enquired, chewing lazily. Another piece of pastry arced over to the pigeon which had been joined by two others.

'That. Don't feed the birds.'

'What are you, the Bizarro Mary Poppins? There's nothing wrong with feeding the birds.'

'Yes, there is.' Her voice was like a piano wire. 'They're vermin. Rats with wings.'

'Yeah, yeah, and they deface public buildings and crap on the tourists. A few crumbs won't hurt.'

With his third offering a flock of pigeons descended to the piazza before them, flapping their wings madly as they cannoned off each other in their greed, their sound like the shriek of demented children. Realizing David was the source of their manna, they moved towards him as one, surging from all sides.

'David!'

Fermay's exclamation was so sharp David's head snapped round towards her in shock. The blood had drained from her face and her eyes were black pinpricks in white, unwaveringly fixed on the advancing horde.

'What is it? Fermay? Are you OK?'

Her entire body was rigid apart from her hand which was trembling uncontrollably. The birds drew closer.

'What is it?' He followed her gaze. The pigeons. 'Is it the birds? Don't you like them?'

Jumping from his seat, he shooed them away, still not sure if he was doing the right thing, but when he looked back at her, it seemed to have done the trick. Her rigidity had gone and the warmth was returning to her face. Slowly she put a steadying hand to her eyes.

David dropped to his haunches at her side and held her wrist. 'You've got a phobia about birds? You never said anything.'

She shook her head, speechless, eyes still glazed from the fear. Overhead the birds flapped and swooped, hungry, always voraciously hungry. Occasionally Fermay's eyes would dart up towards them and then look away. Just checking, in case they returned. Finally she licked her lips and said, 'I hate them. They're like death.'

David laughed. 'They're only birds, Fermay!'

'Don't laugh at me.' Her snapped words were underscored by a frosty glare.

'Sorry. It's just . . . you can understand people being scared of flying or fire, but . . . birds? What are they going to do? Peck you to death?'

'I wouldn't expect you to understand.' Then she said something strange, distractedly, as if she was recalling it. 'Evil takes many forms.'

'What?'

'Nothing. Can we go inside now? I've had enough fresh air.'

Back in the dead air of the Barbican, Fermay relaxed a little. She managed a pale smile and a limp joke and David apologized again for laughing at her.

'I know it's not rational,' she explained, 'but the mind plays strange tricks on you. It makes connections that you can't see.'

'How long have you been scared of birds?'

'Long enough. Since I was a child.'

'What happened? Did you get pecked by one?'

'Something like that.'

The barriers went up as they spoke and David soon realized she was not going to shed any more light on the subject. They walked in silence for a while and then, as they passed the theatre box office, David burst out laughing.

'What's the matter?'

'I just remembered . . . when we first met, you compared me to Bird. I thought it was a compliment, being compared to one of the greatest jazz musicians of all time. But did it really mean you're afraid of me too?'

'You're such a dick, David.' His stupid comment made her laugh and after that she seemed fine. David smiled secretly at his little success.

'Come on,' he said. 'Let's go back so I can play you Birdland. That should be good for a palpitation or two.'

Chapter 15

The room was as hot as a furnace. Sunlight blazed through the window, trapping the heat in the confined space like a greenhouse. As David's eyes flickered open, the radio was playing Martha Reeves & The Vandellas' *Nowhere To Run* in the background, the sinuous bassline tugging him insistently from sleep. His left arm ached and twinged with pins and needles where it was trapped beneath Arlene's head, her warm body deep in sleep and dreaming.

Fermay was the first thing to enter his mind, as she did every morning. The memories that had returned so far, the jumbled thoughts plucked randomly from the time they were together, were painting a more detailed picture of her and helping to explain why he felt so strongly about a woman he had only known for a few weeks. But the memories had prompted as many questions as they had answered. Fermay seemed to have been hiding a well of troubles deep within her, troubles which reverberated back to Broussard. What secrets had she kept hidden from him?

Arlene's eyes opened as he eased his arm out from beneath her. 'Mmmm. Morning,' she said sleepily. 'I didn't crowd you out, did I?'

'No. It was good to have you here.'

'Really? Maybe we should do it again some time.' She stretched, catlike, her body moving against his. The sensation excited him, a prickling electricity that ran up and down his limbs.

'What time is it?' Even her voice sounded sexy.

'Hmmm? Oh . . . 11.10. I better be going soon. I need to spend some time down at Broussard's place, keeping watch.'

'Don't do anything silly, David. Remember, she might not even be there. And this guy sounds like a real psycho, so . . . y'know, be careful.' She kissed him on the cheek.

David rolled out of bed and stretched. 'When it comes to my own skin, I'm walking on eggshells. Trust me.' His bravado was a front which he was sure Arlene could see through easily. But the next step in his search would take him directly into an area of high risk and he didn't want her to know that.

His disguise was pathetic – a pair of Rayban copies borrowed from Arlene and a N'Awlins baseball cap, five dollars from Bourbon Street – but at least it would help him blend into the background if he got too close to Broussard and his cronies. A pair of baggy shorts, a baggy t-shirt and over-sized basketball boots, all 'borrowed' from Scuba's wardrobe, completed the picture. 'Jesus, what a sight,' he had said in disbelief as he looked at himself in the mirror before setting out. 'Someone alert the style police.'

The sun lay heavy across the city and David was secretly thankful for the outfit as he waited in Canal Street for the streetcar. There was only a handful of people hanging around at the stop, most of them tourists armed with cameras and the lazy, relaxed facial expressions of those totally at ease with the world. David envied them.

When the streetcar arrived he was the last to board, the others hurrying for the best sightseeing positions at the front. As he mounted and paid his sixty cents he was surprised to see that the inside was crowded. Some people were even standing in the aisles. There was only one seat free, right at the back, which he slipped into, pulling the brim of his baseball cap low to cover his face.

Despite the crowd, the streetcar was almost silent, the only occasional sound coming from the whispers of the tourists near the front. As it began rolling gently along, David found his head beginning to nod in the lulling atmosphere.

How much longer could he go on watching Broussard's house in the feeble hope that he would catch a glimpse of Fermay? At the start it had seemed a reasonable option, but he had seen no sign of any female presence in the house at all. There'd been plenty of shady figures arriving in cars with smoked windows, dashing to the door as if they didn't want to stay out in the sun too long. But no Fermay. He knew that sooner or later he would have to take the search closer to Broussard. Maybe even break in, search the house. Sure, why not really risk his life?

His thoughts were interrupted by a sudden awareness of a queasy feeling starting to take root in the pit of his stomach. From out of nowhere a strange smell set his nose wrinkling, an odour which reminded him of abattoirs, stagnant ponds and council dumps. His gorge rose then calmed, but all his senses were yelling an alarm. He could taste iron filings in his mouth.

The strange silence of the crowd was not really silence. When he strained he could hear odd words and phrases humming on the edge of his consciousness, disembodied voices, unnatural tongues.

'He hears. He sees.'

'He's here. He's seen.'

With sickening resignation, he looked up.

The figures crowding the streetcar were not what he had thought. The clothes on a man standing with his back to him hung in voluminous drapes and folds as if the frame within was barely more than bone. The skin of a woman sitting across the aisle had no sheen; it was the colour of lard. She clutched a mouldering handbag in her lap and when she saw him looking at her she gave a gap-toothed smile. Something wriggled in her mouth and dropped to the floor.

At the front of the carriage the tourists saw some sight of note and chattered noisily, camera flashes reflecting in the glass. David thought about calling out to them, warning them, and at the same time finding some support for himself, but he knew they would be oblivious to what was around them. They would think him mad, and in that world of madness he was completely and utterly alone. Frustration and weariness misted his eyes.

The streetcar lurched on towards the Garden District like it was taking the scenic route out of hell. David sat rigid, wondering if he should leap off while it was in motion, feeling the sweat trickle down his back. The scent of death hung in the air like an old woman's perfume. The dead moved around in a pale mockery of sightseers and straphangers, faintly remembering the things they did when they were alive – as if to keep doing them gave them some kind of hold on the life that was gone.

An old man with a face as craggy as the moon's surface gazed forlornly out of the window, his fingers soundlessly tapping at the glass in a vain attempt to contact the living on the street without. A small boy, the left side of his head in tatters, wandered in a daze up and down the aisle, looking into the faces of all those present as if searching for a missing parent. And there were more. A fat man rocking backwards and forwards with silent laughter at a never-ending joke. A tall, gaunt woman with staring eyes who relentlessly tugged at her mane of silver and black hair and opened and closed her mouth for a scream that never came.

The whole streetcar was suffused with a sense of extreme melancholy and suffering, but none of the malignancy he had experienced before. They were as aware of him as he was of them, their strangely flat eyes occasionally swivelling in his direction, sometimes mildly curious, sometimes tinged with a longing for contact, always detached and in a state of permanent shock.

For his part, David feared that he was plummeting into a maelstrom. A frightening thought had come upon him that these things were around all the time, silently watching the living go about their business, just a heartbeat and a sudden glance away; and that for some reason he was cursed to be aware of them. Would he spend the rest of his life seeing spectral faces wherever he went? It would destroy him. To make love in a warm bed only to look up and see a mangled corpse face looking over him. To dine with a loved one in a quiet restaurant before discovering an uninvited guest at the table. To encounter the sad, the hateful and the dangerous at every twist and turn, in every private moment. His mind would not be able to cope.

The worst thing, the very worst thing, was that only he could see the apparitions. He was trapped in a minority of one, unable to tell anyone, unable to explain the sudden expressions of shock and disgust on his face. He was being dragged from the real world. Even now he could feel it, that sense that the dead and their twilight land was somehow more valid and important than the world of colours in which he had existed before.

Whenever the dead moved near him he huddled back in his seat, terrified that he would feel the cold-fish touch of their skin,

182

terrified that if he did it would push him screaming over the edge. A woman in the seat in front turned and grinned at him toothlessly. Her left eye was missing and her left cheek was ripped upwards, exposing the bone beneath. Having made eye contact with David she refused to look away, every now and then curiously stretching out her hand to his cheek. When he shied away she would snatch it back and recoil, hissing like a snake, but then a few moments later she would try to touch him again.

Eventually David's dread became numbing and even the scenery outside the car became unreal to him, the dull, grey houses, the faceless pedestrians, the faint honk and grind of traffic. It was hypnotic, and he felt himself becoming lost in it.

Gradually he realized the streetcar was approaching his stop. It was enough to jolt him alert and he half slid, half stumbled to his feet, ready to dismount when they drew to a halt.

The dead woman in front stretched out her arm once more, this time grabbing hold of his t-shirt. 'Where you goin'?' she said in a crackling, dry voice. 'The ride's not over yet.'

There was movement further down the carriage as the other shades turned to look at him, and then, as if they were powered by one intellect, they began to move forward. He looked around, afraid that he was trapped. At that instant, the door slid open.

Before they could stop him David jumped into the sunlight.

He half wondered if they would follow him, but the car's doors rattled shut and then it continued on its way, rumbling down the centre of the avenue until it disappeared in the distance.

David rubbed at his temples as if he could peel open his head and pluck out the memory of the last few minutes. He was desperate to prevent the recent madness from becoming more real than the world around him. He sat on his haunches at the stop and let his breathing slowly return to normal. The strain and stress had turned his heart to a triphammer, a beat too fast for jazz or dancing.

Bang, bang. Bang, bang.

David took up his regular post across the street and a few hundred yards along the road from Broussard's mansion where he could watch without being seen. No one disturbed him, even when he was sitting on the kerb with his feet in the gutter, a Bowery Boy in Fila and Nike. It was like he had become one of the ghosts, going through the motions of everyday life, but unseen by the living. Beth's Walkman allowed him to stave off the boredom of his long watch, his jazz tape helping to restrain any more disturbing thoughts, the trumpets, drums and bass eventually intertwining naturally with the rhythms of his own mind.

Broussard's house was like a morgue all afternoon. No curtains twitched, no one called.

At 7 p.m. David decided to leave his patch. It would give him just enough time to return to Beth's place and get himself ready for work that night. But as he stood up and stretched the aches out of his muscles, he saw movement. The limousine emerged slowly from the side of the mansion at the same time as three people stepped out of the front door. One of them was Broussard; David recognized his bulk. Beside him, a man in a dark suit appeared to be Lynch.

And there was a woman.

David's heart did a sudden flip. She was wearing a black dress down to her mid-calf, a pool of ink in the brightness of the street. A wide-brimmed hat and dark glasses obscured her identity. He only glimpsed her for the briefest moment before she climbed into the back of the limo, but the way she moved, fluidly and confidently, seemed familiar. The car pulled out of the drive, smooth and slow like cream, eased into the traffic and headed along the road away from him.

'Can I help you, young man?' The voice made him start. He had been so deep in concentration he had not heard the speaker come up next to him. It was a woman in her late fifties with expensively coiffured silver hair and immaculate dress. Her expression suggested he was a potential burglar, mugger, drug addict or all three.

'I just thought I saw somebody I knew,' he said, trying to follow the limo's progress with squinting eyes.

The woman began to protest that he had been loitering in the street near her house all afternoon. David made his apologies and left before she mentioned the police, as he knew she would. His mind was whirring frantically. Was it Fermay? It had certainly looked like her, but if Arlene had been there he knew she would have told him that at that distance it could have been Sophia Loren. He couldn't be sure, didn't even dare admit it to himself, despite the excitement that buzzed through his nerve endings.

Was it Fermay? Was it?

That night he could barely contain himself. Both Arlene and Dean, in their respective ways, commented on his newfound *joie de vivre* and although he tried to dampen his enthusiasm in case he was disappointed, David found himself dwelling once more on daydreams of his reunion with Fermay.

Arlene was particularly pleased at his transformation. David confided the cause of it to her. She smiled sweetly and told him not to build up his hopes. Although she wanted it to be true for his sake, there was disappointment mingled in with her advice.

'So what do you do now, David?' she asked, drawing on a cigarette. 'Go in there, guns blazing?'

'Don't worry, I won't act rashly. When I do make my move, I'm going to make sure nothing can go wrong. There's no point in finally getting back together with Fermay if it only lasts five minutes before Broussard's monkeys start using me for target practice.' He paused thoughtfully. 'If I can break in, it would be easy to hide away in a place that size until the middle of the night. Then I can get to her room . . .'

Arlene didn't look convinced. 'Isn't there an easier way?'

'I'm open to offers.'

'So why don't you break in tomorrow, David?' Arlene's anger rose to the surface. It was the first time she had become annoyed with him. 'If you're going to get shot or beat up you might as well get it over with.' She turned and marched away before he could reply.

Surprisingly his dreams were not of Fermay that night. They were populated by creatures, half-living, half-dead, that wandered through endless rooms in a giant crumbling mansion. Arlene and Dean and Charlie were there, but David could not tell which side of the divide they were on; they were animated but their skin and eyes looked dead.

He woke early, the dream fading shortly after. Beth had already gone to work so he ate a makeshift breakfast of what was left in the cupboard, made a mental note to pick up some groceries, and then stepped out into the sunny morning. The air was fresh from a squally overnight storm and a light breeze stirred the hanging baskets suspended from the colourful balconies. A neighbour he had not seen before leaned over her railing and waved to him cheerily.

Dauphine's place was only a few minutes away. He had decided to turn up early to jump the queue on any appointments she had, and unannounced because he knew she would not see him if he did try to make an appointment. It was still a gamble as to whether she would allow him over the threshold, but he was confident his determination would carry him through.

Her face darkened when she opened the door and saw him standing there. 'Whatchoo doin' here?' she said with irritation. 'I thought I tol' you not to come round here.'

'I need help and advice, Dauphine. Don't drive me away.' He added reassuringly, 'No one will know I've visited you. I'll keep it a secret.'

She read his face for a moment and then stepped aside to let him in, saying, 'There are no secrets.'

Her parlour was as cool and relaxing as on his first visit. He paused to examine a crystal ornament with a tiny flower frozen at its centre, preserved for eternity in its moment of glory, and a handsome marble statuette of Orpheus, but all the time he could feel her eyes upon him.

'You're lookin' like you didn't heed Dauphine's advice to stay out of trouble,' she said when he was sitting across the table from her.

David touched his face automatically. 'It's healing now.'

She nodded sagely. 'You know why I don't want ch'oo comin' round here, boy? 'Cause I don't want to look like that.'

'Nobody will find out, Dauphine. Believe me.'

She dismissed his words with a wave of her hand. 'Speak to me.'

'I keep seeing dead people,' he said flatly. 'They're all around me, everywhere I turn.'

Dauphine's face was unflinching and unsurprised. She shrugged. 'Some people have the power.'

'But I never used to have "the power" and now I do. I need to know what is happening to me.'

She began to shuffle and deal her Tarot cards randomly as she thought, picking up each exquisitely designed card and examining it as if she had just seen it for the first time.

'That's not all,' he continued, becoming more animated. 'I keep hearing this music in my head, just snatches of a passage, but it won't go away. It's haunting me. I first heard Fermay humming it just after I met her. She always did it when she was in some kind of trance.'

Dauphine looked up from her cards. 'Sing it to me.'

David tried to hum a few bars and then shook his head. 'I can hear it inside my head, but I can't quite seem to get it out.'

Something like relief crossed her face. She returned to her cards. 'You're in a jam, boy, but I feel sorry for you 'cause it's not your fault. You're just a poor, misguided fool who's been pulled into somethin' too big for him. An' all because of the heart. It's always the way. Fools in love are the worst kind. So,' she said, shuffling and dealing, shuffling and dealing, 'what can I tell you? Let me think.'

'For a start, you can tell me why it's happening to me.'

'You were just in the wrong place at the wrong time. With the wrong person. You've been touched by the dark world, just once, just a soft stroke, but it was enough and it's pulled you halfway over the dividing line. Now half of you's in the world of the light an' half of you's in the dark.'

Her words sounded strangely familiar. 'I'm *totally* in the dark,' he replied in annoyance. She was speaking in riddles again. 'There are so many things I can't remember. Maybe something in the cards will explain?'

She nodded noncommittally.

'But these dead people – these ghosts – can I really see them? Or are they all in my mind?'

'The dead are around us all the time. Most folk can't see them, but that don't mean they're not there. If they died in a bad way, if it was sudden, or if they were sad or angry or sufferin', they

187

hang on. They won't go on. Most of the time they pay no attention to warm folk, but every now and then they realize some poor boy can see them an' then they start lookin' at him. Lookin' at him an' worse.'

David felt sick in the pit of his stomach and he wished he'd eaten more breakfast. 'Can they hurt me?'

'Some of them can. The bad ones. They've got a lot of hate eatin' away inside 'em, an' they get jealous when they see folk walkin' around who aren't sufferin' like they are. The sad ones won't bother you none. There aren't many good ones. They move on quick. They got better places to go. There's others – ones who want you to help 'em. They're the ones who can move on if you give 'em a hand, sort out their problems, the things that are holdin' them back. They'll try to communicate with you, but they can't all talk. You met any of them, boy?' Her question was phrased knowingly.

He thought of Marsayle pointing at the picture in the Jazz Museum and nodded.

'You ought to listen to 'em. Do you a lotta good.'

'OK, so I listen to them. I sort out their problems. I make sure they get a decent burial and I tell their Aunty Mabel they really loved her. Where does that get me? Why should I suffer? What have I ever done that has meant I should spend the rest of my life looking at dead things?'

'Some folk wouldn't see it as punishment . . .'

'Yeah? Well I do. I'm only concerned about one thing: finding Fermay and getting our lives back. I just want to know from you if I'll be sharing her with the spirit world when we do finally get together.'

Dauphine smiled, a secret, knowing smile that infuriated David because in it was the confirmation of what he had believed: that she knew much, much more about what was happening to him than she would say.

'Damn it, Dauphine . . .'

'Treat me with respect, boy.' Her voice was a whiplash.

'I'm sorry.' He calmed himself down. 'It's just there's so much I need to know and I can't understand why you're not telling me.'

She held up the Tarot card of The Fool. 'Mis-ter Easter, I am tellin' you everything you need to know – you're just not hearin'. Too busy listenin' to the sound of your own voice, like all young folk.' She tapped the card she was holding to underline what she was saying. 'You're on a long journey and you've still got a good way to go. You'll be a different man when you get to the end. Maybe a better one, maybe not – depends which road you go down. We all make a similar trip, Mis-ter Easter, and we all make our own choices. Why should you be any different? If you don't open your eyes an' learn things for yourself, you're going to be in big trouble. I can't help you. You've got to see those holes in the road yourself. I'm doin' as much as I can for you, 'cause you're not a bad boy, but Dauphine won't be puttin' her own neck on the tracks. Just remember . . . knowledge is a valuable tool an' a powerful weapon. You open your eyes an' your mind, an' you'll find that out yourself.'

David wearily rubbed a hand over his face. 'What are you scared of, Dauphine?'

'Same as you. Pain, death an' eternal suffering.'

He took The Fool card from her and laid it on the table in front of him. With his head bowed as he studied the illustration, he said, 'I think I've found my girlfriend Fermay. When the time is right I'm going to get her, and then we're out of this city and away. I want to leave this madness behind and I'm scared that I can't.'

'You have my sympathies, you truly do. It's a fact of life that folk are always gettin' what they don't deserve. You have to be strong.' Her eyes were unusually caring, a chink in her emotional armour. 'You're close to the dead, boy. They're all around you – gettin' closer.' She held the thumb and forefinger of her left hand half an inch apart. 'That close. You've been touched by the hand, just a little. Just enough to lead you to the edge of the grey world. It's a gift and a curse. You must have been close to losin' it, but the love of God pulled you back from the edge.'

'Losing what?'

'Your life.'

Her words ripped through the Fog Zone. There was something there, but it refused to materialize. He felt a glacial shock at the thought of what could be hidden in his mind.

'You had one foot in the grave an' it's still there,' Dauphine continued. 'You're brother to the spirits as well as your fellow man now.'

'That's comforting,' he said bitterly. 'Tell me this doesn't have anything to do with what happened to Fermay. Tell me it's just a bizarre, nightmarish coincidence.'

Her sphinx-like smile was enough of an answer.

'Jesus! What *is* going on here?'

'You came to this city at a bad time,' she said quietly. 'It's changed. Something's gone sour. Most folk can feel it though they probably don't recognize it. Since the year turned there's been a cloud over N'Orleans, a cloud of evil.'

Her words triggered a response in his mind, memories of what Fermay had told him on a cold day in Covent Garden.

'They've set something loose, something terrible, and it's gettin' stronger. I can feel it on every street. I don't go out much any more.'

'*Who* has set it loose?'

'Hush. I won't talk about that. Just heed my words. The storm's brewin' an' pretty soon it's goin' to break. This black stuff, this evil, it's goin' to come down on all our heads. I can't leave N'Orleans – it's in my blood and bones – but you can. Get out of the city. Now.'

'Or?'

'Or you die.'

'Is that in the cards?'

'It's writ all over your face.'

'Pleasant thought.' He tried to lighten the atmosphere, but it clung oppressively. 'I will leave – when I've found Fermay.'

'Don't wait for her. You're wastin' your time.'

He shook his head. 'Don't say that.'

'It's up to you if you won't listen, Mis-ter Easter.' She shrugged. 'I'm just warnin' you.'

'You're talking in riddles, same as always, Dauphine. OK, there's something bad coming down. Maybe it's a *cloud of evil*. Maybe it's Count Dracula. Maybe it's Santa Claus gone bad. Whatever it is, it's not going to stop me finding Fermay. It's just one more thing to add to a lost memory, a song that I can't get out of my head, a missing girlfriend, and the contents of the world's cemeteries following me through the streets. I've taken so much over the last few weeks, I can take a little more.'

She held out her hands to say that it was his choice – and, he knew, his burden.

'There's one other thing. You're pretty good with these cards. Are you any good at fortune-telling?'

Her laughter was deep and musical. 'Go to a fairground, boy. You want a tea-leaf reader or a crystal-ball gazer. I read cards.'

'You can't tell the future?'

'Without the cards? Sometimes. The future, the past, it's all *now*. You just have to listen carefully.'

'Well listen to me.'

Concern crossed her face. 'No.'

'Why not?'

'*You* haven't listened to what the cards said.'

David felt cold. He didn't know why he was asking her this, but he had a desperate urge to find out – good or bad. 'I don't care what it is. Tell me.'

Dauphine saw in his face that he meant it. Reluctantly she reached out and took his hand, holding it between her chill palms, and then slowly her eyes flickered upwards until all he could see were the whites. It seemed as if the room had turned cold, so cold he expected his breath to frost over. The sepulchral silence lasted for almost five minutes, and when she spoke her words were frozen in the air.

'You are sitting in a warm room. There is music in the air. A record is playing, old and scratched, crackling. The music box has a trumpet, gold like a horn, but it is chipped and damaged by age. The needle reaches the centre, but the record does not stop. It keeps going round and round. A clock ticks in the background, a pendulum swings, but the hands never go round. It is always one time, one moment. There is no window in the room. The walls are cream and cracked. The floor is bare boards. You know what to do when the woman cries out. You are sitting in a warm room.'

Her eyes flickered up and down before revolving to normal. They were wet, but David couldn't tell if the tears were those of strain or sadness.

191

'I don't know why I ask you these things, Dauphine. I always find myself more confused and disturbed. Is that all there is in my future? I sit listening to music? That sounds ominously like my past, even down to the cracked walls.' Dauphine did not respond to his smile. 'Is there any more?'

'Death,' she replied bluntly.

An icy wind blew over him. 'Mine?'

She shrugged, giving nothing away. 'I don't know. There is always death, many kinds of death. The Tarot is all about death – death of the past, death of character, change, moving on.'

'That's life.' He smiled again, weakly. 'That's a bad joke.'

'I can't tell you more. There's some things which shouldn't be discussed in case of what you bring down 'pon your shoulders.'

'That old cloud of evil again, eh? I better dig out my umbrella and raincoat.'

Her smile worried him; there was too much sympathy for someone who acted so emotionless. 'I helped you two times, Mister Easter. Don't come back again. I don't want trouble at my door.'

'Third time is the charm, Dauphine.'

She led him to the door, emotionless and distant once more, but then she repeated what she had told him before. 'You listen to the spirits now, Mis-ter Easter. Do you a lotta good.'

David thanked her, but this time she did not slam the door quickly. He could feel her eyes on his back, questioning, worrying.

He was sure she thought he was walking off to die.

Chapter 16

The fog rolled into New Orleans the following morning. Cold and damp, it drifted along the river at dawn, spreading across the Vieux Carre and into the city beyond. There was much talk about the unusual weather phenomenon on the TV and radio. Meteorologists were baffled. Conditions were just not right for fog, they repeated, as if that was enough to charm it away. There was talk of pollution from industries up-river, of freak chemical spills and toxic clouds. The only thing that people could agree on was that it was *Just Not Right*.

It reminded David uncomfortably of England, of grey November mornings, choking back the car fumes on the way to work. It was melancholic in the way it dampened the normal joyous spirit of New Orleans, left sounds huddling moodily down into the gutter, music stilborn in the bars. On the street he felt the ghosts were even closer, just feet away, draped in the swirling, grey cloak. Eyes pressed heavily against him, but when he turned there was no one there. Half-heard words floated into his periphery, swept back into the billows before he could grasp them. The Fog Zone had seeped out of his mind while he was sleeping and now he was living in it.

'Do you feel it?' Arlene asked him when he arrived at Charlie's Place. She was hugging her arms around her for warmth and security.

'What?'

'This fog – Jesus! Don't you feel it? My nerves are just shot to hell when I'm out there in it. It's like if anyone suddenly spoke to me, I'd just scream, y'know. There's something, I don't know . . . a feeling . . .'

'Something bad?'

'Yeah! Like there's something bad out there watching me, like it's using the fog to hide itself. Shit, like it's hanging over the whole city, know what I mean?'

David knew. *A cloud of evil*.

'I just get this feeling that something awful's gonna happen.' She reluctantly freed her arms to light a cigarette. 'Maybe it's a premonition. You reckon I'm psychic? My mom had the second sight. Knew when her sister was gonna die and everything. It's been there at the back of my head for a few days now, like a migraine's gonna hit me between the eyes, and it's been getting worse. You reckon there's something in it?'

He shrugged. 'Maybe. Maybe it's just the fog.'

'No. The fog's made it worse. I wonder what caused it?'

A cloud of evil.

For the hour before opening, David studiously kept out of Dean's way; he was in no mood for the usual petty, fruitless confrontation. He carried out his pre-opening chores quickly, efficiently and silently and then hung out with the band as they set up their equipment on the small raised stage.

The Dedication All-Star Ensemble were as laid back off-stage as they were hot and sweaty in front of the crowd. A multicultural crew, they mixed as if there were no barriers apart from Us and Them. David had caught three of them smoking grass behind the speaker stack and for a moment they bristled until he smiled and made a joke of it, and then he was accepted as part of the team. Their drummer, Mickey O'Connell, was the most studious. A long-hair with wire-framed spectacles, he knew his jazz like he'd learnt it at Bible School. David spent a few minutes every night discussing with him the relative merits of their favourite performers. O'Connell had an opinion on everyone, no matter how obscure.

The leader of the band was Boney Lee, the cool, well-spoken son of a mixed-race marriage. The first time they met he'd complimented David on his suit which meant he was as OK as anyone could be. David was impressed by his attention to detail; the antique gold watch and chain which he kept in his waistcoat pocket and the gold-embossed initials on his trumpet case which was itself made of the finest leather.

'Got to keep old Gabriel happy,' he'd say, patting his horn as he fitted the mouthpiece.

That night he came across David in a quiet, hidden place behind the speakers. David was in a trance, staring into his increasingly crumpled photo of Fermay as if he was willing it to give up even more secrets. Lee peered over his shoulder at the picture.

'She was a strange one all right.'

David's mouth gaped stupidly. 'You know her.'

'Yeah. Well, not exactly. I've seen her around, y'know. She was in here one night, checking us out.'

The shock of the revelation was like a punch in the face. Suddenly David believed in fate. 'Tell me about her.'

Lee responded with a grin to the feverish gleam in David's eye. 'She has you hooked, don't she? She's a looker and she has, how shall I put it, a certain style, but she wasn't my type. No way.' Lee took the photo, staring at it squinty-eyed and concentrating. 'Is she your girl?'

'She was. We lost touch.'

'Yeah? Funny you and her being together and me remembering seeing her, but I guess most of the bands in the Quarter would remember her face. She loves her music. She checked out every band on the circuit. Knew what was hot and what was not. I admire that in a woman.' He laughed and snapped his fingers.

'And she thought the Dedication All-Star Ensemble were hot?'

'At the risk of my head swelling too big for my hat, I must confirm that that is the truth. Not seen her around for a while though. The last time must have been . . . oh . . . last year, before Christmas.'

'I've been trying to find her. Even tried the local rag, but I guess musicians don't read newspapers. That's one of the reasons I'm over here.'

'Good luck to you, man. She's a real handful.'

'What do you mean?'

Lee eyed David searchingly and then asked, 'How close were you?'

'Very close.'

'Then I shouldn't say anything.'

'I'm a big boy now, Boney. You don't have to hide things from me.'

'OK,' he said with a shrug. 'She came up to see the band after the set. We were all ready to talk to her, if you know what I mean. We'd all seen her during the show. She had a table close to the stage and after we came off Bodie remarked how classy she looked, better than our average fan. You know what some of the chicks are like in here!' His eyes never left David's face; he seemed to be choosing his words carefully. 'From the moment she walked up, I could tell there was something wrong. Her eyes, man, they were all over the place, like all the time she was looking for a way out, like she had to be constantly on guard. They were hunted eyes, dark rings under them. She couldn't have slept for days. And her cheekbones were like razor blades, dark, like her diet had gone on for four weeks too long. She started talking about bands and things, and you know how it is when someone's living on their nerves, they just talk and talk, running off at the mouth, never staying on one subject long enough to get a handle on it. She was like that, y'know? I got about five words into the conversation and then I gave up. Just let her talk and twitch and mumble. When she lit a cigarette . . .'

David's growing expression of bafflement suddenly erupted in a bout of head shaking. 'No, no, Fermay doesn't smoke.'

'Fermay? That her name? Nice name. Well, she did then, David, and her hand was shaking like a three-day drunk with the D.T.'s If anyone was on the verge of a nervous breakdown, she was.'

David continued to shake his head, a subconscious reaction to the thoughts bouncing around like a pinball inside. That wasn't Fermay. It couldn't have been. She had never been that way with him.

But he knew Lee wasn't making it up. Fermay must have been like that before she came to England.

Lost in his thoughts, he suddenly realized Lee was watching him closely. The trumpet player placed a sympathetic hand on David's shoulder. 'Sorry if I didn't paint a very good picture of her, man, but that's the way it played to me.'

'It's OK, Boney. It seems like there's a lot I didn't know about her.'

'That's why they say you should never play poker with a

woman, David,' Lee said with a laugh. 'They always keep a few cards back to hit you with when you least expect it. Well, I've got a show to get ready for . . . got to make sure old Gabriel's bright and gleaming. Look after him and he'll look after me.' He smiled, adding, 'Seems to me like you're still burning a big candle for this Fermay chick and . . . well, if you ever need anyone to talk to, you know where to find me.'

'Thanks, Boney. I appreciate that.'

Lee saluted and slipped out to the back of the stage, leaving David alone to examine his photograph once more.

'Nice place you've got here.'

David looked across at the man next to him. He had a pork-pie hat pushed to the back of his head and a pair of dark glasses that reflected the gleam of the club's lights. He was rocking gently backwards and forwards on his heels, using one hand on the bar to steady himself.

'It's not my place, pal,' David said. He had paused to rest his feet after a tough session waiting tables.

'You may be right,' the man said. 'But there would be some who would say you earn a piece of this place with every bit of labour expended. And your life, I'm sure, is richer for it.'

'My life, but not my wallet.' David tried to get Dean to bring him a club soda, but the barman ignored him.

'Ah, but which is more important on the road to the hereafter – money or experience?' The man chuckled throatily. 'Heh, enough of that dangerous talk. Still, it is a nice place. Would you join me in a drink?' He threw back a bourbon and released his breath approvingly like pressure from a steam engine.

'The boss doesn't like me drinking with the paying custom. Guess he doesn't want me to get ideas above my station.'

'I guess you're probably right.' The bourbon drinker tugged at his closely trimmed goatee beard thoughtfully and then said, 'Hot time in the old town tonight. There's a storm brewin'.'

'Maybe it'll blow that fog away.'

'Oh, I'm not talking about *weather*, my friend. It's something far worse than that. It's a storm of sourness, of bad feeling and hatred, and it's sweeping low like a hurricane. And it'll do more damage, believe me.'

David watched the stranger out of the corner of his eye. His words sounded uncomfortably familiar. 'Do I know you?'

'Me? Heavens, no. But you know him.' He jerked a thumb over his shoulder in the direction of the heavy shadows at the back of the club. David turned slowly and scanned the room. As if on cue, the crowd watching the band parted and he could see straight through to the rear.

Buffalo Marsayle was there, seated at a table, his staring eyes locked firmly on to David's.

David felt the world spin. There was that old, familiar feeling of discorporation, that sucking at the very essence of his being when reality faded into the background and the twilight world took hold. In that centre of life and music and fun, David could see only death.

This time Marsayle was not alone. With horror, David saw there were others around him, dead people, shades, a dark parody of a drinking party out for the night. Two men were sitting at the table next to him, eyes just as accusing, shot glasses, real or insubstantial, laid out before them. Others, men and women, stood in a tight group, unmoving, watching. Their faces were as one, emotionless, flimsy plastic sheets laid on to pallid flesh, but their black eyes were screaming of horrors undreamed.

They were watching David.

He shivered, trying to avoid their gaze, but even when he looked away he could feel their eyes heavy upon him. There was nowhere he was safe from them.

'Shit,' he muttered under his breath.

'The gang's all here,' the stranger continued. 'Let the festivities commence.'

David looked at him again and this time he could see the skin had no bloom of warmth and that his chest did not rise and fall. When his sleeve pulled up slightly, purple patches were visible on his flesh.

He turned to David and smiled a yellow-toothed smile. Then he took off his sunglasses. Behind them his eye sockets gaped blackly.

Fearfully, David took a step back. His nerves jangled madly. No one else in the bar was paying any attention to them.

The stranger replaced his sunglasses. 'The lights in here are too bright. They hurt your eyes.' He laughed at his joke.

'What do you want?' David tried to sound confident, but his voice betrayed him.

'You keep ignoring us, old friend. There's something very important that you have to do, yet you just keep turning your back on us when all we want to do is help.' He smiled like a shark. 'You're not imagining this. You must know that by now.'

'If you want me to do something, why don't you just come out with it. Tell me.' There was hysteria in his voice, all the repressed tension close to the surface.

'Rules of the game, old friend. We all have to play by them. I can tell you one thing – you keep ignoring your obligation and you'll make us very angry. Very angry indeed.'

'To ignore it, I first have to know what it is,' he protested.

The stranger continued, 'We're watching you, old friend, and at the moment we're waiting. Giving you the benefit of the doubt, as it were. There are others who aren't as nice or patient and they're getting closer to you. Your time is running out.'

'Why doesn't Marsayle say something to me? Why does he stare all the time?'

The stranger's smile grew tight. 'The cat got his tongue.' His glass had mysteriously refilled itself and he knocked back another shot of bourbon. 'Your good health. You're sure you won't join me? No? Ah well, better hurry along now, old friend, you've got a lot to do before this storm blows itself out. Just remember, we'll be watching you.'

He turned and walked out through the crowd, disappearing into the shadows. David looked to the back of the room. Marsayle and his crew were still there.

David tried to go about his business, but he could feel the constant, damning pressure of their eyes upon him, never wavering. The real people, the warm-blooded, living drinkers and music lovers, seemed almost insubstantial in comparison. When David served them drinks, he had the odd sensation that he could see right through them, as if they were filled with mist.

The dead never left him alone all night. When he stood at the urinal, he was suddenly alerted by the earthy smell of the grave to discover one standing next to him, staring at him askance. He discovered another in the stockroom, sitting on a crate of Dixie. There was a ragged, bloody bullet-hole in the centre of his forehead. David tried to ignore him, but as he bent down to pick up a bottle of Jack Daniels, the spirit moved in close – examining him almost curiously from only inches away.

He could feel the soft flutter of their fingertips on his neck as he cleaned tables, sense them walking behind him as he moved to the bar and back. Everywhere David went, they lurked, tormenting him silently until he wanted to scream at them. They were driving him to the brink and the only way he could cope was to go inside himself, to pretend it was all quite normal. And that was the worst thing of all.

By the end of the evening, it seemed to David that the club's only clientele were the dead. They held sway over all. Only when the last customer had departed did he notice they were gone, and even then he could sense their presence, as close as a whisper in the dark.

They had staked their claim on him, and David knew then they would never let him go.

Chapter 17

The fog had gone. David hung out of his bedroom window and looked up and down the street, amazed at the sudden change in the weather. A warm breeze caressed his face and the sun cut stark shadows into the road below, firmly underlining the message that everything was back to normal. David didn't believe it. The fog might have gone, but whatever came with it was still around.

His head was thumping and he quickly withdrew it out of the bright light. Beth was already up, enjoying the secret pleasures of a solitary Saturday morning. She looked up in mock horror when David walked into the lounge.

'Hey, I advertised for a room-mate, not one of the walking dead. You look like you just walked out of a George Romero flick.'

'Thanks a lot. I'll return the compliment some time – like the morning after your next vodka binge.'

'Arlene told you about that? I'll kill the bitch. So what's the problem? Not sleeping too good?'

'You could say that.' He shambled past her to the kitchen and made a cup of super-strong coffee before taking up a lounging position in the threadbare easy chair that seemed to fit the angles of his body. The smoke from Beth's constantly-smouldering cigarette made him faintly nauseous.

'So, like, at least your face is healing.'

'We should be thankful for some things, shouldn't we.'

Beth was sprawled in the middle of the floor in a pair of cut-off denim shorts and a t-shirt which looked like it had been hers since she was a teenager. Around her were scattered a jumble of pictures and photographs, scores of them, a patchwork of glossy colour and black and white.

'What are you doing?' He wanted to talk, aware that idle chitchat would keep his mind off the massed armies of black thoughts waiting to attack him.

201

'This? Just work, y'know, school work. Teaching isn't a nine-to-five job like attorneys or whatever you did before you dropped out of the human race. I have to keep coming up with projects and stuff so I can fill the empty minds of my hideous kids and make sure they don't turn to ways to make teacher's life hell. You think you got badly beat up. You should be standing by the classroom door when the lunch bell rings.'

'I'm sure they'll enjoy their origami.' He motioned towards the heap of paper around her.

'Fuck you, smart mouth.' She turned away from him, but he could see a smile on her face.

'I hope you don't talk like that to the children.'

'Believe me, they've got dirtier mouths than I could ever muster. Plus they take more drugs than I do and they know how to blow the top off a beer bottle at fifty paces with a Saturday Night Special.'

'Sounds like a tough school.'

'Yeah, they don't buy comics, they subscribe to *Soldier of Fortune* magazine. But, y'know, we've all got our crosses to bear. Whoever said life had to be happy? I see myself as a spiritual missionary. Mother Theresa of the third grade.'

David stared into the swirling blackness of his coffee and listened to the rhythmic hoof-falls of a horse making its way up the street with a cartload of tourists. He yearned for those simple pleasurable weeks he had shared with Fermay in his cold, damp flat.

'Shit, you are one moody son of a bitch!' Beth had been watching him closely. 'You spend so much time brooding and moping, you're like Batman with the bats in his head in Wayne Manor. So you got a few bruises and you can't find your girlfriend, y'know, like, so what? Life goes on.'

'Life goes on.' He repeated her words and let them drop to the floor.

'I don't know what Arlene sees in you.' She lit another cigarette, throwing her dying lighter across the room in the direction of the wastebin. 'Look at me. My love life's like Pearl Harbour. Do I complain? A little maybe, but I don't ruin the scenery for everybody else.'

The smoke floated around her, clouding her face, but not her words. David wanted to tell her how much more he was suffering than she imagined, that he had walked into a nightmarish world and somebody had turned off the light and locked the door behind him. He wanted to describe how every time he saw her he spent minutes scanning her face for signs of life, checking for the warm beat of blood in veins, the flare of breathing nostrils.

'You're obviously sold on this Fermay woman – you spend enough time talking about her. What does she mean to you? What makes her so special?'

'What does she mean? Salvation.'

'Why couldn't you just say sex like everyone else? You're always blowing things up into such a big deal. You're like one of my kids, y'know? Get back down to the real world.'

David bristled at Beth's assault. 'Everyone tries to judge what Fermay and I had on their own terms. But it was bigger than a normal relationship. It wasn't just sex. It wasn't even just love. It was life itself, boiled down and put into a bottle. OK, I'll tell you what she means to me. She means never having to be lonely again, never wanting another woman, not having to spend all your life searching for something you can never find. She means love when you've never tasted it before. And she means arguments on wet grass, kissing in doorways while the world walks by, and alienating your best friend. That's what she means.'

Beth was slack-jawed at his outburst until, after a brief break, she whispered, 'Romantic.'

'Cynic.'

The atmosphere dissipated and they found humour together. David was surprised to feel his headache ease too.

As he sipped his coffee, Beth returned to her school project, clipping pictures to size, pasting them on to stiff, coloured card, writing out headings in blocked letters with a sturdy felt-tip pen. She worked diligently, humming to herself as she composed and created. Her actions revealed her dedication to her job, the labour of love that her teaching career secretly was. David had not seen her so at ease with herself; all her fears and worries, her neurotic bursts and nervous energy were lost in a small task and thoughts of her children.

'What kind of project is it?' he asked.

'The history of Mardi Gras,' she replied distractedly. 'It's our biggest annual celebration and I figure the kids should know about their heritage.'

Then he saw it, half obscured by a pile of other photographs, but the merest glimpse drew his eyes like a magnet. There, easily visible on a black and white picture, was a bird's head upon a man's body. He had seen it before . . . when Buffalo Marsayle had appeared to him in the Jazz Museum, drawing him like a fish on a line until they stood in the adjoining Mardi Gras Museum before the picture on the wall. The picture of the bird-headed man.

David jumped from his chair and plucked the photo from the pile. 'Hey!' Beth protested.

'This picture! Tell me about this picture!'

'What is wrong with you? One moment you're a three-toed sloth on valium, then you're a coffee addict on amphetamines. You've got a serious problem.'

'Just tell me about this picture.'

With irritation she snatched it from his hand and studied it before referring to a book beside her. 'Costume of the Krewe of Aidoneus,' she read. 'OK? Satisfied? It's a costume from one of the Mardi Gras krewes.'

'That's right. That's what the label said. *Krewe of Aidoneus.*' David was transfixed by the image: the inhuman mask, its beak cruel and sharp, large enough to rip out a man's heart if it was real. The beady black eyes, staring and emotionless. The flowing, almost regal, white robes. He took the photo back from her, unable to remove his gaze from it. Other memories and thoughts tumbled along in its wake; Willie in the Prince of Wales talking about what he had seen in the alley, the man with the bird mask. Fermay's response. The voice he had heard in the tomb.

Aidoneus is the Devil.

He wondered if Moose had managed to track down any information on the krewe. Maybe it was time David chased him up.

'What do you mean, "That's what the label said"?' Beth was

looking at him like she'd eaten something disgusting. 'What are you on?'

'I'm high on hope,' he said, recalling a slogan from the London clubs. 'Tell me about the krewes and what they have to do with Mardi Gras.'

'Maybe you should join my class on Monday,' she replied tartly. 'It would do your education the world of good.'

'Just answer the questions.'

'OK, OK. Jesus.' She lay on her back, stretching out her legs across the photos and cuttings, and blew a big cloud of smoke into the air. 'The krewes organize the Mardi Gras each year. They have ever since the tradition started. What are they? I guess you'd call them secret societies. There's a whole bunch of them, all with mythological or semi-mythological names like the Mistick Krewe of Comus and the Krewe of Rex. It used to be a society thing, y'know, the idle rich getting together to put on a good show and getting drunk into the bargain. Now there are krewes of all types. Gay krewes. Women-only krewes. The only thing that links them is they keep the identity of their members a secret – in a fun way. It's nothing sinister. The climax of the celebrations is a parade of floats and that's when they all come out of the woodwork, dressing up in cheesy costumes – not forgetting the masks – and throwing out charms and gifts to the assembled masses.'

'What about the Krewe of Aidoneus?'

'They're just one of them. I don't know anything special about Aidoneus. Why are you so interested?'

'I don't know yet. I'm just listening to my . . . inner voices.'

'I'd steer clear of that if I were you. Like, you've got enough problems.'

'How did it all start?'

She shook her head and swore under her breath. 'Hey, I get paid for lecturing. I don't do free sessions.'

'I'll clean the bathroom. Just get on with it. This might be important.'

'Clean the bathroom! Jesus! I've been looking for a man like you all my life. All right. They say the French settlers brought Mardi Gras to N'Orleans. Y'know, Iberville the explorer and his

205

cronies when they sailed up the Mississippi in . . .' She dredged her memory. '. . . 1699. He named the place where he landed Point du Mardi Gras and marked it with some kind of celebration because it was the day before Ash Wednesday, and the start of Lent. I hope you've had some kind of religious education so I don't have to get into that whole thing.' David motioned her to continue. 'The city was founded in 1718 and the Mardi Gras celebrations continued, although at that time they were mainly in the big houses and ballrooms. Poor folk weren't going to be pushed out and they made sure there was some street dancing and partying. The Spanish governors who took over banned it all. No one likes to see people having fun, right? And you can't blame it on the miserable Spaniards because good old Americans continued the ban when we took over the city. The creoles in the French Quarter finally convinced the city fathers it would be a good idea to have fun again in 1827.' David was amused at how Beth's voice had slowly changed, taking on the expressive sing-song stylisms of the teacher.

'It all got out of hand pretty quickly,' she continued. 'The celebrations turned to riots, fighting in the street. Residents were up in arms demanding Mardi Gras be banned for good. It looked like the whole tradition was dead in the water until six men who'd just moved into the city from Mobile, Alabama decided to save the day. They held a meeting with thirteen friends in a room over the Gem Bar on Royal Street and came to the conclusion that only they could keep the carnival going, and then only if they could bring some kind of order to it. They formed a secret society to further their ends and called themselves the Mistick Krewe of Comus. They invented the term *krewe* at that meeting.'

David stared out of the window as he listened. Across the street he could see a woman moving lazily around her apartment. She had a figure like Fermay's, the same confidence and sense of purpose in her movements, like a lioness patrolling her den.

For that one moment he had a sensation of falling, of events hurtling past him at breakneck speed as he plummeted towards a bone-crushing impact. Of what possible relevance was a Mardi Gras society? How was it connected to the hauntings that had plagued him to the edge of madness? All he wanted to do was find Fermay. Why couldn't he just be left alone to locate her in peace?

A sharp rise in Beth's voice signalled that she was aware that his attention was drifting; another teacher's trick. 'Comus decided on a theme for the first parade and that practice still goes on,' she continued. 'They certainly touched something in the public. Within a few years there were secret societies springing up all over the place. Another of the big krewes, the Krewe of Rex, formed in 1872 and they ensured the Royal colours were taken as the official colours of Mardi Gras.'

'What Royal colours?'

'You obviously never had a classical education. Purple, green and gold, signifying justice, faith and power.'

Justice, faith and power. He had faith and he wanted justice. The only one he was missing was power.

'What function do these secret societies perform? Apart from the obvious?'

'They perform a very useful function,' Beth replied with mock gravity. 'They allow dull, rich businessmen and society leaders to dress up and act ridiculous in total anonymity. That release prevents them bottling things up within their straitjacket of conformity and then suddenly going nuts with a rifle in a crowded mall.'

'A boys' club for overpaid white men.'

'I was being a little harsh. That's just a small part of the krewes' attraction. And it's not just for white men. People of colour got their own krewe in 1916, the Zulu Social Aid and Pleasure Club. Each year they have a masked King Zulu to lead their parades. Louis Armstrong was the most famous King Zulu. He did it in 1949.'

'Sounds like everyone in New Orleans is in a secret society.'

'Maybe they are.'

'Are they dangerous?' he asked. 'Are they like secret societies throughout history, ganging up on the little man, the individual?'

Beth laughed. 'Are you some kind of conspiracy nut? These guys are just in it for fun. They may dabble in magic and ritual, or present a façade of mysticism, but make no mistake, they're only interested in the motto *Laissez les bon temps rouler.*'

'And the Krewe of Aidoneus is just one of them?'

'Not even a major player. They never really have a fundamental role in Mardi Gras. They're always there in the background. What's the big interest in them? You want to join up.'

'I'm curious.'

'Yeah, right. Why do I get the feeling there's something you're not telling me?'

David ignored her, lost once more in his thoughts. Dauphine had told him to listen to the spirits and that was just what he was going to do.

David met Moose at the Café du Monde, on a table at the back, far from the street, where they would not be seen. Moose slipped into the seat opposite, grinning as wide as ever, and declined an offer of coffee and beignets.

'Can't stay too long, man. This place is crawlin' with cops. They're all along the waterfront, asking questions about that stiff they pulled out of the water with his head lookin' like a watermelon that got dropped from the fifth floor. Don't get me wrong, man . . . I always stay on the right side of the law. My momma brought me up to know about truth, decency and honesty. It's just I know a lot of folk who don't know 'bout those things. It wouldn't be good for my reputation if they thought I was on speaking terms with the blue boys, you know what I'm sayin'?'

David nodded. 'Do they know who the murder victim was?'

'Some bum. They thought he was a society guy at first – that's why all the interest. They wouldn't have wasted the PD's time and money if they knew he was just some drifter. They were fooled 'cause he was wearin' a tuxedo. Some smart guy in the precinct traced it back to a thrift shop in Houma. Two more days and they'll disappear like they'd never been here an' we won't hear another word about it.'

Briefly an expression of seriousness crossed Moose's face. It was the first time that David had seen any hint that there was more to the hustler than a cartoon grin and a jaunty attitude. His mask came back quickly; Moose was a good actor. 'So, man, I bet you want to know if your money's been well spent?'

'I was getting worried because I hadn't heard from you.'

'This kind of thing ain't easy, man. Not when you're dealing with jokers like this Aidoneus crowd.' He glanced around him when he mentioned their name, his voice dropping to barely more than a whisper. 'To tell you the truth, man, I'm not too happy that I took this job on. The more I find out about this group, the more worried I get. One thing's for sure – they like their secrets. And they don't like snoopers.'

'Are you telling me you can't find anything out?'

'I never welch on an agreement, man. I'm just being *careful*. It's taken a little time, but I think I'm getting close to a guy who might be able to help you out.'

'How long will it take?'

Moose shrugged. 'Soon, man. Don't rush me.' He looked around again and stood up. 'Gotta run, man. Don't like to stay in one place too long with all these cops around. But let me give you a bit of advice. Don't mention Aidoneus to anyone, y'hear. It'll get back to them. They got ears everywhere.'

As he turned to go, David said, 'Moose, do you know what Aidoneus means?'

'Yeah, man. It's another name for the Greek god Hades.'

'The Devil.'

'That's right, man. The Devil himself.'

Chapter 18

The dead had not disturbed David for days, a neglect that was almost as unnerving as their increasingly regular manifestations. As he sat in the morning sun at the Café du Monde, he wondered if they had finally decided to leave him alone. Had he been haunted enough? He doubted it. It was a lull before the storm.

For once Moose was on time, sashaying flamboyantly through the crowd towards David's table with a triumphant grin on his face. Without saying a word, he sat opposite David and laid his palms down on the table, his fingers wide apart. Then he said, 'It's good news day, man. You got your money's worth.'

'I never doubted you for a minute, Moose.'

'There's only one problem . . .'

'I haven't got any more money, Moose. You've drained me out.'

He looked disappointed, but brightened almost immediately. 'No problem, man. I'll take an IOU.'

'Very decent of you,' David said sarcastically. 'So . . . , Aidoneus.'

Moose nodded. 'Weird guys, man. They're like ghosts, always fading into the background. But despite all the odds, I came up with the goods. I found a guy who says he knows more than anyone else outside of the krewe an' he'll tell it all to you . . .'

'. . . if the price is right.'

'Right!' Moose snapped his fingers, and then said in a lowered voice, 'They've got some big secrets, man. Big secrets.'

'Like what?'

'I can't exactly tell you, man, but let's say they're not one hundred per cent on the side of the law, if you know what I mean.'

'Like?' David pressed impatiently.

'Slow down, slow down! Wait till you see my man. He knows it all.' David got the impression that Moose's contact had not revealed anything. 'I've fixed it for you to meet him tomorrow night at a bar called Tipitina's. You know it? No? It's famous, man. Famous! A regular N'Orleans landmark. He'll be at the bar. He's got long hair, grey, tied in a ponytail, and glasses. Weird-lookin' guy. His name's Bill Ligios. Got other names too, but that's the one he'll be usin' tomorrow. Tell him Moose says "Hi".'

'You're not coming with me?'

'No way, man. I never go out after dark.' He stood up. 'Gotta move. Can't stay in the same place for too long. You tell ol' Bill he owes me a favour.'

And then he was gone once again, merging into the crowd as quickly as he had arrived.

Tipitina's was on the edge of the Garden District, off the beaten track for tourists, on a long street which seemed to lack any glamour in the rain which came down in sheets from the night sky. Arlene had told him of the famous names who had performed there, the jazz geniuses and the blues legends. The Neville Brothers called it their home away from home. Professor Longhair was its guardian angel and spiritual guiding light.

David ran from the cab with his collar up and his jacket clutched tightly, but it didn't prevent him getting drenched. He had never seen rain like it. Each drop bulleted down from the heavens to turn the road and sidewalk into one swirling torrent.

In the foyer he shook the rain from him and stomped his feet. A long room stretched to a large stage at the end, the gloom illuminated by spots of light along the bars on opposite walls. Overhead the ceiling soared up into the shadows like the roof of an aircraft hangar. A brief feeling of guilt came over David as he recalled the lie he had told Charlie to get off work for the night.

'I'm sick, Charlie,' he had said on the phone. 'Too sick to come in tonight.'

'You're sick in the head, boy,' the club boss responded with a throaty chuckle. His unusual good nature had made David feel worse.

As he walked into the main room he could see why Ligios had chosen the place for a rendezvous. The subdued lighting provided a discreet atmosphere which kept faces hidden until they flared briefly in the sudden bloom of a cigarette lighter. And when the band came on stage, all eyes would be diverted in that direction, guaranteeing anonymity in the heart of the crowd. He stepped into the heart of the club past a bronze bust of Professor Longhair, its cold metallic eyes fixed eternally on the stage. The punters were thin on the ground, due either to the earliness of the hour – in New Orleans terms – or the downpour. They stood in ones or twos along the bars, guarding Dixies or B-52s as they waited for the entertainment to begin. Bo Diddley rattled away on the sound system.

David spotted Ligios instantly; Moose's description barely did him justice. He was alone at the end of the bar, hunched over his drink like a mourner at a funeral, his grey ponytail lying lank on his back. There was an air of solitude about him, enforced rather than by choice, and as David closed on him he could sense other things: shabbiness, both in dress and attitude, and the bitter whiff of mean-spiritedness.

'Bill Ligios?' He stood just behind Ligios' left shoulder.

Ligios turned around slowly like he had been called out to a gunfight in a Wild West bar. 'Yeah?' His eyes narrowed into a rodent stare.

'Moose says "Hi".'

'Oh yeah. The limey, right?'

'The limey.' David pulled up a stool and ordered a Dixie. He didn't want to shake Ligios' hand; he thought it would be a little too clammy. 'Moose said you could help me.'

'Maybe. Information is a valuable commodity, and it's my bag.' He opened a rectangular tin on the bar and proceeded to construct a roll-up of such minimalism that David was convinced it would be gone in two puffs. 'The Moosemeister says you're checking out the Krewe of Aidoneus, right?' David waited for him to continue as he lit up. 'If it's for your college thesis you'd be safer sticking to one of the other krewes. These guys are bad.'

'Bad as in good or bad as in bad?'

'Bad as in your worst fucking nightmare.' Smoke swirled around his head, but his eyes didn't water or wrinkle. 'I knew one of them once. He was only small time, on their fringes, but he

212

was a fully paid-up member. All these other krewes are filled with society types, bankers and tennis coaches, all Armani suits and aftershave. This guy would have slit your throat and dumped you in the river if you looked at him in the wrong way. He was a mean mother, but the way he told it, he wasn't alone in Aidoneus.'

'Real charity workers.'

Ligios laughed without separating his teeth. Snick, snick, snick. 'The other krewes won't have anything to do with Aidoneus. They're the black sheep of the krewe fraternity. This is all under the surface o'course. Up front everyone is all smiles and million-dollar handshakes like they're best buddies working for the greater good. The other krewes know there's something wrong with Aidoneus . . . they just don't know what it is. And it's not easy to find out. Aidoneus take their secrecy seriously – very seriously. The other krewes treat it like a big game. Charades on the big stage.'

'But you know something, right?'

'Something. Not a lot. Like I say, they're difficult to get into. Members don't talk to outsiders because they know what will happen to them if they do. Aidoneus appeals to people through fear and greed. It's not a joke. Anyone who starts asking questions about them gets stonewalled at first. Then they find they're being *persuaded* not to ask any more questions.'

'They're dangerous?'

Ligios ignored his question. 'This guy I knew, he was the weak link in the chain. There's always one. His problems were worse than anything Aidoneus could threaten him with. He was a junkie, a smackhead. At least he was at the end. When he first got involved with the krewe he was just a regular guy, but the pressures they put him under . . . he was weak. Smack was an easy option.' There was contempt in his voice, like he was one of those people who couldn't abide anything weak because it reminded them too much of their own shortcomings.

Ligios took a long draught of beer and smacked his lips. 'I called round his place one night. He was flyin' high on the snowbird, rambling and raving, talking about all kinds of weird shit. I asked him about Aidoneus. A lot of what he told me didn't make sense 'cause of what he was on, but the bit that did told me what Aidoneus was really about.'

David already knew Ligios was an opportunist. His sneakiness blared like an alarm in every movement and facial expression. David finished his beer and decided to oil the wheels. 'You want a drink?'

Ligios jumped at the offer. 'You're OK,' he said, greedily finishing the warm, flat beer in his own bottle.

While they had been talking, a young guitarist had walked on to centre stage, his shyness frozen in the coloured spotlights. He plugged his Les Paul into an amp. David watched him while he waited for the drinks to arrive, recognizing the unfocused eagerness and nerves of the support act. The guitarist was young and serious, snappily dressed, and there was a glistening sheen of sweat on his brow. Briefly he looked into the audience and managed a flicker of a smile before bowing his head to play.

David was surprised at his skill. His fingers scurried across the fretboard like a veteran, picking and dancing with a mad jerkiness. The music he produced was frantic at first, but eventually it eased into familiar blues riffs given new life by a dazzling technique. He was a star in the making. David was so impressed he subconciously held his breath, mesmerized by the lone figure engrossed in his own world. He wondered if this was how people had felt when they saw the young Jimi Hendrix.

When the beer arrived the spell was broken and he glanced around the club to see how many others had been privileged to witness the brilliant performer. His slow scan halted by two figures standing next to the bust of Professor Longhair. The signs registered instantly, obvious through familiarity despite their subtlety. The staring, unblinking eyes. The faint grey tint to their skin. The stiffness of their limbs.

Even here, he thought. Was there nowhere he was free of them?

The dead watched the stage, like moths before a candle, as bedazzled as any living member of the audience. David wondered if they could still appreciate the music, warming whatever spark of soul remained within them, or if it merely reminded them of what they had lost. They seemed to be enjoying the performance, if that was possible, although there was an air of sadness around them.

As he stared, one of them turned its head and looked at him. For a second its face was blank, and then it winked, its mouth splitting in a knowing grin, at once mean and amused.

David shivered and turned back to the bar. He gulped at his beer and almost choked as it bubbled up and sprayed down his chin.

'See someone you know?' Ligios asked.

'I have friends all over the place,' David replied. 'Tell me what your man said about Aidoneus.'

'From what I could make out, they've got some kind of hidden agenda – I don't think even he knew exactly. Like I said, he was small-time. But he heard enough to know the Mardi Gras was only a front. Randy used to run smack for them, picking it up at the docks and distributing it to pushers around the city. That's when his problems started. What a feeb. Everyone knows you don't sample the wares.

'Drugs were just a part of it,' Ligios continued in his lazy, drawling voice. 'According to Randy, these guys are like the Mob. If there are a few bucks to be made, they're in – prostitution, gambling, pornography, you name it. Fast cash and dirty.' He laughed. 'If all those charity bigwigs knew where their fat cheques were coming from!'

'If they're that big, that influential, someone must know about them. The police, for instance.'

Ligios' face darkened. 'They're very careful. Randy was scared of them. Nobody crossed them. Nobody.'

'Apart from a junkie with loose lips.'

'Yeah . . . Randy. He died a few weeks later. O.D.'d.' The way his voice trailed off implied he was not convinced that was the sole cause of death.

'Are *you* scared of them?'

He shrugged, fixing his eyes on his beer bottle. 'I keep out of their way.'

'Unless there's some money to be made.'

'We've all got to eat.' He sipped his drink, then added, 'I'm careful.'

David was intrigued, but he wanted more. The connections were still not apparent.

'Is that all you know?'

'No.' He emptied his beer and waited for David to buy him another. 'I know one of the big men involved. At least I know where he lives. It was the one piece of information Randy had that was any good. He'd found out by accident, following the guy he reported to to a meeting, and then following one of the others from there. He thought it would be good insurance if he ever fucked up. And he wasted it by telling me when he was high as a kite.' Ligios, like the seasoned informant that he was, had saved the best information until last.

'Can you show me where he lives?'

Ligios nodded, but he remained silent. David slid some cash across the counter, money he had borrowed from Arlene, and it was snatched before anyone could see. For a moment David wondered if he was wasting his energy on a wild-goose chase when he should really be concentrating on finding Fermay. But Buffalo Marsayle's dead stare, lingering in his mind as it always did, convinced him otherwise.

Ligios gave a vulpine smile. 'My car's out back. I'll take you there.'

The journey was shorter than David anticipated. They had barely begun to cruise through the rain-drenched empty streets before Ligios was bringing the car to a halt in the umbra between two streetlamps. With a hollow feeling, David realized the destination before Ligios pointed it out.

Broussard's house was ablaze with light in the night, opulent but not outstanding, a normal house in a normal street. It was a mask; secrets lived behind it.

'He lives there,' Ligios said. 'I don't know who he is . . . I don't care. But look at that place. Who said crime didn't pay?'

David could barely hear him; his head was spinning with converging thoughts. Like the mystical serpent that eats its own tail, his lines of enquiry had folded back upon themselves. It was all connected! He thought he had been pursuing *two* mysteries – Marsayle-and-the-krewe-and-the-ghosts, and Fermay. But there was only one. Just one, and it was all the bigger and more frightening for that.

With this realization came the knowledge that the unknown had been manipulating his life: his search for a missing girlfriend; Broussard and his attempt on his life; the dead that were haunting him at every turn.

All intertwined.

But more frightening than that was one simple connection. He thought about Fermay – and the dead.

Somehow they were linked.

Chapter 19

David lounged in the armchair in Beth's sitting room, staring at the TV with the sound turned down. He was not really watching it, merely allowing the flickering picture to lull him into a state where he could concentrate on the jumbled thoughts swishing around in his head like the contents of a washing machine.

Arlene slid on to the sofa, her knees tightly together, her hands clasped on the purse in her lap. The wrinkles around her eyes seemed to have faded slightly, or perhaps it was just the make-up. In fact there was a bloom about her, a brightness that gleamed.

'How's Scuba?' he asked.

'He's gone away for a few days. Lying low, I guess.'

'Relieved?'

'You betcha. I needed some time on my own.'

'It's doing you good.'

'Flatterer.' She almost blushed. 'So what's wrong?'

He raised his hands as if the weight of the world was upon them. 'Do you ever feel life's a steamroller pounding you into the asphalt each time you try to direct it?'

'Every day around 10 a.m. Don't tell me you've only just found that out?'

Her smile briefly freed him of his burden. 'I'm afraid Fermay's tied up with a bunch of crooks,' he said despondently. 'I knew her guardian wasn't a saint after what he had done to me, but now it seems like he's some kind of gang boss.'

'You still think she's being held against her will?'

'Yes.'

'Then go to the cops.'

He shook his head. 'What could I tell them? I *think* my girlfriend is being held prisoner by a man I *think* is the new Al Capone? That would get me a few laughs, wouldn't it? All I've got is rumour and gossip.'

'They'll still listen, David. Like, the cops aren't my favourite

218

people in the world, but, y'know, they might be able to give you some advice. They might have a file on this guy. What you've got to tell them could be the break they're looking for.'

David thought about what she said and decided that it was worth a shot. He had nothing to lose.

'And,' Arlene continued, 'if you tell them about this guy he won't dare do anything against you.'

That sealed it.

The police precinct was like a hundred others he had seen on TV cop shows, filled with recognizable characters, even recognizable faces. David wondered if police precincts all over America had slowly mutated, adopting the template presented to them by the TV networks. *Hill Street Blues* equals Anywhere, USA. There was a dinginess to the interior, not enough to appear rundown, but enough to let people know *Work Is Done Here and we have no time to be tidy*.

Second thoughts were already infiltrating his mind when he presented himself at the desk. They're going to laugh at me, he thought. *They're going to humiliate me*.

It was nothing so obvious. The cop behind the desk let his mouth twitch dismissively beneath his bristling moustache while listening to David's story. David had honed it to what he thought was a simple and effective tale: his girlfriend had gone missing and he had circumstantial evidence that she was being held against her will at the house of her guardian. That was a lie, of course; all he had was his own instinct, suspicion and fears, but if it gained him access to a detective it was enough.

'So is this Missing Persons?' The policeman eyed him like he was time-wasting pond life.

'Not exactly . . .'

'What exactly?'

'I just told you . . .'

'Kidnapping? Assault? Imprisonment against will?'

'That's more like it.'

'That's more like it,' he repeated as if David had sworn at him. 'Wait here.' He turned and punched out a number on the internal phone. The desk clerk's words were muffled, deliberately

David guessed, and he didn't like the tone. Finishing his conversation, the clerk turned back to David and said, 'He'll be out in a minute. Sit down.' He motioned to a row of rickety chairs.

The detective looked bored and world-weary. His eyelids were permanently half-closed like a dog on a hot day and nothing held his attention long enough for him to focus on it. With a deep sigh, he waved for David to follow him. They passed through a room of raised voices and tapping computer keyboards, yellow walls glaring sickly beneath the strip lights. Through the window the setting sun provided a fiery contrast, turning the sky a charnel red as it disappeared beyond the horizon.

The detective eased behind his desk and signed on at his computer terminal. He pointed to an empty chair on the other side of the desk. The lack of verbal communication was starting to irritate David, but before he could voice this, the detective was firing questions at him in a clipped monotone. David gave his name and nationality, but for some reason he decided to give his address as the Sonesta; he was still paranoid about anyone knowing where he lived.

The detective listened emotionlessly, dutifully tapping the report into the computer, while David explained about his search for Fermay and his fears that Broussard was holding her against her will.

'Broussard's involved in some dirty business,' David stressed.

'Yeah? Like what?' The detective took a mouthful of coffee from a plastic cup on his desk, grimaced, and then tossed it into his wastepaper basket.

'Drug smuggling, for one.'

Instantly the detective was attentive, his eyebrows raised, his gaze fixed for the first time on David's face. 'Whaddaya know?'

'Just what I heard. Broussard is involved with one of the Mardi Gras krewes, Aidoneus, but it's just a front for criminal activities.'

'You got proof?'

'No, but it should be easy to get.'

The detective mused for a moment, staring blankly at his computer screen. Then he said simply, 'Wait here,' before disappearing into the activity at the centre of the large, open-plan office.

David wasn't kept waiting long. Within minutes the detective was striding back across the room with another man in his wake, their faces serious and hard. His companion was tall with silvery hair and an ashen complexion so that he seemed to have had the colour bleached out of him. His cheeks were hollow and his skin lined like someone who had battled against a debilitating illness.

He stuck out his hand – the first one to have done so – and shook David's. 'The name's Krugman,' he said in a throaty voice. 'Kowalski told me what you had to say. I think we should talk. Let's go somewhere more private.'

Krugman was obviously the superior. Kowalski slinked back behind his desk as the grey man took David into an office with a glass wall looking out over the main room. It was airy and dark with pot plants dotted around and an expensive leather sofa along one wall. Krugman motioned for David to sit.

'Coffee?' he asked.

David nodded and Krugman poured him a steaming cup from a pot on a table near the outside window. 'I seem to be getting the five-star treatment now,' David pointed out. 'Ten minutes ago I felt like I'd mugged a tourist.'

Krugman sat on the edge of his desk, relaxed but unsmiling, uncommonly at ease compared to his colleagues; the casualness that comes from power. 'You've got to remember these guys are overworked and underpaid. They're dealing with the scum of the city all day every day. I'm sure you can forgive them a little bad humour. Smoke?' He proffered a packet of Marlborough. David declined. 'So,' he continued, 'the Krewe of Aidoneus.'

'You know them?'

'I know of them. They're very well respected. *Very* well respected. A lot of charities are better off for their good work. And they always put on a good float for Mardi Gras and a good party afterwards. What you told Kowalski doesn't seem to be in line with that.'

'One of the men involved in running the krewe is this rich bloke who owns a huge mansion in the Garden District. Eugene Broussard. You might have heard of him.'

221

Krugman thought for a moment and then raised his hands and shook his head. 'I don't recall hearing his name. But this is a big city. I don't know everybody.'

'Broussard had me beaten up and left for dead. He's got a mean streak a mile wide behind his smooth exterior. He controls what Aidoneus does – drugs, prostitution, gambling – according to my information. And he's holding my girlfriend against her will.' David felt the heat of anger when he thought of Broussard.

'Right. Your girlfriend. What was her name again?'

'Fermay Grey.'

'Nice name. Lyrical.' He waved through the glass window at Kowalski who had one eye on a newspaper and one hand in a carton of McDonald's fries. He dropped both when he saw Krugman beckon to him and hurried across the room.

Slightly out of breath, he poked his head around the door, wary of stepping over the threshold. 'Yes, boss?'

'Have you checked out that name?'

'Yes, boss. Fermay Grey. No listing. No driver's licence. No Social Security number. As far as the authorities are concerned, she doesn't exist.'

'OK, Kowalski. Thanks.'

When Kowalski had closed the door, Krugman turned back to David who leapt in before he could speak. 'I'm not making this up.'

Krugman shrugged. 'There are plenty of people in America who aren't on official records. The legacy of the sixties – all that hippie paranoia about Big Brother watching. Maybe your Fermay Grey is one of them.' He paused briefly and looked into the depths of his coffee cup. When he spoke again his voice had grown harsher. The pretence at conviviality was gone. 'So, you expect me to believe you?'

'What do you mean?'

'Well, it's a fucking unbelievable story if you'll pardon my French. You wander in off the street, some tourist, and tell me a pillar of the community is some kind of gang boss. Then you start making all these other accusations for which I have to take your word because there's no proof – just your "information". Maybe I should just go round there and arrest him now.'

David's ears burned, but he could understand Krugman's point of view. 'I know . . .' He paused, searching for the right words. 'I know it sounds flimsy, but it's all true.'

'Well, let me tell you a fact about the law. It doesn't matter if it's *true*, just as long as it can be proved. Are you going to give me some proof?'

'I can't give you proof about the drugs and prostitution and all that, but if you know Broussard is involved surely you can stake him out and pin something on him.'

'Like, I've got men and time to waste on your say-so.'

'To be honest, I don't care. I just wanted to help you out so you'd help me. He had me beaten up and stuffed in a grave in the cemetery. That's a fact.'

'You want to fill out a report on that?'

'No, I want to find my girlfriend. I know he's got her there. I *know* it. She wouldn't stay in that house with him of her own free will. I know he's tied up in all this other stuff too and I think if you can get Fermay away from him, one thing will lead to another.'

Krugman tapped his pen on his pad and thought about what David was saying. 'This could work out well for you,' David continued.

'Can you get me any more information?'

'I might be able to.'

'If you're fucking wasting my time you'll be down in those cells so quick you won't know what hit you.'

'I'm not wasting your time, believe me. I wouldn't be here if I wasn't sure. I know the consequences.'

Krugman sighed. 'Maybe I believe you, maybe I don't. To tell you the truth, we've heard the word about this fucking Aidoneus krewe, but we've never been able to pin anything on them. People don't talk. Even with the Cosa Nostra you get some slimeball ratting, but not with these fuckers. Everybody's too scared. Nobody's ever mentioned this Broussard guy in connection with them before, though. How'd you find out about that?'

'I can't tell you.'

Krugman raised his arms in the air. 'There you fucking go again! How am I supposed to do my job if you're tight as a clam?'

'I'm sorry. I was sworn to secrecy.' If he was less honourable he might have thrown Ligios' name into the arena just to see him harassed by the police. The small-time crook deserved it.

Krugman studied David's face so intently he made him feel he was under a microscope. The grey man was reading him, trying to see if he added up. 'OK, let's say – and God knows why – that you've got something. How many other people know about this Broussard connection?'

'I don't know. I haven't told anyone.' David paused. 'Look, I'm not trying to be obstructive here . . .'

'Yeah, yeah, I know,' Krugman said wearily. 'I'm just protecting my ass. If I go sniffing round some rich, society guy without good reason I'm putting my job on the line.'

'Can you help me?'

'Well, I'm not going to send you away just in case this whole fairy story is true. Maybe we should start with the girl. That's one way into it. I'm going to take some notes, OK?'

'Go right ahead.'

Krugman sat behind his desk and scribbled on a thick pad. 'Where did you meet her?'

'In London. She was on holiday . . . vacation. She picked me up in a bar.'

Krugman nodded, still scribbling. 'How did this Broussard guy get hold of her. And why?'

'I don't know. I mean, I know he's her guardian, but I've lost part of my memory. There's a period around the time we separated that just won't come back. I don't even remember coming to America.'

Krugman looked at him with a *What next?* expression. 'Excuse me?'

David elaborated. 'Pieces of it keep coming back . . .'

'But?'

'Not the important things. Not yet.'

Krugman stared for another full minute until David began to feel uncomfortable. Somewhere someone was whistling the theme to *The Odd Couple,* but in the office the silence seemed leaden. For a second the atmosphere strained to breaking point, and then Krugman laughed loudly. 'I don't fucking believe it.

224

You've got no proof, and you're an amnesiac! If I didn't know better I'd think I was being set up here. Candid fucking Camera.' He threw his pen across the desk in mock disgust.

'What about Fermay?' David asked.

Krugman's laughter seemed to have broken the ice. 'Look, I'll do what I can. You've convinced me that you *think* you're right, but you've got to be patient. I can't head straight down there with a SWAT team and kick down the door.'

'All I've done so far is be *patient*. I can never decide on the right move so I just sit around doing nothing.'

'Best way,' Krugman said with a tight smile. 'People who go blundering in get their fingers burned.' He swallowed his coffee and crunched up his plastic cup, tossing it the full length of the room into a basket with unerring aim. 'So how long are you planning on staying here?'

'Till my money runs out,' David lied once more.

Krugman nodded sagely. 'Yeah, I'd do the same if my wife upped and vanished on me. Some things are more important than anything, right? You've just got to do them, whatever happens to you. Are you keeping in touch with your people back home?'

David shook his head. 'There's no one back home.'

Krugman rose from his desk and stretched, groaning as various bones clicked into place. 'I'll go get the file on Aidoneus. We'll run through it, see if there's any more you can add. Then I'll decide what I'm going to do about you and your flights of fancy.' He laughed harshly. 'Can you spare the time?'

David nodded. What a stupid question. He'd wait twenty-four hours a day if it got him any closer to finding Fermay.

'OK . . . I might be a while. The files are kept on the other side of the building. Help yourself to coffee and if you want anything to eat, call Kowalski. We'll discuss what we can do about your girlfriend when I get back.'

The door clicked behind him and the room suddenly grew quiet. The hubbub from the main office was muffled by the glass, a dim background drone that was almost restful in the shadowy office. David closed his eyes and pictured Fermay's face floating

225

in the dark. How much longer would it be before he saw her again?

Through the window he could see the moon, large and full, an ivory eye. The sky was clear above the rooftops, although the streetlights drowned out any stars which might have been sprinkled there. During the day it had grown hotter and hotter; it was still uncomfortably warm and even though the office was air-conditioned David could feel his shirt sticking to him along his spine and under his arms. Fog one day, torrential rain the next, and now a heatwave. What was happening? There was no stability any more. And certainly none in his own life: no home, no mundane job, no old friends.

And now where was Krugman? It seemed like he'd been gone for almost half an hour. David's irritation was compounded by another sensation, nudging gently on the edge of his perception, an odd feeling. Like someone was calling to him faintly, but just beyond his hearing.

He looked around curiously. Then, through the glass, in the main office, something shifted, a trick of the light. Unwillingly, David recognized the experience. Slowly the ambience changed; the shadows shifted of their own accord to new, unnatural positions and the very air seemed to sing. His stomach did its usual freefall flip and there was a snap as reality popped inside out.

Buffalo Marsayle stood in the centre of the brightly lit room, tall and erect, while detectives wandered and chatted around him and hookers and dips slumped sullenly in chairs nearby. Yet those living, warm-blooded men and women seemed indistinct and grey, like ghosts, while Marsayle, in contrast, had bloom and substance. His unblinking stare, locked on to David and for one moment all of Marsayle's bitterness and anger leapt along it, striking David with such force that he could not find the strength to power his arms and legs.

'What now?' David whispered. He had the certain feeling that Marsayle could kill him if he wanted to. Stop his heart dead. Suck the air from his lungs. Contempt radiated from the dead jazz player's cold eyes.

226

Slowly, Marsayle moved. David was prepared for a slow advancement across the room until death was in Krugman's office with him. Instead Marsayle merely raised his right arm and pointed. His stare never left David's face.

For a long moment David watched the pointing spectral figure until curiosity overcame the fear that had built within him. Marsayle seemed to be pointing to the window on the outside wall of the room.

His skin crawling, David shakily raised himself from the sofa and walked over to the window in Krugman's office, all the time keeping one eye on Marsayle.

The window looked out on to a courtyard surrounded by police precinct buildings two floors below. Two patrol cars were parked in the shadows near one wall, but there was no sign of life. As he watched, another car drove smoothly into the courtyard, its headlights washing whitely over the buildings. It swung around in an arc and came to a halt. There were no police markings on it.

Immediately two men climbed out and walked quickly across the yard towards a lighted entrance to David's right. He recognized them the moment the light coloured their faces.

It was Lynch and Frantz.

Before they could enter the building, Krugman walked out and shook them warmly by the hand. There was a moment of animated conversation and then the three of them entered the building together.

David's senses suddenly screamed in alarm. *Move! Get out of there.* Krugman had tipped off Broussard. The policeman was involved. Maybe he was even a member of Aidoneus.

Trying not to appear panicked or conspicuous, David stepped out of Krugman's office into the main room. Marsayle was no longer there; everything was back as it had been. Why had he aided David once more? If Marsayle had not appeared, David would have waited in Krugman's office until Lynch and Frantz arrived and his life would have ended up in their hands. He did not know what Marsayle might want in return, but he had just time to act on his warning.

Kowalski was lost in his newspaper and everyone else was

immersed in their own particular troubles. Near the window a woman had burst into tears, sobs convulsing her body. She began to draw attention, allowing David to make his escape. Fixing his gaze on the floor, he ambled in the direction of the exit.

'Hey. Where are you going?'

David recognized Kowalski's gruff voice. He glanced up, sizing up the distance to the door, wondering whether to make a dash for it. It was too far.

He turned and smiled. 'The john.'

Kowalski pointed in the opposite direction, to a door at the far side of the room leading into the heart of the precinct. 'Out there. Turn left. Don't get lost.'

David nodded in thanks and spun round on his heels, trying to hide the worried expression on his face. That way would take him in the direction of the returning Krugman with Lynch and Frantz.

He glanced back at Kowalski. The detective was watching him closely. He pointed towards the door once more.

David had no choice. He walked towards the door without wishing to be seen to be rushing, yet anxious to get out quickly. Slipping through it, the office noise faded behind him as he found himself in a long, dingy corridor with several rooms leading off it. He paused, listening for Krugman and the others approaching, but he could hear nothing.

Which way? He looked right and left, made his decision and turned left, afraid to run in case his footsteps attracted attention.

The corridor turned sharply to the right and he continued along it, cautiously stopping every now and then to listen, his mind racing ahead of him. Police stations would, he presumed, have only one public entrance with the rest of the exits carefully monitored or secured. He suddenly thought about security cameras and checked above him. Nothing. But it was something else to think about.

Rounding the next corner, he was confronted by a stairwell and the sound of someone coming up it. He recognized Krugman's laconic voice. Hurriedly he back-pedalled, selecting one of the doors off the corridor. The office within was empty and obviously surplus to requirements, the only furniture an old table with a bent leg. Sheets of paper were scattered across the floor.

He pushed the door to, leaving a small crack so he could eavesdrop on Krugman and company. His heart was pounding so much he doubted he would even hear what they said.

Lynch's voice came to him first, cold and almost robotic. 'That little jerk must have a charmed life.'

'Don't worry.' Krugman's voice was soothing. 'You'll get a chance to make sure. He's sitting in my office right now, dreaming of his lady love.' Laughter followed from all three of them. 'Boy, is he in for a shock. Where are you going to take him? To Pontchartrain?'

'Yeah, somewhere where he won't be found any time soon. If we weigh down his body, he'll stay at the bottom of the lake.'

'Mr Broussard says we can't make any mistakes now.' This time it was Frantz. 'Things are too finely balanced.'

'If we fuck up now, we fuck up big.' Lynch again. 'There's too much at stake – for all of us.' The last four words were intoned darkly and ominously.

'And a lot to gain,' Krugman stressed. 'The kingdom of heaven on earth. It's a big prize and it's worth the risk.'

'I'm still worried,' Frantz said. 'When a storm this big is building, people get hurt in the crosswinds. People get killed.'

'Don't worry,' Lynch snapped. 'We've only got this kid to worry about. Everything else is going fine now. Once the little prick is dead meat there'll be nothing in the way.'

'Happy days are here again!' Krugman said in a singsong voice, punctuating it with a laugh.

Their voices faded as they marched around the corner in the corridor with only the echoes of their footsteps signifying their passing. There was little time for David to consider what he had overheard. Krugman would raise the alarm as soon as he discovered his office was empty. If David was not out of the building by then, they would shut down all exits and methodically search the precinct until they found him.

His heart was still triphammering as he moved back out into the corridor and hurried to the stairwell. His few options were already flashing through his mind. If he tried to get out through

229

the courtyard there was a chance he would be seen from one of the myriad windows overlooking it. His best bet would be to go through the basement garage. He had passed the downward ramp to the employees' carpark when he'd arrived at the precinct and he recalled there was only one bored and distracted cop in a security box manning the entrance barrier. Traffic going in and out would be thin at that time of early evening. There was a chance he could slip out without the guard seeing him. A slim chance.

More voices floated up from the bottom of the stairwell as he pondered his choice. Two men, climbing the stairs slowly. If he had to keep returning to his hiding place he would never make any headway. Looking around, he spotted a service elevator nearby, 'For Maintenance Use Only' sprayed across the door. Anxiously he thumbed the call button. Shifting from foot to foot to release the tension, he flashed nervous glances at the stairs. He heard the lift trundle into life, rattling and clanking as if it was in its last days.

The voices drew closer.

As the backs of their heads rose above floor level, the lift arrived with a clunk and the doors rumbled open. David leapt in nimbly, hammering the basement button with the palm of his hand as he took refuge at the back wall out of sight. After what seemed like an age the doors finally closed and the lift began its slow, downward journey. David dropped to his haunches and let the air whistle out between his lips in relief.

There was a thick odour of petrol and exhaust fumes hanging in the starkly lit concrete basement garage that greeted him on his descent. Cars were dotted around irregularly, but most of the parking bays were empty. It took David a split second to scan the basement and satisfy himself there was no one around. The security cameras roved dangerously in the corners.

He fell to his knees as if he had been poleaxed. Had he been quick enough? He prayed the duty officer had been preoccupied with the latest bestseller or the sports reports and had not been watching the screens. Like a large beetle David scurried across the dusty floor among the cars, Gregor Samsa looking for a way out of his life.

He came to a halt next to a patrol car, resting against the wheel arch to catch his breath. So far he had been lucky. No one had spotted him. But ahead of him lay an expanse of thirty or forty yards of open floor before the next car which he could use as cover. If he made that he would be across the floor and on to the exit ramp. Holding his breath, he steeled himself for the dash, knowing that Krugman could be raising the alarm by now.

Before he could move, the door of the patrol car swung open with a juddering creak right across his path. David went rigid with shock. There had been no one in the car; he had checked before considering his run. Unable to contain himself, he crept forward and peered around the frame into the front seat.

His breath choked in his throat. Seated behind the wheel was a policeman, the upper part of his blue shirt stained dark and wet with blood. His skin was patchworked with the greyness of long-time death. An angry red hole marred his temple where the bullet had penetrated and David could see part of the back of his head was missing where it had exited.

Slowly it turned to look at him and smiled with grim satisfaction. 'Hey kid, wanna ride?'

David could smell the belching stench of the grave on the blast of air which evacuated the dead cop's mouth. He was not alone. Sitting next to him was a little girl, about six years old. She was wearing a white summer dress and her blonde hair was braided into plaits. In stark contrast, her face was bright blue and black around the eyes and nose; her tongue protruded, purple and distended. Around her throat were marks where fingers had been ground in to choke the life from her. Her hand rested in the dead cop's lap, an eternal caress for her teaser and tormentor.

'Suicide is painless,' the cop said. 'It brings on many changes.'

David stumbled backwards, but the dead man moved like lightning, grabbing his wrist and hauling him forward until foetid breath blasted David's face from only six inches. 'Don't go,' he said. 'We've been alone so long, Susie and me. Nobody plays with us now. But you can. You can see us. Stay and play. Susie plays very well. I've taught her lots of games.'

The dead were everywhere, paying for their lifetime sins in a purgatory where few of the living could see them, David realized.

'You're nearly one of us,' the dead cop continued. 'Stay and play.'

'I'm not one of you!' David yelled, yanking his arm away. He rolled over backwards on to the concrete floor.

'You were that close to joining us.' The cop drew his grey thumb and forefinger close together, reminding David of a similar comment by Dauphine. 'At the last minute you missed out. But you're still near enough, near enough to touch. All it will take is for one of us to reach out and pull you over the edge . . .'

'No!'

He slammed the door with such force that the car rocked. Through the window David could see the interior was now empty. Realizing time was running out for him in more ways than one, he turned and ran.

Ignoring the security cameras, he concentrated on one last, frantic, win or lose, dash for freedom. His pumping legs carried him past the final car and on to the ramp in a matter of seconds. Ahead of him was the guard's booth. The cop had his head down in some magazine. David kept running.

As he neared the booth he heard the radio within blare into life. 'All exits, look out for Caucasian male, mid twenties, black hair, attempting to leave the precinct. Could be dangerous. Repeat. Could . . .'

The adrenaline surging through David's system kept him going at maximum speed. He didn't even look at the guard as he passed, dodging under the security barrier and then taking a sharp left out of the building, weaving through the traffic like a man possessed as the guard's angry voice floated behind him. And then he was in the crowds and in the backstreets before there was any chance of pursuit, breathlessly putting as much distance between him and the precinct as he could before he rested.

Finally he slipped into an alley and slumped to the ground behind a pile of cardboard boxes. His throat burned from the exertion. His head ached from the strain, his hands trembling from delayed shock.

In that alley, the knowledge dawned on him that he could trust no one. The Krewe of Aidoneus had members anywhere and everywhere, their mesh of misdoings closing about him. And the dead, they too were getting closer and more daring. Marsayle might have *saved* his life, but the dead cop had confirmed what David suspected: that some of them – the ones that resented those who were still warm and quick – *wanted* his life.

There was no escape.

Chapter 20

'I'll tell you, David, I don't like her.'

Willie was adamant. He avoided David's eyes and there was a sour expression on his face that he made no attempt to hide.

'I don't want to hear, Willie.'

Willie swigged on his beer and peered at the stage in a pretence of interest at the roadies setting up the equipment. The Jazz Attic was full to bursting, a shoulder-to-shoulder logjam that pushed the temperature up to a summer heat-wave despite the winter chill outside. 'You're mad, David,' he said, almost whispering, his eyes focused on a red amp light. 'You used to be down to earth. In control. This woman has got you acting like a zombie. You're so under her spell you can't see what's really happening. You're like a junkie who can't accept his favourite recreational drug is killing him a little each day.'

'Don't call her "This woman".' David's annoyance gushed out. 'She's got a name. Fermay Grey. Use it.'

'Listen to you. Need another fix, David? You're getting rather irritable.'

David shook his head dismissively and looked away into the crowd. It was too smokey. He couldn't breathe.

'Maybe she's not a bad person,' Willie continued, on a roll now, 'but she's got secrets. She's hiding things from you. You can't trust someone like that.'

'Why don't you just accept her, Willie. It's like you don't want me to be happy. And I *am* happy with Fermay. Shit, neither of us has got much in this life. Let me have this one thing without giving me a hard time about it.'

Willie rounded on him, his cheeks flaring. 'Do you think I'm so fucking selfish?' he hissed. 'After all these years, do you think that?'

234

David backed down a little, astonished at Willie's emotion. 'No, but . . .'

'I've got an objective viewpoint of your relationship, David, something you can't see from within your cosy little cocoon. And despite what you might think, I have your best interests at heart. I can see how much you've changed. You blindly accept everything she says, however ridiculous it sounds . . .'

'You call it blindly accepting, I call it trust.'

'This is about more than dialectics, David. She's leading you down a road where, at the very least, you stand to get emotionally hurt. And badly. Who knows what things she's involved in? Certainly not you, because she won't tell you. You know as well as I do that she's scared of something. She's on the run. Why do you think she moved in with you so quickly? Why do you think she's so eager to give up her life in America for a man she hardly knows?'

'Despite what *you* might think, Willie, I'm not stupid. I can see she's scared. I know she's running away. But there's one thing you can't see from your objective viewpoint and that's how much we care for each other. Yes, it is hard to believe, but as I keep saying to you, I love her. And yes, I know it's happened remarkably quickly. A few weeks ago I wouldn't have believed it either. Because of that love I know I can trust her. And she trusts me. I won't betray her.'

'None are so blind . . .'

'Don't slip into clichés, Willie. It's always a sign of defeat. You were doing so well until then.' His mouth was sticky, the beer tasted terrible and he had lost sight of Fermay through the crowd.

Willie's sigh was a mixture of exasperation and irritation, building from the very centre of him, like that of a man who has failed in his attempt to argue that two plus two equals four. 'For your sake I'll let it drop . . . for now. You'll never convince me about her. At least until she comes clean about whatever she's hiding.'

'Whatever, Willie. Just as long as you don't bend my ear about it.' Relieved, David spotted Fermay heading back from the bar. Her face was a mask of concentration as she manoeuvred her way through the throng, clutching three bottles of Dos Equis. She smiled when she noticed him looking at her.

'Miss me?' she said, handing out the bottles.

Willie made a vomiting noise in his throat.

Fermay's head snapped round and she fixed Willie with an icy stare. 'Sorry, are you feeling left out?'

'I'm feeling positively nauseous, actually.' David heard the familiar twang of alcohol in his voice. Too much beer was adding to Willie's volatility. David's cheeks coloured slightly, partly in annoyance, but mainly in embarrassment. He felt as responsible for Willie in front of Fermay as he did when he was protecting Fermay from Willie's caustic tongue.

Willie sensed David's feelings and shook his head resignedly. 'I get the feeling I'm no longer required around here. I'm going to hit the road.'

'Come on Willie, don't be like that.' David reached out a steadying hand, but Willie shook him off.

'I'm feeling all green and hairy – a human gooseberry. Catch you later, kids.' He smiled humourlessly and disappeared into the crowd before David could stop him.

'What do you see in such a childish person?' Fermay asked coldly.

David sighed. 'Don't you start.'

They clung together like a sailor lashed to the mast in a storm. Revelling in their drunkenness, they floated on the joyous swell of the crowd responding to the vibrant, uplifting music of the band. The jazz was the best David had heard in weeks, or maybe it was just the company. Holding her there, his arms around her waist, he felt more secure than he ever had done. Together they could face anything.

There was a flurry of snow in the air as they walked home, and it reminded David of Christmas although the holiday had been as wet and dismal as ever. He wished Fermay had been around to share it with him. There would be other Christmases, he told himself.

Fermay wanted to hang around in Brixton High Street

until there was enough snow to have a snowball fight. David told her the Louisiana sun had melted her brain and that they should get home before they both turned blue.

As usual, they began to sing various golden oldies, encouraging each other to join in with mock harmonizing. David's voice broke halfway through a verse of 'No Regrets' and they collapsed together in a drunken fit of giggles.

'I have no regrets,' he repeated, kissing her. 'No regrets at all.'

That started them talking about regrets, in a jokey way at first, but becoming more serious as they progressed, the cold slowly damping the warm flush of alcohol. Eventually Fermay admitted that she did have one regret.

'I wish I had known my parents,' she said wistfully. 'I don't remember them at all. It's like I suddenly existed, out of nowhere, you know, like there's no sense of continuity. I have no feeling that I'm a product of a family or that I have any heritage. Can you imagine what that feels like?' In her eyes there was a look of such loneliness that his heart fell.

'I can guess,' he replied. He waited for her to continue, aware that the humour had faded.

'I lie awake at night thinking about them,' she said wanly, 'and sometimes I can almost see their faces.' She smiled. 'At least, what I imagine they look like.'

'Don't you know?' David asked in surprise. 'Don't you have any photos of them?'

'That wasn't allowed.'

Her comment brought him up sharply. 'Not allowed by whom?'

'I wish I'd known them,' she continued, pointedly ignoring his question. 'So many things might have turned out differently. I miss all those things people take for granted ... family vacations, birthday parties, Christmas. I've never had a Christmas present.'

She smiled sadly as surprise registered on David's face. 'Who brought you up? Jack and Jane Scrooge?'

'A friend of my parents. He was very ... strict.'

'I'll say! It sounds like you've been in prison all your life.'

237

'Yes,' she replied thoughtfully. 'I've been in prison. But now I'm free. And I'm never going back there again.'

David laughed in response to the boisterousness of her proclamation until he saw her hand as she reached out to hold on to his arm. It was trembling. When she saw him stare she moved quickly to bury it in the crook of his arm, dragging him along before he could comment on it.

Leading him up to the door of the house, she pushed him forward with mock roughness and as he delved into his pocket for his keys, she suddenly ran her tongue up and down the nape of his neck. The sensation was like an ice pack to his spine. He rested against the door, indulging himself as her tongue teased and nuzzled. Then, gradually, she slipped her hand around his waist and into his pocket, making circles with her fingers as she approached his groin.

David responded in kind. Blindly, he let his fingers walk behind him, over the warm contours of her belly and then down. Slowly he began to rub, backwards and forwards.

Snowflakes glistened in front of his eyes and melted on the skin of his face which was growing warmer and warmer. For a few minutes they stood there, letting the sensations grow in intensity.

Sudden passion swelled over them simultaneously and they turned and grabbed each other, falling to the wet ground of the front garden, only partially obscured by the scrubby hedge.

Neighbours could have wandered by, stopping to watch this act of passion, and the participants would not have known. The only sensation David was aware of apart from Fermay's warmth was the occasional hot sparkle of snow alighting upon his naked thigh. After they had climaxed they lay together for a moment, still joined, until the cold once more intruded on their world.

When David began to withdraw Fermay pulled him back in briefly, as if it was a sign of a greater withdrawal. Her lips nuzzled into his ear and she whispered, 'Forgive me.'

She wouldn't elucidate, and for the next hour as they lay listening to Charlie Parker in front of the electric fire, she clung to David like an insecure child, her face buried in his shoulder.

David's alcohol-induced sleep had been heavy and he surfaced from it with great difficulty, as if he was swimming up from turgid, black depths with exhausted arms. His first awareness was that he could not breathe. There was something across his face. Suddenly frantic, he flailed madly, fighting for air while grabbing the pillow that covered his mouth and hurling it across the room.

It was Fermay's pillow and she was no longer in bed. The bedroom was empty, frozen in darkness and silence in the chill of the night.

Sleepwalking again, he thought. And this time in her trance she had almost suffocated him.

Shivering and rubbing his hands on his arms for warmth, he padded through to the living room. Empty. His body glowed spectrally white in the light from the streetlamp outside his window. Where was she this time?

Maybe Willie was right, a small voice in the back of his head said.

He eradicated the thought mercilessly. 'Fermay,' he called out softly. 'Come back to bed, baby. It's cold.' *It's fucking freezing*, he thought.

He looked in the kitchen. Perhaps she had rediscovered a penchant for middle-of-the-night snacks. It was empty, dark, the dirty plates from the evening meal piled in the sink.

Maybe she's just in the toilet, he thought. All that beer taking it's toll.

But the toilet door was ajar, the small room in darkness. There was only one other place. The bathroom door was shut. He stood outside listening for any sounds, worrying that her sleepwalking might have taken her outside. Thoughts of her dying of exposure in the sub-zero temperature jarred his mind.

Slowly, he opened the bathroom door. Her perfume reached his nose. She was there; he could sense her although he could not see her. His hand tugged the cord of the light switch and

239

for the briefest second he was blinded, caught in a world between light and darkness.

Then he saw her.

She was curled in the bath, which was empty, naked, almost in a foetal position with her hair tumbling across her face. Its dark sheen was emphasized by the paleness of her skin. His first thought was how white she looked, almost as white as the porcelain of the bath.

But there was a contrasting darkness beneath her. It trickled around her slim limbs, past the corresponding darkness of pubic hair, towards the plughole where it slowly ran down into the drain.

David looked at the scene in fascination which slowly grew into shock, then horror. His disposable razor lay shattered on the floor in a score of yellow plastic shards. The blade was missing.

'Fermay!' he yelled with sudden awareness and a fear that he had felt only once before. 'Jesus! Fermay!'

His knees felt weak and his stomach threatened to give up on him. It was an effort to move, but when he did so he acted quickly. David ran into the bedroom with his thoughts boiled down to just one keening objective: *Make her live.* He snatched his shirt from the chair next to the bed and tore it into ribbons with a frenzied strength as he ran back to the bathroom. His left foot hammered down on to the broken plastic, but he was not aware of the pain or that he left a trail of small droplets of his own blood on the fading carpet.

He grabbed Fermay roughly and pulled her round, smearing blood across her pale skin and over the part of the bath which was still pristine white. With some relief, David saw the lines on her wrist were horizontal, not vertical; it gave him hope.

As he bound the wounds tightly, her eyes fluttered open and she looked into his face with pupils wide and dark.

'Why did you do it, Fermay?' A tiny sob sneaked into his voice. He realized distantly that tears were running down his cheeks.

Her voice was tissue thin. 'There's too much death in the

world. Too much killing. The time I've spent with you, David ... it's been so good. I can't face going back. What we have makes everything else so terrible. I'm so afraid, so afraid of losing it ... so afraid of hurting you ...'

Tenderly he stroked her hair. 'Don't worry. Everything will be fine. You don't have to go anywhere.'

He gave her hand a squeeze and then ran for the phone. Behind him he heard her weak voice say, 'They'll find me soon, David, and then what will happen to me? What will happen to *us*?'

His voice trembled with repressed emotion as he gave the details to the emergency services. The ambulance would soon be with them, he was reassured. As he replaced the receiver he realized he was shaking with the shock. What had happened? A few hours ago life had been perfect. What had caused this madness to engulf them? He could not believe it, and when he shut his eyes everything was as it had been. It was tempting to stay that way, but he faced up to the reality as he had always done.

The light in the bathroom strangely sickened him; it was too bright. It revealed too many flaws. Fermay was cold to his touch, so he placed a blanket around her and held her while they waited.

She sounded delirious, occasionally saying things which made little sense. There was only one moment when she became lucid, her eyes looking clearly into his. She said, 'The dead won't let me go, David. They'll never let me go.' She looked past his shoulder as if there was someone standing in the corner of the room. 'Their eyes ... their eyes are hungry. Don't let them get me, David. I'll be good.' Then she smiled. 'How funny! There's no hope for me.'

'Of course there's hope,' David stressed. 'The ambulance will be here any minute.'

'You're sweet, David,' she said, still smiling. 'That's why I love you. You're the only thing that's made this life worthwhile. But who's going to give me hope in the next one?'

'Baby, that's a long time away,' he said and hugged her.

After that they remained in silence, locked together once

241

more, until David heard the ambulance draw up outside. The crew moved quickly, replacing David's tourniquet by taping her wrists and putting up a bag of blood that began to pump life back into her.

One of the men, a Cockney with a lined, grey face, grabbed David's arm and whispered into his ear, 'She'll be all right, my son. We caught her in time. It's a good job she's not an expert at this.' He added with a thin smile, 'She probably didn't want to do it anyway. A cry for help, know what I mean?'

'Oh, I think she was serious,' David replied wearily. 'I only found her by accident. If I hadn't woken up . . .'

As they walked out into the freezing night, David glanced at the spot where they had made love only hours before. He thought he could see the imprint of their bodies on the ground although it was probably an illusion. He knew then, if he had not known it before, that he could no longer live a life without her. In just a few short weeks she had pulled him inside out and there was no going back.

The hospital was bright and quiet with dead air circulating along its chipped and stained corridors. David waited anxiously in a lonely room under glaring lights while the doctors tended to Fermay, still unsure exactly what had gone wrong with their dream.

The night dragged. He didn't know how long he waited, but there was a dull bruise of dawn in the sky when a nurse came through to fetch him. She smiled and led him to the room where Fermay sat propped up by a mound of pillows. Various tubes snaked into her arms like the strings of a puppet.

'Hello,' she said, both embarrassed and apologetic.

David was shocked by her appearance. Her hair was matted to her forehead and her skin had a curious grey tint. 'Hello,' he replied. He couldn't think of anything else to say.

Her mouth opened and closed silently and then she blurted out, 'I'm sorry, David. God, I'm so sorry.'

David sat on the edge of the bed. 'Why did you do it?'

'You probably won't believe me,' she replied hesitantly, 'but I don't even remember doing it. It wasn't a conscious act at all.'

'If it wasn't a conscious act there must be a hell of a lot of weird stuff floating around in your subconscious.' The sentence stumbled out in a release of tension and then he realized how callous it sounded. 'I thought we were happy together,' he added.

'We were . . . we *are* . . .' She struggled to find words. The effort seemed to exhaust her and she closed her eyes for a moment. '. . . you know me well, even though I've not really . . . spoken about myself. You can see into me. You know . . .' She paused. '. . . there's another side of me . . . that I don't really like. You saw it tonight. Trust me, David, please trust me. You won't see it again.'

'How can someone try to kill themselves and not know anything about it?' David asked incredulously.

'I *think* I know why I did it.' Fermay bit her bottom lip. She looked like a little girl again. 'I think . . . I didn't want to ruin what we had. I wanted to preserve it, before there was a chance for it to go wrong. Because it's so good. So much better than anything I've had before.'

'Didn't you think killing yourself would ruin it? Just a little?' he said bitterly. He knew she was not telling the whole truth, not giving the real reason for her action.

'David,' she continued, 'I don't want *you* to get hurt and I'll do anything to stop that happening. Even if it means killing myself.'

'Don't talk like that!' Irritation snapped his voice like a whip. 'You're nuts, Fermay. I'm starting to think Willie was right. None of the things you're saying make any sense.'

A tear ran down her cheek and he felt like crying himself from the strain of it all. Desperate for contact, he reached over and squeezed her hand. 'Look, we can put all this behind us. Just promise me you won't do it again and we can talk about all the whys and wherefores when you're feeling better.'

'I promise.' He could see she was lying. A different conviction was carved into her face, a rebel stance he could not begin to comprehend.

'OK, you get some rest now. They'll let you home as soon as you're fit and I can look after you then. They'll probably send someone in to give you counselling . . .'

'I'm not seeing any head doctor.'

'It's standard procedure, Fermay.'

'No!'

He shrugged. 'It's your head.'

As he turned to open the door, she called to him. 'You know what the Chinese say, David.'

'No. What do the Chinese say?'

'That if you save someone's life, you're responsible for them for ever. You're responsible for me now, David. We're linked together for all time. I'm sorry.'

'Why are you sorry?'

'Because you don't know what a burden that's going to be.'

Chapter 21

'I can't comment on that.'

The detective's face gave nothing away although his eyes glowered and his brow was furrowed. Then, for the briefest instant the mask slipped, revealing a canine stare, harried and cornered, until his mechanical professionalism reasserted itself. Flashing red and blue light splashed across the scene at regular intervals. Behind him, men in blue with dark faces hurried back and forth in front of the camera.

David watched the TV with a strange feeling of apprehension. He had felt depressed all day, ever since he had woken and realized another chunk of his memory had returned while he slept. Not so long ago it would have been a cause for celebration, another old friend to be welcomed with open arms. But the memories that were creeping back now were darker, disconcerting; he almost didn't want to remember. Fermay's attempted suicide had been a blow of terrible proportions, not only because of her suffering, but because of the troubled depths within her to which it attested. Obviously everything was not right in the garden and there was more to his 'perfect' relationship than he had imagined. It upset him; he didn't want his dream sullied. But how could he have been so blind? Other things had surfaced, odd snatches of conversation or phrases which at the time had seemed insignificant, but which now took on a new, frightening meaning in the light of David's own experiences in the city.

And he knew there was more to come.

A body had been discovered. The news producer let the cameras linger on the scene without comment, allowing it to unfold gradually before the eyes of the channel's viewers. The detective coughed, glanced away, looked for a path through the reporters, realized he was surrounded and then wearily faced the cameras once more. 'There is nothing more I can say at this moment,' he persisted.

'Can you comment on reports that the killing is linked to the murder of the vagrant?' a reporter asked breathlessly in a tone that stressed *Of course it is linked*.

'It's too early to tell,' the detective replied. There was thunder in his face and an obvious desire to swat the reporters away like flies so he could get on with his job.

The camera panned away from him to a black bodybag lying on the dockside surrounded by pools of water. A frogman rested on a packing crate, his face white in the camera lights, talking to a man in a smart dark suit and shaking his head continually. The camera lingered on the bodybag, sweeping from head to toe and back as if to say: *Guess what's in here, folks!*

It flicked back to the detective, who was looking even more harried. 'We've been receiving reports that both murders are ritual slayings,' another journalist said. 'Any truth in that?'

Before the detective had time to answer, a woman with big hair and TV make-up that gave her face a plastic sheen continued. 'And that you have uncovered a connection with other supposedly random killings in the city over the years . . . over many years?'

The detective opened his mouth and closed it. The questions continued. 'Sources say police files were deliberately suppressed, mislaid or misfiled. Incompetence? Or something more?'

'Detective Anderson, is there a serial killer loose in New Orleans?'

'No!' he broke in, anger flaring in his face. 'There's no need to scare people. Everything you have said is just supposition at the moment. We'll know more when we've had time to examine the facts.'

The lights continued to flash: a hellish red, an emotionless blue.

'David, close your mouth. You look like an imbecile.' Beth spoke through a mouthful of meatball po'boy she had picked up from the restaurant two doors down.

The room was dark. Beth had drawn the blinds to keep it cool after the heat of the day and now, with the sun sinking towards the horizon, it was an eerie twilight world, their faces illuminated by the grey light from the TV set. They sat side by side on the sofa, David nursing his beer, Beth her sandwich. Their conver-

246

sation had stopped when the newsflash came up on screen with the words 'Live Report' flashing along the bottom.

David was gripped by the information coming out of the set. Just one whole day after his encounter with Krugman, there was a sudden news report with rumours of police corruption and the suppression of murder files. It seemed too much to be mere coincidence.

He searched the faces of the policemen and detectives wandering in the background behind Anderson; they were tapping their toes and looking idly at the bodybag. Krugman was not there. It was too much to expect that he would be.

'If there is a link between the supposedly random murders, why has it only just been identified?' The reporters continued to harass Anderson. 'Is the killer getting careless?'

'We have established no such connection.' Anderson stressed every word, no longer trying to conceal his irritation.

'Who are the other victims?'

'I thought I just told you we hadn't established a connection!' he snapped. 'The only unsolved cases we've had recently have been drifters.'

The TV suddenly crackled and jagged lines of interference disrupted the picture. It lasted for only a few seconds, but the blare of the white noise made it almost unbearable.

'Shit!' Beth cursed. 'Must be the damn weather screwing up the transmission signals. Maybe there's sunspot activity or something.'

The picture returned with Anderson's face filling the entire screen. It was a typical TV producer's ploy. David noted how no one could appear unruffled in such an extreme close-up. Every movement of the eye was exaggerated into a nervous tic. Beads of sweat stood out guiltily on the brow.

'We will not be making any kind of public statement until,' Anderson stressed, 'Forensics have had a chance to . . .'

Interference exploded across the screen once more. Beth covered her ears and grimaced. 'Turn it off!' she yelled.

Before David had got halfway to the set, the picture had cleared. Only now there was no sign of Anderson.

He was looking at himself.

247

David Easter was staring out of the TV screen. It was his face! The David Easter on the screen was pale and hollow-cheeked. His eyes were open graves testifying silently to the horrors he had witnessed.

He glanced back at Beth. She looked up at the TV set and then returned to the magazine in her lap. She couldn't see it.

David was almost afraid to look again. He pictured his face slowly dissolving into a skull, the flesh mouldering on the bone before his eyes. He compared it to watching death in action.

The camera, or whatever was relaying the picture, pulled back. He was sitting in a room with no windows. The plaster on the wall was cracked and crumbling. There was no sound, but the scene included an old-fashioned record player with a chipped, golden horn. The TV-David stared ahead like a man who had received a sudden bereavement, his face revealing his new-found knowledge that there was no order, joy or hope in the world.

With a shiver, David realized it was the scene Dauphine had described to him, an image of his future.

The TV picture crackled jaggedly once more and returned to the newscaster in the well-lit studio. David flicked his tongue around his dry mouth. 'Did you see that?'

'See what? The atmospherics?' Beth's voice was distracted behind him.

'No. A picture . . . something else.'

'I wasn't looking. It was probably just a trick of the interference. Or maybe we picked up some out-of-town station. Get me a beer, will you?'

Dazed, he wandered through to the kitchen and took a couple of Dixies out of the fridge. What had he seen? A premonition? His image on the screen had looked so shocked, so broken. What secrets could that future David have discovered that had crushed him so?

'Hey, look at this!' Beth's voice was surprised. David returned to the lounge to find her staring out of the window in wonder. Standing behind her, he saw instantly what had excited her.

The sky was on fire.

It blazed in apocalyptic reds and shimmering golds over the

city. Flashes appeared and disappeared in an instant, like starbursts or the flares of distant guns.

'Shit!' Beth breathed in amazement. 'What a crazy effect! I've never seen anything like it. Maybe it's some freak electrical storm. No wonder the TV's screwed.'

'The weather's gone mad,' David whispered in awe.

'The gods are angry!' Beth laughed. 'They've had enough of us messing up the earth. Lights in the sky! Shakespeare would have said it's a portent. The death of a king is imminent! Nature is rebelling!'

'Something's going down.' David was suddenly cold.

The storm was building. Soon it would break.

'So, this cop was, like, one of them?' Arlene looked at David incredulously.

'I'm not being paranoid, Arlene,' David replied. 'He called Broussard's goons. If I hadn't skipped out of there sharpish you wouldn't be seeing me now.'

'Well . . .'

'Christ, I know how it *sounds*, Arlene. Even I've got doubts about my state of mind, so I know everyone else must think I've really flipped. But I know what I saw! Krugman is involved with Broussard and that means he's involved with Aidoneus. And if a senior detective is involved with them, anyone in authority could be. *Anyone*. Who can I turn to? Who can I trust? The answer is no one. It's just me. Just me.'

'David, you know you can trust me . . .'

'Sure, I know that, Arlene.' He squeezed her arm. 'But the simple fact is that I'm afraid to look over my shoulder. It was bad enough before. But now . . . Jesus! I can't go on like this.'

'What are you going to do?'

'I don't know. I'm caught between a rock and a hard place. Everything tells me I should get out, go back to London where I can at least save my sanity, if not my life. But I *can't* go. Not without Fermay. And how do I get her?'

The band came on stage and launched straight into 'Backwater Blues'. David's gaze was automatically drawn towards them, the

249

music releasing a rush of memories of safer times, happier times. He wished he could get back to them.

It was a pointless wish. Here he was, a fox with the hounds pounding the ground behind him. He could almost hear the horns.

Boney Lee slipped into a trumpet solo of startling sensitivity, plucking the blue notes from the air. David could hear colours and taste heartache. He turned to go back to his duties with a feeling of growing despondency.

Arlene caught his arm. 'You've gotta open up sooner or later, David. You can't do it on your own – you've gotta lean on someone before you fall down. I can see it in your face. You're not the same guy who walked in here a few weeks ago. There are lines there that weren't around before. You're gonna break down if you're not careful.'

'I appreciate your support, Arlene, but it's my road,' he said bleakly. 'And I've got to walk it.'

Scuba arrived shortly after 1 a.m. For a moment, David didn't recognize him. Sunglasses covered his eyes despite the gloom of the bar, and a shapeless, black coat hung down almost to his ankles. His physical appearance wasn't all that had altered. It was his confidence that had gone, his cheesy I'm-the-best grin and his arrogant, swaggering attitude. Instead David was faced by a man who looked hunted and scared, shoulders slumped, head downcast.

'Hey, Limey,' Scuba asked flatly. 'You seen Arlene?'

David shrugged. 'She's around. It's not that big a place.'

'Yeah.' Scuba looked at the door. 'I'll wait here until she gets her break. You want a drink?'

'Not while I'm working.'

Scuba slumped against the bar, head down low over his elbows. Dean served him a Dixie which Scuba left sitting in front of him, staring at it like it was the strangest thing he had ever seen.

'Problems?' David asked.

'Yeah, you bet.' It was obvious he didn't want to talk, but David wasn't about to let the subject drop.

'Work problems or women problems?' *Or is it that a drugs gang is ready to shoot your ass off?*

'Work problems . . . I guess.' Scuba suddenly seemed to notice the beer and he snatched it up and poured it down his throat.

Before David could continue, Arlene walked up to them, embarrassment and annoyance playing on her face. 'What are you doing here?' she snapped. David was surprised at the sharpness of her tone.

'We need to talk . . .'

'I'm working.'

'Baby, I'm in trouble . . .'

'You're always in trouble, Scuba. Ever since I've known you you've been in trouble. What's so different this time? Down on your luck? Out of money?'

Scuba shook his head. 'It's bad this time . . . the worst.'

'And why are you wearing those ridiculous dark glasses?'

Scuba grabbed Arlene around the wrist as she went to remove his Raybans. 'We've got to get out of town, baby. For a few months. Maybe a year or two.'

'You're mad, Scuba.' She tugged at her wrist. 'Let go.' Her words were reinforced and threatening. Reluctantly he uncurled his fingers. 'I've got a life here. A job. Friends. I'm not gonna drop all that on your say-so. I'm not your property, Scuba. You can't just pack me up in your suitcase with the rest of your junk. What is it? What's happening?'

He looked at David. 'Not now, baby. Not here.'

Arlene's cheeks tinged red. 'Don't waste your breath, Scuba. I'm not going away with you. If you want to leave, fine, but you'll be on your own.'

Scuba stared at his bottle blankly and then looked Arlene in the face. His mouth was fixed in resignation. 'You're killing me, Arlene,' he said quietly. 'You know I can't leave without you.'

He turned slowly and headed towards the door, easing his way dejectedly among the drinkers. Arlene watched him until he had stepped out into the night.

'Shit,' she said sadly. 'I'm such a bitch.'

'You did the right thing, Arlene.'

'Did I? He needs me and I'm not there for him any more. He's

251

got no one.' She fumbled a cigarette into her mouth, failed to light it first time and then flung it on the floor. 'Shit!'

'Pity is no reason to stand by someone.' David offered her a comforting arm. 'You've given too much of yourself to Scuba. Now's the time to stand on your own.'

'On my own?' She bit her lip. 'Yeah, right, I'm so strong. What's going on, David? Everything's falling apart. How's it all going to end up?' She shook her head in resignation.

David would have answered her, but the same question was playing on his own mind. Life was in a state of flux for all of them. Soon, very soon, he guessed, the new patterns would emerge. And he doubted the picture they revealed would be happy at all.

Marsayle appeared at 3 a.m. The manifestation was alone this time, standing grey and cold in a lonely corner at the back of the club. David caught its accusing stare by chance as he ventured out from the storeroom with a crate of beer for Dean. Marsayle's eyes had always filled him with fear, as if they unlocked some secret room where the darkest things lay. But not this time. David was too weary to be scared. All he wanted was to be left alone.

As their eyes met across the room, something within David snapped. The crate almost slipped through his fingers in his haste to put it on the floor, and then he was round the bar and marching across the club. Halfway through the room an urge to turn and run finally hit him, but he overcame it. Marsayle's face was colder than it had ever been.

For the last few steps, that was all David could see, the eyes staring into him, the mouth a slit of jagged darkness.

'Why?' he snapped before any other emotions came to the fore. '*Why* are you doing this to me?'

In his anger he raised his hand to the spirit. Marsayle's expression did not change, but the stare grew more threatening.

'Do you want to drive me mad?' he continued, his fury wholly unleashed. 'Is that it? Whom the gods destroy they first make mad? Why don't you answer me, damn you? Why do you just keep staring? What have I ever done to you?'

He paused in the futile hope that he might finally be given

252

some information to bring him in from the dark. In that lull his anger dissipated and there was only one question left on his lips.

'What has Fermay got to do with all this?'

Was that a movement he saw on Marsayle's face? Almost imperceptible, a slight shiver like a passing shadow? He persevered.

'Tell me about Fermay. Do you know where she is?'

This time there was no doubt. Marsayle's eyes seemed to fall back into their shadowed sockets and his lips pulled back from his teeth like a cornered dog. David thought the spirit was going to reach out and grab him.

'I can't even be totally sure if she's alive. *Is she?*' His mouth was dry. 'Or is she dead?'

Marsayle's face ripped apart and folded back on itself in a silent scream as its arms thrashed madly at the air. David took a step back in shock, his heart pounding. For another second the spirit twisted and tormented itself in wild convulsions, its mouth wide in a banshee howl that no one living could hear. And then a darkness passed across David's eyes and when it cleared that corner of the room was empty.

David was icy with dread, unwilling to comprehend the connection that had brought Marsayle's wrath to the fore. The mention of Fermay's name had triggered something within the spirit, something so terrible it could no longer hold itself together in the world of the living. How was Fermay tied up in this process? There was a little voice in the back of his head telling him he didn't want to know.

Don't remember, it kept saying to him. *Don't remember. To forget is bliss.*

Charlie called David over when the last punter had left and the staff were busy swabbing the floor and washing the glasses. He wandered wearily into his office with David at his heels and closed the door, hastily sweeping a crumpled copy of *Hustler* off his desk. When he had settled into his chair and poured himself a shot of Jack, he looked at David with puffy eyes and grunted.

'I like you, kid, but you're one weird fucker.' He paused while he lit his cigar. 'Dean says he seen you shoutin' at thin air earlier this evenin' – like there was someone standin' there only you could see.'

'Dean would.'

'You seein' things, kid?'

David shrugged. 'I see lots of things.'

'You know what I mean. You doin' drugs?'

'No.'

Charlie sucked on his cigar and chased it with the contents of his shot glass. 'OK, I believe you. But there's somethin' wrong. Dean said you were actin' like one of those drunks stumblin' and grumblin' down on the waterfront. If you're goin' crazy, boy, I need to know. This is a business here. It's my livelihood. I can't do with you goin' psycho on the customers one night.'

'Charlie, do I look crazy?' As he spoke, he thought of Dean gleefully watching his rant at the unseen spirit of Buffalo Marsayle and then scurrying to Charlie with a sly grin on his face. David's face flushed with anger.

'Boy, far as I can see you're crazy as a coot, but that's normal round here. All I'm concerned about is whether you're scarin' off the payin' custom, an' talkin' to an empty table an' chair is gonna make the tourists nervous.'

'Believe me, I'm not nuts. I'm not going to frighten anyone away. Sometimes I sing to myself. Is that a crime? That's probably what Dean saw.'

'Singin'? You got time to sing, you ain't workin' hard enough. Listen up, boy, I'm not stupid. I can see you fallin' apart. Every day a little bit more. You better sort yourself out, y'hear? Whatever it is that's eatin' away at you, I don't wanna know. Shit! I don't care. Just sort yourself out.'

Though his tone was gruff, David could sense the warmth in his voice, buried deeply lest anyone thought he had a heart. 'I'll sort myself out, Charlie. You'll see.'

He glanced up over Charlie's head and noticed the rows of framed black and white photos of jazz musicians past and present, many of them signed. All the greats were there, several donating personal inscriptions to Charlie.

'You know a lot of good people.'

Charlie grunted. 'All sorta folk have passed through this club. Good, bad, drunks, dopeheads and gentlemen.'

'They seem to like you.'

He grunted again, in uncharacteristic shyness or characteristic boredom.

'You know a horn player called Buffalo Marsayle?'

His belly rumbled with laughter. 'How old d'ya think I am, you dumb shit! That cat checked out a long time ago. A *lonngg* time ago!'

'I meant, do you know anything about him?'

'Yeah. A little.' He chuckled and refilled his glass. 'Well, ain't this a turn-up for the books. I thought you was Mr Memory. Mr Smart Guy who knows everythin' about the history of jazz.'

David allowed Charlie his gloating. 'I never said I knew everything, Charlie. Just a lot.'

'Heh. Maybe. Yeah, I know 'bout Marsayle. That's a famous story. You want a drink, boy?'

David tried not to show his surprise. 'Sure.' It was like the doorman getting a lift from the chief executive.

Charlie took another shot glass from the bottom drawer of his desk, blew the dust out and filled it with Jack Daniels. Then he settled back in his chair with his stogy clenched between two fingers and his thumb, a big toothy grin on his face.

'Let me tell you 'bout old Buffalo Marsayle,' he began. 'Old Hot Lips Marsayle. They said he coulda become a legend . . . if he'd lived longer. He was a star in the makin', the Satchmo of his day. He operated out of some joint in Storyville, the old red-light district, and they say his horn-playin' brought them from all over the South. He was a poor boy made good. His folks didn't have two cents to rub together. They lived in some shotgun shack outside the city, eight of 'em in two rooms. Musta been hell. But Buffalo, he wasn't gonna settle for that kind of poverty. Even when he was a kid he knew he wanted out. He worked his butt off and by the time he was ten, he had enough to buy his first horn. Now this wasn't no shinin' gold classic, y'hear. It was a beat-up, dented old thing that nobody wanted. But he learnt how to play an' he stuck at it an' sweated blood an' pretty soon he was makin' the sweetest music. He started playin' for nickels an' dimes in the streets of the Vieux Carre. He did OK, but it wasn't what you'd call a livin'. Anyways, it wasn't good enough for Buffalo.'

Charlie knocked back his shot, smacked his lips and poured himself another one. His storytelling had softened him. He smiled at the memories with the brass-button brightness of a young boy in love.

'He took himself off up to Storyville when he thought he was good enough an' he begged all the bar owners an' brothel madams and pimps to give him a regular stand. Buffalo was thrown outta more joints than you've drank in. But he kept goin' back an' back an' back, until finally someone gave him a chance, just one night, but that was all Buffalo needed. He played like an angel. They were crowdin' in the door an' pressed up against the window tryin' to get a sight of this little kid makin' the big noise. After that, he never looked back.'

'So what happened to him? How come the rest of us never heard of him?'

Charlie shook his head. 'You know how it is with jazz, boy. It's filled with angels, but there're a lot of devils too. For every note played there's been a drop of blood spilled. The history of the music's covered in it. Gangs, feudin', jealousy, drugs, rackets. It's a surprise that the music ever comes through. Buffalo's career was cut short just when he was on the verge of the big time. It was a mystery what happened, one of the most famous mysteries the music has, but you ask anybody in the Quarter who knows his jazz an' he'll have a theory on it. It's the kinda thing that's ony spoken about at the end of a night of smokin' an' drinkin'. Marsayle's murder. That an' the rest of Lionel Johnson's jinxed crew.'

Charlie laughed at David's puzzled expression. 'Yeah, that's right. It wasn't just Buffalo who met his Maker – it was the whole goddamned band.' He drew on his cigar until the end glowed like a furnace.

'How did they die?' The nerves along David's spine tingled with electricity.

'Nobody knows exactly. It's a fact that Lionel Johnson – Hound Dog, they used to call him on account of his expression when he was down on his luck – ol' Hound Dog hired Buffalo and the others to cut a disc. You know the Lost Record, boy?'

He nodded. With a *frisson* of anxiety, David recalled Willie and Fermay talking about it that first night they met each other at the pub. There were too many coincidences, seemingly unrelated things linking up in a nightmarish network.

'The Lost Record, yeah,' Charlie mused. 'It's a N'Orleans myth. The rarest jazz disc cut. Only one copy made – an' nobody knows where it is. "Night-time Blues" by Lionel "Hound Dog" Johnson. You get that one in your collection, boy, and you'll need a SWAT team to keep it safe.

'Johnson was no talent and he knew it. That's why he got some of the best musicians in the city to make him look good. Buffalo was the first guy he approached an' when he was on board the others were just queuing up to get involved. Now although Johnson played the piano like a man with no hands, he wrote "Night-time Blues" an' by all accounts it was a classic. Folk say it was the best jazz song ever written. 'Course, it's easy to say that seein' as no one's ever heard it – not even the band. Johnson made each musician record their part in a separate booth so no one could hear the complete song bein' played. Said he didn't want anyone stealin' it before he put the record out. They stayed up all night layin' the track down. It was a session from heaven an' the next mornin' they left the studio like they'd been smokin' poppy juice, high as kites on the music.

'Within a week they were all dead. 'Cept Johnson. One went in the river. Another OD'd in the john in some seedy joint. Another had his throat slit an' choked on his own blood. But it was Buffalo that everyone was talkin' about. They found him in his room, sittin' in his armchair starin' at the wall an' smilin'. Only he was starin' 'cause someone had cut off his eyelids. An' that wasn't all – they'd cut out his tongue too. The doctor said it'd been done while he was alive an' the shock likely as not killed him.'

Charlie swilled more Jack like he was washing a dirty taste from his mouth. 'There was a lot of sadness an' beratin' an' wailin' about the death of such a fine man, but it all died down when folk started talkin' about a ritual killin'.'

'Ritual?'

'Yeah. Devil worship, black magic an' all that shit. Folk were superstitious back then – still are now – an' pretty soon Buffalo was forgotten. No one wanted to know.'

'What about Johnson? Did he do it?'

Charlie shrugged. 'The cops hauled his ass down to the precinct along with a lot of other folk, but they'd all got alibis. Johnson could account for himself at the times all the others died. Folk thought it was funny that he didn't put out "Night-time Blues", but he just said he was lettin' it rest in honour of the band's memory. All the test copies were destroyed, apart from one which he kept for himself. Screwed way of thinkin' if you ask me. Most people would have wanted that music heard. Anyway, Johnson hung around the Quarter for a while, pickin' up money from here and there. Somehow he got enough to buy a flash car an' house an' then he just faded away.'

Charlie sat back in his chair and spread his fingers on his desk, his tale complete. Slowly his dour expression returned. 'An' that's the story of Buffalo Marsayle. Any time you want to find out about the great and famous of N'Orleans jazz you ask Charlie. But not in work time, right, boy?'

Outside the office, David caught sight of Dean laughing at him maliciously. David ignored him. He was preoccupied with thoughts of Buffalo Marsayle dying in agony when his dreams of fame were only a heartbeat away. Who had killed him? And why? Mystery was heaping on mystery. Did Marsayle want David to find his killer and avenge his death? Why him, and why now, after all these years?

And what did it have to do with Fermay?

Chapter 22

The night was dark, like the bottom of a well. Clouds obscured the moon. It was the perfect evening for a burglary.

David reclined in the passenger seat and gazed out of the window from beneath the brim of his baseball cap, his nonchalance disguising the fact that his heart was beating out of time and his nerves were like guitar strings. Beneath the tension, however, he felt elated that he had finally found it within him to act. His vacillation had been put to one side, no more a Hamlet to Broussard's King. It was a liberating feeling to know his life was his own once more.

Ligios tapped the steering wheel in four: four time, sucking on a bedraggled roll-up. His face looked ashen in the streetlight. His nerves were on edge; the tension was getting to him too. He'd made no secret of his wariness of Aidoneus, but his doubts had caved in before his greed as David had known they would. The prospect of lifting rare works of art from Broussard's mansion had been too much for him to refuse.

The trees in the boulevard rustled in the warm breeze and the only other sound was the intermittent whizz of passing cars. It was peaceful and lazy, summoning up David's fantasies of sipping mint juleps with Fermay in a secluded garden while the moon slowly climbed into the sky. Soon it would be a reality, he told himself, and this time he almost believed it as he watched and waited.

David had finally been convinced to take the ultimate risk after seeing the woman whom he thought was Fermay climbing into Broussard's car. There was no point carrying out any further surveillance. For once, he had to act with confidence and damn the repercussions. Moose had been difficult to locate, but David had eventually tracked him down and requested an urgent meeting with Ligios. Moose, in his usual efficient manner, had arranged it for that evening in the Old Absinthe Bar on Bourbon where there were too many tourists for either of them to be recognized. David outlined his requirements in very basic terms: he wanted to get into Broussard's mansion; if Ligios could arrange it he was welcome to anything he could carry out of there. At first Ligios had flatly declined, saying he was 'not going to mess with those boys'. But when David described the riches stored inside the house, Ligios had begun to waver. Eventually he agreed. Ligios was a small-time crook, but he was an expert on electronic security systems. If anyone could get in, Ligios could. The raid was set for two days hence.

'Maybe he's just filled the place with his muscleheads and they're gonna beat the crap out of us when we step inside,' Ligios had said nervously. David told him he'd seen no sign of extra guards during his brief visit, but if truth be known the danger barely worried him. He felt fired up like a Tommy preparing to leap out of the trenches into No-man's-land. Ligios thought he was insane and told him so.

An elderly couple sauntered along the sidewalk, enjoying the balmy evening air. The man had silver hair and a face like crumpled paper, hers was a chubby pieface with rosy cheeks. They held hands and smiled at each other, the oldest teenagers in town. David wondered how many years of love lay between them, how many embraces, how many caresses and whispered, secret words. They passed by, oblivious to his presence in the car.

'Are we gonna do it then?' Ligios' tomb-like voice floated through the stillness.

'I guess we are.' David opened the door.

Broussard, Lynch, Frantz and three others had vacated the mansion earlier that evening while the red sun was still crawling down the sky. The mystery woman was not with them. *Fermay* was not with them. They were wearing evening dress and they'd departed in a convoy of cars with Broussard at the head like a king with his entourage. It had been a stroke of blind luck. David had anticipated observing the house for several days before an opportunity arose for them to break in, but there it was on the first night *and* on his night off from Charlie's Place. Ligios had not been so surprised. Broussard was a socialite who spent most of his time partying and mixing in the circles of the rich and famous.

Ligios moved ahead of David, walking confidently, not too fast, not too slow, head down so as not to draw attention. David followed his lead. Even with his eyes fixed on the sidewalk, he could feel the presence of Broussard's mansion, a dark, brooding monster waiting on its haunches. It reflected the man himself, as if it had soaked up some of his spirit over the years.

David allowed himself a fleeting glance at its façade as they turned sharply into the drive, its black windows like eyes, its marble columns like teeth. A single light burned in the room where Broussard had entertained David; the rest was in darkness. They were both sure no one else was at home. During their long watch no other light had come on and no one had entered that room. It was silent. David could taste the remnants of his last cup of coffee in his mouth.

Ligios led the way up the side of the house, fluidly slipping into the shadows, while David wondered if Broussard kept any guard dogs secreted away. That would be just like him, a couple of Rottweilers awaiting their evening feed. His ears were primed for a tell-tale growl or the pounding of approaching paws.

With practised ease, Ligios ghosted up to a large window which looked into the library, his feet barely disturbing the gravel of the path. He slipped his hands around the window frame while peering inside.

Eventually he whispered, 'Pretty good system, but not the best. What is it with this guy? Doesn't he know there are criminals out there?'

He took from his pocket what looked like a Gameboy. There were two wires with clips hanging from it which he fastened to a wire running underneath the window ledge. This he then slit with a knife. A digital display on the machine glowed redly in the dark. Ligios tapped at the keyboard and then turned and smiled broadly at David. 'We're in.'

From a small leather pouch tied around his waist beneath his shirt, he pulled out a rubber suction cup and a glasscutter. The cup adhered to the pane and he cut around it so that when he pulled it away a circular section of glass came with it. Slipping his hand through the hole, he flipped the catch, rolling up the window just enough for them to climb through.

'Easiest job I've ever done,' he said.

As David waited to follow Ligios into the library, he felt unusually cold as if the bricks of the building were leeching the heat from his body. It was an unfriendly house, a dangerous house, and it made its warnings plain, but he steeled himself and climbed over the window ledge.

The room was suffused with a strong aroma of old leather from the hundreds of books lining the walls from ceiling to floor. Darkness pooled in the corners and David was almost afraid to look into them. Inside, the house felt strange, subtly disconcerting. It didn't seem to be the same place he had visited in the bright morning sunshine; come nightfall, it had been replaced by its darker cousin from the other side of the mirror. David realized he was subconsciously holding his breath.

The disturbing atmosphere didn't seem to bother Ligios who was examining a statuette on the mahogany coffee table in front of the large open fireplace. It appeared to be silver. He turned it over and over in his gloved hands, nodding approvingly, before replacing it.

'On the way back,' Ligios whispered, pointing to it.

David motioned towards the door. If Broussard and his men returned before they were out of the mansion, the penalty would be too frightening to envisage.

At the door Ligios turned to him and said, 'Which rooms do you want to try?'

'Every room. I don't want to leave a single one unchecked.'

Ligios gradually opened the door and peered out. A shaft of light came through the gap and bisected the library. All was silent. Over his partner's shoulder David could see a small lamp on a table in the passage which led to the grand reception hall. They moved through swiftly, at first going in opposite directions like a couple in a Marx Brothers film, before agreeing to check the back of the house first.

It was enormous. David really hadn't grasped how far it stretched back into the dark, verdant gardens and then it went up for three more floors, including the attic rooms. He began to comprehend exactly how rich Broussard was when each room they entered surprised him with its wonders. The opulence was

262

dazzling, a world he had only glimpsed in glitzy American soaps. Carpets so deep he felt he was walking on air. Paintings, cracked with age, on every wall, their frames gilt and heavy. Bone china, intricately decorated, crystal, gold and silver. Softly ticking French carriage clocks, antique tables and chairs and dressers, Chinese vases, Japanese swords, wooden chests and Persian rugs. Not only did crime pay, it paid well.

Ligios was like a child on Christmas Day. He wandered through the rooms in a daze, his eyes barely lighting on one object of value before they were drawn to another.

'Fuckin'-A,' he said breathlessly. 'It's Donald Trump's junk shop!'

He would have stayed on the ground floor examining each piece if David had not ushered him out to the hall. The rest of the house beckoned. He had seen nothing that told him of Fermay's presence, but it was too early to become disillusioned; there were still many rooms to search.

The magnificent staircase rose up ahead of them. They both paused at the foot of it, the light from the hall filtering out halfway up. Beyond, there was impenetrable darkness. David was momentarily gripped by a childhood fear, the one that had taken him every evening as he prepared to mount the staircase to bed.

The dark at the top of the stairs.

Every child will say something lives there, something that retreats into the shadows whenever the light is switched on. Ligios' face revealed he was thinking something similar; it amazed David how close childhood always was.

'Up we go,' Ligios grunted apprehensively. He drew a pencil flashlight from his pouch and flicked the switch, the beam slicing through the darkness like a laser.

Nerves jangled as David placed his foot on the first step, his ears alert for the slam of a car door, the sound of approaching footsteps and muffled voices. If Broussard returned while they were upstairs, their escape would be much more difficult. The tension in the air was almost strong enough to taste.

They climbed swiftly, reaching the top and turning right. The flashlight helped direct their way and David's eyes gradually grew accustomed to the gloom. They were soon investigating a maze of bedrooms. The master bedroom, obviously Broussard's, might have been prepared for Louis XIV, it was so gloriously and tastelessly overstated. An ornately carved four-poster lined with heavy drapes dominated the room, a gold silk dressing gown lying across it. Broussard seemed to be obsessed with privacy. Thick velvet curtains covered the window and before them was a large Chinese screen with a red and gold floating dragon on black. No prying eyes would ever see what took place in that protected room. A private bathroom of white marble and gold lay off it.

In a flash of insight, David realized Fermay would have experienced all this richness and glamour as she grew up. She must have been pampered like a millionaire's daughter; how difficult had it been for her to abandon it all? And what must she have thought moving into David's small, grey world? Secrets. She had kept so much from him.

They progressed along an empty corridor, their breath sounding hoarse and laboured in the dead stillness. David could feel Broussard's presence everywhere, hanging in the air like the smell of rotten meat. There were rooms for his lieutenants, spartan compared to his own, but still expensive. An office appeared at the end of the corridor, all the filing cabinets and desk drawers locked. David considered jemmying a few of them open, but it hardly seemed worth it. Records of Aidoneus' drug deals and numbers rackets would mean little to him. There was only one thing of value the mansion could hold. They covered the next floor quickly. Only the attic rooms were left.

'Do you still want to go on?' Ligios emphasized the question in such a way as to leave David in no doubt of the option the small-time crook preferred.

'Of course. I haven't found what I'm looking for.'

'What *are* you looking for? You don't give much away, man.'

'That's right. And that's the way it's going to stay.' David was already thinking ahead. One more floor to go. Would there be enough time?

'Because if there's something big here,' Ligios continued, 'I want to be part of it.' David was already striding out towards the attic stairs. Ligios kept up a few paces behind. 'I've taken all the risks here. I'm not going to settle for any penny ante stuff if there's something more. What is it? Drugs? Guns?'

'Nothing you'd be interested in.'

'Don't play me for a fool, Limey.' Ligios' voice grew harder. David had pushed him as far as he could. 'I'm no sucker and I'm no leg-man. I want a fifty-fifty cut if you're looking at big money.'

'It's personal. A missing person.' David stopped at the foot of the final flight of stairs. The shadows there seemed even darker.

'Missing person?' Ligios repeated incredulously. 'Who is it? Elvis?'

'No, it's not.' Ligios' whining was starting to irritate David. 'It's a woman. Named Fermay Grey.'

At the mention of her name, a blast of icy air swirled down the stairs and past him. He shivered. And hadn't there been something else? Something behind the breeze, on the edge of his senses?

A whisper.

From the top of the stairs.

David strained his ears, stretching out one arm to stop Ligios from moving. Even the drop of a pin would have sounded like a cannonshot in that quiet. There was nothing. The air hummed with silence and that was all.

'What is it?' Ligios hissed nervously.

'Nothing. I thought I heard something.'

'Well did you or didn't you?'

'No. It was just my ears playing tricks on me. Let's go.'

They started to climb the stairs.

David's heart was beating faster with each step. He *could* sense something.

Halfway up the flight, Ligios' torch played over a door at the top, large and black and made of sturdy wood. It was unexpected and architecturally out of place, but it had obviously been installed to seal off the entire top of the house. It seemed to say: GO NO FURTHER.

'If we're going to find anything,' David said, 'it will be through there.' He tried the handle. The door was locked. 'Couldn't have expected any more, could I?'

'There's always something about a locked door,' Ligios said

thoughtfully. The acoustics caused his voice to echo slightly, as if he was at the bottom of a pit.

'That's because it represents secrets and there are two kinds of secrets. The good ones that you want to find out and they want to hide. And the dangerous ones that everyone wants to stay hidden.'

Ligios rattled the handle. 'I think we can do this one,' he said confidently. 'It wasn't installed by a security expert. Look, the door is solid.' He rapped it. 'Take you a day to get through that. But the jamb, that's a different story. Cheap, soft wood.'

His bag of tricks provided a jemmy slightly larger than a tyre iron which he positioned where the door met the jamb at the lock. There was a splintering of wood and a few minutes later the door was ready to be wrenched open. Ligios stepped back to let David do the muscle work.

David took the cold, brass handle with both hands, braced himself, and then heaved backwards. There was a crack, but the door did not budge.

'You're getting there,' Ligios said. 'Try again.'

'Who shot Clinton and made you President?' His sinews ached. He set his feet further apart, grabbed the handle again, and pulled. The crack was louder and this time the door moved slightly.

'One more time.'

'Shut up, Ligios,' David said breathlessly. And then to himself, 'Third time lucky.'

He threw himself into it with such force that the jamb exploded like a gunshot, splintering wood in all directions. The door swung open, throwing David off balance, and in that instant madness exploded out.

The dead rushed from the darkness towards him like a horde of screaming banshees.

Their faces hurtled towards him, bone-white or mouldering, mouths thrown wide with a screech ripped from their suffering souls, hands grasping in anguish ahead of them. There was a score or more, packed on either side of the door, until it seemed like a tidal wave of death.

The shock almost stopped David's heart. He threw himself to the floor in terror, his arms over his head, sure he was going to die. Their presence tore over him like an arctic blast as he clapped his hands to his ears to cut out the pain of their howls. He could smell the grave and see death hanging in the air like a shroud.

The roaring wind on which the dead were riding passed over him in a second and screamed down the stairs, the noise of souls in agony never relenting until it disappeared out into the night.

When silence finally returned, David sat up, feeling sick and shaken. He now imagined the dead waiting behind the door as he and Ligios had climbed the stairs, pressing in closer and closer to express their pain until finally they were released like steam from a pressure cooker.

What were they all doing there, in Broussard's house? Lost souls who wanted to tell the world of their suffering, but doomed to speak only to themselves?

And to David.

David became aware of Ligios staring at him in horror. *Of course*, David realized. *He didn't see them*. All Ligios had observed was David opening the door and then falling to the floor and covering his head in fear. Shakily, David pulled himself to his feet.

'What the fuck happened there?' Ligios was aghast. David could see he was considering abandoning their mission. And why not? Who would want to be alone in the home of a dangerous gang boss with a certifiable lunatic.

'I'm OK. I'm epileptic,' David lied.

'Didn't look much like epilepsy to me. Looked like you were seeing things. Too much acid?'

'It was an epileptic fit,' David stressed. 'Very brief and uncharacteristic, but a fit nonetheless.'

Ligios eyed him warily, still half thinking about leaving. Eventually the greed returned to his face and he smiled hungrily. 'Hey, I can't wait to see what he's got in here. It must be something valuable with a door like that. If there's all those fine antiques downstairs, what's important enough to be stashed up here?'

David was almost afraid to consider the question. They entered the top floor together, one with growing fear and apprehension, the other with boundless greed.

As Ligios' torch ranged along the corridor it seemed as if they had been transported to another building, devoid of the

267

luxuriousness that characterized the rest of the mansion. The walls were bare to the plaster and that was cracked and damaged by age. No rich, deep carpet lay on the floor; it was rough boards. Overhead the lights were merely bulbs on the end of a flex. There was an odour of damp and dust.

The first three rooms were all empty and undecorated to the point of deterioration. According to David's calculations, that left two more. The layout of the floor had been altered at some time and as they entered the penultimate room, he realized access to the final room could only be gained through it.

'Thank the Lord,' Ligios breathed. They were back in the world of money and power. The room was packed with antiques; a little too many so that it resembled an over-stuffed saleroom. 'I thought we'd been caught out,' Ligios continued. 'This must be the storeroom.'

Like the library on the ground floor, the walls were covered by shelves of books. These seemed older. The bindings were cracked and decaying and they reeked of yellowing paper and age, and years of use.

Despite the wealth piled high around them, David felt dismayed that they had discovered no tangible signs of Fermay. He was almost afraid to try the final room. It was his last hope. He looked again at their present surroundings. The centrepiece of the room was a sturdy glass case like the ones used in museums. David's curiosity got the better of him and he asked Ligios to shine his torch inside.

Ligios, expecting jewels, perhaps, or rare coins, sounded disappointed when he said, 'It's only an old record.'

Something twinged in David's mind, insistent, tugging him forward. It had to be, didn't it, he thought. The coincidences, getting closer and closer.

He leaned over the case and peered at the disc which had been reverentially placed on a crumpled black velvet cloth. It was a 78, yet it looked almost brand new as the torchlight illuminated its shiny, unscratched surface. The label was handwritten in a spidery scrawl on paper discoloured with age. The twinge had turned into an alarm, growing louder.

Ligios turned his torch away to investigate some of the antiques nearby.

'Hey!' David snapped. 'Shine it back here. I want to read the label.'

Ligios cursed under his breath, but he did what David said.

Night-time Blues. By Lionel Johnson.

The Lost Record. The final performance of Buffalo Marsayle before his brutal slaying. Yet another part of the mystery came back to Broussard and Aidoneus, another artefact harking back to the past, linked to the present by undiminished strands of blood and terror. Who was it who told him the past and future lived alongside the present in New Orleans? Here was the proof. All times were now, old horrors and new horrors intermingling.

'OK? You seen enough?'

'Yes, but I want that record.' Apart from its significance in the mystery, the jazz buff inside him felt a *frisson* of excitement at the prospect of owning such a rare and valuable disc. And after all, it was a small price to pay for what Broussard had done to him.

He leaned forward and smashed the top of the case with his elbow.

An alarm shattered the silence instantly. David froze.

'Shit!'

Then both he and Ligios moved as one. The alarm was deafening, but it was not any kind David had heard before. It was a deep, sonorous tolling like a funeral bell and it was answered by another somewhere far back in the house.

'Jesus H. Christ!' Ligios cursed. 'You stupid bastard! We gotta get out of here! Fast!' He moved towards the door.

David started to follow him. He stopped three steps across the room and glanced back. 'Hang on. Give me a minute.'

'You gotta be fucking joking!' Ligios yelled at him incredulously. 'They'll be all over this place before you can sing God Save The Queen, you Limey asshole!'

David ignored him. He ran back to the case, dipped his hand through the broken glass and pulled out the record. It felt warm to his touch, like the hand of a friend. Then his eyes were drawn to the final room. Could he leave without checking it? He looked

269

back at Ligios. His ponytail was flapping wildly as he darted around the room stuffing the smaller antiques into his pockets and pouch.

There was still time.

Grabbing the record, and then snatching its velvet bedding as wrapping, David pushed it down his jumper close to his chest. Then he covered the rest of the room in a couple of bounds and yanked on the handle of the final door. It was locked.

More treasures and precious secrets, Broussard? he thought.

With a wish and a prayer he hammered on the door. 'Fermay? Are you in there?'

There was no reply, but he was struck with a strange prickling sensation that ran along the length of his spine. It told him, as well as any voice, that there was someone within. He *knew* it.

He was about to try again when Ligios' steel-sprung fingers clamped around his upper arm. 'Get the fuck out of here!' he hissed, 'or I'm going to pound your fucking skull in.' He was brandishing the jemmy with his other hand. 'I'm not leaving you behind to set me up.'

David roughly threw him off and ran to the door, but Ligios pulled ahead of him, cursing loudly, his pockets bulging with loot. David touched his chest where the record lay, as if he was checking on a baby.

As they piled into the corridor, the first thing they saw was the silhouette.

Behind it, the window overlooking the street framed a few stars in a black sky. David's blood ran cold.

The silhouette moved, shifting the weight of a body that towered up almost seven feet. The true outline was difficult to discern. There was something about it that didn't look right. Something about the head.

'Shine your torch at him,' David said. 'Try to blind him.'

Ligios responded quickly. He clicked the switch and a beam of light cleaved through the darkness, slicing across the body until it settled on the head. It took a second for what they saw to register and then the shock hit them.

The figure stopped moving when the light hit it. A bird's head flared in the spotlight – curved, cruel beak glinting, eyes black and beady. David recognized it instantly. It was the bizarre bird costume he had seen in the photo in the Mardi Gras Museum. The costume of the Krewe of Aidoneus. In any other circumstances David would have marvelled at the mask, a myriad subtle colours shimmering and merging in the glare of the light.

Ligios fumbled and almost dropped the torch and as the light played downwards, David could see their opponent was wearing long, flowing white robes adding a regal, refined touch to the huge frame.

'If we both jump him he won't stand a chance,' David whispered. 'Dazzle him with the torch again.'

Ligios flashed the beam. The beak of the mask snapped open, emitting a sound so hideous David brought his hands to his ears. Then he saw it. Just a glimpse, but it was enough.

Inside the gaping, screeching beak he could see grey skin pulled taut with tendons like cables. Illuminated in the torchlight, at the entrance to the throat was another mouth ringed with razor-sharp teeth, opening and closing, snapping shut with sharp clicks of rage.

It wasn't human.

Ligios must have seen it too for a small cry escaped his throat, a pathetic response in the face of something that should not be. 'What is it?' His voice was dry and paper thin.

'I don't know,' David replied. 'But I think we're in big trouble.'

A reek like a charnel pit radiated from the bird creature. David gagged, nauseous from the smell and from the fear that had its hooks in him, but he wasn't as scared as Ligios who had not had the benefit of David's brushes with the unknown. Ligios was rigid, his pupils shocked black dots. David touched his elbow to prompt him into movement. Ligios rocked and his mouth dropped, but he stayed where he was.

The bird-creature screeched again, half-avian, half-human, high-pitched and keening, chilling the blood.

And then it moved.

It was faster than David could ever have imagined. Its bulk cleared the length of the corridor in a second, the screech rising higher and higher. David only just avoided the sweep of its left hand which seemed to sprout razored talons. He half dropped to one knee, feeling the air whistle over his head. There was a rending noise and five furrows were ploughed in the plaster of the wall.

The bird-creature's other arm swept round and plucked Ligios off the floor as if he weighed no more than a bag of sugar. For a moment he remained rigid and then a fearful awareness dawned on his face. He opened his mouth and shrieked a shriek of madness. It was mirrored by the bird-creature as it threw its head back in triumph, its beak opening wider than Ligios' head.

David didn't wait to see what happened next. His knees popped with the strain as he crawled quickly along the floor next to the wall. Behind him, the bird-creature's noise had taken a terrible turn.

When he had passed the thrashing beast, David threw himself to his feet and ran to the end of the corridor, glancing only once over his shoulder as he turned towards the top of the stairs.

The bird-creature was in a blood-frenzy, rending and tearing at Ligios with its talons. He was jiggling before its onslaught like a puppet in a hurricane; within seconds his body resembled a tattered bundle of rags, hanging limply next to the blood-splattered walls. Then the beast opened its beak as wide as it would go, stretching the tendons on each side. David averted his eyes before the final sickening tearing sound.

And then he was running, down the stairs to the next floor, arms flailing to keep him from over-balancing, his lungs burning, his heart pounding, running, running to avoid that awful noise. As he rounded on to the first floor he realized the noise was drawing closer. It had disposed of Ligios.

And now it was after him.

All that was left was the primal instinct to escape. David cleared the next set of stairs two steps at a time. His landing on the polished floor was awkward and he skidded and fell.

There was a screech of triumph behind him.

Without looking, David knew it was at the top of the stairs. With a shift of his body weight he somehow righted himself and half ran, half tumbled, into the library, slamming the door behind him and tipping over as many chairs and tables as he could. He threw himself through the open window and winded himself as he landed partly inside an inhospitable bush on the edge of the gravel path. Pain flashed through his shoulder and he thought he was going to black out. Only the crashing in the library drove him to his feet.

The car seemed miles away, the other side of the world, but he ran. And he ran. Out on to the street. Towards the car. Almost crying with the exertion, ripping open the driver's door, scrambling into the seat, locking the door. The keys were still in the ignition where Ligios had left them for a fast getaway. He turned them. The engine fired first time. He put his foot on the accelerator.

Before he could depress it there was a crash behind him and the rear end lifted up and then smashed back down. In the rearview mirror, David could see the bird-creature clinging on, thrashing at the metal with its talons. The boot screamed and burst apart. The rear window imploded like a bomb going off. Glass showered on to the back of his head. The bird-creature's arm shot through, accompanied by hungry, slavering sounds.

David slammed the accelerator to the floor and popped the clutch.

The tyres squealed in protest, sloughing the car from side to side like a dragster before finding traction. For the briefest second it seemed to stand still and then David was hurled forward and whipped back as the car reared from a standing start. He hunched himself over the wheel, gripping tightly until his knuckles turned white.

Behind, he could still hear the bird-creature screeching over the protesting howl of the engine. A glance in the mirror revealed it trying to pull its way through the window space. A few more inches and it would be able to rip open the back of his neck to the vertebrae.

The world blurred past outside. With a muttered prayer, he hit the brake with his foot, simultaneously yanking on the handbrake. His head snapped painfully to one side as the car spun round in a 180-degree turn, narrowly missing a parked car. It skidded across the road and then he had his foot back on the accelerator, a tearing of metal resounding loudly before he felt a sudden lightness.

In the mirror, the rear window was empty.

David breathed deeply, suddenly feeling like a blow-up doll with a bad leak. Relief flooded through him, but he knew he could not rest. The bird-creature could not be killed so easily, it was too powerful, too inhuman. It was still out there somewhere.

He put his foot down to get as much space between himself and Broussard's mansion as he could. And as he did so he delved with one hand into his jumper, needing to know whether his precious cargo had survived its journey back into the outside world.

Underneath the protective layers of velvet, he felt his fingers close on a perfect circle.

Long hours passed before he could find sleep that night. Images of Ligios being reduced to a slab of bloody meat formed in garish colours whenever he closed his eyes. And then there was the head of a bird that was not a bird, screeching and screeching as it ripped at flesh.

He had dumped the car in Canal Street and thrown himself into the crowds of the French Quarter, losing himself mindlessly. But there, alone in his room, there was no respite, nothing to distract him from the horror. Occasionally he took the record out from under the bed and considered throwing it away as if that would end it all, but he could not bring himself to do it.

He knew in his heart there was no easy way out for him. His only option was to face up to the unfaceable, to the sequence that was being revealed, and go with it to the bitter end.

Chapter 23

David knew then. As the pale light of dawn filtered into the room like a ghost, the jigsaw pieces of his memory began to slot into place, interlocking gradually until a picture emerged.

He knew.

Staring at the ceiling above his bed, he could see links forming between his now-life and his then-life, between the horrors he was experiencing and the beauty and romance of his life with Fermay. Two sides of the same coin. The bird-creature had been there too, in London. Willie had seen it on a rainy Brixton night standing in a dark alley only minutes before David introduced him to Fermay.

It had started *then*, not, as David had thought, when he first arrived in New Orleans and the dead people started crawling out of the woodwork. It had started weeks before.

It had started with Fermay.

The crowds at Charlie's Place were sparse that night, as if everyone could sense the growing strangeness in the city. Those that had ventured abroad after dark were unnaturally subdued and the normally buoyant atmosphere of the French Quarter appeared stifled; partying seemed to go against the mood of the moment.

The weather had returned to normal, the violent climatic swings replaced by a marked lull, a stillness like the feeling at the apex of a rollercoaster ride. The only thing that remained the same was the music. The jazz, the blues and the soul, defiantly broadcasting from the bars and clubs, a call to arms – a promise of a better life, hope, faith and determination rolled into one. The music went on for ever.

David had remained in the apartment all day, watching the city from his restricted window view. He'd been almost afraid to step out into the open. The world suddenly seemed so alien to

275

him that even the walk to Charlie's Place seemed like a trip along the canals of Atlantis. There were no more guarantees. In his heart, he was convinced Fermay had been locked in that final room at Broussard's mansion, but he was terrified of returning and confronting once more that hideous creature which had destroyed Ligios.

His work in the stockroom was a comfort to him. It allowed his mind to drift, avoiding the strains of conversation, and it kept him away from the eyes which he felt were always watching him. For the most part, he was alone. Occasionally Dean would poke his head around the door to taunt him, and once Charlie appeared to make sure David wasn't 'talkin' to the walls an' all that mad shit.'

Arlene was the only person whose presence he could bear. When she finally ducked into the stockroom to talk to him, they hugged like long-lost lovers, their bodies tightly entwined, their scents intermingling. David was so wrapped up in the comfort it gave him, it took a while before he realized she was crying on his shoulder.

'What is it?' He held her face, knowing there was only one thing it could be.

'Scuba.'

'How did I know you were going to say that? So what is it this time, Arlene? Has he hijacked a shipment from the Medellin Cartel?'

'Don't joke about it, David. It's not funny.' She looked tired and frightened, like the pictures he had seen of women in Communist Russia, old before their time.

'I'm sorry. I didn't mean anything by it. It's just my way.'

'I know.' She gave a pale smile before bursting into tears again, the strain evident in every movement of her body. When the last sob had been stifled, she said, 'I haven't seen Scuba since yesterday. It's no great loss, y'know. Sometimes I like the peace and quiet. It's nice to be on your own, to have time to think. You ever feel like that?'

He nodded, lying.

'Yeah, I thought you would. Anyway, that's . . . not important. It . . . it was today. It happened today.' The breakdown of her train of thought was accompanied by another sob, but she caught herself and then continued, 'I went shopping. I wanted to get myself some clothes, something nice. It always makes me feel better. I was only gone for an hour. When I got back the apartment had been ransacked, not just a few drawers emptied out on the floor, totally, totally ransacked. Everything I own had been taken out and thrown across the room. All the furniture was upside down. Anything breakable had been broken. It was a nightmare, y'know, David?' She sobbed again. 'A total nightmare. Straight away I went and checked my jewellery. Y'know, I've got some things my mom gave me, silly, sentimental things and I wouldn't have been able to take it if they'd been stolen. It was all still there. I keep the box under the bed, but they'd found it and emptied it out. Nothing had gone. I knew then it wasn't burglars who'd done that. No. You know what? They were after Scuba and when he wasn't there they'd wrecked the joint to leave him a warning. Jesus, David!' she said, her voice suddenly rising. 'What would have happened if I'd been there? Would they have wrecked me too? Beaten me up? Raped me? Murdered me? What, David? What? I can't take any more!'

David gave her a hug, massaging the iron out of her neck muscles. 'You can't stay there any longer, Arlene. It's as simple as that.' He whispered into her ear, smelling the fragrance of her hair. It made him want to hold her tighter.

'Where can I go?' Her words were muffled by his shoulder.

'You know you can always come and stay with Beth and me. You don't have to wait to be asked.'

'Scuba wouldn't allow that.'

'You don't have to tell him! If he's still lying low,' *with no regard for you*, David wanted to add, 'just leave him a note to tell him what happened and say you've gone away until it blows over.'

'I don't know . . . he won't fall for it.'

'He'll fall for it.'

She considered his offer quietly before saying, 'OK,' as he knew she would.

'Leave work early tonight and wait for me at Beth's. I'm bound to have to work late and, anyway, you don't want people talking if we leave together.'

'I can cope with that,' she said.

'You might be able to, but I'm sure Scuba wouldn't be too keen if he heard it on the grapevine. When I get back we can go round to your place and pick up some clothes. If Scuba's there, I'll just say I escorted you home and you stay. If not, we get back to Beth's as quick as we can and lock the door. Deal?'

'Deal.'

This time Arlene hugged him, and in her embrace was not only thanks but also hope for the future. David tried not to respond to it.

Four a.m. The dead of night. David slipped out of the door before Dean could find him another futile task that would keep him unnecessarily occupied for a further half hour. It was a chill night and the air was sweet, a sprinkling of stars visible in the sky.

David's footsteps echoed hollowly in the empty streets around the club as he set off at a brisk pace, a little faster than normal but that was hardly surprising. The dark scared him. He'd always loved it in London where it masked the worst aspects of the city and added a subtle trapping of mystery and intrigue, but now he could never be sure what lay in the shadows. Unseen eyes followed him wherever he went. He would never be alone again.

Somewhere far away, a ship sounded its horn as it approached the city along the river, the sound could've been a funeral oration. David shivered and pulled his jacket around him. For some reason it made him think of Fermay. Where was she when he needed her? A long, warm kiss from her lips and a tight embrace in the dark would solve all his problems. The memory of her, emerging as it always did from nowhere, filled him with sadness. He was losing her. His failed raid on Broussard's mansion had been his last real hope. If only he hadn't started to believe. At least then the failure would not seem so awful.

As he walked on, the street behind him was empty. No one looked out of the windows on either side. A breeze stirred the hanging baskets on the balconies.

So why did he suddenly feel something five times stronger than the general feeling of paranoia which always followed him? More than that, his nerves were on fire, warning him of something drawing closer, swooping down like the angel of death. Swooping down.

Like a bird.

His head snapped up. It was there, sweeping across the rooftops, a dark shape silhouetted against the night sky, cruel beak opening and closing. Fear rose within him in a wave. He should have guessed Broussard would have sent it out to track him down – after all, isn't that what he'd done with Fermay in London. As soon as David thought it, he knew that it was true.

For a split second an image of Ligios' tattered body hanging from that beak flashed before David's eyes and then he spun on his toes and started to run, his footsteps like machine-gun fire in the street. The night shrieked behind him. He sprinted faster. Two blocks and he would be home.

Then what would he do? Lock the door? That wouldn't keep it out. He had seen its prodigious strength already, and if he did return to the apartment both Arlene and Beth would be at risk. No, he could not go home. His only option was to keep running until he lost it.

Overhead, the screeching sound reverberated through the night before fading away to leave a blanket of silence. Somehow that was worse.

He took a sharp left at the next block, trying to steer himself away from Beth's apartment. There was a clattering of roof tiles, silence and then a dull thud which David guessed was the creature leaping the whole width of the street.

At the end of the next block he took another left and, in the centre of the street, with the luminescence from the streetlamps pooling out on either side of him, he snatched a backwards glance.

The bird-creature was floating down to the street from the rooftops almost in slow motion, as if it was as light as a feather. It wasn't flying, it was just descending, arms outstretched like a crucifix. Silently it opened its beak wide, a hungry, preparatory gesture.

Then he was running again, fear fuelled. But he realized it was only a matter of time. He could not outpace it. It was too fast, too strong. Perversely he wondered what that first arcing tear from the talons would feel like. Would he black out, mercifully? Or would it be the ultimate agony?

Turning suddenly up a side alley, he hoped to lose the bird-creature in the same way that he'd once lost Lynch and Frantz. The alley was black as pitch and he slammed into a trash can. The impact winded him only for the briefest moment and then he was left running blindly. It only took him a few seconds to realize he had out-manoeuvred himself.

He was in a small courtyard barely ten foot square. There was no exit. Even though he saw the far wall at the last moment, he carried on into it as if it was an illusion and he would magically pass through. In a second, he recovered and spun round, pressing his back tightly against the cool bricks. The other end of the alley was a rectangle of light on to the street. It remained that way for a few seconds and then the bird-creature lurched into view, its huge bulk a silhouette of strangeness. It began to advance with the ponderous gait of something which knows its prey is cornered.

David felt his life slipping away from him. He thought of Fermay, briefly, and wished he had seen her one more time. The darkness all around him was as black and deep as a well, but he could tell it hid no doors or windows. The bird-creature advanced. It seemed hungrier now, its beak click-click-clicking like knitting needles.

There was the thought and then there was the movement, with only the briefest instant before David jumped and caught the bottom rung of the fire-escape ladder which his eyes had plucked from the darkness above his head. Taking the pursuit into the creature's own realm might not be the smartest thing he had ever done, but what choice did he have?

The bird-creature emitted a blood-chilling screech and David could sense it moving quickly towards him as he hauled himself up. He didn't hang around. Like a monkey he scaled the ladder, throwing caution to the wind as he achieved a speed which surprised even him. Then he was clambering over a parapet and on to the roof. The French Quarter stretched out all around, the light radiating up from below to reveal a magical rooftop vista of towers and cupolas, gambrels and secret carvings, steep slopes and flat-tops in Spanish and French style. In the distance the skyscrapers of the financial quarter glittered against the night sky. It was breathtaking, but it didn't slow him down. He moved across a flat section with speed and then on to the gentle red-tiled slopes that neighboured it.

Against his better judgement he glanced back and saw the bird-creature rising like a wraith, above the edge of the roof, its arms aloft.

David caught himself as his foot slid on the slick tiles. Ten feet away to his left the eaves dropped away vertiginously to the street below. He didn't look down. He didn't even consider it, keeping his eyes ahead and moving as fast as was safe.

His foot skidded with each step, but he concentrated on his centre of gravity and balanced like a surfer, adopting a simian half-lope with both arms hanging low. A gust of wind came out of nowhere and rocked him, but he rode with it. In this way he completed the stretch of roof.

He ran across the next one at the apex, one foot on either side, and found he could make quicker time that way with less chance of slipping. At the end he dropped on to another flat roof which ended at a black chasm. There was a gap of about ten feet to the next building and little room for a run-up, the walls disappearing into the blackness of an alley below. There was no fire escape.

Behind him the bird-creature was drawing closer, as imminent and unstoppable as death.

David couldn't afford to hesitate. He took a few steps back, closed his eyes and jumped. There was a brief sensation of flying, and then he crashed half-on, half-off the facing roof, his legs hanging over the void. He could feel the magnetic pull of the drop below him, dragging him down to his doom.

With an effort, he braced himself with his elbows and tried to get some traction on the wall with his toes, feeling like a cartoon character pedalling wildly whilst being plummeted over the edge of a cliff. Finally something caught and he inched himself slowly forward until his knees were on the lip. Then he propelled himself forward into a roll across the flat roof whilst overhead the moon cast a curious eye on his frantic attempt to escape, its butterscotch luminescence bright enough to light his way.

The pain seared his back like fire, erupting at his left shoulder and running down to his right hip. The force of the blow partly spun him around and he saw the bird-creature right behind him, raising its talons for another swipe. Its beak was opening, slowly. At the rim of its throat, David was fascinated by its other, secret, mouth, the ring of teeth that snapped shut, then open, a *vagina dentata*. Its arm, its human arm, moved towards him, sweeping in slow motion to mesmerize its prey. David threw up his arms to protect his face, rolling backwards as he did, and then . . .

He was falling . . . plummeting through the air, debris raining around him.

He thought: *Don't let me die this way.*

Chapter 24

David didn't know if he had blacked out for seconds or if he had lain there for most of the night. Broken tiles and wood covered him and all around was in darkness; every nerve ending in his body seemed to be crying out in pain. Above him he could see a jagged shape lighter than the surrounding blackness in which a few stars twinkled, the wind occasionally moaning through the hole in the rotten, sagging roof through which he had fallen. He had been lucky; two feet either side and he would now be a bloody, mangled heap on the sidewalk.

The haze gradually seeped out of his head, to be replaced by an awareness that the bird-creature could still be lurking on the roof, could even now be progressing towards him. David eased himself out from the debris, making as little noise as possible, and scrabbled around on the attic floor until he found the hatch which let him down into the main body of the house. The windows were dirty and broken, but they let through enough streetlight for him to make his way down to the ground floor quickly. Planks had been nailed across the door, but the jamb was soft and prising two free was as easy as pulling pins out of balsa.

He crawled out into the street nervously, eyes scanning the rooftops. He had considered waiting in the house until dawn, but that left the risk of being cornered by the hideous freak that had already left its mark on him. No, he needed somewhere safer where he could lie low.

'Third time's the charm, Dauphine.'

Her eyes were heavy with sleep, but it only took a second for them to burn with anger. 'I tol' you to stay away from here!' she hissed.

David remained calm, despite his desperation. He had not been so afraid in all his life, and when he spoke it was an effort to keep the tremor out of his voice. 'I've been chased across half the French Quarter by something that's got the head of a bird and the body of a man. If you close this door I'm going to wait here until it finds me – and you as well. I'm sure it's something you wouldn't want to meet. Am I right?'

Fear passed across her face like a spasm. Her eyes grew wide and white and she looked at him as if she wished he would die on the spot. When she glanced over his shoulder along the empty street, David realized she was more scared than he was, and it only took a second before she relented and hurriedly ushered him in. The door slammed behind him and the bolts were pulled across with uncommon alacrity.

'The E'lethri,' Dauphine whispered starkly.

'What?'

'That thing,' she said with loathing. Dauphine allowed herself to rest briefly against the back of the door, her eyes closed. 'Half-bird, half-human. The E'lethri.'

'What is it?' David didn't like to stand so close to the door; it seemed a flimsy barrier in the face of what lay without.

'A guardian of dark secrets and things of power. It is invoked with blood.'

'Where did it come from? What . . .' David struggled to find words.

Dauphine opened her eyes into an unwavering, stony stare. 'Believe me, boy, you don' want to know.' Suddenly her anger snapped, drowning her fear in a red wave. 'I tol' you to stay away!' she reprimanded, furiously waving a finger in his face. 'Now look what you gone an' done!' She continued in an impenetrable patois with hints of the Caribbean in its rhythms and inflections until slowly her anger abated. 'Go through!' she snapped, pointing within.

Night had transformed her parlour into a dark, primordial cavern. One small lamp threw a jigsaw of shadows that hung threateningly on the walls and ceiling. Only when she closed the connecting door did David relax.

'What choo doin', boy? You want to make me suffer? I tol' you I couldn't help you. Why don' choo listen? Why'd you want to bring all this bad stuff to my door?'

Dauphine sat behind her finely polished table, regally resting her hands palms down before her. Her eyes were white and round, accusing, causing David to wonder if he was as safe inside as he thought.

'I don't want to cause trouble for you, Dauphine.' His eyes ranged over her face, looking for a way in, a crack, that would allow him to ask for help. 'But I'm desperate. You know, most of the people I meet these days are dead.' He smiled wryly, a better presentation than the creeping hysteria he felt within. 'Some days they feel more real than the people around me. I've seen a man ripped apart by a beast from hell. I've been close to death so many times it's as commonplace as a trip to the supermarket. Do you know what's worse? I haven't the faintest idea why this is happening to me.' He looked around the parlour. 'Have you got a drink?'

Dauphine's tongue traced around the inside of her mouth thoughtfully, her eyes never leaving him. Her decision was made silently, without the merest hint on her face, and then she rose and fetched him a glass of dark, red wine from a stoppered bottle which she kept in a cupboard. David took a long draught. He would have preferred bourbon or scotch to provide instant, numbing relief, but the wine would do, eventually.

'All these things . . . these awful things happening to me . . . you know about them, Dauphine. You know *why*. I could see it in your face that first time I came to you, but you sent me away . . . Now I'm asking you again. You've got to tell me. You've got to!'

'What choo goin' to do if I don' tell you? Raise your fist in anger?'

David shook his head wearily. 'Of course not. Tell me anything, just keep talking until sun-up so I don't have to face that thing . . .'

In his dejection she found some pity, a degree of tenderness came to her face. 'You don' know what you're asking.'

'No one will find out, Dauphine.'

She laughed dismissively. 'You po' boy! Words have power beyond themselves. Once they're spoken, they're out,' she waved her hand around, 'jus' waitin' to be picked up. These people you're facin' – they see an' hear things that aren't laid before them.'

David drained his wine glass and set it on the table between them, watching intently as the light glinted off its rim. When he spoke again, his voice was quieter but the tension was still there, flexing in every word. 'Do you know what the soundtrack to this is, Dauphine? Banging. The sound of hammers on wood at the back of my head all the time. Sometimes it's just a distant rumble, like thunder. Sometimes it's a cacophony, *bang, bang, bang!* until I think my head is going to burst.'

'I will show you the roots,' she said. 'You must climb the tree yourself.' With this, Dauphine beckoned to him and led him into an even gloomier room at the rear of the house. Heavy drapes covered the windows but the atmosphere was imposing: the furniture was dark, antique wood and the carpets strangely over-patterned. Dauphine motioned to David to sit in a wing-backed armchair while she lit a stubby candle on a small table in the centre of the room, its flickering flame releasing the soothing aroma of bay leaves. Then she closed the door to the parlour and took a seat in another armchair just out of David's field of vision.

'The lines which brought you to this point stretch back years,' she began. 'Before you were born, before I was born. Like most things, it started with one thought. An evil thought in an evil man.'

'If it started years ago, how did I get dragged into it? How did Fermay?'

'You were unlucky.' She watched David closely as if trying to decide what to say and what to keep hidden. 'Your girl, she was trapped in the web a long, long time ago.' She rose, suddenly seeming tired and aware of all the problems bearing down on her. From a small box on the side, she took a pinch of powder and sprinkled it on the candle flame. It sparkled and crackled and a new, stranger aroma filled the room. 'Things are comin' to a head,' she said, shaking her head despairingly. 'After all this time. All the death an' the blood an' the heartache of years, it's all been leading up to now. If I was a different person . . . if the Lord gave me strength . . . I would do somethin'. But that's not the way it's goin' to be. I'm fated to sit back an' watch the night draw in like an ol' woman in her rocker on the porch.'

A sad smile crept on to her face. 'You don' want to know about that. You jus' want to know about your girl. I know there's no point in me tellin' you to leave well alone. It's too late for that now anyhow. But if you're goin' to get her back you're goin' to have to pay an almighty price. It might jus' be more than you have. Whatever you say to me, I'm not goin' to get involved in what's happenin' in the here and now, but I'll show you what *has* happened. I'll show you what started all this an' then you'll know what you're up against. What you do with the knowledge, well, that's up to you.' She returned to her chair.

David felt punch-drunk. Nothing made sense to him any more. 'What do we do now?' he asked.

'Jus' close your eyes and concentrate on my voice. Listen very carefully to what I have to say. I'm goin' to tell you about a time an' place long ago. Heed now,' she whispered. 'And learn.'

Her voice remained on one level, calming like the voice of his mother at bedtime, and with the cloying clouds of scented smoke wafting around his head, David found himself succumbing to the soporific atmosphere. He soon allowed himself to drift into a peaceful world where it was a balm to relinquish all responsibility and be towed along by that warm, rich voice.

'Back round the turn of the century,' Dauphine began, 'N'Orleans was Sodom an' Gormorrah and Jerusalem all rolled into one. There were plenty of churches an' chapels for the god-fearing folk, but there was somewhere to go for the other kind too, those who liked to enjoy themselves. Now I'm not sayin' the Devil had a place of his own in town – maybe he did an' maybe he didn't – but he sure dropped in to call from time to time. It's his place that concerns us. They called his place Storyville.

'It was named on account of it bein' the idea of one Alderman Sidney Story. He believed, an' rightly so, that you can never get rid of the trash in any city, the whores an' the gamblin' dens an' the gin joints. So one day Alderman Story had a fine idea. Why not put all the trash in one place that they could call home an' that way they'd keep the rest of the town clean. It worked fine, for a while. From 1897 it was a palace of sin an' a temple of dazzlement. If you wanted the finest woman in N'Orleans, she was waitin' there in Storyville, all warm an' rounded an' perfumed. Back then seven hundred women had their names in the Blue Book – that was Storyville's Yellow Pages to heaven an' hell. Whatever your pleasure, alcohol or junk, you could find it up there in Storyville.

'For me, the finest thing in those houses around Basin Street was the music. There were two hundred houses of pleasure with a trumpet in every parlour. Satchmo blasted out the hottest sounds around. Jelly Roll Morton an' King Oliver were cookin' up a storm. The Basin Street Blues was alive an' kickin' an' the whole of Storyville was dancin' to its tune. Course the pimps and the madams loved those boys! Folk used to come up to the whorehouses jus' to see the show of their lives. An' then they'd stay for dessert. Jazz wasn't born there, but Storyville slapped its ass an' sent it screamin' into the world.

'Yes, it was a fine old time. They shut it down in 1917. The navy, in their hypocritical way, couldn't take the sinnin'. They locked the gates on the Alderman's playground, threw out the women an' watched the jazzmen go north lookin' for work. N'Orleans has never lost its sense of fun, but it's never had a time like it did back then. Back then, it was Wonderland. Open your eyes.'

It took a second or two for her order to register. David had been drifting in a velvet pool, Dauphine's languorous voice his only link with reality. The candle smoke wafted coolly around his nostrils with the scent of summer gardens on a long afternoon. With a tremendous effort he forced his eyelids to open.

The sensations hit him with the full force of a blood rush to the brain. The night air was cold on his skin. Yelling, laughing voices and muffled music reached his ears. His nose wrinkled at the odours of cooking, beer and cigar smoke.

He was standing on a busy street, the rutted mud of the road beneath his feet. The shock of the transmigration caught him full force and his legs turned to hot toffee. 'What! Where are we?'

Dauphine's fingers closed around his upper arm and he started again. 'What's going on, huh? What happened to your house?'

She did not answer.

'This is a dream, right? I'm still sitting in the chair in your back room, drooling out of one corner of my mouth. Your voice, the candle, those things you were saying . . . you've put me into some kind of trance, hypnotized me?' David waited for a response which never came. Then he simply shrugged and said, 'Play the all-powerful witch-lady if you like, I don't care. If you want me to believe you've magically transported me back eighty years, fine. I know all you've done is put me into a heavy theta state so I'm more receptive to your suggestions.'

Dauphine seemed unperturbed by his accusations. 'There are dreams and there is reality and there are dreams.'

'That and other mumbo jumbo. Where are we supposed to be?'

'This is Basin Street.'

Though he knew in his mind it was a dream, his senses told him otherwise. He could smell the thick spiciness of strong gumbo wafting through the open window of a bar's cookhouse and the tang of aromatic smoke from roaring wood fires. His skin bloomed at the chill of the night, while his ears caught the beat of the music – a score of competing songs, in different keys, in different tempos – bass, trumpet, saxaphone, drums. Nearby a woman screamed and then shrieked with laughter as she dodged the hands of a grizzled, leering man in his derby and Sunday best.

It was as Dauphine had described it. The street was bustling despite the lateness of the hour, a playground for those hungry for the pleasures of the flesh. The women were beautiful, the *crème de la crème*, an orgiastic delight of high cheekbones, full lips, thick lashes, and wide, wide grins with pearly white teeth. They wore fine ruffled dresses of taffeta, imported silk and velvet. Through the open doors and windows David could see others in skimpier dress.

The men were drunk or sober as judges with little in-between, furtive or imbued with a bombastic *joie de vivre*, prowling in groups or marching with single-minded determination. The noise was enough to wake the dead. Indeed a sign over the door of one bar said in a florid script: *Tonight let us party for tomorrow we may die.*

'Great place,' David said. 'Sex, music and alcohol all in one spot. It's a supermarket for sinners.'

'A good choice of words,' Dauphine said darkly. 'Let us walk.'

His attention wandered from face to face, from doorway to window, like a schoolboy in the House of Fun. They avoided the entrance to a honky-tonk where a group of men clustered, their tempers rising in a welter of grunts and shaken fists. David stepped over a big-boned labourer who lay face down in a pool of vomit outside a barrel-house.

A jazzband was in full swing in a cabaret called the 101 Ranch. David paused outside, watching the musicians through an open window as they jolted uncomfortably on a cramped stage. They were white, their faces contorted by the passion of their playing.

'That's the Original Dixieland Jazz Band.' Wonder was evident in his hushed voice. 'They really made it big. They proved white boys could play the jazz.'

'They *will* make it big,' Dauphine corrected.

A few doors down towards Beauregard Square, David was stopped in his tracks by the sound of a honking trumpet. A prickly shiver ran down his spine. The style was instantly recognizable and he was determined not to believe it could be so, but he could not stop his heart quickening. Squeezing past the crowd in the doorway of a brothel, he could see the young musician, his eyes shut tight, light dancing around his head as he milked the soundtrack of his soul from the trumpet. His foot doubled the beat and, with amazing skill for one so young, he stressed accents around the rhythm.

'Satchmo.' David gaped in awe, a golden moment that he would always remember, a magical, shining beacon – Louis Armstrong before he set out on the road to fame.

He would have stayed there for the whole set, bedazzled, but he felt Dauphine's insistent tug on his arm and reluctantly followed her back on to the street.

'I want to meet him,' he said. He realized he had been holding his breath. 'Jesus, Dauphine, I just want to shake his hand!'

She fixed a cold eye on him. 'Don't you go forgettin' why you're here.'

David could not resist one last backwards glance as the sense of loss overwhelmed him. Here was something he would never experience again. 'Can they see us?' he asked as a drunk lurched across his path.

'That's a strange question for someone who thinks he's dreamin'.' Dauphine smiled ironically, but offered no answer.

It troubled him. It was all too real, every sight, sound and smell, even the occasional breeze that ruffled his hair.

She must have seen the doubt on his face, for she added, 'No, they can't see you. They're too deep in their lives.'

'Deep in their lives,' he repeated. 'I remember when I was like that.'

Dauphine stopped outside a brothel with no name and motioned to the open door. 'We're here.'

In the hall, David could see a dark-haired woman in a basque and stockings sitting provocatively in a wooden chair, one leg draped over the arm, her crotch prominent. Dauphine led him past her, ignoring the room to her right which was raucously alive with drinkers and romping women. A thick fug of smoke clouded the air, while in the far corner was an empty stage with a battered, upright piano, its white keys gleaming in a cheesy grin.

David looked the hooker in the eye as he and Dauphine mounted the stairs to the first floor, but she did not blink or meet his gaze. He felt like he was dead.

At the top of the stairs, they doubled round on to a landing lined with flaking, chipped doors. From behind them, David could hear grunts and gasps and the sound of punished bedsprings. The crack of a whip or a belt echoed dully through one of them.

Dauphine paused at the foot of the second flight of stairs, looking into the darkness at the top. It reminded David of Broussard's house. An air of apprehension clouded her face and her eyes darted uncomfortably from the dark summit to David. He could see she was considering turning back.

'Nearly there?' he asked. She nodded slowly. His voice seemed to spur her into action and she started to climb the stairs with the reluctant insistence of someone embarking on a loathsome task.

When his eyes had adjusted to the gloom at the top, he noticed a thin strip of flickering light at the end of the landing. He realized it was shining through the gap at the bottom of a door and the way it ebbed and flowed told him it was radiating from a flame, a candle or an oil lamp.

'Is this what it's all about? Whatever's behind the door?' he whispered.

Dauphine did not answer, her gaze fixed on the strip of light as she walked. When she reached the door, she did not hesitate, one twist of the handle swinging it open. David stepped in front of her, drawn by a powerful magnetism that had the feeling of destiny about it.

He stood in the doorway, wanting to scream, thinking he would vomit.

The room lay before him like a vista on to hell. It was small and decaying with paper peeling off the wall in huge flaps, the paintwork blistered and cracked. The floor was bare boards, splintered and stained from years of abuse and it was sparsely furnished with only a rickety wooden table, a chair, a metal bed and, incongruously, a shining black piano. On the table, a candle guttered in the draught and cast unpleasant shadows around the room.

There were two occupants.

One had his back to David. He was black and naked as the day he was born, the skin of his wiry back gleaming like polished leather and dappled with droplets of sweat which ran in a tiny rivulet down the crack of his behind. David could tell from the streaks of grey in his tight, curly hair that he was in his fifties. His hands and forearms were red.

On the bare, iron springs of the bed was a woman. She was screaming, but the only sound which emerged from her gaping mouth was a strange, strangled gurgle. David saw with horror that she had no tongue and that the red around her mouth was not lipstick.

Her hands and feet were tied roughly to the bed frame with strips of her own clothing, and her wrists and ankles were rubbed red raw where she had struggled vainly. Her garish underwear, revealed where her outer clothes had been torn away, marked her as one of the brothel's residents and drew attention to the ghastly pallor of her skin. Her eyes were wide and glazed with confusion at the unjust hand that had been dealt her.

Her body had gained another orifice: a gaping wound from sternum to belly, sucking and breathing as the blood bubbled out. The man must have had his hands up to his wrists in her intestines.

David wanted to run forward and grab him, throw him across the room, but he was rooted. He could do nothing but observe.

The man turned slowly, his lithe muscles rippling beneath his skin. He had an erection. For a moment, he surveyed his hands, watching as the blood ran down them and drip-drip-dripped rhythmically on the floorboards. His face was blank, but there was a coldness around the eyes which hinted at a soul as barren as the surface of the moon. Shaking himself from his moment of contemplation, he strode across the room and sat at the piano. Red droplets of blood splattered across the virginal keys as he raised his hands and began to play, an expression of almost orgasmic pleasure filling his face.

Behind him the woman writhed violently and then relaxed, her strength exhausted. She stared at his back in despair, but he was oblivious to her, lost in his music, his head rolling backwards and forwards passionately.

At first his fingers pulled out random, dissonant notes, but the more he played the more they began to come together into a complex tune, layer building upon layer. The strata of richness kept David transfixed.

He had heard the music before. It came to him as if through a dream, the smallest part of it overheard somewhere, only a few bars maybe, but it had driven itself to the back of his mind and taken root there. He recognized its themes, notes that seemed to whisper: *There is no meaning to life, only black despair and the void*.

David's heart was beating faster, driven by an excitement that felt like a drug, while his skin tingled with arousal. Slowly he became aware of a pain in his wrist and when he looked down he saw Dauphine's fingernails were biting into his flesh. Her face was filled with panic, but her voice sounded a million miles away, drowned out by the swamping waves of music. She appeared to be shouting, but David could not make out the words.

His eyes were drawn back to the pianist whose fingers darted across the keyboard, seemingly without conscious thought, like those of a man possessed. David felt a red haze slowly fogging the edge of his vision. Then Dauphine's face was in front of his, her nose only inches from his own. She was still shouting.

This time he could just hear her. 'Don't listen! Don't listen to the music.'

It was a strange thing to say and David laughed at it. He turned away, still smiling, relishing the powerful intoxication induced by the strange composition.

Dauphine slapped him across the face so hard that his ears rang, and then she passed her hand slowly across his face and all sound vanished – the music, the pathetic, dying gurgle of the woman, the moans of illicit sex, the braying and barking of the downstairs party room. A ringing silence settled across the room, but the pianist still ran through his demented motions, now resembling some madcap character from a Mack Sennett movie.

Dauphine's face was still before him and she was mouthing the words *Don't listen* over and over again. He wanted to do as she said – he knew deep down that it was important – but the music was like a drug. He could hear it right then, fighting its way through the noise vacuum, very faint, not yet a threat, but growing louder. And he welcomed it.

She raised blood with her second slap, her palm catching the edge of his lip and splitting it, shocking him to his senses. He nodded to her with sudden acceptance and suppressed his hearing until the music disappeared again. Relieved, Dauphine moved back to his side and they watched the silent tableau together. Blood was smeared all over the keys, making their silent music a symphony of death.

David could sense something was going to happen; there was a rise in atmospheric pressure and the room grew darker. As he watched, the woman died, her breath trailing out in one long, final gasp. The pianist reached the crescendo of his masterpiece of jazz.

Then it happened, as if a switch had been suddenly thrown.

The walls of the room blew out with the force of a nuclear blast and a brilliant white light flooded in. David felt he was looking into a different world, a cold, alien environment that would snuff his life in an instant if he ever entered it. He felt the uncaring eye of the void upon him as if he was no more than bacteria squirming in a petri dish.

The pianist faced the light, his stained arms raised, his eyes shut in silent supplication, and then he began to speak. The words were lost to David, but he was aware of their pleading. Cajoling, begging. Something answered with a voice that was not a voice. David felt a lurching dread.

There was a blackness moving in the light, a shimmer, a shadow, and it was followed by others, a multitude surging forward, a legion. One of them erupted out of the glare like a lightning bolt, towards the pianist. He screamed soundlessly and the light winked out, taking the sputtering candle flame with it.

David stood in darkness; he groped out blindly for Dauphine. When his hands did not make contact, he began to stumble around, moaning her name. Then he began to shout.

Then he began to scream.

His eyes snapped open and he saw her face in front of him. At first he thought she might be concerned, but no emotion registered; there were just her eyes looking deep within him. With a feeling of relief, David glanced around. They were in the back room at Dauphine's house. The blue candle had gone out and the only illumination was that filtering under the door from the parlour.

'A dream. I was right! A dream. But what did it all mean?' The sound of relief in his voice was almost a caricature. Slowly his aching fingers uncurled from the chair arm where they had been gripping tightly.

Dauphine did not answer him until they were sitting on opposite sides of the table in the parlour, and then she said simply, 'That was how it began.'

'Who was the man?'

'Lionel Johnson. They used to call him Hound Dog.'

'I know about Lionel Johnson. That music . . .'

'They say the Devil has all the best tunes. That was one of them. Johnson was a no-talent, no-hoper, but he knew where to go for inspiration. He listened good when that music came through from the other side and he put it down on a record.'

'"Night-time Blues."'

'"Night-time Blues." Only it wasn't just music, it was a spell, powerful, powerful magic. He made that record so that anyone who heard it . . . well, that don't concern us.'

'Tell me. It might be important.'

'No.' She was adamant. 'If someone ever tells you to listen to it, *don't*. That's all I'm goin' to say about that.'

'Would it kill me?'

'That's all I'm goin' to say.'

David considered telling her that the only copy of 'Night-time Blues' was now in his possession, hidden under his bed, but he thought better of it. The fewer people who knew that the better. Now he could understand why Broussard had preserved it, why it was valued beyond its rarity. 'Did he really kill that girl?'

Dauphine nodded soberly. 'He thought he'd found a short cut to a better life. But anybody'll tell you, there ain't no short cuts.'

'She was a sacrifice, right? Just a piece of meat in offering to get what he wanted from . . .' He remembered the white light, the shapes within it. 'From . . .'

'That poor girl was a teaser to get the Dark's attention. He wouldn't have got the music without her and . . . well, he sure got somethin' in return, but it wasn't what he expected. He never did get to play no Radio City. He got somethin' else, somethin' that proved more valuable to him. There was a price to pay, though. There always is.'

David considered her words, the connections building rapidly in his mind. 'So what's Johnson got to do with Aidoneus?'

'He set them up. He formed the krewe with one thing in mind – to get the power he wanted. They were the holders of his song an' they were there to see his business was done, even after he was gone.' She poured another glass of wine for David and this time had one herself. 'What Johnson was told that night, no man should ever hear or think about. A pact was made an' sealed with that girl's blood. Johnson had to provide souls, hundreds of them, killed in the right way at the right time. His band were the first, the men who helped him record his song, an' that served two ends 'cause none of them could ever get together to play that terrible music again. Johnson might have been a waste of time an' space, but he wasn't a fool. He knew he couldn't get all those souls in his lifetime – an' *that's* why he set up his krewe, as a cover, to see the killin' was carried on after he was dead an' buried.'

'That doesn't sound like much of a deal. What use is it to him when he's dead?'

Dauphine smiled coldly. 'I tol' you he wasn't a fool. When that last soul is offered an' the Evil comes rushin' into this world, Johnson comes back too, all fired up an' filled with the power to do what he wants.'

Finally David asked the question he had wanted to ask at the start. 'What's Fermay got to do with all this?'

Dauphine shook her head and refused to meet his eyes. 'That's for you to find out.'

'Why won't you tell me?'

She shook her head once more, this time silently.

'And that music. I'm sure I've heard it . . .'

'You forget that music!' Her tone was so harsh it brought him up short, before she added simply, 'It calls the Dark Side.'

The importance of the record to the krewe slowly dawned on him and he realized that if his life had not been on the line before, it certainly was now. The E'lethri had been hunting through the night for him. Perhaps all of the Krewe of Aidoneus were out on the streets with orders to reclaim the record at any cost. Still, he was not about to return it. It was his ace, the one thing he could use to bargain for Fermay.

'You got any more questions, boy, or can I get back to my sleep?'

'Yeah, I've got a few. How come you know so much about this?'

'Eugene Broussard and me were lovers.' Her words were so baldly stated she seemed matter of fact, but the sour expression on her face told differently. 'When I was a girl and not so wise as I am now. He was always a powerful man an' he took my heart from me right from the start. I was just a fool in love . . . until I found out about Aidoneus an' what they were plannin'. I walked right out of there. He lets me keep on livin' 'cause I sit here like an old woman, doin' nothin', sayin' nothin'. . .' A fleeting expression of self-loathing crossed her face.

'And do you know how many souls they need to get what they want?'

The fear in her eyes was unmistakeable. 'Not many.'

'That body in the river, the one with the head smashed in . . . all those deaths the police are investigating . . . ?'

She nodded.

'I've *got* to know about Fermay, Dauphine.'

'You take my advice, you'll forget her.'

'I can't do that.'

'I know.' Her voice held a hint of sadness, or pity. 'You stay here, you're goin' to lose. You're goin' to lose everythin'.' The shutters went down once again. 'I'm not sayin' any more. You've seen how it started. You've seen what you're dealin' with.'

'You showed me that to frighten me off, didn't you? It won't work, Dauphine. I'm living my life with the dead now. Nothing else can disturb me. I accept it all . . . all the darkness.'

'I keep tellin' you, boy – there's some things worse than the dead.' She smiled grimly.

'I'll find Fermay,' he said. He leant over the table and held out his hand which Dauphine took hesitantly. 'Thanks for all you've done. I know how difficult it's been for you. Every bit of imformation helps. Even seeing Johnson . . .'

'You never know,' she said disturbingly, 'you might meet him again one day.'

The journey back to Beth's apartment was not far, but with his gaze fixed firmly on the skyline it took him longer than expected. Come the first light of dawn, he was surprised to realize his fear had diminished. Part of that was due to the disappearance of the darkness, but part of it was because he felt empowered now he realized the true worth of the record. It made him a target, but it was also his defence. He only felt true relief, though, when he had locked the door behind him and retreated to his room. There was a note on his bed from Arlene. She had waited for him, as they had agreed, and when he had not materialized she had decided to go back to her place. She was worried, didn't know what to do, afraid Broussard had got to him again. He should call her the moment he got in, the note said.

When he did, she sounded on the edge, as if she had not slept all night – which was probably true. David didn't tell her about the E'lethri or what had happened with Dauphine; he didn't want to make things any worse than they were. He put her mind at rest with a little white lie about someone following him, and said he had lain low all night. It seemed to do the trick. He promised to help her out later that day. When he hung up, he felt more alone than he had ever done.

Beneath the bed, the record was calling to him. David reached down and took it out, turning it slowly in his hands, finding it teasing and comforting.

Should he play it? Despite what Dauphine had said?

He wrestled with the idea for a long moment and then put the record back under the bed; there was plenty of time for playing records. Right then, all he wanted to do was sleep.

Chapter 25

Four hours of sleep was all David could manage. Warm, reassuring thoughts of Fermay and memories of happier times kept getting swallowed up by other images.

Several times he awoke suddenly, sure he could hear a dull, rhythmic banging in the room, but there was nothing there. Finally he could take no more. Feeling tired and strung-out he dragged himself from his bed to face a day which to most people would have seemed sunny and filled with possibilities.

Outside the door, he hopped on to one of the horse-drawn carriages that hauled the tourists around the Vieux Carre. It was hiding in plain sight; no one ever looked at tourists. They were ghosts, fleeting images in a place in which they didn't belong. His driver was laid-back, drawling out his commentary with a smile and a well-rehearsed quip, punctuating each joke with a flick of the reins. The journey was lazy and soothing, but David couldn't help looking at the rooftops, even though he doubted he would ever see the E'lethri in broad daylight in a crowded place. A woman leaned on her balcony and smiled seductively at the driver, wiggling her hips when he wolf-whistled in reply.

'An' that's where Tennessee Williams used to sit writin' in the lazy afternoons,' the driver said. 'I'm sure he won't mind me sayin' that the view's prettier these days.'

The mid-morning sun was hot and David was glad of his baseball cap which he had pulled low, although occasionally a cooling breeze blew by, fresh with the scents of flowers from some balcony garden. David settled back into his seat and noted with some surprise that for a moment his worries had disappeared. New Orleans still held its magic.

But it wasn't long before he realized there had been a palpable change in circumstances during the night. On a street corner a man doffed his hat and smiled at him. David nodded in reply until he noticed the man cast no shadow. Then he saw his clothes in more detail, rotten and stained with the mud of a shallow grave. When he let his eyes wander around, seeing the city for the first time that morning, death was everywhere.

A woman shambled along the sidewalk, shocked and distressed, bumping into walls and lampposts. When David passed, she looked at him and her eyes widened with recognition. An old man stood on a balcony facing the sun, serene and thoughtful, his hands behind his back, and a colourful handkerchief rakishly blossoming from the breast pocket of his white suit. A bullet had taken out his right eye. He turned and waved to David when the carriage passed beneath. A naked man, his wrists bound, wandered aimlessly across the road in front of them, smiling with a mouth filled with broken teeth.

There were more, too many to catalogue, each with their story waiting to be told. David saw at least twenty of them before they reached Jackson Square, all of them acknowledging him as he rode through.

The individual manifestations no longer frightened him – he had seen too much – but he was troubled by their collective appearance and by their recognition. It signalled something, although he was not sure what. Perhaps they recognized that a crucial time was approaching, a pivotal moment when life and death would be held in balance.

Or perhaps they were simply preparing to welcome David into their ranks.

David tipped the driver and moved quickly from Jackson Square through the crowds to the riverside. Moose was easy to find, still working his turf loudly and with good humour. He was David's last resort. There was no one else who could get him back on track in his search for Fermay.

'Hey, man, what's wrong with you? You look like you've just seen a ghost.'

'That's right.' David chewed on the inside of his lip. 'I need some help. Can you talk?'

'Sure, man. Shoot.'

'Ligios is dead.'

'Yeah?' Moose didn't seem too surprised. 'Wondered why he wasn't hanging out last night. What happened?'

'He got caught the other night – inside the house.'

'Clumsy, man, very clumsy. Ol' Bill should've known better.'

'I've got to go back inside or something. We didn't finish searching the place.'

Moose shook his head. 'Not wise, *at all*. It's too soon. They'll be waitin' for you.'

'I'm desperate. There might be some information about my girl in there. I've got to get to her.'

'Sorry, man, can't help you. Give it a couple of weeks, maybe a month. We'll try then. When things've quietened down.'

Further along the path, near the docking point for the steamboat *Natchez*, two men stepped across the streetcar tracks and began to walk towards them. One half of David's mind couldn't help but wonder if they were dead. Their gait seemed sluggish and their heads were bowed, but the brightness of the sun made it difficult to tell. He shivered. Why was that always his first thought: are they dead?

'Maybe there's another way,' he continued. 'Do you know someone who . . .'

'This is a bad time, man. Everybody's nervous. The cops are antsy about those killings an' the TV guys are giving them a hard time for not doin' anythin'. Nobody wants to take any risks.'

The two men drew closer. There was something about them, something familiar.

'I can't afford to wait,' he said, still watching over Moose's shoulder. And then he recognized them.

It was Krugman and one of the detectives from the precinct.

They were trying to appear nonchalant, but David could tell they were zeroing in on him by the way Krugman occasionally glanced along at him.

'Keep talking, Moose,' David said, looking straight into his face. 'Don't look round. There are two cops walking towards us, plain clothes. They're after me – only they're bent cops. They're involved with Aidoneus and if they catch me, I'm a dead man. I'm going to make a break for it soon and I suggest you do the same. I know a lot of things they don't want me to know, and now they've seen me talking to you – let's just say they won't take any chances.'

'Thanks a lot, man.' Moose looked worried, his eyes darting from side to side.

'Just run, Moose, as fast as you can.'

Krugman had obviously recognized that they were going to make a break and was already moving in by the time David looked up. His hand was inside his jacket.

'Run!' David yelled. He turned and sprinted along the side of the streetcar tracks without checking to see if Moose was following.

'Stop!' Krugman's voice barked out angrily, but whatever else he was shouting was drowned out by the shrill whistle of the *Natchez* and the rattle of an approaching streetcar.

'Shit, man,' Moose said breathlessly at his side. 'They got their guns out.'

The first shot was a warning, ricocheting off their path. To their left, across the tracks, was a high wire fence, while to their right was the river. The only way was ahead, at least for a hundred yards, but then David could see a gap in the fence which led through into the French Market.

A shower of concrete exploded on the ground where the second bullet hit. Krugman was still yelling, but the competing noise of the streetcar ahead drew even closer.

'Get on the tracks,' David gasped.

'What?' Moose seemed to be flagging beside him.

'Get on the tracks! They won't shoot at us in case they hit the streetcar.'

Without breaking step, they left the riverside walkway and moved into the path of the streetcar which bore down on them mercilessly. Bang, bang, the wheels rattled. Bang, bang.

A third bullet zinged off the tracks, hot metal on metal.

'My heart, man! My heart!' Moose sounded frightened now. His sunglasses slipped from his nose and he threw them away. 'Shit, man! I don't need this!'

The streetcar was only yards away. David could see the driver's face, framed in shock.

'When I give the word, jump to the left,' David said. That would put the streetcar between them and the detectives. 'We'll go through the fence, split up.'

The juggler appeared from nowhere. Or maybe he had been hiding at the side of the track where David hadn't been looking. That hideous death's-head, that chalky-white face, eyes black-rimmed and wild. His hand was moving through the air and there was something in it, something silvery. His arm came down suddenly and then across, and bright red spurted out in a jet. Moose gurgled and disappeared from view. With a screech the streetcar surged into them. David jumped. There was a noise like screaming, like agony, and David realized it was Moose, his voice drowned out by wheels locking on metal before he was suddenly cut off.

They had killed him. Knifed him and then left him to die so it looked like an accident.

David didn't stop. With tears of anger in his eyes, he dived through the fence, running as fast as he could, dodging this way and that through the jumble of the French Market, the face of the juggler engraved on his mind. If only he had known that the bizarre performer was involved with Aidoneus when he had watched him on the steps of the cathedral. If only . . . but that wouldn't have saved Moose.

Hell closed in around David as he ran. The streets and people passed in a blur. For one strange moment he felt he had been running ever since that first time when he had leapt from the streetcar on his arrival, and everything since had been a dream.

Only when exhaustion finally overtook him did he stop and look behind. Krugman, the other detective, the juggler – all lost. He realized then that it was impossible trying to carry on as he had been; the dark forces aligned against him were drawing closer and if he stayed in New Orleans any longer his life would most definitely be forfeit.

'You know what, honey, you look like death.' Arlene lit a cigarette, tossed back her hair and posed in the filtered light from the stage. A golden halo surrounded her head as the smoke drifted upwards.

'Nice choice of words, Arlene. Thanks a lot.' David finished his secret beer and dropped his bottle on her tray.

'This is the first time you've been out of that stockroom all night. What've you got in there? Some grass and a cheerleader?'

'I wish! Arlene, things are getting bad. I've been hiding out all day – since this morning anyway – and I was in two minds about coming into work tonight, but . . . well, I wanted to see you. Say goodbye.'

'*Goodbye*?' Her smile faded quickly. 'Where are you going? What's happened?'

'I'm getting out of town, for a few days anyway. Maybe a few weeks. If I want to keep living, I've got no choice. Those guys who beat me up are getting too close and next time they won't let me walk away.' He pulled another Dixie from his pocket and knocked off the cap on the edge of a post. 'There's no way I can get close to Fermay when things are so hot out there. It seems like there's someone watching out for me on every street corner. It's getting so I'm afraid to go anywhere there's a crowd. My guess is that if I stay away long enough, it will all cool down. Then I can come back and carry on looking for Fermay.' There was a little voice in his head telling him that he was running away, that he was abandoning his task because he couldn't face up to it.

'You're sure she's . . .'

'Yeah, I'm sure she's alive and I'm sure she's with Broussard, only I've got no idea if he's keeping her at his house or somewhere else. Shit, Arlene, I'm so confused!'

'A rest will do you good.' Arlene tenderly held her palm against his forehead, pretending to check his temperature, but really just wanting contact.

'Moose is dead.' The words seemed terrible in their baldness.

'What?' Arlene looked horrified, her hand going to her mouth in shock.

'They got to him this morning, slit his throat and left him to die under a streetcar.'

She stared at him and then she said, 'I'm going with you, David.'

He shook his head adamantly. 'You can't.'

'You need me.' It was a simple statement, but powerful, and they both knew she was right. 'I'll stay with you, look after you until you get back on your feet. I can watch your back, y'know, let you know when the goons are coming.' She laughed, then smiled, then looked serious again, trying to find an emotion that fitted.

David carried on shaking his head. 'You've got a life and a job and a boyfriend. You can't afford to give up all those things.'

'I'll still have a life. The job – hey, it's not like I'm a Cindy Crawford, y'know. And Scuba, I need him like a hole in the head. Maybe this will shake up my life, get me out of the rut I've dug myself into. Y'know, David, this could be good for me!'

'And maybe you're just putting on a happy face so I won't think you're throwing everything away for a worthless dickhead from London.'

She hugged him so suddenly it startled him. 'You're a friend, David, and I care about you. I want to help.'

'I don't—'

'Listen, jerk, I'm coming whether you like it or not.'

Finally David relented; she was a big girl now, she could make her own decisions. 'OK. As long as you know what you're getting into. It might be dangerous.'

'Who cares? It's better than dying of boredom. Where are we going?'

Where *were* they going? He hadn't even thought about it, so preoccupied was he with the pure act of escape. 'I don't know. Just out of the city somewhere. We could bum around.'

'If you want to get lost, Louisiana is the place to be. There are a lot of swamps and hickvilles out there. When do we go?'

David could not bring himself to travel anywhere at night; the dark was too dangerous. 'Dawn,' he said.

After Charlie's Place closed, Arlene ordered a cab to take them to her apartment. David slid down low in the back seat, never even raising his eyes to look out of the window, and Arlene surreptitiously held his hand in the dark.

She lived on the top floor of a crumbling old block with stairs that creaked with each step and an odour of damp permeating everywhere, but when she opened the door to her apartment David could smell flowers, polish and the crisp smell of kitchen cleaners. The lights were on in some of the rooms.

306

'Shit.' Arlene swore under her breath and hovered on the threshold as if she couldn't decide whether to enter or go back down the stairs.

'What is it?'

'Arl? Is that you?' The slurred, drunken voice of Scuba floated out of the kitchen.

Arlene ignored him and turned to David. 'I just want to pack a small case in the bedroom. We don't have to be here long.'

They had to pass the kitchen as they walked along the corridor. Scuba was slumped on the floor next to the open fridge door, an empty six-pack scattered around him and a dwindling bottle of cheap vodka clutched in his hand. He cut a pitiful figure, unshaven, unkempt, but his physical appearance wasn't the worst thing. The air of confidence and arrogance had been crushed from his eyes. Now he just looked scared.

'Arl, what . . .' His eyes focused on David. 'What are you doing here, Limey?'

'Leave him alone, Scuba,' Arlene interjected angrily. 'He's helping me pack and then I'm getting the hell out of here.'

'Where you goin'?' It was painful to watch the thought processes played out on his face. 'With him? With that wimp?' His voice rose angrily as he tried to pull himself to his feet. 'You're not leavin', Arlene!'

'Who do you think you are, talking to me like that?' she snapped. 'You treat me like shit. You're never around when I need you. Shit, Scuba, you're never around! I've had enough of all the crap you've given me. I'm getting out. From now on you can do what the hell you want!'

With an effort, Scuba pulled himself to his feet, temper raging on his face, and then he staggered forward with fists bunching like a street fighter. Halfway across the kitchen he changed, the fear suddenly returning. He looked around nervously as his hands slowly unclasped.

'You can't leave me, Arlene. I *need* you.'

'You should've thought of that before.'

Scuba held out his hands in a pathetic pleading gesture. 'They're after me, Arlene. I don't know what to do.' His voice cracked. For the first time David wondered if it was the krewe.

They were into drugs as they were into every other criminal activity, and if that was the case Scuba stood little chance.

'Who? The drugs gang?' Arlene's face lost some of its harshness, but there was not as much sympathy as David had expected. Before she had jumped when he had spoken, but now their situations had reversed, as these things did in relationships. 'I warned you, Scuba, but you wouldn't listen to me,' she continued in a softer tone. 'You can't mess with these guys. They're not human beings, they're machines. They just want the folding green and no excuses. Anything less and you're an obstacle in their way.'

'I know that now, Arlene. Jesus H, if I could go back . . .' Tears formed in his voice. 'They wanna rub me out. They've got an enforcer . . . shit, SHIT! They think I'm still in Baton Rouge, but it's only a matter of time before they come back here looking for me. I've gotta get out, and you've gotta come with me, Arlene. You've gotta! We could go back to Crystal City, hide out for a while. They'd never find us there.'

'Scuba—'

'I know I've treated you bad, Arlene, but I won't be like that again. It's the truth. We'll be like we were when we started out. You remember that? You remember the good days?'

David could see from Arlene's face that she could. There was fondness there, maybe even love, but it was a memory, nothing more, and it disappeared just as quickly.

'Sorry, Scuba, it's too late for all that now. I'm sorry you got yourself in this mess, but it's *your* mess. You sort it out. You've gotta grow up sooner or later . . . I can't carry on being your mom. I'm leaving town for a while. You'll find somewhere to go and if you're still around when I get back, maybe we can talk then.'

As she started to walk down the hall towards the bedroom, something erupted in Scuba and his anger returned like a hot geyser, fuelled by drink and desperation. His hands were fists again as he barged out into the hall, yelling, 'Arlene, you bitch! You're coming with me!'

Arlene whirled, frightened by memories. Her hands automatically went to her face.

Before Scuba could advance towards her, David had grabbed him, throwing him back into the kitchen. In his drunkenness, he teetered off balance and then crashed into the fridge before sliding down to the floor and his original position among the beer cans. The impact knocked the fight right out of him, but there hadn't been much there to start with. If he had been sober and his old self, David couldn't have tackled him, but now he was like an old dog which had been whipped one time too many. David left Scuba staring in shock at the floor, and as he walked away the sound of uncontrollable sobbing floated out behind him.

Ten minutes later, as they hurried back to Beth's apartment to wait for sun-up, David asked Arlene if she was doing the right thing.

She smiled tightly and said, 'We all have to take risks to get what we want out of life, David.'

He found it difficult to sleep, but when it did finally come it was filled with dreams that were not dreams. The past streamed back into his head, Fermay and Willie and London, vibrant and filled with life, the Fog Zone giving up its secrets . . .

Chapter 26

'God, I love this city!' Fermay hooked her arm through David's and slid in close. The look of wonder on her face that rarely seemed to disappear filled him with a warmth that he had not felt since he was a child. She watched everything, the people, the cars, the shop windows, as if seeing them for the first time. Occasionally she would tug him over to look at some insignificant thing with unrestrained glee and he would have to skip and hop to keep apace with her. Somehow she saw the magic, where he could only see the mundanity, yet he experienced it through her and felt like he was being reborn.

The Sunday morning shoppers in Camden Market crushed and jostled in their frantic search for bargains, a dinosaur herd driven to hunt by a hazy race memory. The majority of them were under thirty and uniformly dressed in black: leather jackets, Levi's, Doc Marten boots, mohair jumpers, long overcoats, a thrift-shop congregation worshipping at the church of Punk and Goth – a now-fading religion that had had its heyday. At times, though, the crowds seemed too much for Fermay and she said so. She had always had a problem with too many people, the legacy of her lonely childhood.

'Maybe we should have gone to a market which doesn't attract any customers,' Willie said acidly. His sour expression seemed to increase in line with Fermay's wonder. 'Where all the goods are really expensive and there's no variety. What do you say, Fermay?'

'Shut up, Willie.'

'What is it with you and the rest of humanity anyway?' Willie haphazardly flipped through records on a stall with the bored expression of someone who knew he wouldn't find anything of interest.

Fermay delved into a box of rare groove discs and did her best to ignore his jibes. 'So I had a sheltered upbringing, so sue me. I didn't get the chance to hang around a lot of people. It seems weird to me, all these people in one place.'

'Poor little Rapunzel up in the tower. Let down your hair, let down your hair!' Willie looked over at her to see what effect his mockery was having, a slight, supercilious smile on his face.

Fermay showed no sign it was having any effect.

'Come on you two,' David interjected wearily. 'Let's try to get through at least one hour without you sniping at each other.'

'You know I come here every Sunday in the hope that I might find some rare jazz record that I haven't got in my collection.' Willie changed the subject almost reluctantly. 'You'd think I'd realize by now how futile it is. All I do is mooch around the stalls for a couple of hours and then I end up going to the pub and getting pissed for Sunday lunch.'

'You're a creature of habit. You wouldn't want it any other way.' David moved in to stand between them.

'Just once I'd like to stumble across a record that really excited me. Something from the fifties. Maybe earlier.' Willie's eyes sparkled behind the thick lenses of his glasses. 'Yeah! Something no one else has. I dream about it sometimes. A stall filled with really crap records like those Hot Hits albums from the sixties, all scratched with dog-eared sleeves. I flick through them and there, right in the middle, is the rarest jazz record in the world! I ask the stall owner how much he wants for it and he doesn't know how valuable it is. He says it's mine for a couple of quid. I take it home, lock myself in my room and excite myself. That's my dream.'

'Some people have fantasies about Madonna and Julia Roberts. You know. *People.*'

'Who wants that when you can have records? They don't kick you out of bed in the morning. They always provide you with enjoyment. The *perfect* relationship.'

They moved on, pushing through the crowds like explorers in the jungle, Fermay pausing at all the clothes stalls, picking up garments, feeling the cloth or leather, checking the stitching, occasionally enquiring about the price. Overhead the sky was a powder blue with only two small, meandering clouds scudding across it. It would have been easy to think, even with the cold, that winter was already behind them and spring and its fresh start just around the corner.

They walked along the towpath of the canal in silence, listening to the sounds of a jazz quartet playing 'Saints' to the young and lazy sipping cappuccino in the open air. David felt happy there. Being with Fermay provided him with a feeling of boundaries collapsing.

The aroma of vegetarian chilli bubbling in a pot attracted them and they ate a large serving with pitta bread while sitting on a wall. Fermay remained quiet, watching the shoppers go by with a fascinated eye. David couldn't tell if Willie's constant sniping was starting to bother her, but he guessed it probably was. Any normal person would have been irritated by such a relentless assault.

Willie, in contrast, was in high spirits. 'Two more stalls, that's all. There are some tucked away at the back. They might have something.'

'Why don't we just go for a beer?'

'Because I'd never forgive myself if I missed something I really wanted.'

'How would you know?'

'You know what I mean.' He paused. 'What happens if they're selling the only copy of the Lost Record?'

'Not that again.' David chewed on his pitta bread, trying to ignore the pain in his gut from the chilli.

'And why shouldn't I be fascinated by the rarest jazz record in the world? You go to any record fair and there's always somebody muttering about it, normally the obsessive types with dirty anoraks and personal hygiene problems. Nobody knows where it is. Probably tucked away in some collector's vault.'

'It's a myth.'

Fermay had spoken for the first time in a quarter of an

hour. She looked over at Willie coldly and repeated, 'It's a myth.'

'It might be.' Willie took off his glasses and buffed the lenses urgently on his handkerchief, a habit when he was irritated. 'But if that's the case, there are a lot of people who believe in it.'

'A lot of people believe in flying saucers and the Loch Ness Monster, but it doesn't mean they're there.' Fermay screwed up the paper that had wrapped her pitta bread and held it tightly between her knees. 'People who spend their lives looking for that record are wasting their time.' She looked into the dark waters of the canal and seemed to lose herself in her memories. She continued abstractedly, 'And if it did exist it might not be worth finding. It might be . . .' Her voice drifted off, her glassy eyes focusing somewhere far away.

'Well, I'm an agnostic,' Willie said dismissively. 'I'll keep an open mind. Maybe I'll look for it when I'm over in New Orleans, spend a little holiday time trawling around the record shops.'

'Are you thinking of going to New Orleans?' David interjected.

'Maybe. I've got the money set aside and I've got some time owing.' David felt a little irritated that Willie had not mentioned it before; and they had also promised each other that they would visit the city together. 'If the record does exist,' Willie continued, 'someone there should know about it.'

'It's a myth. Forget it.' Fermay stood up and walked along the towpath.

'There goes little Miss Moody,' Willie sneered quietly. 'Jump up and run after her, David. Can't you hear the dog whistle?'

'Eat shit and die, Willie.' Baffled by her attitude, David followed her and caught her arm. 'What's wrong?'

Fermay shook her head, staring out across the canal to the houses and shops beyond. 'I don't know. I'm just irritable. I woke up with a strange feeling about today . . . oh, maybe it's just PMT.'

'It's probably the fact that you hate Willie.'

'I don't *hate* him, David, really. I dislike him. I think he's an arrogant, selfish jerk. But I don't hate him.'

'Just try to get on with him – for my sake.'

'OK, OK . . .' Fermay froze mid-sentence, her gaze fixed on a point somewhere over David's shoulder. As he watched in puzzlement, waiting for her to explain what she had seen, the blood drained from her face and her mouth formed an 'O' of shock.

'Fermay?' David grabbed her arm, feeling the muscle rigid as stone beneath his fingers. When he turned round, following the line of her frightened stare, there was nothing there – just the familiar Camden panorama of shops and houses which greeted him every Sunday.

Then he saw it. Or thought he did.

On a rooftop, moving quickly, a dark shape visible only for a second before disappearing into the glare. David squinted, not quite sure if his eyes were being tricked by the distance and the quality of the light.

He had to be mistaken. It looked for one moment like a giant bird.

'Fermay . . . ?' He turned round, but she was already walking quickly back the way she had come, towards Willie who was still playing with the remains of his pitta bread, flicking chunks of it on to the towpath for the pigeons. Her volatility still surprised him. Her occasional moods were difficult to comprehend, seemingly without reason or trigger. It was entirely possible she didn't like the architecture or the position of the sun in the sky, he thought with slight irritation, but as soon as the notion crossed his mind, he felt guilty about it. He had seen her face. He had seen the fear and shock there. Something had disturbed her.

Something bad.

David looked back at the skyline. Roofs were flat or sloping, aerials protruding starkly. The sun was bright and rising slowly. There was nothing out of the ordinary. But the more he thought about it, the more he was sure he *had* seen something, just briefly, passing across a dead spot in the glare.

314

A giant bird?

Sure. And a pink elephant.

They cut short their browsing and returned to Brixton amid Willie's protestations and unanswered questions. David managed to calm him and persuade him to take them back to his house for coffee, while Fermay remained mute in the back of the car, shrunk down in the seat.

Behind the locked door of Willie's house and away from the windows, she slowly began to return to normal. As she wandered around the lounge, picking up magazines or browsing through the extensive record collection, Willie watched her with something close to contempt.

'Nice collection,' she said eventually. 'You've got all my favourites.'

'It would be better if I had the Lost Record,' Willie replied with pointed antagonism.

Fermay spun and glared at him with such cold hatred, the words died on his lips. 'It's a myth.' Each word was turned out with a coating of vitriol. Even David was chilled.

'*Yes*, I was scared, Davey.' Fermay played with her chicken madras, mixing her rice in with her fork like a child at its first school dinner. 'But please don't ask me about it. It was nothing to do with Camden or the people there, I just . . . I don't want to talk about it.'

David wondered how far he should push the issue. The more he got to know her, the more he realized she was hiding something from him. At the start of their relationship he had overcome his worries by telling himself that she would open up once they grew closer, but now they had been seeing each other for weeks. The icy grip of winter was preparing to become the open hand of spring. They had exchanged gifts; the talisman for their relationship – the poster she had given him – hung on the wall. And still he was no closer to probing the darkness that lay at her core.

'How do you like the restaurant?' he asked, changing the subject.

'Hmm, nice wallpaper. Red flock. Clashes with the carpet perfectly.'

'You don't go to an Indian restaurant for the decor. You go to punish your intestines with a selection of spices that are alien to your body's normal diet.'

'Oh. The culinary equivalent of a horsehair shirt. I can live with that. Punishment is good for the soul.' She swallowed a forkful and nodded appreciatively. 'I'm glad you didn't bring Willie along.'

'I thought we should have some time on our own. Time to talk. We don't do that very much.'

'Of course we do.'

'Not *really* talk – not about the things that are important to us, that drive us. We skirt around the big issues.'

'Yeah, well, what can I say? The big issues are overrated.'

A couple on the next table paid their bill and left, allowing David to raise his voice above a whisper. He ordered another beer before he began his tirade.

'Fermay, I don't know how you feel about you and me, but we're not going to go very far if you keep erecting this barrier between us. If all you want to do is have fun, then fine. But if you have any aspirations for anything more, then we have to talk. And soon.'

'Talk about what?'

'Secrets.'

Fermay stared at her food for what seemed like an age, until David saw a tear fall from her eye and splash in the centre of her curry.

'What is it?' he asked frustratedly. 'I can't work out your reactions.'

From behind her fringe, she said quietly, 'I knew it would come to this eventually. If I carry on as I am, I lose you. But believe me, David, if I told you everything that has happened to me in my past, I'd lose you too. And that would be worse because then you'd hate me. Anyone who knew all about me would hate me.'

David reached across the table and grabbed her hand, his grip reassuring, but in its tightness also a desire to dispel her self-pity. 'Fermay, for an intelligent person, you're really not very perceptive. Do you think . . .' He repressed the sound of his voice, but not the emotion. 'Do you think there is anything you could tell me which would dampen even slightly my feelings for you? Fermay, I love you.' He searched around anxiously for the right words, 'I love you more than life itself. I remember when I was very young, my mother trying to explain true love to me. She said it's when you love someone more than you love yourself – and when you're prepared to give up your life for that person.' David paused, making the words he was about to say too heavy by far, 'Fermay, I would give up my life for you.'

'David, don't say that! Don't ever say that!' Her shocked face and fearful eyes seemed an overreaction to his words, but he cut her short and continued.

'If I feel that way, how could I ever stop loving you because of anything you might say? There is nothing in your past that could make me love you any less.'

There was a flicker of something across her face that might have been hope. 'I wish I could believe you, David, more than anything else in the world.'

'You can. You just have to have faith.'

She smiled.

From the restaurant, they wended their way through the dark streets to the Jazz Attic, the place where they had first met, a place that held power in their relationship. The band on that night was not very good, and although the music was technically brilliant, it had no soul. Neither of them cared. It was fun to be out there, laughing, drinking, sparking off each other with an energy that had been building for weeks.

At one point, when the music thundered through the speakers and the lights flashed purple, then gold, David looked into Fermay's face and thought: *This is it. For life.* He didn't know she was thinking exactly the same.

Romance had come into his life stealthily, unbidden, stealing away his past and offering him a future. In that one spot, in that one moment, David realized Fermay had given

317

him salvation from a life as grey and unfeeling as stone. He could never go back and he never wanted to.

Surprisingly, when Fermay spoke she gave voice to his thoughts. 'You've saved me, David,' she began. 'I never believed in the good things until now. I just hope . . . I just hope I can escape what I've left behind. I don't want that spoiling everything that lies ahead for us.' She gave him a tight, clinging hug. 'I'm going to tell you everything – I've decided. You're right. I've got to do it. It's the only way I'll be able to leave the past behind. I just hope you won't shut me out when you hear what I've got to say.'

'Never. When do you want to talk about it?'

She considered his question with her eyes shut and then said adamantly, 'Next week. Just give me a few days to prepare myself. There I've said it now! There's no going back.' Even in the brightly coloured lights from the stage, David thought she looked momentarily pale.

'Don't worry. Things will work out fine.'

'Of course they will. But what if . . . ?'

'No buts.'

Fermay laughed. 'No buts.'

The band crashed into a laughably soulless version of 'Saints', but it sounded like the greatest music on earth. David and Fermay went to hold each other at the same moment, bumped bodies and tangled arms, then laughed. Finally they kissed. For the first time it wasn't a kiss of desperation, a holding on to fill a hungry need. It was a sealing of their love. To David, the night radiated like a beacon. If he suffered for the rest of his days, he would still die happy, for right then he had experienced perfection.

He pulled back and looked into Fermay's eyes, past the fear and the worries, and there it was in her too. A light that would never go out.

'Here?'

'No, no, a bit to the left.'

'Bollocks. Are you mad? To the *right* and down a bit.'

Fermay and Willie glared at each other across the room

318

while David held the framed poster next to the wall and looked from one to the other; their pretence at cordiality was collapsing with unnerving regularity.

'Come on, make up your minds,' he snapped. He was perched precariously on a kitchen chair that had not been new twenty years ago and his arm muscles ached from awkwardly manipulating the picture back and forth across the wall. He waited five seconds for an answer and then said with exasperation, 'Fuck it, it's going *here*.' He rested the picture carefully on the floor and hammered a nail into the wall with three hard blows. It slipped into the plaster and brick with worrying ease.

Fermay and Willie remained silent as he hanged the picture, adjusted it three times until the bottom was horizontal, and then stepped back to admire his gift.

'Perfect,' Fermay said.

'Certainly cheers the old place up,' Willie said. 'But that's not too hard to do. Even Dracula could get depressed in this dump.'

'Well I like it,' David replied. 'When you live in a morbid hole, the rest of your life seems brighter.'

'Very philosophical. Why don't you crack open the beer and the wine – that should brighten up your life even more.'

Fermay fetched the drinks from the kitchen and handed them out. She had done a good job preparing the party on a small budget, and even though most of their cash had gone on booze, she had still managed to work up a small buffet. David had tried to sample it several times during the afternoon, but she had fended him off violently, telling him he was like a small child waiting for his birthday party. That was almost true. The hanging of the picture was only an excuse for what he really enjoyed doing: relaxing and hanging out with the people who meant the most to him in the world.

David tossed the hammer on to the sofa and Fermay quickly snatched it up and placed it in easy view on the bookshelf. 'You'll forget to give that back,' she chided.

A mocking smile sprang to Willie's lips. 'Listen to mother.'

David flashed him a black look, but Fermay didn't seem to hear as she headed to the kitchen to fetch more food and drink.

'It's bizarre, this party for just the three of us,' David said, as he riffled through his CDs. He pulled out 'A Love Supreme' by John Coltrane.

'We've never been particularly hot on the friends front, have we,' Willie replied. 'We're such an antisocial couple of bastards. I suppose in that respect Fermay fits in very well. She's just like us. We've got our own little world, tightly enclosed, and the rest of the universe keeps out.'

'Yeah, well, they'd only ruin it if they came in, wouldn't they? Sometimes, though ... don't you think we'd benefit from a bit of contact with the rest of society?'

Willie thought for a moment and then smiled broadly. 'Nah. Fuck it. Hey, did I tell you? I've finally made the big decision.'

'What's that?'

'When to go to New Orleans. I was sick to death of us talking about it and never doing it, and with your girlfriend going on about it all the time, I just upped and booked a flight and hotel.'

David felt a twinge of jealousy, but he knew it was unfair. 'I hope you have a good time, you bastard. You better bring me back a present.'

'Of course I will. The best.' Willie glanced over at the pile of booze. 'So are we allowed to get pissed?'

'Of course we're allowed to get pissed – as long as you only vomit in the toilet. And that's me talking, not Fermay, before you ask.'

'I never vomit. I'm a man. I can take my drink.'

'Macho, very macho. I'm impressed.' David ripped at the ringpull of the can of Guinness and swallowed a mouthful, grinning as it went down. It was going to be the first of many.

Willie and Fermay hid their antagonism well for most of the evening, and David knew it was for his sake, but he could still sense it just beneath the surface like a pike in a lake. It had been growing over the weeks and it showed little sign of abating. Sooner or later something would give and David didn't want to be there when it happened. They were both volatile people, although Willie, with all his logic and belief in rational thought, controlled himself better. David wondered if he would have to choose between them, something he would resist doing at all costs. After all, they fed different aspects of his psyche. Willie was his childhood friend, his link to his past and the days of wantonness and irresponsibility. Fermay was his love, his link to the future. How *could* he choose between them? Deep down, though, when he allowed himself to think about it, he knew that really there was no choice at all.

Fermay smiled at him, a secret smile that Willie did not see, and in it were all the reasons why he loved her. He had even found himself thinking about settling down with her. David Easter! The original fly-by-night. Love does strange things to a man.

She lit two candles and placed them on either end of the table. 'What say I tell the future of you two ambitious, thrusting gentlemen?' she said, picking up her pack of Tarot cards.

Willie eyed them sneeringly. 'Oh deary me, the female Russell Grant. I'll pass on this one, thank you very much.' He adopted a mock-serious tone. 'As a humanist, I have no time for mumbo jumbo. Besides, I have no desire to know my future. I prefer it to remain a mystery. That way I'll get more surprises.'

David nodded in agreement. 'Yeah, let's give the future a miss. My teachers always said I never had one, anyway.'

'And you've certainly proved them wrong, haven't you, David-boy. You've got a great job in a record shop. Lots of prospect of making manager in ... oh ... fifteen years ...' Willie smiled tightly at his winning point.

'If you were Donald Trump I would take heed of your opinion, but ...'

'Yes, yes, I know.'

'OK,' Fermay said, cutting in. 'How about if we do a more general reading? Like what's happening now?'

'Sure,' David said, eager to please. 'Whatever.'

Fermay dealt the cards and began to talk, spinning tales, weaving humorous anecdotes and witty observations into a sharp analysis of their lives at that moment. David was entranced. She showed such skill and charm he could not see how anyone could fail to be bowled over by her. But when David looked up at Willie his face was blank and unimpressed.

It irritated David more than he could express, to the point where he wanted to grab his pal and shake him and tell him not to be so blind. Fermay knew she was making no impression on Willie, David could see that, but she didn't care. All her attention was focused on David. Willie was not allowed to intrude into their world.

When she had finished, David wouldn't let her clean the cards away until he had fetched his camera from the bedroom and handed it to Willie.

'Take one for posterity – and don't cut off any heads. I want to remember this night.'

'Why should you ever forget it?' Willie said sarcastically.

David shuffled up next to Fermay on the sofa, his intoxication caused by more than alcohol. Fermay snaked her arm around him and pinched his behind where Willie could not see. David reached back and squeezed her in return.

'Ready?' Willie took off his glasses and focused the camera. 'Say something witty.'

The flash was blinding.

And after that the drink flowed: empty cans and wine bottles piling in a growing hillock in one corner. David slumped in the armchair with the sagging seat and realized that at some point during the previous hour, alcohol had got the better of him. He was capable of little more than staring at the clock on the mantelpiece, although it kept drifting out of focus and he had to cover one eye to bring it back. In the background was the CD which had been set on repeat because no one could be bothered to get up to change it. His tongue had given up long ago when his conversation had slurred out of control and Fermay and Willie had been forced to talk to each other.

With a misty detachment, he watched them side by side on the sofa, their body language speaking volumes. They were each leaning on an arm, as far from each other as they could get on the same seat, their eyes never meeting. When they spoke it was as if they were talking to the room in general, rather than to each other, and it was obvious that here were two people who could barely tolerate each other's presence.

David remembered hearing the conversation drift on to the subject of jazz, as it so often did. It was as much an obsession in Willie's life as it was in David's, but the similarities ended there. David loved to listen to it and watch it performed. Willie, with his extensive collection of rare recordings taking up most of his home, wanted to *own* it. Willie asked Fermay what bands she liked and Fermay replied with the detailed knowledge of someone who had lived the jazz life. They compared notes, half-heartedly, on different styles and performers, on composers new and old. Fermay asked Willie about his collection and that allowed him to expound at length on the sources for his discs: the specialist shops and collectors' fairs; the way he had it ordered, filed and cross-referenced under musical styles, performers, decade, country of origin; the speed with which he could find any record.

His voice droned on in the background like a bee in a summer garden, and David drifted and drifted, floating on the waves of alcohol, in and out of the conversation, picking up snatches of sentences here, half-heard words there . . .

And then, through the fog, he could hear voices raised angrily. Somewhere down the line the conversation had turned into an argument. Willie was raising his hands in the air, pleading and cajoling with growing annoyance and vehemence. Fermay was shouting at him to shut up, to forget it, that he was mistaken, that it did not exist, occasionally turning her back on him, her dark hair thrashing as it did when her emotions were charged.

323

'Of *course*, you know where it is. I can tell! Little things you've let slip. You know too much about it,' Willie was saying.

'Drop dead! Leave me alone.'

The record. The stupid Lost Record that intrigued Willie so much. *Did* Fermay know something about it? She had denied it, but the way she was talking . . .

'Why don't you just come out and say it?' Willie said with exasperation. 'You don't fucking like me.'

'You're right, I don't like you. You're not a nice person. You're dragging David down, and you're trying to split him and me up. I'll never let that happen. *Never*.'

'If he stays with you it'll be the worst thing that ever happened to him. *You're* the one that's dragging him down, leeching off him. You don't care about anything, only about—'

'I don't care about anything apart from him and me, that's right. That's all that matters. The rest of the world can go to hell!'

'Shit!' David watched Willie hurl a half-full can across the room as if he was watching the scene through a gauze. 'In an ideal world, somebody would just take you out.'

'Take me out?'

'Permanently. Bang. One clean blow to the head. Do us all a favour.'

'Funny,' Fermay replied frostily. 'I was thinking the same about you.'

David saw the look that crackled between them and realized he would never be able to reconcile them. Then he thought of his mother, and his father. And then he slipped once more into the soothing alcohol pool. But as he went he had a terrifying feeling that he might never see the light again.

PART 3

The Late, Late Show

*'They have sown the wind, and they
shall reap the whirlwind.'*

Hosea (8:7)

Chapter 27

The grey waters of the Mississippi roiling beneath the bridge looked strangely inviting, reminding David of the Thames 3,000 miles away in space and a life away in time. He remembered how magnificent London's river looked from the top of The Monument; a shining, silvery ribbon stretching to the horizon, inspiring in its timelessness. He wondered what it would be like if he jumped. Beneath the slow-moving waters of that wide, old river he could let himself drift away, finally finding peace in a secure grey world.

'Too much thinking isn't good for you.' Arlene rested an affectionate hand on his shoulder.

Her eyes were a sparkling crystal blue in the early morning sunshine. David looked back at the deep water. 'I was thinking about escape.'

'Escape's this way, honey.' She pointed south-west across the bridge. 'We can lose ourselves in the bayou for as long as we want. Nobody goes right out there. I guess the Cajuns in the interior like their secrets too much, and the tourists stay around the edges where it's safe. If we can find a place to stay, it'll be like dropping off the edge of the earth.'

David felt reassured by her strength and he was bowed by the extent of her sacrifice for him. 'I appreciate you coming, Arlene.'

Her cheeks flushed slightly. 'Don't think about it, sugar. You would have done the same for me.'

They stood at the beginning of the bridge for almost an hour, breathing in the carbon monoxide and the oily petrol fumes as the cars and lorries trundled past their thumbs. Eventually an open-backed pick-up rumbled to a halt next to them, its paint job camouflaged with primer and rust. The driver leaned over the passenger seat and examined them through the open window.

'You folk lookin' for a ride?' he asked.

'We ain't standing here for our health, mister.' Arlene flashed a flirtatious smile. She could turn her sex appeal on and off like a grandmaster of seduction.

The driver was in his fifties with a ruddy face, sun-tanned and wind-blasted, his eyes grey behind silver-framed glasses. A dirty, white kangol shielded his head.

'Wa'al,' he said, rubbing his chin thoughtfully, his eyes twinkling teasingly, 'no one gets to ride for free. What can you offer me?'

David bristled at the comment, as protective of Arlene as she was of him, until he saw there was no lasciviousness in the driver's face. 'How about this?' He pulled out of his pocket the jazz cassette which had been his sole entertainment and a close friend for so long.

'Music.' The driver laughed with hearty approval. 'That's good enough for me, people. Hop in!'

Arlene wiggled up next to the driver and David sat on the outside, resting his elbow on the window where the breeze could refresh him. The driver cheerily shook hands with them and introduced himself as Will something-or-other, a French surname that David didn't catch. He snapped the cassette into a machine haphazardly wired beneath the dashboard and hummed along to the first track.

'The music of life,' he said, swinging his head to the rhythm. 'We Cajuns, well, music was invented for us, folks. It's in our blood. You can always make a Cajun happy by giving him a gift of music. So where are you folk going?'

'Oh . . .' Arlene smiled falsely as she searched for an answer, '. . . around.'

'I'm over from England for a few weeks and I wanted to do some sightseeing,' David interjected. 'Arlene said it would be great to get a cabin in Cajun country, somewhere off the tourist track.'

'See how real folk live? Good idea.' Will cracked his gum. 'So you got a place lined up? A friend of mine's got a place to rent out, ain't much, but I could axe him . . . ?'

'That would be nice,' David said quickly.

'There we are. Problem solved.' Arlene gave his thigh a secret squeeze. 'Now we can sit back and enjoy the journey.'

Across the bridge, the road rolled on ahead of them, the

industrial environs of the city eventually giving way to a flat landscape filled with flat buildings, car lots and drive-in restaurants, and then scrubby, wind-blown countryside. The whir of the traffic and the rhythm of the music was soon joined by another sound, the drone of Will's voice. Talking was his hobby in the same way that for some people it's train-spotting or stamp-collecting. If there was a lull in the conversation he went into overdrive, filling it with a jumble of words and sentences until there was smooth consistency once more. The weather, politics and the highs and lows of his life blurred into one, punctuated by loud, off-key singalongs to David's tape. His questioning was superficial and didn't force David to confront any of the things he was trying to forget, leaving him instead to sit back and drift along in a limboland of meaningless noise.

The grey-streaked sky had threatened rain all day and by the time they were deep in the countryside, fat drops had begun to burst on the windscreen. It quickly became a torrent, sheeting across the road as they turned off the highway and followed a series of minor roads into the heart of the bayou. As the clouds rolled over, obscuring all sight of the sun, they brought with them an oppressive atmosphere.

The road followed the channels that crisscrossed the wetlands, occasionally passing the Cajuns' wooden homes hunched over the water like ancient anglers waiting for the fish to jump. A gaggle of children squabbling on a rickety wooden jetty, oblivious to the downpour, stopped and waved as Will rumbled by. He blasted his horn in reply.

They came to a halt outside a single-level white house which looked as if it had been constructed from old packing crates and unwanted timber. It could only be reached by a deeply rutted driveway which was turning into a sea of mud in the rain. Cypress trees clustered blackly around it on three sides, but there was a path through them to the levee at the rear.

'You folk wait here,' Will said. 'I'll see if he's in.' The thin wisp of smoke that rose from the chimney signalled that someone probably was.

Will emerged from the house a minute later accompanied by a tall, gaunt man with a wiry black beard, an off-brown felt hat pulled tightly on his head. They beckoned and David and Arlene hurried through the cloudburst to the protection of the roughly built porch.

'Here he is,' Will said, slapping his friend across the shoulders. 'He goes by the name of Duchayne. Don't know if it's his first name or his last – he's never said. Me, I call him a lyin', cheatin' weasel, but you folk don't know him well enough yet.' He laughed loudly at his own humour, but only the barest flicker of a smile crossed Duchayne's lips.

Arlene introduced both herself and David and explained once more that they were looking for temporary accommodation while Duchayne listened and nodded. 'Well, cher, I think I can help you folk out,' he said after she had finished. 'My cousin died and left me a place just a ways from here. It's no palace, but it's clean and it's got light and heat. You're welcome to it for . . . say . . . fifty bucks a week.'

David would have haggled, but Arlene accepted the offer and paid the cash up front.

Their 'holiday accommodation', as David called it, was a shack, no more, no less, but it was dry and the pounding rain revealed they would not have to worry about any surprises from a leaking roof. Duchayne gave them a key, although the door could have been forced with one thrust from the shoulder, and then the Cajun handed over some clean linen for the bed, wished them well and left them to settle in, happy in the knowledge that he had concluded a good deal.

'Welcome to paradise,' David said, slipping his suit on to a wire hanger and arranging it on the outside of the wardrobe. The inside smelled of mould.

Arlene threw the sheets haphazardly on the bed and sprawled across it, her legs, long and slender, sending seductive alarms off in his head; she arranged them naturally to maximum effect.

'Well, y'know, it's no Sonesta Hotel, David, but we haven't all got such high standards, know what I mean?'

'I've lived in worse places than this,' he replied, rising to the bait. 'There are squats in Brixton that make this seem like a bijou residence.'

'Oh, you hard man.' For one moment, in the confident

330

warmth of her smile, he almost succumbed. It would have been so easy to clamber on to the bed next to her, to nuzzle up into the crook of her neck, to feel some human warmth. The desire was almost irresistible.

He returned to unpacking what few possessions he had. 'And I bet there are cockroaches.'

The rattle of the raindrops on the corrugated roof was at first like gunfire and then strangely comforting. A draught came through the dust-smeared window that looked out towards the water, soothing in the humid warmth of the day, and adding to an atmosphere that was refreshingly relaxing and lazy.

'I'll sleep out there,' he said, pointing to a threadbare sofa covered in stains and patches.

Arlene gave him a look which told him he didn't have to, but she nodded reluctantly in agreement.

The cabin felt reassuringly secure, but David could not shake the feeling that he had not really escaped, and at times he would turn suddenly and look out through the window into the grey and green countryside. And see nothing.

The three days following were calm and quiet. David would rise at first light, eager to leave his troubled sleep, and walk out among the black boles of the cypress trees, breathing deeply of the clean air. The cries of the swamp birds as they took flight into the dawn sky was unusual music to him.

One morning he saw an alligator swimming sinuously out into one of the wetlands channels. It was only as long as his arm, but it provided a moment of pure excitement. He felt stronger for being away from the city and its 'cloud of evil', but he knew the moment he set foot back in New Orleans it would swallow him and taint him once more. Looking out over the water, he kept asking himself one question: was he man enough to face up to his destiny or was he still the frightened boy he had always been, hiding away and letting life pass him by?

Early on the second evening Arlene plucked up the courage to head out to a nearby store to phone Charlie. Her attempts to explain how she and David had been forced to skip town because of trouble were drowned out by a rising tide of abuse and curses.

'He didn't take too kindly to being left two workers down on his busiest night of the week,' Arlene told David afterwards with great understatement.

'But will you still have a job when you get back?' David asked with concern.

'Who says I'm going back?'

David pressed the point and Arlene finally admitted she thought Charlie would forgive her. 'He's a sweetie at heart. He won't leave me high and dry.'

'Do you want to go back?' he asked.

'No,' she said confidently. 'I want to stay with you.'

On the fourth evening they opened a bottle of wine which David had purchased on a grocery-buying expedition with Duchayne. After a hot chilli cooked by Arlene, it was cool and soothing and they drank it from chipped mugs in the moonlight, a communion shared in prayer for happier times. By the time the bottle was empty they felt closer than they ever had done before.

The night birds sounded mournful in the dark, lost souls loose in the trees. And when Arlene laughed, her voice sounded just as much a part of the natural world around them. David watched her move through the cabin, carrying the mugs to the sink; through his alcohol haze, and when the moonlight caught her through the dirty windows, he thought she was Fermay. There was the same mix of vulnerability and strength, summed up in something as simple as the way she held her head when she was listening or the manner in which she pushed strands of hair behind her ear.

On previous nights she had undressed in the bathroom, wrapping a robe loosely around her before going to bed, but not this night. The atmosphere was different. It was right, alive with magic. She had looked into David's face and seen complicity.

In the half-light she began to undo the buttons of her blouse. She half turned away from him, but not so much that he couldn't see her breasts when the thin material slipped from her arms. Her nipples were erect. She eased her skirt down her legs, feigning ignorance of his gaze.

David felt the heat rise within him. Somewhere deep down a dam had burst and the bottled need for contact and succour came

332

rushing to the surface. He needed her for more than sex. He wanted her to make him whole again.

Sparks flew when his fingertips scraped the warm skin of her shoulders before they traced down her arms, and then moved round to her breasts. He wanted to say something, but he knew it would only turn out crass and laughable so he put his mouth to use on the back of her neck, working it around until he could feel the softness of her lips. She dragged him back on to the bed as his hands moved over her body.

Being within her was like being within himself, an act of perverse geometry that Euclid would never have grasped. He pounded harder and harder so she would swallow him up and free him, but he always seemed a hair's breadth away from the ultimate release. And when they both came, in a tidal wave of orgasm, it was a split second apart.

David awoke several hours later. It was still dark outside and the only sounds were of water, insects and the occasional night bird. Staring into the shadows of the ceiling, David felt guilt eating away at him. Not only had he betrayed Fermay, he had also used Arlene, a woman who had done him nothing but good. It would have been easy to dismiss it as a mere moment of passion, but he knew Arlene hoped for more. Seconds before she had climaxed, she had whispered 'David, I love you' into his ear. He had not responded.

He slipped out of bed, feeling Arlene shift in her sleep and moan. Looking down at her, her dyed blonde hair tousled across the pillow which her arms hugged, he felt a warm wave of affection. He pulled on his boxer shorts and walked into the sitting room which was illuminated by two broad bands of moonlight shafting through the cabin's windows on either side of the door. It reminded him of Fermay sitting in a similar moonbeam in his lounge thousands of miles away.

'Where are you?' The words came out unprompted and he was surprised at how loud they sounded in the still of the cabin. It was almost like calling to her across the ether and for a moment, as his voice rang out clear and sharp, David would not have been surprised if he had heard Fermay answer. His lovemaking with

Arlene had only served to emphasize the emptiness he felt within. His life felt barren without Fermay. In the dark all the clichés seemed true. He wondered if he could live without her.

Sleep was no longer an option. Outside the dark and the trees looked inviting, a soothing world. Quietly he reclaimed his boots, jeans and shirt from the bedroom and dressed leisurely, listening to the wind around the cabin.

The night air was aromatic, heavy with smells he had never encountered in London. The insects and birds and the lapping of the water merged into one, the comforting whisper of nature that was never heard in the city. *kkk-kkk-kkk, caw, carooo*. It was as mesmerizing as Thelonious Monk in the heat of a solo.

He stepped out from the porch and felt the squelch of moist ground beneath his feet. The butterscotch moon provided more than enough light. Among the stars, two lights flashed red and white, a plane swooping down to New Orleans airport. David tried to remember his own arrival, the type of plane that brought him, the airport security check, passport control. Nothing surfaced as he wandered through the water channels. He felt lost.

The sudden urge to return to Arlene's side was strong. He wanted to hold her, to leech her warmth. Nature seemed to have hushed in sympathy. One moment he could hear the insects and the birds and the water, the wind and the leaves; the next, nothing. The effect was so jarring that he started suddenly, wondering if he had gone deaf.

He hurried back the way he had come, but he could see no sign of the cabin or the path that led to its door. There was just the trees and the sky. And the silence.

He saw the first one out of the corner of his eye. Initially nothing registered, but there was a subliminal warning which drew his gaze back after the half-glimpse. Slowly his eyes focused on the dark shape silhouetted against the lighter sky, hanging from the branches of the tree ahead of him. Further on he could see another one, and off to the right, another. And another. And another. They were like some strange alien fruit, huge and bloated, dangling limply on a thin stalk. He squinted, imagining the fruit dropping to the lush vegetation and bursting open on impact, the pungent, white, fleshy insides breaking out through the tough skin.

He was closer now, and the original silhouette took on more shape. Suddenly he knew what it was. In his revulsion the only thing that came to mind was Billie Holiday singing throatily.

Strange fruit. Hanging from the trees.

It was a man. A dead man. The noose around his neck was snug, the rope taut to the lower branches. The strain of being hoisted off the ground had pulled his head from the top of the spine and it lolled to one side at an excruciating angle. The lips were drawn back from the teeth and the tongue was distended, swollen and green. Despite the agony of the last moment, the rest of the face was placid, and there was a calmness around the eyes as if they had spent too long watching TV. The body swung from side to side in the breeze, keeping perfect time, the pendulum of a hideous clock.

The other bodies he could see, six in all, looked the same. Naked skin glistening in the moonlight. Lynched. By who? The Klan? Some other radical group? Did that kind of thing still happen in the nineties? From the lack of decomposition, he could only guess that the horrific act had happened recently. With a growing feeling of apprehension David became aware again of the silence which cloaked the bayou.

Then the corpse opened its eyes and looked at him.

It was alive, but not-alive, another denizen of the new world he had entered. That world tilted under his feet and he yelled, 'What do you want?'

Slowly it raised its arm and pointed at him. Behind it, further into the trees, the other hanging men seemed to be pointing too.

The hypnotic swing of the rope drew his eyes. Slowly, almost imperceptibly, and still keeping perfect time, it began to unravel where it was tied around the branch. For an instant it slipped, jerking the body down an inch before continuing its agonizing unwinding while the hanging man's hollow eyes continued to bulge, his fingers opening and closing, opening and closing.

There was death in his face.

Bang, bang. The blood pulsed in David's brain. Bang, bang.

*

He was in the lounge of his parents' home. Outside it was dark, a sudden storm pounding with thunder, rain lashing against the French windows. It had only started as he had walked up the path to the front door, but it had taken hold with unbelievable speed and intensity. Inside the lounge, however, it was warm and cosy. Two small lamps emitted just enough light to see by, but the shadows that lay beyond them were comforting. In the fireplace, flames sputtered from the white and black remains of a log. He was seventeen years old.

'It's very late, David.' His father sounded weary. There was darkness under his eyes and the lines on his face were drawn in dark relief in the half-light. David always remembered him this way, glasses studiously dangling on the end of his nose, grey hair pushed back behind his ears or looped up over his bald patch, but his grey eyes crystal-clear and intelligent.

'I know that, Dad, but I've got to talk to you.'

'Very well.' With faint irritation, his father motioned David to take a seat on the sofa just as he would have done to one of his students at the university. He did not join David. Instead, he stood with his back to the fire, one elbow resting on the mantelpiece. 'Is this going to take a long time? I've got a paper to finish and—'

'It won't take long, Dad.' David was aware that he was fuelled by nervousness.

His father audibly sighed and signalled to David to proceed.

David looked up, aware that he had never really known his father. He always seemed to be on the brink of it, of experiencing that warm closeness that only fathers and sons knew, but then his father would withdraw into a cloak of books and letters and words. Once, when he was very much younger, an entire month went by without David setting eyes upon him. During the day he had laboured in his study, deciphering ancient texts, burying his head in the dust of history, and only emerging when David had been long in bed. When David arose the next day his father would already have been at work for two hours.

'Don't disturb Daddy,' his mother had said to him. 'His work is very important. He needs his concentration.'

Books and dry intellect were his father's world; emotions and human warmth were not. But David loved him nonetheless, that distance allowing him to build up a perfect paternal image, unsullied by reality. It was his mother who was the villainess.

'Dad, it's about Mum.'

'Oh?' He raised one silvery eyebrow and smiled patronizingly. 'How is she tonight?'

'Dad, she's having an affair.'

David thought it would hit his father like a thunderclap. He expected sudden, angry denial, perhaps a slap to the face, then rage, but his father simply smiled benignly. His voice was quiet and still. 'I don't want to know what your mother does, David.'

The words struck David harder than a slap. 'You can't keep burying your head in the sand, Dad. That's all you ever do! Problems never enter that little office of yours, but that doesn't mean they don't exist.'

'David!' The veins were standing out on his father's forehead. David only remembered seeing them like that once before, when he had spilled Pepsi on a text book. 'David, go to your room.'

If he had only done so, it could all have been swept back under the carpet, forgotten and smoothed over so life could go on as usual. But he couldn't stop himself.

'No, Dad. You've got to hear me out.' He licked his lips. His mouth was dry. 'Mum is having an affair. I caught her at it . . . in a car.' Hot tears stung his eyes. 'In a bloody car. It . . . it was parked at the sports ground near the university. Her blouse was undone and . . . he had his hands all over her.' David took a deep breath to hold back the sobs that wanted to force their way out. 'It was Alan Garston . . . The bastard! The bastard! Every week she says, "Oh, I'm just going out for a drink with Alan. He's such a nice man." *Bastard!*' The tears blurred his eyes so he could not see his father. His own hurt was too much.

'Go to your room, David.' It was as if his father had not heard a word he had said.

'If you didn't spend so much time in your office with your blasted books this would never have happened!' Spittle flecked from his mouth in childlike rage. 'You're her husband, for God's sake! How can you be so blind?'

Even quieter this time: 'I *knew*, David.'

337

'You knew!' David's voice rose sharply. 'And you haven't done anything?'

'When you grow up, son, you'll realize there's a world of difference between knowing and accepting.' He sighed, and in the quiet of that room it sounded the saddest thing in the world. 'When I first found out I thought it would destroy me.' He swallowed loudly. 'I felt like all my self-respect had been taken away, but the thing that kept me going was you, David. As long as you didn't know . . .' He swallowed again, and for one brief moment David thought he was going to break down. '. . . as long as you didn't know, I could still pretend everything was how it used to be. That's the only way I could keep going.' His shoulders sagged until he resembled a sack of firewood and at that moment he looked much older, as if all the strength had been sucked out of him. He slumped against the mantelpiece so awkwardly that David thought he would stumble.

'You've got to face up to it, Dad. You've *got* to talk to her. Or she'll leave you for good. Don't be weak.'

'Is that what you think I am? Perhaps it's true. It's so much easier to pretend . . .' He looked into David's eyes, as if searching for what his son truly thought of him, and when he found it he nodded sadly. 'All I wanted, David, was for you to see me as a good father, someone to look up to, not some cuckolded old fool who couldn't keep his wife happy. I didn't want you to see me as that.'

'I don't, Dad. It's just . . .' He stopped. He couldn't find the right words any longer.

'Without your belief in me, I've got nothing.'

The fire gave one dying crackle and the embers turned slowly from red to pink. David became aware of the aroma of pipe smoke around his father, a smell that had comforted him since he was young, and he had to fight an urge to hug the dejected figure and tell him it would be all right. Emotions had never been expressed between them in the past and it was a little too late to start.

'Face up to it, Dad,' he said simply. 'Do what has to be done.'

There was a faraway look in his father's eyes and it seemed he had not grasped the problem or the urgency of solving it. 'I'll think about it, son. I don't really have much choice now, do I? You go to bed. It's late.'

David did as he was bid but found it difficult to sleep. Two hours later he found it difficult to sleep ever again.

As soon as he heard the retort, he was out of bed and running, naked, along dark landings, down the dark staircase, and in his mind anger began to surface as he realized his mother was still not home.

The lounge was cool, the ashes white in the grate. The two lamps still provided a semblance of cosiness, but there was a strange smell in the air: gunpowder and something else, an indefinable sticky odour.

His father was seated at the bureau. In his lap was the shotgun which had been in his mouth. Behind him, on the wall, was an unusual Rorschach blot which David stared at for several moments, trying to work out what he saw in it. There was a bird falling from a speckled sky. There was a boy, his arms held wide.

His father had left a note. David read it over and over, but it might as well have been written in Sanskrit for all the sense it made. He did not need to read the words to understand the meaning, though. He deciphered it easily.

It said: *David killed me.*

He was suffocating. There was a dead weight across his chest, crushing the life from him. His eyes snapped open to see the hanging man's face pressed against his. David could smell the reek of death, the flowering decay.

In horror, he broke the grip the hanging man had around his own body, flinging himself backwards with the force of his exertion. And as he hit the ground he began to reorient himself. He saw that he had been mesmerized by the horrific replay of memory that had left him rooted to the spot even while the corpse made ready to seize him. As it stared, he felt himself going under again . . .

Water splashed his face. His eyes widened as the storm broke overhead, forked lightning slashing the sky as rain sheeted down through the trees. There was a perverse attraction in wondering what it would have been like to feel his life slip away in its grasp.

He deserved it. For all his selfishness. Join the dead! He was only a moment away from them.

Instead David broke the spell. He rolled over on to his stomach and hurled himself forward blindly, and then he was running through the trees and bushes, as much escaping from the hanging man as trying to escape from what was inside his head. Later he marvelled that he had not plunged into the depths of some sucking bog, but that would have been too easy, he thought bitterly. That would have ended his suffering.

The sun came up on the storm-torn wetlands with a wan, yellow light that revealed broken branches, torn vegetation and scattered detritus from far and wide. After running until his legs had almost crumpled beneath him with exhaustion, David's clothes were sodden and he was shivering in the morning chill.

He somehow met up with Duchayne, the Cajun's bright eyes shining above the grizzle of his beard. A hat that was almost a museum piece topped his curly head and he clutched a fishhook and line close to his body.

'*Bonjour,*' he said warily, his eyes skimming over David's dishevelled appearance.

David nodded wearily.

'It's not best . . . to go for walks in the storm. The lightning, you know, and all these trees . . .' A little laugh.

'I look comical I suppose.'

'I'm sorry, *mon ami*, it's just . . . you're quite a sight at this time of day.'

'The trouble with you, Duchayne, is you don't understand good English character. There's nothing like an early morning stroll in the rain for cleansing the soul.' It was an effort to speak and even more difficult to summon up humour, but he found the conversation calming.

'Yes, yes, I'm sure. Me, I prefer to fish.' Duchayne held up his hook and line which swung back and forth, the barb glinting in the dawn light. David watched the pendulum effect and had a lucid remembrance of the hanging man, his swinging feet marking out time on death's clock.

'Tell me,' David asked, 'have there ever been any murders round here? Not just murders, lynchings?'

Duchayne creased his brow in thought. 'Recently?'

'Not necessarily. This century.'

He nodded. 'Sure, back in the fifties. A few blacks got hung up in the trees. Ev'ryone thought it was the Klan at first . . . till they found a white man hangin'. I know the Klan offed a few white folk in their time, sympathizers, white niggers they called them, but this didn't seem like one of them. He was some fat banker from the city.'

'Who did it?'

Duchayne shrugged. 'They never caught no one.'

'Have you heard of the Krewe of Aidoneus?'

'Don't know them from Adam, *ami*. The krewe? Some of those Mardi Gras types, right?'

'That's right. Mardi Gras types.' David's mind was already elsewhere.

'You look troubled, *ami*. You need something to cheer you up.' Duchayne leaned against a cypress tree and looked up at the trailing Spanish moss for so long that David thought he had drifted off. 'Tonight,' he drawled lazily, 'we're having us a little party – a *fais-dodo*. Good music, good dancin', good food, good drink.' He looked David in the eye and smiled knowingly. 'You bring your woman. Have a good time. Take it easy.'

'Well . . .'

'No excuses, *ami*. You come, enjoy yourself. Paul's Bar. You know where that is? Course you do. The music starts at seven.'

It seemed fitting: a goodbye party. 'OK, we'll be there.'

Duchayne laughed heartily. '*Bon*! Drink and make merry.'

'I'll wear my best suit. My wedding and funeral suit.'

David peeled his wet clothes off in the main room of the cabin and towelled himself down before climbing back into bed. Arlene had hardly moved since he left, her breathing slow and regular. He felt an urge to check his bag under the bed and the prize it contained, the record. He ignored it, but as he lay there he could hear it calling to him, the monster under the bed. Arlene's naked back distracted him and he felt a tingle run through his numbness. Beneath the sheets it was warm. He moved up close and slipped his arm around her, resting his palm on her smooth belly where it rose and fell steadily.

The urge to make love with her came over him again – and this time he *really* wanted to make love with her. She woke to his touch and their union was tender and sensitive, filled with long kisses and slow caresses. At one point he looked up and was shocked to see figures crowding around the bed, dead people, their eyes not judging, not feeling, their arms by their sides. Just watching. He closed his own eyes and when he opened them again they had gone.

Arlene's body looked tanned and healthy against the whiteness of the sheet. David stroked the skin of her arm, feeling the hairs prickle erect.

'Want to tell me about it?' Somehow she knew he had been to hell and back.

He lounged back on the pillow and stared at the ceiling, only really coming to terms with it then himself. 'I've been haunted by the death of my father since the night it happened. I thought everything was my fault, in the way that adolescents always do. It affected me so badly, Arlene. For years it's left me afraid to take any kind of action or responsibility in case things turned out as bad as they did with my dad. But last night I went through it all in my head, sort of relived it, and I just don't think I can blame myself any longer.'

'I could have told you that, David. When somebody commits suicide, that's a choice they make themselves.'

He nodded. 'But I always thought *I* had forced my father to do it. But, you know, there were other things he could have done. He could have opened up to me . . .'

Arlene lit a cigarette and inhaled. 'They say suicide is the supreme selfish act because all it does is hurt those left behind.'

'I don't want to blame him. I can't, I loved him. But I just don't feel like blaming myself any more.' He felt like the bag of rocks he had been carrying on his shoulder had suddenly been discarded. 'I feel like a new man, Arlene. I feel like I can really face up to all the hideous things that have been tugging at my life. Jesus, maybe I can even find a solution!'

She put the cigarette in the ashtray next to the bed, and rolled on top of him. 'I'm pleased for you, honey. So where do we go from here?'

He smiled and then kissed her. 'We go to a party.'

Paul's Bar was a low, brick-built utility building without any character and only a Bud sign to signal its identity. It was like a hundred other bars that David had seen on the route out of New Orleans, but what was taking place within set it apart. They could hear the music long before they entered. Arlene described it as the rhythm of life because of its whirl of fiddles and accordions, harmonicas, guitars and drums. It raised David's spirits, as music always did, and for a time he thought everything really was going to be OK.

The bar was packed to bursting, with all generations represented, from the very old to the new-born. It seemed like the entire town and surrounding area was there. David and Arlene edged round the floor, marvelling at the flamboyant, intricate steps practised by the dancers. Duchayne and Will were drinking beer together at one end and they nodded in greeting as David and Arlene approached.

'Wild!' Arlene said. 'You don't get this sort of atmosphere at Charlie's Place.'

David ordered two Jack and cokes and then they squashed into a corner where they could get a better view of the room. The *fais-dodo* was hypnotic in its thunderous evocation of vibrant emotions, but David felt unable to concentrate on it. Eventually he turned to Arlene and said without preamble, 'I'm going back to New Orleans tomorrow.'

Arlene's head jerked round in surprise. 'So soon?'

'It's sooner than I planned, but . . .' He sighed. '. . . it's later than I thought. Sometimes you can't sit back doing nothing, however much you want to. Oh, listen to me . . . I sound like John Wayne!' He laughed and threw the Jack Daniels down in one. 'What I mean to say is, hiding away is not a positive action.'

'It'll positively save your life.'

'Life's overrated.' Her frown made him smile and add hastily,

343

'Don't worry, I'm just being glib. I only want one thing in this world, Arlene, and there's no point living without it.'

'Fermay.' Her face lost its gleam.

David gave her a hug, but it wasn't out of guilt. 'Sure, Fermay. I've been a kid all my life. My growing up stopped when I was seventeen and since then I've been the eternal teenager with too many hormones and not enough responsibility. The good thing about these last few days is that it's made me face up to myself. You've helped me do that, Arlene, and I love you for it.'

'Yeah, I love you too, David.' She laughed, a little sadly, but she took it better than he'd thought she would, and that maturity was part of the reason he liked her so much. 'Well, I gave it my best shot. Can't win 'em all, girl. But we're still friends, right? That means something.'

'Of course it does.'

'So now what?'

'You've been saying that to me ever since we met. Well, first I'm going to head back into New Orleans. You don't have to come with me if you don't want to, but I *have* to go. Then I'm going to avoid Broussard's thugs until I can get in the same room as him, just the two of us, face to face. And I'm either going to bargain with him or else I'm going to beat the shit out of him until he tells me where Fermay is. I haven't quite decided yet.'

'You're crazy.'

'That's right.'

Arlene shook her head, laughing. 'My lunatic friend! You know nothing's going to go according to your plan, David. You'll get to N'Orleans and they'll pick you up and put a bullet through your head.'

'Maybe, maybe not. To tell you the truth, I haven't got a plan. My problem is that I've been sitting down making plans as an excuse not to do anything; it's been a good way of fooling myself. But not any more. When you've lost your fear of dying, there's nothing to stop you doing stupid things.'

The band stepped up the tempo, drawing more people into the whirlwind on the dance floor. Heads bobbed up and down. Bodies came together then sprang apart. There was music and drink and laughter, and life ruled.

Briefly, a dark shadow fell across the proceedings. David watched the crowd intently and then turned to Arlene and said, 'I'll be back in a minute.'

'Where are you going?'

'I've just seen an old friend.'

David strode around the floor, smiling back at the people who smiled at him. He felt calm, at ease. He didn't find what he was looking for on the other side of the room so he carried on through to the toilet which was strangely empty, despite the number of people in the bar. Slowly, he turned round, surveying the room. Nothing. He did it once more and Marsayle was standing in the corner.

The jazzman looked immaculate, hair pomaded and shining; suit, that perfect performance suit, clean and with creases like razors. Only the eyes and the sheen of his skin gave him away.

'Hello,' David said. He looked unwaveringly into Marsayle's eyes.

Marsayle did not reply. He seemed to hover in and out of focus as if David's vision was misting over.

David continued, 'I know about Aidoneus and Lionel Johnson and the record. It was wrong of me to try to leave my responsibilities behind. You've got to realize, I was scared. I still don't understand why you chose me and I'm not sure I've got the power to do whatever it is you want. Revenge, I guess. Freedom from all this moping around dark corners. I just want you to know that I'm going back. Even if I can't do what you expect of me, I'm going to give it my best shot at getting Fermay back. I'm going to find a way through to her. And who knows – maybe by doing that I'll somehow do what you need?'

He paused, waiting automatically for a response. If his words meant anything, it didn't show on Marsayle's face.

'You know, life would be a lot easier if you spoke to me.' Another pause. 'Well, I can't hang around here all night. I want to make the most of my last few hours in the country.'

Marsayle was still staring as David turned and walked out of the toilet, and he could feel that stare on his back for the length of his walk through the bar.

*

That night he and Arlene did not make love. They merely held each other, falling into a deep, dream-filled slumber, and in those depths David could feel his Fog Zone stir, as he knew it would. There was not much in it now and he knew the Zone was saving the worst for last.

Chapter 28

Twilight crept through the bayou behind them as they headed towards the city. Will sang along to his jazz tape, but with little enthusiasm, his attention focused on the sky above New Orleans. It was a sight which fascinated them all, but no one mentioned it as if they all sensed that it was so much more than a meteorological phenomenon. Heaven was burning. As the sun set behind them, the sky flared an apocalyptic red with occasional flashes of gold and silver, so quick they seemed like ghost images on the retina.

Finally Arlene said in awe, 'Atmospherics again.'

'Red sky at night, shepherd's delight.' Will snapped his gum.

David stared into it until he felt he was floating in a sea of flames, knowing in his heart that it was a portent; nature was screaming at some affront to the established order. The cloud of evil was descending upon the haunted city.

When Will dropped them on the outskirts of the French Quarter he seemed apprehensive and in a hurry to head off to his cousin's house on the other side of the city. He told them he felt like he did on the night before his brother died. 'No rhyme nor reason to it. Just a feeling.'

The evening was as fragrant as the first one David had spent in the Vieux Carre, the scent of flowers mingling with the aroma of good Louisiana cooking. Not far away in the main streets of the Quarter, they could hear the first signs of the hubbub that was to come as the crowds headed to the bars and clubs in search of good music and the fine N'Orleans high life. Soon the streets would be thronging, busier than they were during the day, the perfect time for David to lose himself.

Next to the river, as the heat of the day faded, Arlene stepped forward and gave David a hug that told him everything he needed to know about her feelings. Her own special scent comforted him as she stroked the back of his neck, her voice muffled deep in his shoulder.

'Y'know, you're a good guy, David.'

'Just give me the Nobel Peace Prize and be done with it.'

'Don't go doing anything foolish, right? I don't want my best friend to end up dead.'

'I'll be careful,' he replied, knowing that *careful* wouldn't mean much in the face of the odds.

Her eyes were a little misty when she looked into his face, but she was smiling. 'You saved my life, y'know?' She laughed. 'I don't think that all guys are jerks any more!'

'Have you decided what you're going to do?'

Arlene nodded, suddenly serious. 'I've thought about it a lot since we talked. Y'know, David, the things you say . . . I'm not very good at putting it into words. I'm only a waitress. All I know is how to get good tips and stay one step ahead of the creeps . . . but the things you say, they made me think about looking after other people and caring for other people and, well, just being, y'know, responsible. Scuba's a jerk and he's selfish and he doesn't think, but somewhere inside him there's the guy I fell in love with. The decent guy. He needs me, David. He's lost without me, I know that. He'll probably wind up dead in a gutter if I'm not there to look out for him, and that's what I'm gonna do. If he's still around, we'll skip town together, bum around just like he wanted. You never know, it might work. One thing's for sure, I'll never let him walk all over me again, even though I think he only did that to hide how much he needed me. Maybe I'll save him from himself, pull the good guy back to the surface. What do you say?'

'I say if anyone can do it, you can, Arlene.' Then he gave her a hug in return and was almost afraid of letting her go. 'So it's goodbye. I'll miss you, Arlene. You might not know it, but you've done as much for me as you say I've done for you. Thanks.'

They kissed one final time, as lovers and friends, and then Arlene smiled and said, 'I gotta go do my duty. And if everything works out for us both, we'll meet up at Charlie's Place some time soon. Is that a deal?' He nodded. 'Good! Love you.' She turned and headed along the street quickly, not looking back. David watched her until she disappeared into the swelling crowds.

As he set off into the heart of the French Quarter, his mind turned to the task that lay ahead of him and he tried to put it all into some kind of order as if that would make sense of the madness. Lionel Johnson had established the Krewe of Aidoneus to achieve some ultimate power for himself and his followers. He had petitioned for, and received, the support of some higher force and he had locked the knowledge and strength he had received into the notes of a song which he had recorded for posterity.

David felt the record in his bag pulling at his arm and with that awareness came the desire to take it out and look at it. It was calling to him, telling him to play it, to listen to the music, to get lost in it . . .

The krewe had carried on Johnson's mission after his death, a job of murder that began with Buffalo Marsayle and ended . . . where? The faceless corpse in the river? The other mysterious deaths that had been swept under the carpet in the city over the years, maybe even the hanging men in the bayou? All of them sacrifices, their souls stored until there was enough to tip the balance. To bring down the *cloud of evil* on the day Johnson and his followers would hit the jackpot.

And Fermay was part of all that. She was an innocent brought into the darkness by her guardian, Broussard. And when she'd escaped, they'd hunted her down and fetched her back using what power they had already created in the form of the E'lethri.

Events were rushing towards a resolution and David was being carried along in the flow. He didn't care about the big picture, the struggle of evil on a grand scale. That was just a backdrop and he was not going to be sucked into it. His aim was to find Fermay and get away. The rest of them, even New Orleans, could go to hell.

David soon realized things were moving quicker than he realized. The dead were everywhere now, standing on street corners in glassy-eyed groups like a parody of the Mardi Gras, riding on the back seats of horse-drawn carriages, sitting at bars waiting for company that never came. Some of them looked at him like bystanders who had just witnessed an airline disaster.

They all recognized that events were heading towards an even more terrible climax.

If it even shocked the spirit world, David wondered, how would the living react?

He spoke to some of them, and as he did so he realized that his affinity now was for the dead. He could understand them and their needs and desires, while the living seemed beyond him. None of them answered him, but he could tell they felt he was one of them; no longer was he a stranger to be hated and despised.

On one corner David stood with a group of them – three men in varying states of mutilation, and a woman who had a stake through her side – and together they looked at the sky. The hellish redness was fading as the sun sank low, but he could still see the occasional flash of light which now seemed to be accompanied by a deep rumble. As the darkness rushed up to claim the sky, David sensed a blanket of evil being drawn across the city.

Beth's apartment suddenly seemed a long way away and the crowds had grown much thicker as they prepared to celebrate the coming of night with exuberance. The bars were filling up. Dixies and Jack Daniels were oiling the wheels of enjoyment ready for a long ride through till dawn. David wondered if their fever was an anticipation of what was about to come down upon their shoulders.

A boy of about eight was playing in the street. There was the mark of a tyre track across his face and his head was misshapen. He ran up to David and stared at him before returning to the gutter. *Stay cool*, David told himself. *Keep your head clear.*

As he headed quickly along Chartres Street, David was forced to take a sudden detour. The krewe were out en masse too, either looking for another victim or preparing for their own black celebration.

Or, David thought anxiously, perhaps they knew he was back in town.

Lynch stood at the corner of Jackson Square and Chartres talking to a huddle of serious-faced men. Beyond him, further along the square, Frantz was speaking animatedly to the juggler who had killed Moose. David fought back a wave of loathing.

When Lynch started to lead the group towards him, he dodged up St Peter Street, thinking he could always loop around the top of the Quarter and come at Beth's apartment from lakeside. He had only travelled a few yards when he noticed a police patrol car parked at the junction with Bourbon. The windows were dark and he could not see who was sitting within, but he knew that there was a chance it was Krugman. He was caught in the middle.

Quickly scanning the buildings on either side for a place to hide, he saw the big crowd that was gathering outside Preservation Hall. Impulsively he headed for the front of the queue and, ignoring the protestations, pushed his way in, throwing a few dollars at the teller as he slipped by. An old man with silvery hair, who must have been dead for fifty years from the clothes he was wearing, silently applauded David's passing.

When he stepped into the cramped room, undecorated for decades, instantly he could see why it was called Preservation Hall. Time stood still in those four walls. David had intended visiting the hall on several occasions, aware of its reputation as the home of jazz, but he had always been deterred by the long queue that snaked outside. It seemed like everybody in the city always wanted to see one of the twice-nightly performances by the house band which kept up the hall's tradition as *the* prime jazz venue.

He was too tense to appreciate the music. With the krewe swarming like an army of ants, he knew that when he did finally step outside he could be picked up at any moment. So it was a credit to the jazz's quality that eventually it did ensnare him in its uplifting spell. The band hammered out their songs with an unmatched virtuosity that made David close his eyes. Each lick told him of love and happiness, but at the back of it, like all jazz, there was a darkness waiting to take over.

Sometime during the fourth number it came: that old familiar warning. They were there, his close friends, his kindred spirits. The space that had been left at the back of the hall was now full of familiar faces. Marsayle was at the centre of them, watching the set.

Perhaps they came every night, David thought, an audience of ghosts with memories so powerful it tormented them. The music was the link, the silver thread that joined the land of the living and the dead. If only the band knew who was watching them. Would they still play with such gusto?

He felt suddenly cold, like he was standing next to an open grave. Marsayle had raised his arm and was pointing to the exit. David knew better than to ignore him. He pushed his way through the crowd, muttering apologies, and stepped out into the corridor. When he looked back, the rear of the hall was empty once more.

Out on the street he saw the police car had gone and his route was now open to him.

Night had fallen completely by the time he made it back to Beth's apartment. With some relief, he discovered she was not there and all the rooms were in darkness. He washed and shaved quickly in the light of a streetlamp that streamed through the window, slicking his hair back with Brylcreem and ironing his best white shirt. He dressed carefully in front of the mirror, paying particular attention to detail. Top collar buttoned, gold cufflinks fastened, tie selected. Finally he put on his best suit, his wedding and funeral suit. Then he was ready.

He considered leaving his bag with the record in his room, but he could not bring himself to do it. He felt uncomfortable without it.

In the lounge he went hunting for the one item he still wanted, eventually finding it in a bottom drawer cluttered with newspaper clippings and old cassettes. It was a handgun, quite small, but powerful enough to take out any intruder which was the only reason Beth had bought it. She had shown him how easily she could manage it one quiet Sunday afternoon and then had laughingly told him she was too afraid to use it. David examined it carefully. It frightened him too.

In the end he had decided to adopt the most basic approach. He would burst into the mansion and hold the gun at Broussard's head until he showed him where Fermay was. Desperate times required desperate measures. He took the ammunition from the box next to the gun and loaded it as Beth had shown him, before slipping it inside his jacket. He winced when he saw how it pulled the lines of his suit out of shape.

Now he only had to wait, doing nothing until sun-up; the night belonged to the krewe, but in the daylight he'd take his chance. In the kitchen, he grabbed the last two bottles of Dixie from the fridge and headed back to the lounge to kill time. The darkness made it difficult to do anything but think, but he couldn't afford to put on a light in case it attracted attention. As he lay on the sofa staring into the gloom, he became aware of a strange smell, difficult to place. The odour was so odd and so disconcerting he felt obliged to investigate. It seemed to be emanating from Beth's room.

The door was ajar. He punted it open with his toe, the noise of his shoe on the wood sounding far too loud. The curtains were drawn and the darkness was impenetrable within, but the smell was stronger. Apprehensively he closed the door behind him and fumbled to switch on the small bedside lamp.

Beth lay on the bed. A pool of her dried blood had soaked through the sheets, with more of it darkly staining the carpet. Her throat had been slit from ear to ear. And there was more. Both her eyes were gone, darkness filling the sockets where they had been gouged out.

David clapped his hand to his mouth in shock. He had to turn and run before the nausea overcame him, slamming the door behind him.

Poor Beth. She had done nothing, but her death had been virtually guaranteed from the moment she'd agreed to take him as a lodger. The Easter curse continued.

He tried to stop himself trembling. He had to think clearly. The mutilation was a sign of the krewe. They had obviously tracked him down and Beth had paid the price. He couldn't stay there a moment longer. Snatching up his bag, he ran to the door and down the stairs without looking back, desperately trying to think where he could hide next.

Charlie's Place was full and sweaty when David arrived. He slipped past Washington at the door with a pale grin and found a spot at the back of the club where he could wait without being troubled. When the crowds thinned out at 2 a.m. he steeled himself and then marched across the room and hammered on Charlie's door.

'Go away.' The deep, mahogany voice sounded bored and weary.

David walked in and closed the door behind him. Charlie's expression changed from irritation to surprise and then to a sarcastic smirk.

'Well, holeee shit. If it ain't the wanderin' white boy.' After the initial recognition, his face slowly darkened. 'You got some nerve comin' round here, boy. Droppin' me in the shit like that. How'm I supposed to run a business when the staff go for a walk round the countryside every time the fancy takes 'em?'

David slumped into the chair in front of Charlie's desk. 'I need to hang out, Charlie. Just for a few hours. Until the sun comes up.'

'Well, sure thing, boy. An' if you're good I'll cook you breakfast. Shit!' His cigar rolled around his mouth furiously. 'Ever since you came here, I've had nothin' but trouble. Fights. A stabbin'. Disappearin' staff. You're not good for business, boy!'

David had little energy for an argument. Reluctantly, he stood up and started to walk towards the door, no longer knowing where to turn.

'Sit down.' Charlie barked the order harshly. 'I don't know what kinda goddamn trouble you're in and I don't want to know. Just tell me you haven't dragged Arlene into it.'

'No, I haven't. I wouldn't do that. She's off with her boyfriend trying to sort her life out.'

Charlie shook his head tiredly. 'You kids, you're lives are just a mess. I learned a long time ago not to get screwed up like that.' He sighed and rested his spade-like hands in front of him. 'You can stay in the stock room. Just don't touch any of the goddamn beer, y'hear? You want me to find somewhere for you to stay?'

'Thanks, Charlie, but I'll be OK. Things will sort themselves out tomorrow, one way or another.'

Charlie pulled open his bottom drawer, took out his bottle of bourbon and poured himself a shot. 'Don't go gettin' yourself killed, boy. That's all. Now get the hell outta here. I don't want to see your white face again.'

David awoke with a crippling pain in his kidney where a crate was pressing into him. His head was stuffed with cotton wool, his mouth dry and sticky. He wondered how long he had been asleep. His watch said 3.50 a.m. The club would be closed, but the staff should still be clearing up.

Standing up, he shook the kinks from his legs and opened the door on to the sound of muffled voices. They seemed to be arguing. David walked along the corridor and peered out into the main hall. Charlie and his bouncers were standing at the door haranguing someone outside. Further back stood Dean, intently watching the confrontation. There was no one else in the club.

After about five minutes the argument reached a crescendo and then Charlie spat out a stream of expletives and slammed the door, locking and bolting it. He spun on his heels and strode towards his office, the bouncers close behind like well-trained pit bulls. Halfway across the room he caught sight of David.

'Get your ass over here!' he bellowed.

David approached him cautiously. 'What's happening? Trouble?'

'Too damn right it's trouble! And you're the cause of it! I don't know what you done, boy, but the whole goddamn world wants a slice of you an' now they're threatenin' to get the cops on *my* tail.'

David tensed. They had found him. He had to get out. 'Charlie . . .'

'They were a coupla stuffed shirts with necks that were too big, and one of those mothers was wearin' shades! Shit! At night. That's a bad sign.' Charlie laughed humourlessly. 'I told them if they didn't get their asses off my property, my boys would hit them so hard they'd have to look up to tie their shoelaces.'

Charlie was taking a big risk protecting David, and they both knew that. There was nothing David could say without embarrassing him except, 'Thanks, Charlie.'

'Don't thank me, you no-good punk. We look after our own here – whoever they are.' He shoved his cigar into his mouth and muttered something unintelligible before marching towards his office.

Then it came. The tap on his shoulder. David started, expecting the worst, but when he turned it was only Dean. 'What?' he snapped, anticipating a snide comment.

'Looks like they found you, Limey. No escape from justice, right?' Dean's face was hard and triumphant. David knew before he said anything else that Dean had put the krewe on his tail.

'Did you tell them where I lived as well?'

'Sure I did.' He smirked.

David struck him once, hard, in the middle of the face. Dean went down like he'd had his legs chopped from beneath him. When he shook his head and looked up, there was blood streaming from his nose. 'They fucking killed my friend,' David hissed.

'With any luck, they'll get you next. I want Arlene, Easter, and I'll do anything to get her. You came in here and pushed me right out of line, but now you're going to get your dues.'

David made to hit him again and then thought better of it. It was futile. There was a lead weight in his heart when he thought about Beth, about her brightness and her love of teaching. All gone because of some stupid jealous youth's desire to bring a little love into his life. David looked back at Dean mopping his nose and realized they were alike, both of them desperate for love, both of them in pursuit of a woman. But where David had been optimistic, Dean had become bitter and hollow. There was a sour taste in David's mouth at the thought that he could have ended up like that.

'Everybody gets what they deserve, Dean,' he said. 'I'll get mine, and believe me, you'll get yours.'

David decided there was only one real alternative to walking outside into a confrontation he could never win, and that was a small window in the band's dressing room. It looked out on a filth-strewn alley. It was normally locked, but he knew where the key was kept. Come the dawn, in two hours, it would have to be his escape route. Accordingly he prepared himself for a tense wait in the darkened room, but it was only five minutes later when he heard a loud crash and then a series of panic-stricken cries.

'Put it out!' someone shouted. 'Shit! Put it out!'

David ran out of the dressing room into chaos. The club was on fire. A pool of flames blazed in the centre of the floor, spreading quickly on a liquid wave and surging up one of the supporting pillars to the ceiling. Shards of glass were scattered around where the Molotov cocktail had exploded.

Charlie rushed round the room cursing, stamping impotently at isolated pockets of flame, while Dean wielded the club's single fire extinguisher expertly. He might as well have been using a soda syphon. The two bouncers yelled something about calling the fire service before disappearing out of the door. And then it was just the three of them. The heat was turning David's cheeks slowly scarlet. It was his fault. Just like everything else. Charlie had been nothing but good to him, and David, like the pariah he was, had led disaster to his doorstep. Overcome by guilt, he ran forward, desperately wanting to help.

As he reached the pool of fire, something strange began to happen, something which made the flames suddenly fan outwards and the smoke billow in unnatural ways as if there was a wind at the heart of the fire. Charlie and Dean were oblivious to it as they concentrated on their futile attemps to save the club, but it stopped David dead in his tracks.

The flames sucked in and out, breathing, spreading tendrils along the floor, up chairs and over tables to the walls. Charlie and Dean danced half a quadrille among the fingers of fire, stamping and spraying with no result. The smoke curled, twisted and folded in on itself. There was a moment when everything was suspended, an almost poetic balance of fire and air, and then in a huge gust a wall of flame roared out and dispersed.

Standing at the centre of the now muted fire was the E'lethri. For a second it focused its black eyes on Charlie, Dean and David and then it held back its head, opened its hideous beak and let out a chilling war cry. The moment the shriek tailed away the E'lethri was moving. Its muscles and tendons rippled sleekly under its flowing white robe as it fixed its eye on Charlie and surged towards him.

Charlie threw up his hands in horror, as the E'lethri bore down upon him like a juggernaut. At the last moment, Dean threw himself into the E'lethri's path in a desperate attempt to save Charlie's life; wielding the fire extinguisher clumsily, he clubbed the creature harmlessly on the side of the head.

The E'lethri followed through with its arm and caught Dean just above his right ear. There was a wet ripping sound as his head came off his shoulders and bounced into the flames.

Charlie was frozen, a pitiful prayer on his lips. At the last moment he closed his eyes.

The E'lethri didn't stop to destroy the bodies as it had done with Ligios.

David turned and ran. He knew he would be next. The E'lethri was like a force of nature, primal, unstoppable. He could wave his gun at it, maybe plug it with a couple of bullets, but it would be like firing into the heart of a hurricane.

He reached the dressing room with the creature's cry in his ears, rising above the crackle and snap of the inferno which was consuming the club. The window was open as he had left it. He dived into the gap and wiggled through, expecting at any moment to feel a clawed hand snap round his ankle and rip his leg from its socket. His fall was awkward and he landed on all fours, winding himself. But clutching his bag with the record tightly in one hand and fumbling for the lame security of the gun with the other, he was up and off.

Where could he go?

Chapter 29

The large building that loomed ahead of him out of the dark, its tower illuminated by the white beams of spotlights, resembled an ice-cream castle. David recognized it as the rear of St Louis' Cathedral which overlooked Jackson Square. Through the tears of exhaustion which blurred his eyes, it seemed to call to him, offering sanctuary, a place to hide. It was a long shot, but it was all he had. Perhaps the E'lethri would not be able to enter a house of God.

He spotted the tiny side door as he ran down Pirate's Alley towards the front of the building. It looked like it was rarely used, but it was an opportunity he could not pass by. Even the large padlock fastened across it did not deter him. David pulled out his gun as he ran and putting one arm across his face, he fired two shots at the padlock, bursting it apart. He was faintly surprised that he'd even hit it, and that he had not been hit in turn by a ricochet or flying metal, and then he was kicking the door open like a madman. It grated noisily on the floor and then ground to a halt, leaving a space just big enough for him to squeeze through. As he did so, he looked back and saw the E'lethri was only feet away. Slamming the door hard, he pulled two large bolts at the top and bottom, and then he waited for the impact.

Nothing happened.

There was no sound at all outside, as if the moment David shut the door, his pursuer had disappeared. Head bowed, he turned and walked along a short, dark corridor into the main body of the cathedral. It was surprisingly light within. The spotlights illuminating the outside shone through the tall, stained glass windows and filled the building with a dazzling display of colours that painted the walls and ceiling in a magnificent celebration. David looked up and around him in awe and for a fleeting instant was overcome with the wonder of it all. He slipped into a pew facing the altar, rested his head, closed his eyes, and thought of Fermay.

He looked up at the altar when he opened his eyes and this time he saw the vibrant painting on the wall behind it. He remembered it instantly from a guide book. It showed St Louis standing on the steps of the Notre Dame, heralding the Seventh Crusade, with the rest of the saint's life depicted on the six stained glass windows. David examined each one carefully, following the life of King Louis IX through his trials and sacrifices to his eventual canonization. The message seemed obvious: you have to suffer before you can be saved. And an act of sacrifice wins the ultimate reward.

Sure, he thought cynically. *It's just like poker. The bigger the stake, the more you stand to win. And lose.*

He tried to imagine the scene outside the cathedral, the darkened faces waiting in the shadows, in the alleyways and doorways, waiting for the moment when he would have to walk out. It was like the final minutes of Butch Cassidy and the Sundance Kid only there was no freeze-frame to preserve him for all eternity.

He walked slowly up the aisle to the altar where he paused and stared at the cross. In a sudden rush, the faces of Charlie, Beth, and Moose flashed across his mind, people who had all been prepared to help him in some way, and who had all paid the final price. His sadness was strong and biting; he owed them a debt. They were not innocents. They were not good, nor were they bad. They were just human beings who had suffered.

He thought about his mother and father then, freely and without the urge to suppress the images, wondering more than anything where his father was, if he was being punished eternally for the crime against life that he had committed. Of all the ghosts he had encountered, the one he really wanted to meet was his father. Just to see him again! And it was with that thought that David greeted the dawn.

Gradually at first, but then with increasing speed, the rays filtered through the stained glass windows, throwing fiery reds and brilliant blues across the inside of the cathedral. The effect seemed even richer and more vibrant than that created by the spotlights during the night. Looking at the expanding spectrum, David felt a refreshing calmness come over him. He waited until the entire nave was touched by the sun's rays and then he rose and with a steady step walked towards the door through which he had entered.

The street wasn't empty, but David could see no living thing. The massed ranks of the dead were waiting for him. They stood on either side of the door, a gauntlet of hideous apparitions. Marsayle was among them.

David shivered and looked straight ahead of him. 'Broussard!' he yelled to the still, peaceful street. 'Come to me.'

Silently, the long, black limousine glided along Royal into his line of vision at the end of Pirate's Alley. It came to a halt and the rear door swung open so David could just make out Broussard sitting inside. There was a ripple through the throng of the dead like a breeze through a forest.

'I want to make a deal, Broussard,' David continued. 'You can have the record. You can have me. I'll give myself up freely. In return I want just one thing. I want to see Fermay again and I want some time alone with her.'

He waited. The dead had started to shift, become agitated. After about a minute in which David thought Broussard was not going to reply, the big man eased himself out of the car and stood on the sidewalk. His supercilious smile reeked of triumph. He held up both arms in a welcoming gesture. 'We have an agreement.'

Tentatively, David began to walk towards him. The moment he left the cathedral the dead on either side erupted in a deafening roar, tearing at their hair and beating themselves repeatedly. Almost overwhelmed, David closed his eyes and walked straight on, sensing them crowding closer, hearing their shrieks increase until he thought his ears would burst.

Then, in a single instant, there was silence. He opened his eyes and looked around. The dead had gone. Broussard stood before him, smiling and beckoning to him to climb into the car.

As the limo pulled smoothly away, Broussard turned to him and said, still smiling, 'Of course, you know you will die.'

David did not reply.

Broussard continued as if he was explaining a minor problem to a small child. 'It really is unavoidable. To say you've been an irritation is an understatement. You were like a rat, although a very handsome one, scurrying through tunnels a few feet ahead of us. But the network was finite and the exits limited. We knew with patience we would bag you before too long.' Broussard looked down at David's bag, held safely between his feet. 'Give me the record, David. I know it's in there. I can feel it.' He was grinding his teeth in anticipation.

David dipped into the bag and pulled it out. The record gleamed darkly in the early morning light, so mundane a prize to claim so many lives. Suddenly he didn't want to give it up, but before he could reconsider Broussard had snatched it from him. The big man held it lovingly between his hands, shifting it every now and then so the light shone from every inch of its surface.

'If only you knew what you were carrying around with you,' he said softly.

'I know more about it than you think.'

'Oh?' Broussard looked at him with surprise.

'I know about Lionel Johnson and the woman he sacrificed in the attic in Storyville. I know that because of that he was granted some kind of power. And that power was hidden in the music of a song and only released when the song is played. I know that he recorded it and then murdered everyone who played on the record.'

Broussard nodded, smiling. 'Yes. But do you know what the music *does* when it is played?'

'No.'

'No.' His smile was tighter, more satisfied.

'How is Fermay?' David could restrain the question no longer.

'Ah yes, young Fermay.' Broussard laughed at a joke that was not apparent. 'The world is changing before your eyes, the old order is falling, and all you can think to ask about is your loved one. How sweet.'

'I don't care about the rest of it.'

'No, of course not. When you're young, things like love do seem so terribly important, don't they. Truth to tell, I never experienced it myself. It always seemed to entail a negation of the

362

self. Yes, Ms Grey is well, or as well as can be expected when her freedom is denied her.'

David fought back the urge to cry with relief, but even so, his eyes misted over and he was forced to look at the still empty streets until the emotion had passed.

'If that record is as important as you say, why didn't you do a better job of guarding it?' David said when he had regained his composure. The last street of the French Quarter passed by as they pulled across Canal heading towards the Garden District.

Broussard's face darkened. 'We had grown lax. We never expected anyone would attempt to seize the record and we certainly never thought anyone could escape the E'lethri. You surprised us, Mr Easter.'

'You owe me for exposing the flaws in your security. You should be able to get it right from now on.'

'No need. The time for that has passed. Tell me, who told you about Lionel Johnson?' His fingers flexed subconsciously as if he was searching for an imaginary throat.

'No one.' David would not break Dauphine's trust. He knew that if he mentioned her name, Broussard would have her killed instantly. 'A little bird.'

Broussard shrugged. 'Again, it hardly matters now.'

'What is going on?' David finally snapped, 'What do you hope to achieve?'

'Ultimate power,' Broussard replied matter of factly, gazing out of the window. 'The power over life and death, good and evil. The ability to walk with the gods.'

'That's the trouble with you people – no ambition.'

'A sense of humour is tremendously important in life, David. Believe me, you're going to need it.' The big man settled back into the leather seat, stretching out his legs with a sigh. 'It all comes down to souls. *Chi* or *ka* or life energy, call it what you will. That's the currency that the higher powers deal in. If your account is full, you can buy whatever you want, it's as simple as that. What Lionel Johnson wanted was eternal life and unlimited wealth. He's dead now, but he'll get it very soon. He knew he would be allowed to return. The krewe, well, the Krewe of Aidoneus will be the chosen ones in a new era. I suppose you can draw an analogy with the business world. When a new chief executive takes over a company, he favours all those who will be loyal to him and punishes all those opposed to his new regime.'

'So who's the new Chief Exec?'

Broussard boomed with laughter. 'It's not as simple as that, David. Let's just say that we're creating a climate where select members of the Krewe of Aidoneus can use power as they see fit.'

'By bringing down a cloud of evil.'

'Oh, who have you been talking to! Evil is an emotive word to frighten small children and devout Catholics. It has no real meaning. We are talking about the rule of Self. Self-determination. Freedom of choice.'

'Your freedom of choice.'

'Exactly. "Do as thou wilt is the whole of the law," as that fat charlatan Aleister Crowley said, but he had the right idea.'

The car pulled into the Garden District, only a few blocks from Broussard's mansion. David felt a mix of emotions as they drew near, a dread of his impending doom and a tingling excitement that threatened to rise up and overwhelm him at the prospect of seeing Fermay once more.

'All those people in the Krewe – surely they don't all know what's happening?' he asked. 'If they did, you wouldn't have been able to keep the deaths a secret. It would have leaked out at some point.'

'Every army needs its generals and its troops. The Krewe of Aidoneus has a large number of foot soldiers who obey orders at peril of their life. Most think we are a highly effective criminal gang, cornering the market in drug smuggling, prostitution and gambling – which, to a certain extent, is true. Only a specially selected few, twelve in all, understand the true agenda. The inner cabal. Self-perpetuating, we pass our information down the line. When one dies, another takes their place. The mission is all, as it has been for the last fifty years. In that way, information is controlled and protected and mysteries remain mysteries. Our vision has remained pure and that is why we are so close to achieving it.'

'How close?'

'Oh, very close.' He chuckled. 'Very close indeed. All those drifters, those out-of-towners, those people who crossed us, their deaths were leading up to this moment, this very day. Magic works, you see, David, whatever else you might think in this technological age. You saw a very small part of it in the E'lethri, which we have been able to summon for several years now. When Lionel Johnson received the gift of music, he also gained the ability to store the life energy released from sacrificial deaths. Of course, the deaths had to be carried out in a certain way to ensure the free flow of that energy, but the music and the record saw to that. That is its power. The equation dictated to Johnson was quite simple. When enough energy was stored up it would become a key that would unlock a source of dark and terrifying power. And now we are very close to achieving Johnson's dream, to getting what we have all wanted for so long. In fact, we need only one more soul, David. Just one, and that will be yours. Quite apposite, don't you think? After all the trouble you caused us. And because of your links to Ms Fermay Grey.'

'What's Fermay got to do with all this?' David said, refusing to picture his own fate.

Broussard smiled a smile of pure malice. He gazed out of the window and said simply, 'You'll see.'

The limousine slowed down as it approached the mansion and then it was turning across the road and into the drive. They had arrived.

'Take him upstairs to her,' Broussard ordered, unable to control his smirk.

Lynch and Frantz stood on either side of David and roughly gripped his arms. The house seemed less threatening in the dawn light, but it was as if the darkness and menace had not gone, merely retreated to the furthest reaches of the building until night fell once more. David was led quickly up the first flight of stairs, along the landing and up the second flight. The stark, undecorated part of the house seemed colder than the rest. They passed the spot where Ligios had been killed and David could see dark patches still staining the walls and floor. The antique-stuffed room where 'Night-time Blues' had been kept was in darkness, but neither Lynch nor Frantz put on the light. They led David straight to the door at the rear. It was the one room he and Ligios

365

had not searched when they broke into the house, the room where he'd sensed a presence, but had got no reply. To have been so close! Lynch kept the key to the room on a chain around his neck. The lock turned with a click and then David was suddenly shoved in like a piece of meat being thrown to a lion. Before he could get his bearings, the door was slammed and locked behind him. There was complete darkness.

'Fermay?' he whispered.

No reply.

Clumsily he fumbled for a light switch next to the door. His fingers closed around one and he flicked it, illuminating a bare bulb hanging from a flex in the middle of the ceiling.

A woman sat on a chair near the far wall, her head bowed forward in her hands, her elbows resting on her knees. Her hair had fallen across her face so it was impossible to see her features, but it was unmistakeably her.

'Fermay?' he asked again, louder this time.

She looked up.

Her hair was unkempt, her clothes dirty as if they had not been changed for weeks. She was wearing the same dress as when David had seen her climbing into Broussard's limousine, although at the time he had not been sure it was her. And now he could see why. Her weeks of imprisonment had taken their toll. Her skin was so pale from being locked away from the light, it almost had a milky, translucent quality. There were tears in her eyes.

'What have they done to you?' David said, choking back his emotions.

'It's the price I pay for abandoning my duties.' Her voice was hoarse.

She pulled herself shakily to her feet and walked towards him. David's joy at seeing her again was almost uncontrollable; he was shaking as if he had the ague and his blood burned in his veins. But this wasn't the same woman he had known in London. She seemed broken, her eyes flat and dead.

'Why did you come, David?' she said weakly. 'Now they'll kill you.'

'I was dead anyway, Fermay. Without you.'

His love for her, repressed for so long, surged to the surface and he threw his arms around her so tightly he thought he would crush the life from her. It was all he wanted and if their stories could have finished then it would have been his perfect ending.

Slowly she pushed herself back so she could look him in the face and her eyes roved across his features, taking in every detail, preserving the moment for all time.

Then they kissed. It was soft at first, the greeting of long-parted lovers, but then it became harder and deeper, encompassing all the desperation that raged within them. In the centre of the vortex, David felt something strange happening to him, like he was being sucked inside himself, plummeting into an area he knew only too well.

The Fog Zone.

Only one memory was still locked inside it. Only one, but it was the worst one, the worst one of all.

'Not now,' he pleaded to himself. 'Please. Not now.'

The kiss had been the key. The images came rushing out of his subconscious in all their horrific glory and there was nothing he could do to stop them.

Chapter 30

The night was cold. David's breath plumed frostily, clouding upwards towards the orange streetlamp. Would winter ever go? With his hands thrust deep into his pockets, he headed into the chill wind and hurried towards the flat, drawn by the thoughts of warmth and comfort and Fermay waiting for him. He almost felt sorry that he had gone to the Jazz Attic on his own, but it *was* a weekday night and Fermay had not been as keen to see the band as he had. She had been quite happy to stay in the warm and watch TV and play records. And who could blame her? he thought with a shiver. She had made the right call again; the band had been awful.

A cat glided across the road ahead of him, its eyes flashing with basic cunning. In the distance he heard the rumble of a train, clack-lack, clack-lack, and the throaty roar of a motorcycle accelerating away at great speed. He smelled the dirty stink of a wet city.

The party had been a success, despite Fermay and Willie's constant bickering. It gave him a warm glow to think back to it, its memory homely and comforting in the cold. He was surprised at his own thoughts; he never thought he would ever admit to liking something that was 'homely'. If only he hadn't got so drunk. He would have liked to have appreciated the latter part of the evening as much as the earlier, but after ll p.m. it had disappeared in an alcoholic haze and he had suffered for it the next day. Still, there would be other times.

David turned into his street and winced mentally when he saw the house. Grimy. Run-down. Depressing. It had never bothered him before, its peeling paint and mouldy walls simply not an issue when it was just a place to hang his hat. But now . . . perhaps it was time to look for somewhere new. Somewhere brighter and cleaner. He resolved to discuss the matter with Fermay at the earliest opportunity.

He had the key in the deadlock. It turned. Clack. The door swung open and he breathed in the familiar musty smell of aged carpets and yellowing wallpaper. A sound caught his attention, dim, muffled.

Bang, bang.

The door closed with a click. Overcome with curiosity, David put his foot on the first step. What was that noise? He strained, but it was hiding behind doors, behind walls.

Bang, bang. A pause, a few seconds. Then, bang, bang.

His foot eased on to the second step, then the third, and above, and then he was on the landing. The sound was louder, a drummer monotonously exercising one wrist in boredom. The boards on the landing creaked with every step, *eek-kk*, *eek*, each one an explosion of sound that ruptured the stillness of the house. Streetlight flooding through the dirty net curtains on the window at the end of the landing cast stark, angular shadows across the floor.

His fingers scraped the smooth, cold surface of the bannister as he rounded on to the second flight of stairs and through the gloom he could make out his door at the top. The dull, intermittent rhythm was coming from behind it. David felt strangely apprehensive, all thoughts of the party and his quiet joy suddenly forgotten. His skin was prickling and his throat felt dry, an inexplicable warning of something he could not guess. He climbed the stairs slowly, the muscles down his neck and back taut and painful.

He was at the top of the stairs. His hand was on the door handle. He was turning it slowly. Slowly. Click. The door opened a fraction. The door swung open. He looked in. He saw.

The scene froze as his mind disassembled it and then gave meaning to the visual signals. There was an atomic explosion of blinding white light at the back of his head as the synapses fired as one.

Bang, bang.

Bang, bang.

His heart leapt as it always did when he saw Fermay. Her beauty blinded him to everything else, cutting through the

369

half-light like a beacon, dazzling, intense. Her face turned towards him as the door swung open, her skin a lustrous white, illuminated by the moonlight through the bedroom window, her lips ruby red, slashed wide in surprise. Patches of shadow obscured her eyes and her hair was a swathe of darkness shifting around her head.

'Fermay,' he whispered, entranced by necessity because he did not want to perceive the surroundings which his peripheral vision had already noted and dismissed.

There was music in the air. At first he was not aware of it, but then it sneaked up to the boundary of his hearing like a breath of wind or the rustling of leaves on an autumn day. He recognized the construction of an old jazz tune, the excitement of a trumpet, the rumble of drums, the mania of a guitar. It was reminiscent of something he had lived with all his life without truly listening. The strains were entrancing, weaving skeins through the air. He could not tell from where it was coming. Magic, he sighed. Magic.

The hammer was in Fermay's hand, held aloft, a prosaic trophy. Moonlight glinted off the metal that remained unstained as it hung there for a second, poised at the top of the arc. David held his breath in anticipation. Then it came down with force.

Bang.

And again, rapidly.

Bang.

A whimpering giggle escaped Fermay's mouth, a small sound that spoke of a soul lost to the void. It told of a life without self-determination, an unwilling puppet.

Willie lay on the floor, near the inviting curve of her thighs as she half sat, half sprawled on the bare boards, one hand resting in a viscous pool. Willie's hand was as white and delicate as porcelain. His leather jacket, his prized possession, was soaking. Willie would never have let his jacket get so wet, David thought.

Bang, bang. The hammer beat out its double rhythm once more.

Willie's head was missing. No, that was wrong, he knew

that as soon as he thought it. Willie's head was there, but it was missing. David laughed fleetingly at the mad humour of it. It was there in the lumps of grey, the shards of white, the mounds of indistinguishable matter splattered in a wide jelly around him.

And the hammer came down, although there was no longer any need for it, as if Fermay was trying to expunge all evidence of a hated act. So her life could carry on as normal.

Oh Willie, David thought. Why couldn't you leave well alone? You kicked through the ashes and fanned the flames into a forest fire. Fermay had always been like a beat-up, malfunctioning factory boiler, pressurized until the needle was edging to the limit of the red. David had recognized that. He had tried to ease the pressure gently before he could reach the core of the woman he loved. Willie had been oblivious to her subtle dangers.

Bang.

Recognition slowly surfaced through the mists of the eyes that had been staring at him. Like a patient coming out of a coma, she asked unbelievingly, 'David?'

The hammer slipped from her fingers and clattered into the sticky puddle and tears welled up in her eyes, one bubbling over on to her cheek and then on to the floor. 'I did it for you, David!' Her voice rose into a shriek of anguish. 'I did it for you! I could feel it coming over me, the fever, the killing fever, and I knew I had to do it soon. It's within me, like a cancer. I couldn't fight it.'

She looked at her hands aghast, the skin stained bright red from her elbows to her fingers, and then she sobbed hysterically. David was rooted, dumbfounded. Eventually her sobbing subsided and in between gasps of breath she continued. 'It was him or you, David. When I realized I had to do it, I knew I would be drawn to him or you. It has to be someone I've seen or spoken to during the three days before, so the emotions are at a pitch. I chose him because it could never be you, David. Never. I love *you*.'

Her eyes turned glassy for an instant and in a small voice that he could barely hear, she said, 'And now it's over.'

Resolve seemed to flood her system as she stood up quickly and walked away from the body without a backward glance. She paused briefly next to David and he could see in her face thoughts of a future that might have been. The depths of the sorrow that he saw there were immeasurable; he thought he was going to drown in it.

Gently, she placed two bloody hands on his white shirt and kissed him on the lips. When she withdrew it looked like he had been blasted with a shotgun. Then she was past him and away down the stairs, her heels clacking rhythmically on the bare boards.

Bang, bang.

Bang, bang.

Chapter 31

David came screaming out of his mind like a banshee, bringing with him a feeling of such abject horror that he honestly hoped he would die. He had never experienced loss like it before, not even when his father had died. This time he had lost everything: his future, his love, his salvation. The Fog Zone had dissipated and everything had fallen into position and now he knew why he had lost his memory in the first place. No mind could cope with what he had seen. His consciousness had retreated in shock at the sight of his love covered in the blood of his best friend. That sight had almost shattered him completely.

Now, as if he was watching a stranger through a gauze, he could see his actions after that moment when the shock had taken over . . .

He had wandered the streets in a daze searching for Fermay, hanging around at the locked doors of the Jazz Attic like some ghost drawn to the happy memories of his life. Eventually, through that half-aware state, he realized Fermay would not be back. David knew instantly where she had gone – to the only place she really knew, the place that had been calling her. Home.

New Orleans.

Despite everything, their bond was still there, strained but unbroken. He could forgive her anything. *Anything*. Even the worst crime of all. And he could not let her go from his life, for what else remained? Only the emptiness he had felt before, made infinitely worse by the still-remembered weeks of fulfilling joy he had experienced with Fermay.

He could not let her go.

He returned to his flat as the morning started to come up, grey and cold, just like the body that was lying in the congealing pool on the floor. His mind did not make the connection with Willie, with the warm, breathing person who had accompanied him for

373

most of his life. It was just an object, he kept telling himself. Just an object.

With revulsion he took Willie's house keys from his trouser pocket – even they were sticky – and then he hurried across Brixton to the quiet backstreet house where Willie had lived, and let himself in. David might have been able to scrape together the money to follow Fermay by calling in a few favours, but he doubted it. There was an easier option. Willie would no longer be able to go on his dream holiday to New Orleans, but David could. As he walked into the bedroom, he saw the suitcase packed for the flight that weekend and the small travel bag lying next to it. The travel details were stuffed in the front pocket and at 9 a.m. he phoned the agent. It was easy for him to pose as Willie and get the pre-paid airline tickets and hotel booking changed into the name of David Easter.

Collecting the traveller's cheques and US dollars from the bank was just as easy. Willie's credit card paid for them – David forged the signature easily – and the teller didn't even notice the payment slip was signed in Willie's name and the cheques in David's.

For a time he stood in his flat staring at the body, wondering how long it would be before it was discovered. Days? Weeks? When the smell got really bad and the neighbours started to complain?

Then he waited for the day of the flight. Time passed in the flat in a blur. At one point someone knocked at the door, but he never answered, and eventually the footsteps receded down the stairs. He remembered turning the key in the lock one last time, standing on the cold, grey street with his bag clutched tightly to his side and then nothing.

The shock must have hit him wholly then. There was no recollection of the journey to the airport, the flight, the connecting flight, his arrival in New Orleans. He must have been operating on only the most basic level until, gradually, his consciousness had emerged from the corner where it had been hiding, pulled out into the opening by the banging of the streetcar wheels which sounded to his taut mind like a hammer pounding on a wooden floor again and again and again . . .

*

374

And then he was back there, in that small room, his emotions threatening to tear him up as he looked into Fermay's pale, sickly face.

'Why?' His voice croaked. He could only muster one word.

Fermay took his hand and led him across the room, pushing him on to her seat while she knelt before him. 'Your question implies that I had a choice, David,' she said in a small, tired voice. 'I didn't. It's part of my nature, imprinted upon my character. It's an involuntary action, like . . .' She struggled for the correct words, '. . . a sneeze.'

'A sneeze?' David's incredulous exclamation veered towards hysteria. 'You murdered my best friend!'

'Yes. Yes, I did.' She stared down at his hands cupped gently in her own. 'You followed me here. You found this house . . . You must know something about Mr Broussard . . . about Aidoneus . . . ?'

David's laughter was bitter and strained. 'You mean all this madness that you kept hidden from me, from the man you were supposed to love?'

'I didn't tell you because I wanted to protect you, can't you see that? Knowledge is dangerous.'

'You could have protected me more by not talking to me that night at the Jazz Attic. By not moving in with me. By not telling me you loved me.' The moment he said it, he regretted it. He was hurt, and disoriented, and yet despite what she had done, he didn't regret meeting her or any of the time he had spent with her. He could never do that. 'I'm sorry. I didn't mean that. Yes, I know about Broussard and Aidoneus, Lionel Johnson and "Night-time Blues", about the killings . . .'

'Then you know it all!' She raised her head and closed her eyes with relief.

'Except one thing.'

'What's that?'

'*Your* involvement in all this. That's the only thing that matters to me. Broussard can have whatever he wants. He can bring down a plague of frogs and turn all of New Orleans into his zombie slaves for all I care.'

'There's more than that at risk, David. What Aidoneus is planning will affect everyone. It—'

'I don't care!' David grabbed her wrists tightly, feeling like he was on the verge of madness. 'I just want you back with me. I want things how they were, in London, in the flat. Just you and me. We can forget the rest. If there's a way, tell me!'

Fermay shook her head. 'There isn't a way, David. Can't you understand that I'm at the heart of all that's happening? I'm the essential component in the plan, the lynchpin.'

'Tell me.' David let go of her hands and sat back, dreading what he was about to hear.

Fermay sighed and reluctantly began. 'My parents died when I was very, very young, you know that. I think Mr Broussard had them killed. I can't be sure, but I would guess that's what happened. He chose me, even at that age, at four or five, for the part I was going to play. Mr Broussard looked after me, gave me food, clothes, saw to my education, but there was no love, no caring. He was like a farmer breeding a calf to become a prize cow. It all seemed quite normal to me because I didn't know any different . . . until I started reading books, and then I started asking questions. I soon learned that wasn't the thing to do. If there's one thing Mr Broussard knows about, it's discipline, and he trained me well. Like a dog. So I kept quiet, carried on living my non-life, until my eighteenth birthday and that's when they decided I was ready.'

'Ready for what?'

'To become the prize cow.' She laughed humourlessly. 'To take over the role that I had been prepared for. To . . .' She laughed again, and this time it chilled him. '. . . become a killer.' The memories made her wince, but she continued. 'They brought me into this room, sat me down on this chair and told me about the krewe, about its past, its reason for existing and its future. Until then I thought all these men I had seen since I was a child were just involved in arranging the Mardi Gras floats and the biggest, flashiest balls in town that only the richest and most important people attended. I couldn't believe what they were saying . . . well who would? I thought they were teasing me, playing some kind of stupid joke for my birthday. And then they told me the part I was going to play. I laughed. That was the punchline, I thought. Shy, quiet, loveable me doing things like that? Then they took out the record, *that fucking record*, and put it on the music box over there.'

David had not noticed the record player on the table in the corner until then. It was old and it had a huge, golden-coloured horn that was chipped and battered. With a shiver he realized he had seen it before, on the TV in Beth's apartment during the unreal transmission that had corresponded to Dauphine's prophecy.

'They switched it on,' Fermay continued. 'Then they shut the door and locked it. They came back for me two days later.' She bit her lip and a small droplet of blood erupted like a bud on a rose. 'It changed me. That music, the music that Lionel Johnson bought with a life, it's filled with a dark power. It's like a computer virus, going straight to the heart of the system where it sits and gnaws away, changing everything, corrupting. I listened to the music and it transformed my mind, it transformed me. Every now and then I can hear it running through my head like a tape loop.'

David nodded soberly. 'Sometimes I can hear it too, just a few bars of it. I've not heard the record, but I know what it is, from the nights when I disturbed you when you were sleepwalking. And then . . . at the end . . . at the end, with Willie . . . You were humming a song and it worked its way into my mind. It was "Night-time Blues", wasn't it?'

'Even hearing a part of it changes you. Not totally – you have to hear all of it for that – but enough to take you away from the life you had before.'

'I saw dead people . . .'

Fermay gave David's hand a sad, comforting squeeze. 'I know what you went through. They've been all around me since I was eighteen. Mostly they leave me alone, but that's because I think they're scared . . . of the power, of what Aidoneus is doing . . .'

'What *did* the record do to you, Fermay?'

'It programmed me to kill. Aidoneus doesn't get its souls from just any murder. The killing has to be a ritual, carried out by one specific person, the Avatar. When the Avatar kills, the soul is added to that total – waiting to tip the balance.'

'You're the Avatar?'

'There have been a few down the years. When one dies, another one takes over, someone who has been groomed for that position since childhood. You don't know what it's like, David. To have that virus running away at the back of your head. Most of the time you can act like a normal person, but when it decides to come forward, when it's time for another killing, there's nothing you can do to stop it. It's like a mist comes down over your eyes and you're filled with a hunger which you know won't go away until you've satiated it. When that happens I become more than human. My strength, my speed, my drive . . . it's all channelled into killing.'

'And that's what happened at the flat . . . with Willie?'

'The person I have to kill . . . it has to be someone I've known for three days. In the past the krewe always picked up the victim and locked them in this room. I'd visit them each day, talk to them, find out all about them. That way when I killed them the emotions were charged.' She bit her lip once more and this time the blood burst forth and splashed on to the back of her hand. She rubbed at the spot for long after the blood had been wiped away. 'I thought I'd escaped in London, so I wasn't prepared for it when it came over me. I could feel it coming over me a few days before and I thought I could control it this time, through my love for you, and I tried, God, I tried, but in the end all I could do was make sure you weren't the target. But then I had to find someone else, someone I knew . . .'

'And Willie was there.'

'He called round while you were out. When I saw him at the door, grinning and still talking about that damned record, I knew he was the one. I invited him in . . . I saw the hammer you'd used to hang the picture . . .'

'Wasn't there anything else you could do?' David felt nauseous at the memories that sprang to mind, the image of Willie, or what was left of him.

'David, don't you think I would have found a way out if I could? To save you and me I would have done anything. But

378

when Willie arrived, I knew that was it . . . it was all over. I would kill him and lose you . . . I knew you could never forgive me that. It was the thing I had dreaded from the moment I met you. There was nothing left for me but to come back here, running back home like a stupid kid. In my little fantasy world I'd dreamed I could escape all the killing and the blood, create a new life for myself like normal people have. A life where there was love and not death, tenderness instead of suffering. I had that for a while, David.' Tears filled her eyes and as the long-suppressed emotions poured out her face once more began to resemble the woman he knew. 'Can you realize what it's like to see heaven and then know you can never go there again? That killing . . . what they expected me to do . . . it destroyed me. It turned me into something worse than an animal. I realized I'd have only one chance to get away. I suppose I knew there was no escape when the E'lethri appeared in London . . . you know about the E'lethri?'

He nodded.

'Even there, more than three thousand miles away, they'd managed to find me. I was lucky that over that distance the power was weakened. The E'lethri knew I was in the city, but it didn't know exactly where. It was only a matter of time till it tracked me down.

'In the end it was me that ruined things, not them. *Me*. So I came back here . . . to this shithole . . . this nightmare. I had to accept that that was all there was for me. The only other option was to kill myself, and the music in my head won't let me do that.' Fermay wiped away the tears and gave a short, unbalanced laugh. 'So, David, what do you think of your lovely little Fermay now she's accepted that all she can ever be in life is a butcher, sending the innocent to slaughter?'

David looked into Fermay's face and felt the world swinging away from him; he was almost dragged back to the lunatic existence that had possessed him on the way to New Orleans. But then she blinked and smiled a smile without cynicism or fear and it was London once more. He smiled back.

'Let me help you.'

'Oh David,' she sighed. 'Haven't you been listening to a word

I've been saying? *I kill*. I suck up souls so evil men can exert their will on the world. I'm damning us all with my very existence. There's no hope any more.' She paused. 'For either of us.'

Her final words brought home to David what the future held. His death, the death he had almost come to accept, would be by her hand. When the blood lust claimed her once more and she attacked him with whatever weapon the krewe provided, his last sight would be her face, crushing the life from him. No wonder Broussard had laughed. It was the supreme irony, the most devastating blow David could have imagined.

'So I'm to be your last victim,' he said almost to himself. 'The one who finally pushes everything over the edge.' Then he grinned at her, a lopsided honest expression. 'My mother always said I'd have a big role in life.'

'Don't joke, David. I can't cope with this any more. I thought my last one would be another old drifter who I'd meet a few times and . . . but not you, David. Not you!' Her voice rose suddenly and David had to grab her to calm her down. 'How can you even talk to me after what I've done?'

'It wasn't you, Fermay,' he whispered into her ear. 'I know the real you, what you're like in your heart. You're a good person. This was something you were forced to do against your will.'

'Still, I've sinned,' she said hopelessly. 'You can't wipe all this blood off my soul.' She looked down at her hands as if she could see it there upon them. 'Look at me, Lady fucking Macbeth.' Another sob.

David looked around the room, Dauphine's prophecy electric in his mind. From some deep well within him he had found a new source of hope, very small and slightly polluted, but he was sure he could use it to save her. It didn't matter if he died, as long as Fermay survived free of all the corruption.

'I'm going to save you, Fermay.' It was a stupid comment, but the confidence and optimism in his voice redeemed it.

'No one can save me,' she said bitterly. 'I was lost from the moment I was born.'

David walked over and hammered on the door. 'OK, let me out of here! I'm ready!'

Then he returned to Fermay and gave her a hug of such

ferocity that her feet left the floor. They kissed passionately and in the darkness behind their eyelids it could have been the Jazz Attic again.

Before he left, David said with a smile, 'I'll be back.'

'Sure you will,' Fermay replied bleakly. 'Just don't wish for it to happen any quicker than it does.'

Broussard sat in the chair where David had first met him, a large glass of bourbon in his hand despite the earliness of the hour. He seemed completely relaxed. The room was warm and sunny and smelled of sweet summer gardens.

'Was your reunion as romantic as you expected?' Broussard asked snidely. 'And,' he added pointedly, 'have you said your goodbyes?'

'I'd like to insult you, but I can't think of any words that are bad enough.' David slumped into a chair, his lack of sleep taking its toll on his aching joints and heavy eyes. Lynch and Frantz took up a watchful position next to the door.

'A singular lack of imagination on your behalf. I certainly have no difficulty conjuring up words to describe you, Mr Easter.' He swirled the drink in the glass and knocked back half of it. 'I don't normally take spirits at this time of day, you understand, but I felt the need for a celebration. I feared at one point you might upset the plans we had spent decades formulating.'

'How could I do that? I didn't have any plan myself. I was just trying to stay alive and get sane.'

Broussard laughed, a patronizing and arrogant sound. 'You had no idea of the value of the thing you stole.' The record had already been returned to its resting place upstairs.

'What could I have done with it that could have stopped you?'

'You don't think I'm about to tell you, do you, even at this late stage? Suffice to say, I am quite relieved to have the source of our power back. It has been returned to its case upstairs until the moment when we need it no longer, a time not too far into the future. One more soul, Mr Easter! Just one more, and this tired old world comes crashing down to be rebuilt by a shining new vision.'

'I don't care about all these big plans, Broussard.'

'No, of course you don't. You have a small ambition. You

would quite happily settle for walking away with your true love. Sadly, even that tiny dream will not come true. Would you like to know what will happen, Mr Easter? In a little while Mr Lynch and Mr Frantz will take you upstairs and lock you in the room with Ms Grey. Shortly the spirit of the Avatar will possess her. If she can find something in the room to use as a weapon she will beat you to death with that. Otherwise she will tear you apart with her bare hands. Don't think that because you are a man and she a woman that you will be able to stop her. You will be like straw before a whirlwind. And then . . .' He raised his glass until the sun caught it. '. . . our day will begin. Shall I tell you what will happen when we are given the power?'

'No.'

Broussard's cheeks flushed with anger.

'What I want to know is, what will free a person from the duty of the Avatar?'

Broussard's eyes widened with surprise and then he burst out laughing. 'Always the dreamer, Mr Easter! The eternal optimist, hoping for a *deus ex machina* that will free your love so you can elope together.' Laughter burst forth once more, cruel and mocking. 'Shall I raise your hopes? Yes, why not. There is a way, a quite simple way. If another person plays the record, then the current Avatar is freed of the burden. There is a catch, of course . . .'

'The person who plays the record becomes the new Avatar.'

'Very good, Mr Easter. You *have* been paying attention. Only one person can be the Avatar and the power is never transferred. An Avatar kills for Aidoneus until death. Strangely, they die young. Perhaps they burn out from the sheer horror of the task they perform, who knows? Your young Fermay cannot have long to go.'

Anger swelled within David, but he fought it back, knowing that above all else he had to remain calm. There was a thin film of sweat covering his back and he felt his stomach muscles clench in anticipation. Broussard was watching him intently, and for one frightening moment David was sure he knew what was going through his head. But then the big man broke his stare and rose,

382

swaggering over to one of the large windows which looked out across his tranquil gardens.

'Such a beautiful day.' He folded his hands behind his back like an officer inspecting the troops. David watched the spot between his shoulder blades, imagining a knife plunging again and again into the flesh.

'Soon we must prepare to receive the power,' Broussard said dreamily. 'It will be a gruelling ritual, mentally and physically demanding, but the results will be so sweet.' He turned back to David, excited like a child. 'I will be able to raise the dead, did you know that? Lionel Johnson will be the first, but there will be others.'

'I've seen enough dead people to last me a lifetime,' David said drily.

Broussard closed his eyes and fantasized, inhaling deeply as if he could smell his success. 'I will have the power to snuff out lives with a thought.'

'You seem to do that already.'

'No.' He smiled tightly. 'Literally, with a *thought*.' Broussard savoured the idea and then said, 'I have never met a man so dispossessed of the concept of power. You are an intelligent person, I can see that. You are well aware of the great stakes that are before us, yet you show no interest. The world will literally change overnight, but all you are concerned with is your own world, your tiny sphere of existence. I find it difficult to comprehend.'

'That doesn't surprise me.'

'And there is also the matter of your death – and believe me, you *are* going to die. The way you sit there, so calm and so peaceful . . . it's as if you don't care?'

'If I die, I die.' David looked past Broussard into the garden where he could see movement amongst the shrubs and trees, shapes emerging out of the harsh sunlight shadows.

'What does it feel like?' Broussard continued with relish. 'To know you will die horribly in a matter of hours? Do you have a sense of loss? Are you afraid? Do you wish for redemption?'

'I'm very philosophical about it.' The truth was that fear gnawed away inside David like a giant rat, but it wasn't just a fear of death. For the first time he was afraid of losing something of value, someone who depended on him. It was a burden he had never experienced before.

The shapes in the garden were moving closer, the dead advancing upon the house. David watched in fascination as they glided towards the windows like a dense fog, faces so blank and grey they might have been made of stone. There were men and women of all shapes and sizes, colours and ages, even the very young. He saw a baby, barely a month old, walking as it never had done in life. He saw magnificent clothes mouldered or bullet-ridden, and funeral shrouds in tatters, skin hanging like cloth, and exposed bone. And once he even thought he glimpsed Marsayle holding Moose by the hand at the head of the grim procession. It was a grey wave of death flooding towards the house; the despair and bitterness brought in with the surf were almost tangible.

They know it's nearly the end, he thought. *They've come to witness the last act.*

The dead pushed forward until they were packed tightly against the glass, swarming against every window, hands pressed on the panes. Wherever David looked he could see them, waiting, waiting.

Broussard was not aware of the eyes upon him as he wandered around the perimeter of the room, gripped by the vision of his terrifying new world. Without warning he stopped in his tracks and said, 'The time is getting near. We must prepare.' He grabbed hold of a shelf and tugged it towards him and with remarkable ease the whole rack of books slid forward to reveal a doorway behind. It was poorly lit, but David could make out stairs leading down.

'These old houses often have little secret doorways and hide-aways,' Broussard said. 'In those days there were always things to hide from, the threat of crime from the city, jealous lovers. Come.' He placed a hand on David's shoulder and guided him forward to the top of the stairs. Lynch and Frantz were close behind.

The air was dank and cold after the warmth above. David

could hear sounds down there, people talking, a bark of laughter, a cough.

The stairs led into an old cellar which stretched for the length of the house, the stone walls slick with damp and mildew. Nine men were gathered there, some sitting in leather-backed chairs, others talking quietly in pairs. David instantly recognized the juggler who had murdered Moose. He was still wearing his garish make-up and his cold, cruel eyes followed David's path across the room like a falcon's.

In one corner of the cellar, chains and rusty manacles hung from the walls above an old mattress covered in dark stains that had spread out across the flagstones of the floor. David could not bring himself to look at it for too long.

'Here we all are,' Broussard said cheerfully. 'I thought it right that you meet everyone.'

'In all the best restaurants diners have the opportunity to view the meat before it is cooked,' a tall, gaunt man with piercing black eyes said coldly. His comment was followed by a ripple of sadistic laughter.

'Shall I do the honours?' Broussard continued. 'Of course you've met Mr Lynch, our enforcer, and his assistant Mr Frantz, two lions who perform the most herculean of tasks. And Mr Krugman, our eyes and ears in the city at large. This is Meikel, our assassin.' He motioned to the juggler, but seemed to shy away from touching him. 'Meikel rarely speaks and never to strangers. He is as silent as the wind and as uncompromising.' Meikel remained immobile, his gaze fixed on David, and in it David could sense the hunger of a predator waiting to feed.

Broussard moved among the others, naming them and describing their strengths and contributions to the krewe that had elevated them to the inner circle. The gaunt man was a pornographer who controlled the krewe's interests in prostitution. There was an obscenely fat man called Leduc who Broussard ominously said 'loved children', and a sharply dressed character with silver hair whom Broussard described as, 'our communications expert, our Mercury.' And there were others, their faces flaring in David's mind for the briefest moment as he saw the hardness and icy determination that characterized them all. They were men who had raised themselves above the rest of humanity by eradicating all compassion and joy from their lives. Their sole motivation was the brutal pursuit of power at any cost.

'And there you have it,' Broussard said. 'The new pantheon for a new age, ready to ascend to Olympus and look down on feeble humanity beneath. We will have no need of other gods.' He licked his lips. 'Power is its own master.'

'When's it going to start?' Krugman asked. He looked nervous and a tic had developed underneath his eye.

'Very soon,' Broussard said to him. 'The Avatar is almost ready. But first I want to give our final offering a taste of what is to come, an appetizer, if you like, to accustom his palate to glorious suffering.' Broussard's speech was accompanied by a ripple of appreciative laughter through the gathered krewe members. He pushed his face in close until David could smell his breath and then he whispered, 'Are you ready?' before nodding to Lynch to lead David along to the far end of the cellar.

A large black screen covered the entire wall. It was placed so close to the bricks that there couldn't really be anything behind it, but Broussard took up a position next to it as if he was about to unveil a work of art. Lynch and Frantz gripped David's arms tightly, but he had no intention of struggling. His attention was focused on the curious screen, then, as he stood before it, he could hear something – a faint buzzing like an out-of-tune radio and his skin prickled in response. Broussard had become suddenly serious, and the other krewe members were watching silently.

With a flourish, Broussard pulled back the screen and David was momentarily blinded by the sudden white glare which flooded the room. The buzzing rose sharply until it reached an irritating pitch that made his ears ring, and it was accompanied by a nauseating odour like a chemical dump on a hot summer's day. He gagged and swallowed, steadying his stomach.

Gradually, his eyes accustomed to the light and as they did so he realized it was something he had experienced before, whether in his mind or in reality. The light was not really light, in that there was no source. It was part of the atmosphere of the place he was viewing and it had other qualities to it; taste, texture, things that made it almost like a fog, although it did not swirl or move with air currents. Looking into that brilliant whiteness, David experienced a sensation of floating like the white-out which people lost in an arctic blizzard often mention. It was impossible to tell where the ground lay, or even if there was any ground, and perspective and depth did not exist. It was an alien world, inhospitable to humanity, and it terrified him at the very base of his being; he felt like it was sucking him in, like it was trying to swallow his soul. Was this how Lionel Johnson had felt when he'd looked into the same vista that night in the attic in Storyville?

Dimly, he became aware that Broussard was yelling something, trying to make himself heard above the insectile buzz. In response, Lynch and Frantz began to drag David forward, despite his rigid limbs, until he was on the edge of that doorway through to the unknown. The stench grew more intense the closer he got and he held his breath to stop himself vomiting. As he neared he had the strangest sensation that he could see things moving in the whiteness, drawing closer.

'When you die,' Broussard shouted, 'this is what it will feel like!'

He motioned and Lynch grabbed David's wrist and pushed his hand into the white. There was a moment of nothingness and then his nerves exploded in pain, a thousand sensations of agony, as if his hand was engulfed in fire, as if razor blades were being drawn across his skin, as if he was being eaten by maggots.

David screamed, a cry of torment that rose up from the very heart of him, but it was not just because of the pain. In a flash of lucidity that had begun when his hand entered the white, he saw one of the shapes that moved within it. At least he saw its form, but his mind could not give it a name. He screamed a scream that tore at his throat and then he threw himself back with a lunatic strength that took even Lynch and Frantz by surprise.

As he lay on the cold stone floor recovering, his memory of that fleeting instant winked out as if a section of his mind had been seared away. But he knew that what he had seen was more terrible than anything he could ever imagine and he could still remember feeling its hunger; he had encountered something that wanted to consume not just him, but the whole human world.

Hands helped him roughly to his feet and then he stood before

Broussard, shivering and depleted by his experience. The room was dark once more. Broussard had hurriedly replaced the screen and he seemed, behind his mocking exterior, almost as terrified as David.

'Do you still not fear dying?' Broussard said softly. 'The pain you felt was just a pale shadow of what your soul will endure when it has been torn from your body.'

'Those things . . .'

'Do not speak about them!' Broussard's voice was diamond hard. 'The power will flow through here and into our world and it will be channelled through us. Can you begin to understand now what is at stake?'

David ignored him. He was fighting to retain his composure, and prepare himself for what he knew he had to do. Whatever he had seen behind that screen had only added fire to his determination. He knew he could not afford to wait any longer.

Breathing deeply, he drew himself upright and looked Broussard firmly in the eye. 'Go to hell,' he said, and he meant it.

Broussard laughed and turned to the others who all seemed shaken and unnerved; the unknown was obviously a much more daunting prospect when it was before them and not merely an abstract concept. Broussard sought to calm their fears, saying no one can be prepared for a view across the fields of god. And then, as they warmed to his speech, he began to talk about the power that would be granted to them. He spoke like an officer readying his troops for one final push.

At that moment, on the threshold of a terrifying world, David knew it was time.

He pulled out the gun.

Broussard stopped and looked at David in surprise, before laughing as if he had witnessed a gesture of grand stupidity. David tried to appear confident although he knew he had as much chance of hitting Broussard as blowing the head off a pin at fifty yards. He tightened his fingers on the trigger even as, behind him, Lynch was moving.

Broussard was eyeing him more warily, edging behind a pillar, 'You are being quite foolish,' he said menacingly. 'This will get you nowhere. It will only mean more pain before you die.'

David ignored him. He could hear Lynch creeping up on him. With a sudden turn, he fired.

The bullet ricocheted across the room, before embedding itself in the wall yards away from Lynch who was grinning with the realization that David had no control over the weapon. 'You should leave these toys for the big boys,' the krewe member said patronizingly.

David took aim and fired once more and this time the bullet headed straight for Lynch. He threw up his arms in a futile attempt to protect himself, but the bullet whizzed by and smashed into his left cheekbone which exploded on contact. He fell to the floor clutching his face.

David didn't wait. He scrambled for the stairs out of the cellar. But before he could get to them, someone ploughed into his legs and knocked him to the floor. He rolled on to his back, winded, as the body jumped on to him. It was Frantz. The enforcer started to pound David around the head with his meaty fist, smashing and smashing until David thought he would lose consciousness. The pain was intense.

He still held the gun between their two bodies and Frantz was trying to keep him destabilized so he didn't use it. David pulled the trigger without thinking of his own safety.

The blast almost raised Frantz off David's body, and with a shrug David managed to roll him to one side. There was a hole in his stomach.

The others had held back afraid, and before any of them could move, David reached the stairs, clearing the steps two at a time. He bounded into the study, on the verge of collapse, and closed the bookcase door behind him. He knew it would not delay them for long, but it would give him enough time to do what he had to do.

His attention drifted briefly to the dead who still massed at the windows. He could sense a rise in the pitch of their emotions, although their expressions seemed dispassionate, and he bolted out of the door.

David had made it to the top of the first flight of stairs when he heard the angry sound of pursuit behind him. He paused in his escape and half turned. He felt alive. Directed. No longer a ghost.

'You're scum, Broussard!' he shouted. 'You'd smash down everything I believe in to get what you want. Well now I'm going to do the same to you.'

David fired off another random shot and while the krewe's inner circle was ducking for cover, he was bounding up the stairs. He half expected to confront the E'lethri, but his journey was unimpeded and his feet pounded up to the top floor. Then he was sprinting along the corridor and through the room where the record had originally been stored.

Behind him he heard someone shout, 'He's going to destroy the record!'

But that wasn't enough. Not for him. He snatched the record from its case.

The door to Fermay's dingy prison was open. Lynch had left it ajar, knowing her spirit was broken and that she would not attempt to escape again. David grabbed a wooden chair from the outer room and took it with him as he burst in.

Fermay started in shock when he entered, her face, if possible, even paler. David wanted to hug her, but there wasn't time.

'David! What's . . . ?'

'It's too late for talk. Just do as I say. The krewe are on my heels.'

'David?'

'Hush. Get out there and hide. They won't pay any attention to you at the moment. They're too interested in me because I've got this.' He held up the record.

'Oh God! Oh David . . .'

'Find yourself a room and lock yourself in. Don't open the door under any circumstances. OK? I love you.' He grabbed her by the shoulders and thrust her out as the sound of running feet drew nearer. Next he slammed the door and jammed the chair under the handle.

And then he was alone with the past, present and future merging quietly into one. The noise outside faded into the background.

With shaking hands he placed 'Night-time Blues' on the

ancient record player, cranked up the handle and lowered the clumsy needle into the groove. He pulled up Fermay's chair and sat with his head and shoulders bowed, staring blankly at the wall, his breath catching in his throat. This was the moment when he gave it all away, and for what?

He knew. He was paying the ultimate price, his immortal soul, for the ultimate prize, an immortal soul.

The air was filled with a dusty crackle and a hiss like wind down a tunnel from another age, and then the music started . . .

He was sitting in a warm room. There was music in the air. A record was playing, old and crackling. The music box had a trumpet, gold like a horn, but it was chipped and damaged by age. The needle reached the centre, but the record did not stop. It kept going round and round. A clock ticked in the background, a pendulum swung, but the hands never went round. It was always one time, one moment. There was no window in the room. The walls were cream and cracked. The floor was bare boards. He knew what to do when the woman cried out. He was sitting in a warm room.

The music was in his head. At first it sounded like a simple jazz song, a throbbing double bass plucking out slow and sultry notes before a piano joined in and, then, blasts of Marsayle's haunting trumpet. Gradually the tempo increased, as did the volume, until the individual instruments were lost in a maelstrom of sound. Round and round it went, round and round, hypnotic but not soothing. It was the sound of war machines trundling across a blasted landscape, the sound of swords clashing in anger, the sound of hammers on a wooden floor. It pulled him and spun him around until he could be aware of nothing else, his thoughts punctuated by screams of brass and gunshots of drums.

'The music,' he sighed, entranced. 'The music.'

And then, just as quickly as it had soared, it died down. He was aware, vaguely, that the record had played out long ago.

The music was in his head.

It was playing over and over again, no longer drowning out his senses, but coiled like a snake at the back of his mind, the new soundtrack to his existence. And as it settled into its groove, he could feel other parts of him changing too, synapses firing differently, altered chemical flows, the reprogramming of his mind.

As this took place, the sound of a woman screaming his name intruded in his head. It was Fermay, somewhere distant in the house. He hoped she had locked herself in. He knew what he had to do.

Everything that he was was departing him, if only for a while. A film like blood came down across his eyes, transforming the world with scarlet hues. Hot metal flowed in his veins, electricity crackling through his sinews. He was reborn, a god of retribution. Resurrected.

It was as if he was trapped within a robot that was acting independently. The chair was removed from under the handle. The door was opened. The room without was distorted, a view through a bottle glass. People were moving within his field of vision, strange loathsome creatures that he had to destroy. Their eyes bugged in a caricature of fear, their mouths wide in a scream he could not hear.

The first one he encountered looked strangely like Lynch. The enforcer vainly tried to defend himself, but his left arm was snapped at the elbow. The robot was moving too quickly to comprehend. Entrails tumbled. An arm fell to the floor. Lynch was gone, out of sight.

The others were rooted, and then they were trying to run, but there was no point. No hope. The silence grew more intense. The red film grew thicker. David could not see at all.

Chapter 32

The clock in the warm, sunny reception room was ticking lazily. The rest of the house was quiet and still. David sat in Broussard's comfortable leather chair, his fingertips pressed tightly together before his face, humming a tune dreamily to himself. The soothing chirrup of birds singing a spring song and the sweet garden scent floated in through the half-open window.

All was right with the world.

David was looking at Broussard who was returning his gaze. The big man did not blink. His eyes were glassy, a little frightened, a little wide. His skin was pale, his lips pursed as if he was about to deliver a gentle kiss to a loved one. The head was on the mantelpiece, between the carriage clock and the porcelain figure. David held his gaze for a moment, and then looked out of the window, across the tranquil garden with its well-edged lawns and colourful blooms. He half expected to see someone there, but it was deserted apart from the birds and the insects.

His joints ached and his limbs were weary, but he stood up and stretched like a cat, forcing his tendons and sinews to come back to life. How long had it been? He checked his watch. An hour, that was all.

An hour.

The body of the juggler was tucked behind the chair like a pile of old magazines hastily hidden when unexpected visitors called. David eyed it matter of factly and then stepped over it; he was concentrating on discovering the rest of Broussard's corpse. As he moved, he caught sight of himself in a large, gilt-framed mirror hanging on the wall. He started in shock. His first thought was that a bizarrely dressed intruder had walked into the room while his back was turned. The reflection showed a man frozen in hellish red. Blood covered him from head to toe, plastering his hair, staining his skin, making his suit so sodden it clung to him. Gradually he became aware of the discomfort as if his sensations were slowly returning. He looked at the face for a long moment, still seeing a stranger while recognizing the form.

Flashes of memory exploded in his mind, but he stifled them just as quickly. It was too much. Too horrifying. Too unbelievable.

With renewed vigour, he hurried out of the room, the numbness fading as his eyes began to see what was around him for the first time. The scene outside the door was even more horrific and David snatched his hand to his mouth involuntarily. The blood, so much blood everywhere, like a charnel house. He wandered through the mansion in a daze, stepping over dismembered limbs and body parts, slipping on entrails and brains, offal so badly butchered it was difficult to identify. The elegant, expensively decorated home had become an abattoir where beasts had been disposed of with furious efficiency.

And he wondered what kind of wild animal could have done this, what soulless, inhuman beast? But he knew and his mouth was whispering the name over and over again. His ears would not listen.

In the room where the record had been kept, David tripped over the side of meat that had been Lynch. He skidded in a pool of grue on to his knees, until he was looking at his reflection in the viscous puddle.

He remained that way for a minute and then he began to sob, softly at first but with increasing intensity until his whole body was wracked and gasping. In that moment he was aware of what had happened to him and how he had damned himself for all eternity. For love. He had sacrificed so much for her! His immortal soul, an insubstantial thing but so valuable and now so lost.

As he cried, the door of the far room opened and footsteps hurried towards him, hands pulling him to his feet where arms encircled him with a love greater than love. Fermay held him close like a child and stroked his head, smearing blood across her clothes and pale skin.

Eventually he pulled back and looked at her with red-rimmed eyes. 'You're safe,' he said, blinking away the tears.

Fermay was crying too. 'It's over,' she replied.

David tried to show he was happy for Fermay, but he knew that although it was over for her, it was only just beginning for him. 'How did you avoid it . . . me?'

'I locked myself in a room downstairs. I could tell from the screams that you were working your way through the house systematically. The first few tried to confront you. When they fell, the rest scrambled to escape, but you were too quick for them. I heard Broussard outside the door mumbling and trying to summon the E'lethri and then you were on him and he was cut off . . .'

'In more ways than one.'

'I heard you pass by and then when everything had grown quiet, I slipped out and came up here. I . . . I don't know . . . I've been locked up here for so long, it's the only place that I feel safe.'

'Yes, you're safe.' David repeated his earlier comment. 'You're free of it?' he asked anxiously.

She nodded. 'When I heard you start to play the record, I ran, and as I ran I felt it leave me. It was like a weight lifted from my shoulders, like a giant bat had suddenly taken flight. I could almost hear its wings . . .'

'And then it entered into me.' David felt cold and his throat seemed to have shrunk to the width of a pipe cleaner.

Fermay took his hand and squeezed it tightly. 'Oh, David. I'm so sorry.' She hugged him; the blood was getting everywhere. 'I know what you've sacrificed for me, David.'

'My soul.' He paused. 'My eternal soul, damned for all time. And I'll keep on killing, over and over again, whenever the spirit of the Avatar comes over me.'

'If I could take it back—'

'No, I did it to save you, Fermay. That's the only thing that matters. That you're free of it now. That there's a chance for you to redeem yourself.'

'We could get someone else to play the record?'

He shook his head. 'I couldn't wish this on another human being. It's my burden. I've got to carry it.'

There was one tear in her eye, but when she wiped it away there was confidence in her face. 'There's got to be a way out for you, David. Someone, somewhere in the world, will know a solution. We'll just keep travelling until we find it. I'll be with you. I'll be your strength and I'll be your protector. And those times when the Avatar spirit takes you, well, I'll lock you in a room until it passes. We'll save your soul, David. Together. We've just got to have faith.'

David helped Fermay up from the floor and put his arms around her, suddenly feeling more exhausted than he ever had done in his life. Was she right? Could they find a way out together?

She looked him in the face and asked quietly, 'Do you regret doing what you did?'

'No,' he replied without having to think. 'I'd do it again tomorrow, and every day until the end of the world. If it saved you from the suffering you were going through, then it was worth it.'

'You saved me from more than just mental anguish, David, you gave me back my soul. I've got a chance. I can seek absolution . . .' Fermay choked off her words as the memories came back.

'How did you cope with it?' he asked her, his eyes wide. 'It's like there's someone else in my head all the time, whispering to me. Sometimes I can make out the words. Awful, awful things. Telling me to kill, to carry out atrocities.'

'I learned to accept it as part of my life.' It was a cold statement that hid a lifetime of suffering.

'Is that it then?' he asked. 'Have I sold my soul down the river?'

Fermay didn't answer.

'Or does it mean something that my intentions were good? Can you be damned for committing an act of evil if you do it to save someone's soul?'

Fermay could see he was starting to lose control again so she quickly grabbed his arm and led him out of the room, along the stark corridor towards the stairs. 'There must be hope. You didn't just save me, you stopped them too . . . the krewe. All the ones who knew how to complete the ritual are dead. The rest of them are just small-time gangsters.'

They walked silently down the stairs, until at the bottom

Fermay said, 'You won't be alone, David. We're going to be together now, for all time, and I'm going to look out for you.'

They avoided the front door, not wanting to be seen coming out of a house filled with corpses, and slipped out into the garden through the study, wandering among the flowers and shrubs until they came to rest beneath a tree where they could enjoy the feel of the sun on their skin. The warmth soothed David and he found himself almost believing Fermay's message of hope. He felt it even more strongly when he looked across the garden and saw Marsayle standing in the shade of a willow tree, alone once more. For the first time he was smiling, only the faintest impression of pleasure on his saturnine face, but a smile nonetheless. David guessed that the jazzman was pleased with the outcome that had seen the destruction of the krewe. Could he return to the afterlife now? David didn't know, but Marsayle did not seem unduly troubled.

He was holding something at his side, and as he raised his hands David could see it was his horn, as gleaming and golden as the day it was made. Slowly he put it to his lips and began to play.

The tune started off slow and quiet and David thought it would develop into a dirge, a mournful evocation of the life and dreams that he had lost. Instead the tempo gradually increased and the flourishes became wilder and more joyous, until Marsayle was playing a vibrant, gleaming celebration that boomed with happiness and with the promise of a wonderful life. He continued his dazzling solo for five full minutes, matching the natural resplendence of the garden with the colours of his sound, until the shadows around him grew darker and he slowly faded from view.

David realized the tears were streaming down his cheeks, but it was not through sadness or self-pity. Rather he found himself crying for the happiness he had finally achieved.

It was Marsayle's gift to him, a magical gift of the music of life.

Fermay saw his tears when she opened her eyes after sunning herself, and with concern she asked him if he would be all right.

'I want to leave all the death behind,' he said, wiping his face. 'We can't go back to London, with Willie—' He bit off his words. 'We can't stay here. Where do we go first? Vegas? Havana? Rio?'

'Let's just hit the road and find out. There's enough money stashed in that house to keep us going for a while. We'll just keep travelling, David, and sooner or later we'll know where we're going.'

They kissed under the tree and then they walked through the garden and out on to the street, Fermay leading and David following. Anyone who saw them would have been impressed by the confidence in her step and saddened by the weight which seemed to bear down upon his shoulders in contrast. But as they progressed they drew closer together until they were walking in step, side by side, looking towards the horizon. They were a curious couple, filled with mysteries and conundrums, and it was obvious they were meant to be together. Those who saw them as they passed could almost feel the invisible bond, as powerful as magic, as uplifting as music, eternal and unbreakable.

And if sometimes a darkness did cross their faces, it only stayed for a while. It was banished with a kiss or a whispered word or, more often than not, a song played on a battered cassette recorder. The music never left them, a constant soundtrack of joy and strength and hope for the future.

The BSFA takes you beyond your imagination

The British Science Fiction Association is your key to the many worlds of Science Fiction. You will discover everything you always wanted to know about SF in Britain — and more. Six times a year *Vector* brings you interviews, book reviews, and incisive articles in one of the leading critical magazines on SF. Six times a year *Matrix* brings you right up to date with all the news, plus film and magazine reviews. Six times a year *Paperback Inferno* gives you a searing overview of paperbacks in the UK. And three times a year *Focus* provides a unique forum for every SF writer in the country.

All this for just £12 a year. If you enjoy science fiction, join the BSFA. Write to Joanne Raine, Membership Secretary, 29 Thornville Road, Hartlepool, Cleveland TS26 8EW. In North America: Cy Chauvin, 14248 Wilfrec St, Detroit. MI 48213, USA. Rates $25 sea/$40 air.

CRITICAL WAVE

THE EUROPEAN SCIENCE FICTION & FANTASY REVIEW

"CRITICAL WAVE is the most consistently interesting and intelligent review on the sf scene."
- Michael Moorcock.

"One of the best of the business journals... I never miss a copy..." - Bruce Sterling.

"Intelligent and informative, one of my key sources of news, reviews and comments." - Stephen Baxter.

"I don't feel informed until I've read it."
- Ramsey Campbell.

"Don't waver - get WAVE!" - Brian W Aldiss.

CRITICAL WAVE is published six times per year and has established a reputation for hard-hitting news coverage, perceptive essays on the state of the genre and incisive reviews of the latest books, comics and movies. Regular features include publishing news, portfolios by Europe's leading sf and fantasy artists, extensive club, comic mart and convention listings, interviews with prominent authors and editors, fiction market reports, fanzine and magazine reviews and convention reports.

Previous contributors have included: MICHAEL MOORCOCK, IAIN BANKS, CLIVE BARKER, LISA TUTTLE, BOB SHAW, COLIN GREENLAND, DAVID LANGFORD, ROBERT HOLDSTOCK, GARRY KILWORTH, SHAUN HUTSON, DAVID WINGROVE, TERRY PRATCHETT, RAMSEY CAMPBELL, LARRY NIVEN, BRIAN W ALDISS, ANNE GAY, STEPHEN BAXTER, RAYMOND FEIST, CHRIS CLAREMONT and STORM CONSTANTINE.

A six issue subscription costs only eight pounds and fifty pence or a sample copy one pound and ninety-five pence; these rates only apply to the UK, overseas readers should contact the address below for further details. Cheques or postal orders should be made payable to "Critical Wave Publications" and sent to: M Tudor, 845 Alum Rock Road, Birmingham, B8 2AG. Please allow 30 days for delivery.